FAVORS
AND
LIES

FAVORS AND LIES

A novel by

MARK GILLEO

THE
STORY PLANT

ALSO BY MARK GILLEO:

—

Love Thy Neighbor
Sweat

The Story Plant
Studio Digital CT, LLC
P.O. Box 4331
Stamford, CT 06907

Copyright © 2014 by Mark Gilleo
Jacket design by Barbara Aronica Buck

Print ISBN-13: 978-1-61188-145-5
E-book ISBN: 978-1-61188-146-2

Visit our website at www.TheStoryPlant.com

First Story Plant Printing: July 2014

Printed in the United States of America
0 9 8 7 6 5 4 3 2 1

ACKNOWLEDGEMENTS

—

I would like to thank a few people for their continued support and willingness to read draft manuscripts, share their knowledge, and answer crazy questions out of the blue. So in no particular order . . .

Thanks to Lou Aronica for believing in my first three novels. Thanks to Jim Singleton for being my long-standing sanity check and questioning every location, character, and motive. Thanks to Tim Davis for the same, and for providing line by line editing of the first draft. You have more patience than I do. Thanks to Dave Allen for reading and for answering numerous random law enforcement questions. Thanks to Sergey Sirotkin for your Russian advice and fifteen years of friendship. (I am sad to report I was unable to keep any of the Russian that I initially included in the manuscript as Sergey determined all of it to be "undignified.") Thanks to Sue Fine and Dan Lord for both their names and for reading various drafts of the book. Thanks to Michele Gates for enthusiastically reading whatever I pass to her. And a special thanks to Chey Wilson and Tobias, whoever they are.

Last but not least, I would like to thank my wife, Ivette, for all of her support.

CHAPTER 1

—

"This city eats souls," the cabbie ranted.

Dan Lord stared out the rear window trying not to respond to the driver. From the back seat of the yellow cab, Dan caught a glimpse of his reflection in the metal trim of the security glass. He admired the tamed gray locks that danced above his ears and adjusted the thick-framed glasses, which slid down his nose with each bump in the road. He ran a hand along his two-day-old stubble, satisfied the growth provided the desired unkempt European flair.

The cabbie glanced into his rearview mirror and continued his paid-by-the-mile viewpoint.

"Don't get me wrong, this city looks great on the evening news with the Mall in the background. The outline of the Washington Monument just shimmering in the reflecting pool. Cool water at the feet of Abraham Lincoln . . . 'All men are created equal,' my ass."

"I think Thomas Jefferson said 'all men are created equal.' Lincoln wrote 'government of the people, by the people, for the people . . ..'"

"Well then, I've been underselling Lincoln all this time because 'government for the people' is an even bigger pile of horse excrement. It may have been true a couple hundred years ago, but it's not true today."

Dan offered an olive branch and struggled to focus on his task for the evening. "This city has its fair share of problems."

"Nothing 'fair' about the share. At least Vegas is honest. They come right out and call it Sin City. But it has nothing on this place. Nothing. People here are conservative and pretentious on the surface, but behind the curtains this place supports a volume of ill-repute unseen since Lot's wife turned into a pillar of salt looking over her shoulder on the way out of town."

The name of the city is Sodom, Dan thought.

"These politicians come to town, ride around in waxed limos and executive sedans, heading from one buffet to the next. And who pays for it? We do. And don't forget the lawyers."

"Can't forget the lawyers," Dan agreed, going over the plan for the next hour in his mind.

"It never ends. New politicians and lawyers invade this town with every new administration. Everyone promising change. Changes to the system. Promises made with bits of food from the public trough dripping from their chins."

This guy should have a talk show. Dan tapped the manila folder in his lap, cracked the window a couple of inches, and let the driver's ranting fade into the noise of the traffic.

If Dan wasn't on the clock, he would have told the driver the city still had a chance. That there was at least one person still shining hope in unseen places—illuminating dark corners where blue collars and hired help shared secrets with those vying to be king. *The rub of the classes*, Dan called it. It was where he operated. Where he lived. Where he thrived. He knew the popular hotel suites, the private clubs with no signs on the doors, the call girls who fed pent-up sexual appetites that normal sex with the wife, or a kinky intern, couldn't satisfy.

For the oblivious masses lost in the shuffle—the teachers, the cubicle dwellers, the engineers, the working class with dirt under their nails and callused hands—the rub of the classes in the most democratic city on earth wasn't something discussed over meals-in-a-bag and frozen instant dinners in front of the tube. For the majority of the population—a sliver of whom came to town each year as tourists for the history and culture—DC was simply monuments and museums buffered by architecture unseen outside of Europe.

And there was no place dirtier.

D.C.

Dirty City.

Dan was on the clock, working to clean it, one soil stain at a time.

—

The cab pulled to the curb on one of the city's myriad one-way streets and Dan spoke through the holes drilled in the security glass. "What's the damage?"

"Nineteen even."

Dan stepped from the back of the cab and slipped a twenty through the front passenger window. "Keep the change."

"Thanks, big spender," the burly driver replied, shoving the cash into the front pocket of his sweaty shirt.

Dan bent at the waist, his manila folder in hand, and peered into the open window. The glare from Dan's light blue eyes subdued the driver's bravado, bringing a moment of long-sought silence to the interior of the car. The cabbie muttered something unintelligible and the car pulled away into the evening rush-hour traffic.

Dan straightened his dark blue suit and red tie before heading down H Street. The business side of the White House sat just beyond Lafayette Square to his left. As a white male in a suit, within spitting distance of the White House, Dan was perfectly camouflaged. Despite the changing face of American society and the dual terms of President Obama, those making the rules remained largely as they always had been—lily white. An hour watching C-Span was the only proof needed.

Dan walked deliberately to the corner of H and Sixteenth streets and silently mingled with a half-dozen likeminded suits waiting for the light. The pedestrian signal changed from an illuminated red hand to the depiction of a person walking. The crowd moved. Dan took three steps towards the street and then froze at the edge of the curb. He scanned his environment for a mirror reaction from anyone in the vicinity. Sometimes the best way to see if you are being followed is to stop. It was a standard counter-surveillance move, an ancient ritual likely perfected a hundred thousand years ago by an animal on the Serengeti trying to avoid becoming dinner.

The sidewalk around Dan emptied as the pedestrian signal on the far side of the street began to countdown. Dan swiveled his head slowly, finishing with a glance over each shoulder. *No one*, he thought. *At least no one on foot*. Walking against traffic on a one-way street mitigated most of the possibilities of being trailed by car.

He waited until the countdown on the pedestrian signal reached five and then crossed the street illegally in the opposite direction, dissecting a group of lawyers and think-tankers on their way to a local watering hole to finish their briefs and pontifications for the evening.

On the far side of the street, Dan turned right and headed back in the direction from which he had come. Once again he checked for surveillance. *Nothing.*

Near the end of the block, with a taxi queue ten yards ahead, Dan checked his watch with a casual glance and turned left down an alley without looking back.

He passed several Dumpsters and looked up at the darkening sky framed by the buildings on both sides of the alley. A light scent of urine wafted through the air. Under a fire escape near the corner of the building Dan turned again. He followed a staircase downward, his hand running along a worn metal handrail, his shoes trampling cracked concrete steps. Three stories above the urban crevasse, room rates started at eight hundred a night.

Dan forced himself to relax. Feeling out of place was the single greatest contributor for being spotted in an area where one had no earthly business. But with the appropriate behavior and movement, a man in a suit in an alley was no more out of place than a man in overalls in the lobby of an office building. Properly portrayed, every appearance could be overlooked.

Dan reached the bottom of the stairs and admired the collection of discarded cigarette butts thrown half-heartedly at an empty coffee can resting just outside the door. He took one more calming breath and pushed through an unlocked metal door that read "Exit Only" in neat white print.

Unlocked doors were goldmines. Half the buildings in the nation's capital were circumventing million dollar security systems with propped open doors. A brick here. A doorstop there. If you knew where to look, an employee with a smoking habit could be better than a week of surveillance. Not to mention cheaper and less risky than paying off a doorman.

Inside the building, Dan entered an elbow-wide foyer facing

another door. He watched the light under the closed door and waited for the telltale movement of people on the other side to abate. When the timing was right and the movement ceased, he pulled the knob.

An attractive blonde in an off-the-shoulder red dress took a breath of surprise. Dan muted his response and without pausing pointed towards the men's room with his chin. "Wrong door."

The lady in red smiled and Dan followed through on his impromptu ruse and entered the restroom.

"Shit," Dan whispered, looking into the mirror over a granite sink with gold fixtures. He had rules. One adjustment in the plan was standard. Two put him on notice. Three unforeseen adjustments to a plan and he aborted—immediately and without exception. There was little he could do about the woman in the hall so he pushed it aside. *That's one*, he thought. *A little early for an adjustment.*

The lower-level backdoor at the Hay Adams Hotel was a direct line into the living room of the elite. Off the Record—the appropriately named bar in the basement of the Hay Adams Hotel—boasted a history as long as its client list. It was where the rich blew off steam. People with faces too famous to enjoy a quiet drink in Georgetown or along Connecticut Avenue. Faces from the morning paper and the evening news. Off the Record embraced customers who didn't mind overpaying for drinks or the forty bucks it cost to valet their cars. Money was rapidly becoming the last legal barrier for keeping out the riffraff.

The Hay Adams Hotel, and its subterranean watering hole, was public. Dan could have chosen to walk through the lobby. He could have nodded at the bellhop and doorman as he strolled in unquestioned and unmolested. He could have slowly crossed the ornate wood-paneled entrance and past the polite scrutiny of the front desk as he made his way to the stairs. But why announce your arrival when you didn't have to? Especially so close to payday.

In the mirror in the bathroom, Dan checked his hair, his face, his glasses, his teeth, his fingers. He peeked inside his manila folder. He exited the room and walked through the lone swinging door into the bar. He located his target before his first foot hit the deep burgundy carpet. He completed his room assessment by the time his second foot landed. Nine men and four women, he calculated, parsing his headcount before anyone noticed he was in the room. Five men at the bar, two of them seated together, most likely co-workers. Two women alone at a table on the far side of the room in similar black dresses. *Waiting for dates*, he thought. A table of three huddled in the opposite corner, far enough away to be out of most contingency scenarios. Dan added four more to the headcount for the bartender and waitresses, and a final addition for the lady in red who was now in the bathroom.

Dan stepped out from the dark corner near the bathroom and approached a man in his early fifties sitting alone at a table, his hand caressing a glass of Maker's Mark.

"Judge McMichael," Dan said, sitting quickly without invitation.

The judge tried not to look surprised but the corners of his eyes betrayed him as they danced towards the entrance of the bar.

"The back door?" the judge asked.

"Bathroom window," Dan replied straight-faced.

"Am I at the correct table?"

"Yes. Thank you for following instructions."

Dan didn't take his eyes off the judge. The judge looked older than his pictures in the press. More stately. Fifty and fit with large hands and sharp eyes. The lighting was romantic—enough light to see the judge, but dark enough to erase cosmetic imperfections from across the table. Perfect call-girl ambiance.

The judge stared back across the table at a short grey mop of curls and wild blue eyes dancing behind thick black-framed glasses. The judge's eyes dropped to Dan's hands and the manila folder on the table. Dan noticed the judge's attention and he covered one hand with the other, both on top of the folder.

"Why don't we both agree to keep our hands on the table," Dan suggested before getting to work. "See the two guys at the far end of the bar?"

The judge turned his head slightly.

"They are with me."

The judge nodded.

"I will make this short and sweet. Your wife has divorce papers for you to sign. She also has an agreement regarding alimony and the custody of your stepson and stepdaughter. She says you have been refusing to sign these documents and have threatened her and her children."

"Do you know who I am?"

"Yes. Judge Terrance J. McMichael. Born in Naperville, Illinois. Educated at Princeton. Law School at Dartmouth. Judge for the United States Court of Appeals for the District of Columbia Circuit . . . also known as the DC Circuit. Wife is named Cindy. Stepdaughter is Caroline. Stepson is Craig."

"And you are?"

"Someone willing to ruin your life. Your wife hired me to make a request on her behalf. You are a highly intelligent man so I'm going to assume you heard my request the first time and that I don't need to repeat myself." Dan paused for effect. "You *are* going to sign the papers."

"Do you have any idea what I can do to you?"

Dan slid the manila folder into the middle of the table and opened it. The first photograph showed the judge's wife with raccoon eyes, her nose broken, swollen to twice its normal size. Her torn and blood-drenched clothes were on full display next to her. The photo was taken in a bathroom, the reflection of the cameraman, the judge's stepson, clear in the mirror.

"She fell," the judge said.

"Well, as convenient as that explanation may be, I think sympathy will wane when the public sees the next pictures."

The judge waited for Dan to turn the next photo in the stack. Sweat beaded on his forehead.

"Those are bruises on a ten-year-old girl. Your stepdaughter." Dan flipped to another photo. "If you notice, there is a telling shoe print on her back, which I imagine is a little bigger than your wife's size."

"What do you want?"

"I told you what I want."

"Whatever she is paying, I'll pay more."

"It's not about the money . . . well, not entirely. Besides, whatever she pays me is your money anyway."

"You motherfucker," the judge quietly hissed. The veins in his neck bulged.

"Certainly all those years of schooling must have linguistically prepared you better than that."

The judge took a sip of his drink, his hands shaking slightly. Dan stole a glance of the room as the judge's eyes dipped beneath the edge of the upturned glass.

The judge returned his glass to the table but didn't release his grip. "You are aware that blackmail is illegal."

"I'm asking for your cooperation. I'm not asking for money. Though, now that you have offered money, it wouldn't be blackmail if I accepted."

"You won't get away with this. You don't become a DC Circuit judge without friends. You don't serve on a court that has bred more Supreme Court Justices than any other without knowing people."

"Don't let pride get the better of you. You're not the first person I've made a deal with. You won't be the last. Not in this city."

Dan let the statement sink in before he continued.

"You have one week to sign the papers and file them with the court. If I don't hear from your wife by then, I will release the story to the press and to certain people at the Justice Department who may not share your enthusiasm for unmitigated power. Certain people who believe the oath they took means something. I should also mention if something should happen to your wife between now and the filing of the papers, the photos and taped testimony from your wife and children will go public. If your wife mysteriously changes her mind in the next, say, month or so, the photos and her testimony still go public."

"How do I know you won't go public after I sign the papers?"

"You don't." Dan paused. "Are you familiar with the Lady Justice Statue, the one with a woman holding a set of scales?"

"I *am* a judge."

"I appreciate that sentiment, but given your non-judicial behavior on other fronts, I didn't want to take anything for granted."

"Your point?" Judge McMichael grunted.

"The Lady Justice Statue depicts your current situation. On the one hand you have the possibility of me going public if I don't hear from your wife by next week. The weight of this possibility is driving down one side of the scale in Lady Justice's hand. On the other side of the scale is the possibility I will go public with your information regardless of what you do. I would consider this side of the scale far lighter than the other."

The judge glanced quickly at the front door of the bar. "I can't do it in a week. I need more time for my attorney to review the documents before they are filed."

"Judge McMichael, a man of your talents can have this done before you get up from your seat."

The judge finished his drink and he set the glass on the table with a thud. "Anything else?"

"One thing." Dan pulled out the last photo in the folder. "I recognize the woman in this photo so I'm sure you do as well, particularly given the lack of clothing. Nice socks, by the way. And your partner's knee-high red fishnets are very naughty. So before you do anything rash, remember it's more than just you and your ego at stake."

The judge brooded, his anger visible in his eyes, the corner of his lips quivering.

Dan continued. "I'm offering you the path of least resistance. I suggest you take it." Dan took another look around the room and waved at the two men at the bar who waved back in a look of inebriated recognition before turning towards one another and resuming their conversation. The rest of the bar's occupants were still in their respective places. All systems checked. Nothing out of the ordinary.

Dan readied to stand and added another condition. "And if something happens to me in the near future, before or after the documents get filed with the court, the photos and taped testimony go to the press. I have a secure website with some unique programming. If I don't log on in pre-determined increments, well, you get the picture. And so will everyone else."

"Are we done?"

"Follow the rules and you will never see me again." Dan stood. He gestured towards the folder on the table. "You can keep those copies for your records."

———

When Dan left the table the judge frantically removed his cell phone from his pocket and made a call to the off-duty police officer posted in the lobby upstairs. Then he waved over the waitress and ordered another drink. A double.

The judge was still in his seat when the plainclothes policeman briskly crossed the floor of the bar minutes later.

"Did you find him?" the judge asked.

"Nothing."

"How long did it take you to get to the back alley?"

"Thirty seconds. Ten to get outside. Another twenty to run halfway around the block. Plus the few seconds it took to take the call."

"Wonderful."

"How would you like to proceed? I didn't call it in, per your instructions."

"Let it go for now," the judge said. "Check those two guys at the bar and see if they know the man who was just here. I doubt they do. I'll let you know if I need anything else."

"Yes, sir."

The officer spoke briefly with the two men at the bar and then shook his head in the direction of the judge. The judge raised a hand and dipped his head. The officer nodded and left. The judge removed the digital voice recorder from the inside pocket of his jacket. He pressed play, listened for a moment, and then hit delete.

CHAPTER 2

—

Dan took a shortcut through the backdoor of the Aroma Indian restaurant, which shared the alley with the Hay Adams Hotel. He weaved through the restaurant full of patrons and exited out the front door past a confused maître d'. He took his first taxi to Georgetown, and his second cab to DuPont Circle. He shed his tie in the first cab and shoved it under the driver's seat with the toe of his shoe.

In the one-stall bathroom at the Cosi on New Hampshire Avenue, he took off his wig and glasses and threw them in the trash. He removed the blue-tinted nonprescription novelty contact lenses, revealing his natural dark green irises, and flushed the lenses down the toilet. He tussled his matted brown hair with water from the sink and washed the layer of cyanoacrylate—a medical glue—off his fingertips with soap and water.

The stubble on his face was real and he would keep it until the morning. The wrinkles on his forehead were also real and growing in number and in depth, skin aged by a mix of laughter, worry, and sun. He remembered his thirty-ninth birthday party, in all its glamour, celebrated in the bars nearby. He remembered the hangover even more succinctly. Forty, and premature death if he continued down his current career path, was right around the corner. But so far, genetics still allowed him to flash his ID for a beer on occasion. He held firm to his college build—six foot one, one hundred and ninety pounds. The looks wouldn't last forever. Genetics always lost to Father Time. Everything did.

He completed his after-a-job reflection on life and exited the bathroom, holding the door for a college student listening to music on headphones, his nose buried in the latest edition of *The City Paper*.

Outside, Dan walked through DuPont Circle proper and watched the freak show. Druggies and yuppies, straight and gay, lovers and professionals, mingled on common ground from all angles of society's spectrum. He stopped near a chess match on a park bench long enough to determine who was going to win and then continued to the north entrance of the DuPont metro station. Two trains and an hour later, he was on the other side of the Potomac, within walking distance of home.

—

Dan was asleep on his three-piece sectional sofa, his right hand resting on the waistband of his favorite boxers. On the table, a trio of empty red Chinese carryout boxes rested among a stack of unread magazines and a wad of grease-stained napkins.

Once a week he slept on the sofa. For the white picket-fence, husband-and-wife segment of society, sleeping on the sofa was a sign of immaturity, laziness, or a marital spat. For a college student or binge drinker consumed by the suppressant of his favorite indulgence, it simply meant a move to better sleeping arrangements was physically out of the question. But when you grow up in a thousand beds in a thousand locations, sleep was an opportunity not defined by where the activity took place.

But even for a man with unusual work hours, a phone call at two in the morning rarely proved a good omen. Dan flailed his outstretched hand without looking until it found the cordless phone in its cradle.

"Yeah," he answered, his throat dry, raspy.

"Dan, it's Vicky."

He knew something was wrong with the utterance of the first syllable.

"Conner isn't breathing," she said, voice cracking.

Dan bolted upright and shook his head.

"Where?"

"He isn't breathing. His eyes have rolled back. He's covered in sweat," she said, the full emotions kept in abeyance on the other end of the phone bursting their containment.

"Where are you?"

"Home. Oh God, I think he's dying . . ."

Dan's stomach turned as his sister-in-law crumbled into incoherence.

"Call 911. I'm on my way."

Dan grabbed the jeans off the floor near the sofa, jammed on the running shoes by the door, and swiped his keys off the counter.

—

Dan exited Old Town Alexandria going north, hitting the GW Parkway at ninety. He felt himself up for his cell phone, which he had left behind, and then focused on driving. He didn't touch the brakes for the next eleven minutes, cursing through moments of panic. The ride was a blur. A blur of memories, a blur of emotions, a blur of headlights and streetlamps. Snapshots of his nephew coursed through his mind. *Conner. Dear God.* A special kid in many regards, although at nineteen he was no longer a child. In Dan's mind, part of him always would be.

Dan took the ramp onto the Roosevelt Bridge and punched it, the ripples in the water of the Potomac eighty feet below. The car hit sixty on the Rock Creek Parkway and dropped to twice the speed limit on the leafy, well-heeled streets of Northwest Washington. The car zoomed past large brick homes with manicured lawns and an assortment of high-priced imports in the driveways.

Dan hit the brakes in front of his sister-in-law's house and his car came to a screeching halt, the front tires on the lawn. He left the car door open and sprinted for the front porch. He screamed his sister-in-law's name loud enough for the neighbors to hear, tried the front doorknob, and began banging on the large door knocker while fumbling for the extra key he kept on his key chain. He smashed his palm into the buzzer as he slid the key into the lock with his other hand.

He pushed the door open and the darkness of the house was outweighed by its silence. Chills ran up Dan's spine, his body wet with perspiration. He moved through the foyer, feeling the wall for the light switch. He turned into the living room and banged into the side of the doorway as he made his way to the kitchen in the back of the house.

"Vicky!" he yelled again.

He continued through the kitchen, into the dining room, and completed the lap around the first floor of the house, turning on lights as he went. He paused. *The bedroom in the basement!*

He ran back to the kitchen, light now shining from beyond the large island with its hanging cookware. He flung open another door and took the steps to the basement three at a time, losing and regaining his balance as he hit the landing. He turned on more lights as he scanned the room. The basement was as he remembered it. *How long had it been? Two months? Maybe three?* The foosball table was in the corner. The large-screen TV was against the far wall. Two empty leather chairs were parked in front the TV. He scanned the floor and saw nothing but beige Berber carpeting.

His head swiveled left to right as he made his way to his nephew's old bedroom in the corner. The door was shut and Dan inexplicably stopped for a split second as if preparing himself for what he was going to find on the other side. He took a breath, held it, and pushed his way in.

His anxiety passed with a flick of the lights. Nothing. The bed in the corner was made and unoccupied. The closet with its large sliding doors was open and empty, less for an old set of golf clubs and a small pile of out-of-fashion clothes balled up in the corner.

"Bathroom," Dan said to himself, leaving the bedroom with another burst of energy. He yelled his sister-in-law's name again.

He crossed the large, open family room and passed the small kitchenette in the corner where his nephew microwaved pizza and drank beer without his mother's consent. The bathroom door was open and Dan poked his head in long enough to see the empty tub, the shower curtain pulled to the side, a towel hanging in the middle of the rod.

He threw the door open to the laundry room. The light from

behind him sent his own shadow against the wall. Dan blinked to straighten his mind. He yelled out his nephew's name and waved his hand in the air, feeling for the chain to the light bulb hanging from the ceiling of the unfinished room. With a tug of the short chain, the room proved empty.

Dan raced up two flights of stairs and continued his frantic search through the four bedrooms on the top floor. In the walk-in closet in the master bedroom Dan froze in his tracks. The body of his sister-in-law in her nightgown, feet off the ground, face contorted and blue from the belt around her neck, brought a mouthful of greasy Kung Pao Chicken up from the depths of his stomach.

—

Dan sat on the hood of his car in the driveway, staring up intermittently at the stars above. He ran his hands through his brown hair and let the tears dry on his face in the cool autumn air. The flashing lights of the ambulance were mercifully extinguished once the death had been officially declared. A well-dressed Asian detective from the Washington Metropolitan Police made his way from the open front door of the house to Dan's position on his car.

The detective extended his hand and Dan returned the greeting with a firm grip. "Detective Nick Nguyen. District 2."

"Detective. Dan Lord."

The police detective measured Dan's exterior—his hair, eyes, weight. "You look familiar. Have we met?"

"It's possible. DC is a small city in the who-knows-who business." Dan leaned back slightly and casually sized up the detective: five foot eight on a good day, a hundred and sixty pounds when draped in a rain-soaked winter jacket. Meticulously combed jet-black hair. A perfect crease ran vertically down his trousers.

"I hear you were the one who found the body," Detective Nguyen said.

"That's right," Dan answered. "Not the body I was looking for, but I found the body."

"You want to run that by me again?"

"I told everything to the first officer on the scene. The name on the badge was Lawson."

The detective raised his notebook and scribbled on an open page. "How about giving me the rundown? From the beginning."

"You going to pay attention or am I going to have to repeat this a few more times?"

Detective Nguyen looked at Dan and nodded slowly. "I'm sorry for your loss."

Dan nodded back, a gesture he meant as both an acknowledgement of the detective's condolences and a temporary truce. "I got a call at a little after two from my sister-in-law. I arrived on the scene about twenty-five minutes later."

"And your sister-in-law is the deceased?"

"That's right. Her name is Vicky Lord. My brother passed away five years ago October."

The detective raised his notebook again and filled in two more lines in nearly incomprehensible chicken scratch. "Exactly what time did your sister-in-law call?"

"A little after two. I was asleep. When I reached my car the clock read 2:13, so she called a few minutes before that."

"And what was the conversation?"

"She said my nephew wasn't breathing. That she thought he was dying."

"Your nephew?"

"That's right. His name is Conner Lord."

"Did your sister-in-law call the police or 911 before she called you?"

"I assume she did. She wasn't stupid. I also told her to call as I hung up. I assumed the police and EMTs would be here when I arrived. They were not."

"Where do you live?"

"Alexandria."

"That's quite a drive for twenty minutes, assuming it took you a couple of minutes to get dressed, out the door, and to your car."

"You planning to give me a speeding ticket?"

"Did you call anyone on the drive?"

"No. I ran out without my cell phone . . . or wallet."

The detective glanced at Dan's attire and noted the thin gray t-shirt, woefully insufficient for the current temperature. The detective's eyes dropped further to the sockless skin peeking out from the gap between Dan's jeans and the top of his shoes.

Dan continued. "I used my key to enter the house, turned on the lights as I went room to room, and called 911 when I found Vicky. Obviously, the chain of events is a little unusual."

"And then?"

"I took down the body, checked for vitals and performed CPR until the paramedics arrived on scene. The police took another twenty minutes to arrive."

The barb did not go unnoticed.

Detective Nguyen ran through the story once more from beginning to end. "That's your statement?"

"That's my statement," Dan confirmed.

The detective scribbled again in his notebook.

"How much longer will you guys be?" Dan asked, wringing his hands. He wanted a cigarette. Three years of sometimes painful abstinence and the cravings still haunted him.

"Not sure. All indications are that it was a suicide. There's no crime scene to speak of. Everything looks in place."

"In place? Were you listening?"

"Yes, I was. Were you?"

The stare down in the driveway lasted several uncomfortable seconds.

"What exactly *aren't* you saying?" the detective asked.

"There are two things that bother me. Obviously, my sister-in-law believed her son was dead, or dying, in the house, or she felt compelled to have me believe that."

"Did your sister-in-law have a history of mental illness?"

"No. She is, or was, pretty straight-laced. After my brother died, I know she took Prozac for a while. But, hell, I think we all should have."

"A lot of people are on Prozac. There have been studies linking a higher rate of suicide with those taking the drug."

"I saw that *20/20* episode. My sister-in-law is also a devout Catholic, meaning suicide is at the bottom of her list of things to experience. And she has never called me in the middle of the night before. Ever."

"It is possible she planned to kill herself and wanted you to find her body."

"Then why tell me that my nephew's body is in the house, in the throes of death? Why the wild goose chase?"

"Buy some time, maybe."

"Doesn't make sense. My nephew doesn't live here. He goes to American University. Stays in a dorm. Drops by to see his mom and have dinner once a week. On occasion he drops by on the weekend."

"And you're sure your sister-in-law said he was in the house?"

"Yes."

"I guess we're going to have to take your word on that."

"His car is parked in the alley at the rear of the house."

"Is that normal?"

"Every house on this block has a couple of parking spaces in the back."

"Thanks for the info on the car. I'll have it examined. Have you tried to contact your nephew?"

"I called his dorm room from the house but there was no answer. I called his mobile number and left a message for him to call me here, at home, or on my cell. Of course, sitting out here in the driveway, I am not available on any of those lines."

"Well, if your nephew is alive, he should be easy to locate."

Dan looked away, almost speaking to himself. "Dead people are actually easier to find. They don't tend to run."

The detective looked at Dan with curiosity.

"What did you say you do for a living?"

"I didn't."

"Consider me asking."

"Self-employed. I'm a legal advisor. I also maintain an active private investigator's license in Virginia."

"So you carry a gun?"

"Was someone shot?"

"Are you going to answer the question?"

"I have a license to carry a gun. Whether I own a gun is irrelevant to this investigation, unless I'm missing something."

The detective stood stoic, digesting the facts. "So, one more time from the top. You received a call at home from your sister-in-law saying that your nephew, her son, wasn't breathing in her home. You immediately drove over to the house and found your sister-in-law dead, with no sign of your nephew, dead or alive."

"You take excellent notes, Detective Nguyen."

"Are you busting my balls?"

Dan sighed.

The detective paused. "To you, I probably look like a young Asian kid with a badge and a notebook. But Asians age well. Hard to guess our real age. And I'll let you in on a little personal knowledge. I learned from the best detective this fine city has to offer. One of the best, period, regardless of geography. Someone who has investigated more dead bodies than you and I combined will see in our lives. Someone involved in cases you and I couldn't access with a top secret security clearance."

"Very moving. You think the evidence will be impressed with your credentials, training, and previous partners?"

"You aren't very popular, are you Mr. Lord?"

"Look, I have been out here for an hour rehashing my side of the story. In the meantime, my nephew is missing."

"I assure you we are on the case."

"Talk is cheap, Detective."

Detective Nguyen glanced back at the house as a pair of paramedics stepped onto the porch. "Let me get your info," the detective said, flipping to a new page in his notebook. When he was done with his question and answer, he wrote down the car's license plate number and VIN. "I'll see if your story checks out," the detective added. "Are you planning on going out of town?"

"Are you labeling me a suspect of some kind?"

"A person of interest."

"Sounds like a suspect to me. Just a sugar-coated one."

CHAPTER 3

—

Dan was reading the *Post* and drinking a Dunkin' Donuts coffee on the park bench down the block from his sister-in-law's house. He had gone home and changed into a Polartec top and Zip n' Go hiking pants manufactured from high-tech, rip-stop material. He had stopped by American University, gave his story to the campus police, and waited at the station while two campus officers accessed his nephew's room and found it unoccupied. He had left messages with everyone he could think of and then drove back to his sister-in-law's house on auto-pilot, stopping for a dose of sugar and caffeine on the way.

The last emergency personnel had exited the house an hour before, leaving a wrap of yellow police tape stretched between two columns on the front porch. An unmarked dark police cruiser arrived shortly thereafter and Detective Nick Nguyen stepped from the driver's side. He perused the yard and sidewalk as he approached the yellow tape and then ducked under the temporary impediment before entering the house. An hour later he reappeared on the front porch and removed the yellow police tape. He walked across the front lawn and threw the spaghetti of yellow into the police cruiser's trunk.

No longer a crime scene, Dan thought. He gulped down the dark sludge at the bottom of his coffee and threw the cup and newspaper in the trashcan near the jungle gym before heading down the block on foot.

The alley behind the houses was the main thoroughfare for garbage men, stray cats, and teenagers sneaking their dates through backdoors for parentally unapproved sexual gratification. The surface of the alley was uneven, large concrete slabs rising in a medley of angles like tectonic plates rearranged by induction. Dan had been in the alley a handful of times, usually chasing down a runaway baseball that managed to clear the fence, escaping the confines of his nephew's yard.

A neighbor dumping a plastic bag into a large green trashcan startled Dan as he approached the rear entrance to his sister-in-law's house.

"Morning." The man with the white hair and blue pajamas looked curiously up and down the empty alley. "Can I help you?"

"Good morning," Dan said to the retiree in blue pajamas. "My name is Dan Lord. Conner is my nephew. Vicky is my sister-in-law."

"A lot of commotion last night."

"Yes, sir. Not good news, I'm afraid. Vicky passed."

The retiree shook his head and choked up. "Awful. Just awful. What about the boy?"

"I'm trying to get him word."

"Seems like a good kid. Don't know him too well."

"Real good kid." Dan shifted his weight from one foot to the other, his eyes darting suspiciously across his field of view.

"You sneaking in the back door?"

"Something like that."

"Anything I can help with? I've got nothing pressing, as you can see," the neighbor said, lifting his arms to show off his attire.

"I have a few questions for you, if you don't mind."

"Don't mind a bit."

"See anything strange around here last night? Anything strange over the last few weeks? People who shouldn't be in the neighborhood?"

"Nothing out of the ordinary. We're lucky. This is a real quiet street. One of the reasons I moved here."

"That's why I asked. I figured anything unusual would get noticed."

"Can't say I noticed anything last night. Was in bed by ten, sawing logs by ten fifteen. I woke up when the ambulance arrived. Didn't sleep too much after the commotion, though."

"Me either."

"Guess not."

Dan glanced up the alley at his nephew's Nissan hatchback parked neatly in one of the two spots at the rear of the house. "Any idea how long my nephew's car has been parked there?"

"I think it was there Sunday. Not sure about Saturday."

Dan's eyes shot left and right as a police siren wailed in the distance.

"Well, I'll let you get on with your business," the neighbor said. "I assume you aren't walking up the alley for your health."

Dan nodded and continued up the alley to the next yard, stopping to check the doors to his nephew's car and to peer through the windows of the vehicle. With a final glance around, he pushed open the wrought iron gate and entered his sister-in-law's property.

The grass in the backyard was neat and trim. The fall leaves were bagged, sitting on a bed of mulch that would be dormant until spring. A large oak loomed over the yard, a measure of the neighborhood's age, the tree's thick trunk showing that its roots were there long before the human invasion stole its land and cut down its relatives.

The step-up slate patio arched into a semi-circle from the back of the house. The patio furniture was neatly pushed under the overhang of the roof, ready to spend the upcoming winter partially shielded from the elements. The screened-in porch had been winterized—the plants moved inside, the thin carpet rolled up and dragged to the attic.

Dan stepped onto the patio and the house weighed on him. He could never live there. The home had memories, good and bad, but too numerous for Dan to find peace. Besides, he preferred Alexandria when it came to living. Better roads, better services, friendlier police, and of course little things called a congressman and a senator to represent him with their elected hot air.

Dan pulled on the sliding door leading to the screened-in porch. It didn't budge. He moved to the other side of the patio and tried the wooden door that lead directly to the laundry room at the back of the house. He twisted the knob, pushed, and then added his shoulder to the equation. The deadbolt held firm. He bent at the knees and looked at the doorframe for signs of forced entry, telltale scratches, chunks of missing wood.

Nothing.

He used his key to enter and then repeated the inspection on all doors and windows from the inside of the house. Upstairs, he took another look at the master bedroom. He picked up the phone on the bedside table and checked for a dial tone. All systems go.

Downstairs, Dan paced the layout of the first floor several times. Through the kitchen, the living room, down the hall, and around the dining room table. On a wooden plaque near the back-door that read "Welcome Home," a dozen key rings dangled from their respective hooks. Dan flipped through the assortment, found a set that included keys to his nephew's car, and exited the back of the house to take a look at the Nissan hatchback.

He opened the car door and the light over the center of the dash illuminated the black fabric interior. He shuffled through a pile of receipts in the storage bin under the center armrest and re-moved everything from the glove box, putting the owner's manual, a tire-pressure gauge, and a small box of tissues onto the passenger seat.

Dan looked in the back seat, felt around on the rear floors, and then turned back towards the front. He noticed a faded ring mark on the windshield glass, several inches in diameter. He leaned for-ward, took a deep breath, and exhaled onto the glass. Aided by Dan's warm breath, the circular mark appeared more distinctly.

Dan felt under the driver's seat and double-checked the stor-age slits on both front doors. The portable GPS he had given his nephew for Christmas two years ago, which had been attached with a suction cup to the front windshield, was missing. Dan filed away the need to locate the GPS when the phone in his pants started to vibrate. He fumbled through the multiple pockets on his hik-ing pants, glanced at a number he didn't recognize, and hit the talk button.

He sat for a moment staring at the phone, the voice on the other end of the line searching for a response. Dan was frozen, his phone in hand. Something in his mind kick-started. A bubble of subconscious reasoning not yet ready to surface.

"Dan speaking," he finally answered.

"This is Detective Nguyen. We may have found your nephew's body."

Dan cleared his throat. "Where?"

"Underpass, near L'Enfant Plaza. Under the Promenade."

"When?"

"Someone called it in early this morning. The medical examiner got the body about two hours ago. I just found out. I'm still a little light on the details. I was on notice for any white males fitting your nephew's description, but this one initially got listed as homeless. I wasn't on the lookout for an NFA."

"NFA?"

"No Fixed Address."

"I'm not following you."

"NFAs usually don't get a lot of forensic work, meaning the body is moved fairly quickly. Unofficial policy. Homeless people die all the time in this city. Can't have bodies lying on the sidewalk."

"Do you have a positive ID?"

"Not yet. We may need you for that."

Dan exhaled loudly. "Where are you now?"

"On my way to the Medical Examiner."

"Which hospital?"

"Washington Hospital Center."

"I'll be there in a half-hour."

"There may be nothing to tell you in a half-hour."

"Then I'll be there waiting when they do have something."

CHAPTER 4

—

The automatic double doors slid open as Dan approached the entrance. An empty gurney was pushed against the pale blue tile walls under a sign indicating the direction of the medical examiner's office. Dan bypassed the elevators and followed a sign down a flight of gray stairs and stopped in front of a waiting area. Six black plastic chairs failed to entice him to sit.

He spotted Detective Nguyen sitting at a lone desk in an alcove across from the waiting area. The detective hadn't changed since the night before, his clothes more wrinkled, bags now under his eyes. Nguyen flipped through his ever-present detective's notebook and looked up as Dan walked towards him.

"You're here."

"Thanks for calling."

"I think the ME is ready. You ever identified a body before?"

"This won't be a first."

"Then I'll forego the speech."

Dan nodded. His eyes were focused. He forced his feet to move towards a set of swinging doors.

The examination room was devoid of life, save one. Inside the windowless, colorless room, three large stainless-steel tables filled the floor. The table nearest the door was empty. The unmoving occupant of the far table was covered, a toe protruding from beneath a sheet the only hint to its owner's identity. The medical examiner was standing at the head of a body on the middle table.

"Come in, Detective Nguyen," the doctor said. Dark-framed eyeglasses dominated the space between the doctor's cap and his medical mask. His light green scrubs and his white apron were fresh from the laundry pile, yet to be stained by the hazards of the job.

"Dr. Lewis, I have a possible family member with me," Detective Nguyen announced, offering a professional courtesy that gently reminded the ME the incoming audience may not be as callous to certain specifics of the ME's occupation.

Dan followed the detective into the room. The medical examiner met them halfway across the floor. Dan offered a handshake and the doctor—behind the glasses, mask, scrubs, and rubber gloves—raised his hands and waved them in the air, indicating a handshake wasn't a hygienic alternative.

"Sorry we have to meet in *my* office. It makes a visit to the dentist seem enviable by comparison."

"Yes it does," Dan responded.

The ME turned and Dan followed behind him. He held his breath through the last few seconds of hope that the body on the table wasn't his nephew's. Through the last few seconds of hope for a reasonable explanation for everything. As he approached the table, the large circular light above illuminated the pasty body below.

Dan looked at the legs first, his eyes slowly moving up the naked frame until he reached the face. He squinted out a tear, looked away for a moment, and then ran his fingers through his nephew's hair. He nodded and whispered over his shoulder in the direction of the detective, "It's him."

The doctor simply nodded. It was occupational stoicism. Emotions were for the living.

"I'm sorry," Detective Nguyen's said, putting a hand on Dan's shoulder.

"Relationship to the deceased?" the doctor asked.

"Uncle."

"Shall I proceed with what I know?"

"Please," Dan answered, clearing his throat. His eyes were wet. His temples pulsing.

"I'll tell you what I think, and you tell me when I'm right. Fair enough?"

"Sure." Dan slipped into a surreal mode. Half his mind was in the room, listening to the doctor expound upon the evidence before him. The other half of Dan's mind was already asking questions—working what he knew and didn't know beyond the confines of the room.

Dan tuned back into the medical examiner's commentary.

"A male, age nineteen. According to the body temperature, dead eight to ten hours, give or take. Death appears to have been a drug overdose, most likely heroin though I won't know until I get the toxicology report."

Dan interrupted. "Heroin? No way."

"You certainly have the right to that opinion. It would not be the first time my opinion has been sabotaged by medical evidence."

"How long does a toxicology report take?"

"A week. Sometimes longer. I may be able to push it through a little faster—a favor I extend to the friendlier detectives I have to deal with." The medical examiner glanced over at Nguyen and nodded slightly.

"What else can you tell me?" Dan asked.

"There's a recent injection mark on the left arm, the most likely entry point for the drug. It's a small mark in the crook of the elbow. Was your nephew right-handed?"

"Yes."

"That increases the likelihood he injected himself. It's difficult, though certainly not impossible, to inject yourself in the arm on the dominant side."

"Understandable," Dan replied.

"I would check to see if the subject has given blood recently. If he is a college student, a blood drive on campus could explain the injection mark. That is another possibility."

The detective's notebook flipped open and he wrote for a moment.

"In addition to the recent injection mark, the subject also has a burn on the underside of his right arm. The forearm. It was healing well until . . ." The medical examiner's voice trailed off.

"Until he died," Dan finished.

"Correct."

"How old is the wound?"

"I estimate the wound at a week to ten days."

"Then probably unrelated to his death," the detective added.

"A good assumption. The body shows no additional signs of outward wounds. No habitual track marks. No substantial cuts, no abrasions, no bruising. No wounds on the knuckles. There is no evidence, on the outside of the body, that indicates the subject was involved in a premortem struggle of any sort, which, if you connect the dots, would indicate the possibility the subject had been forced to ingest a drug. But without defensive wounds, it makes a forced injection less likely."

Dan absorbed every word.

"There is residual vomit in the throat, which is not surprising. Most heroin overdoses, if that is indeed what we are dealing with, are caused not by heroin itself, but usually a combination of heroin with alcohol or some other drug. Asphyxiation on one's vomit is the most common outcome and thus the cause of death in many heroin overdose cases. This may run contrary to what you have seen in the movies where the victim takes the drug and then falls into immediate unconsciousness. The subject also shows discoloration of the tongue, another telltale indication of heroin overdose."

"What are the other causes of death with heroin?" Dan asked.

"The lethal dose of heroin is quite high: 500 milligrams for a non user, up to 1800 for a regular user. Once again, the toxicology report will solve that mystery. A lethal dose will affect the central nervous system. This will manifest itself first in labored, shallow breathing followed by complete respiratory arrest. The heart will follow a similar path of deterioration."

"Death always boils down to the same two factors. Breathing and heartbeats. Everything else just leads to those," Detective Nguyen added expertly.

Dan glanced at the detective and then back at the medical examiner. "Please continue."

"Internally is where things get interesting. The body shows signs of physical—shall we say—wear and tear."

Detective Nguyen interrupted. "What do you mean?"

The doctor paused and looked at Dan, his long nose pressing

against the inside of his mask. The medical examiner pulled a handful of X-rays off a mobile table and adjusted the overhead light.

"A fracture of most bones results in a very slight overall increase of bone mass in that particular location."

"Which is why it is hard to break the same bone in the same place twice, once the original break has healed," Dan stated.

"Exactly, unusual circumstances notwithstanding. As you can see here in the X-rays, your nephew shows signs of multiple breaks." The doctor flipped through several X-rays with pauses in between.

"There is evidence of at least nine fractures. And those are the ones I can be sure of. Left arm twice. Right arm three times. Both ankles. A tibia. A fibula. A femur."

The doctor paused again. "The femur is particularly intriguing. It's the largest and strongest bone in the body. As substantial as concrete. Obviously, it's not easily broken. Large-scale, high-impact collisions are the usual culprit. Often a collision hard enough to break a femur is also fatal."

Dan could feel the weight of the detective's stare to his right. The doctor's eyes were penetrating Dan from the front.

"Conner studied hard and played hard. All kinds of sports. He had a few breaks over the years that I know of. Jumped out of a tree house once in the backyard and broke one of his ankles and the other leg. Broke his arm once playing tackle football in the school-yard with his friends. I'm sure his medical records would have more specifics."

The detective's notebook and pen magically reappeared.

There was another moment of silence.

"Was your nephew ever in a severe accident? Car, boat? Skiing perhaps?"

"No," Dan answered.

"Well, then, there is one additional possibility. I have seen several cases of severe physical abuse resulting in multiple fractures. Usually this occurs before adolescence."

Dan felt the stares again. This time they were hotter, more penetrating, more accusatory.

"He wasn't abused at home. I can guarantee you that. His

father wouldn't have touched him. His mother was a saint. And my nephew, well, he wasn't the victim type."

"Were you around when he was younger?"

"Around enough to know he wasn't being abused. And you can bet your ass I wouldn't have allowed it to continue if I did suspect it."

The conversation reached a stalemate and the detective interjected. "What about personal effects?"

The doctor moved to a square stainless-steel box at the foot of the table. "We have jeans, a sweatshirt, and a pair of leather shoes from a company named Born. There is some dirt on the shoes and clothes, but nothing that registers as unusual given my understanding of the location of the body when it was discovered. There was no wallet. No cell phone. I did find twenty-six dollars in his pocket."

"No wallet?"

"No."

"So someone stole his wallet but left him with cash?" Dan asked.

Detective Nguyen looked at Dan. "Any ideas?"

"I need to see where the body was found."

CHAPTER 5

—

Dan rode shotgun in the black unmarked police cruiser. They cut across the National Mall and Dan stared stoically at the Capitol on the left before turning his gaze 180 degrees towards the Washington Monument. The car rounded the corner from Ninth Street onto Independence Avenue near the Air and Space Museum and Dan noted the exceedingly empty sidewalks.

The tourist season was in a lull, a break between the masses of 'tourons' as they are called by most government workers who practice avoiding them during the summer rush. A smaller influx of tourons occurred over the holidays, but most of the federal government ran a skeleton crew between Thanksgiving and the New Year. It was a schedule envied by the private sector and yet considered overwork by Congressional standards.

The police cruiser turned left in front of the red Smithsonian Castle.

"Did you know the Smithsonian, the greatest American collection of museums, was initially a gift from a Brit named Smithson?" the detective asked.

"Yes," Dan replied tersely as the car drove under the Department of Energy's Forestall building. The DOE structure was built on huge concrete stilts perched over the road, a reminder of what architecture could be before 9/11 changed everything.

Detective Nguyen pulled the unmarked car into a space along the L'Enfant Promenade, a desolate swath of cobbled pavement devoid of trees that boasted a title far more grand than it deserved. The Mandarin Oriental stood on the horizon a half-mile away, a diamond in a sea of coal, a showcase of possibility for the future of the area.

"This is us," Detective Nguyen said, throwing his official park-anywhere pass on the dash. "Welcome to the most undesirable real estate within a block of the Mall."

"The Mandarin is just up the street."

"Another universe exists between here and there. Don't let the proximity fool you."

Dan followed the detective out of the car and up the sidewalk of the promenade.

"Essentially, this portion of the promenade is a large bridge, though it is hard to tell when you are topside. D Street and the train tracks are right below us. At the top of the promenade are four of the ugliest buildings in DC. An architectural style known as 'brutalism.'"

"Everything sounds better with a name."

"You know the area?"

"I've driven through on my way to the Fish Market. Never walked it."

"There's probably a reason for that."

Detective Nguyen turned right onto a concrete staircase leading downward. The high-walled, concrete staircase—with a twisting landing at the midpoint—was a descent into hell, a path to the abyss underneath the promenade.

"Nice place," Dan said as he eyed the pile of syringes, condoms, and broken bottles that littered the landing as the staircase turned downward.

The detective stopped on the landing and motioned over the edge of the shoulder-high wall. "You ready for some climbing?"

Dan looked at the detective's slight frame. "Are you?"

"Been climbing city walls since I was a kid."

Dan nodded, reached up, and threw his foot to the top of the wall. Without breaking momentum he effortlessly stood, looking down at the detective and then at the depressing terrain below. Train tracks ran ten yards off to the left, the rusted underbelly of the promenade support structure above.

"There's a ladder on the other side," Dan said as Detective Nguyen struggled to get his leg to the top of the wall. Dan offered a hand. Detective Nguyen ignored it and worked his way into a seated position, his legs hanging over the edge.

"Grab the ladder," Dan said.

Detective Nguyen looked at the makeshift chain of shipping pallets and crates nailed together to cover the twelve feet to the ground below. "Not very promising," the detective said.

"There must be another way down. People live here," Dan said.

"There are all kinds of tunnels and paths around here. You want to look for one?"

Dan looked at the detective, smiled, and then stepped off the wall, landing twelve feet below and executing a perfect roll to displace the downward energy.

Dan stared up at the detective and watched as Nguyen's face froze and then melted into a look of disbelief and concern, eyebrows furled. Dan stood waiting below, listening to the detective curse and mumble as he lowered his slight frame down the stack of old pallets.

The ground under the promenade and next to the train tracks was a wasteland. Dirt and clay filled the retaining walls of the shared commuter and cargo rail tracks. Glass shards and rocks protruded from the earth. A dusting of trash, metal fragments, and shreds of discarded clothing littered the ground. The stench of human waste was overpowering. Blue tarps curled around the main support column for the promenade above.

"What a hellhole," Dan said.

"Welcome to the Third World."

"I have seen Third World and this is worse. This is the Third World with guns and crack. Most of the real Third World is just trying to find water and food."

"How about welcome to the Capital City?"

Dan walked in the direction of the support column and a patch of earth unmistakably being used as a shelter for a homeless soul. Several strands of displaced police tape fluttered about.

"This is where they found him."

Dan absorbed the details of the location where his nephew took his final breath. He stepped onto the concrete base of the support column and surveyed the area. "Not sure how someone would have gotten him down here."

"Assuming he didn't overdose and was carried here," the detective retorted.

Dan stepped down from his perch and wiped at the moisture gathering in the corner of his eyes.

"OK, Detective . . . tell me, how does a kid from Northwest DC end up in a shithole like this?"

"My guess?"

"Your best guess."

"The search for a bigger and better high. Starts with a few beers, moves onto pot, maybe a little ecstasy and shrooms, and then onto the really hard stuff—meth, coke, heroin."

"Not this kid."

"You think your nephew is immune? I have seen millionaires strung out on heroin, politicians on crack."

"They have the latter on video."

"There have been others. And I'm telling you no one is immune to a fall from grace. No one. Not even your nephew. And if your nephew was abused as a boy, well, maybe there is more to him than you know."

"Not my nephew. No way. No how. That goes for both drugs and abuse."

"How can you be so sure?"

"Because if I found out he'd been in a place like this, I would've killed him myself. And that would've been enough to keep him away."

"I hope you're right. But that's not the kind of thing you want to tell a police detective on the job. Particularly after the medical examiner said your nephew may have suffered prolonged abuse."

"I haven't abused anyone," Dan said. "And I haven't killed anyone recently. At least, not this week."

Detective Nguyen grunted and wiped some dirt off the front of his grey shirt.

Dan ran through the scenario. "All right. Let's assume he knew this place as somewhere he could get drugs. Does that mean he would come here to shoot up?"

"Generally speaking, drug users like to use their drugs. The scenery is secondary."

The ground rumbled underneath their feet and a single blast of a horn forced Detective Nguyen to turn his head. Dan took several steps forward as a CSX cargo train passed and disappeared into a tunnel that ran under the taxi queue in front of the Mandarin Oriental in the distance.

The surroundings settled and Dan asked, "Who found the body?"

"Anonymous call."

"How often you get calls on dead homeless people?"

"Anonymous calls?"

"Yes."

"Depends on the time of year. Depends on the location of the body. We had one last year around Christmas turn up at the Capitol. Had throngs of tourists calling in. The guy was frozen in the seated position right smack on the front steps of his elected officials' place of work."

"Appropriate if he was trying to send a message to Congress."

"People freezing their asses off usually don't think that deeply."

The detective walked around the support column and moved the pile of blue tarps on the ground with his foot.

"Looks like someone lives here, at least part-time," Dan said.

"Probably more than one person. It's got a roof above, it's isolated, it's close to the Mall, close to tourists. Easy access to high-quality panhandling."

"Isolated . . ." Dan repeated, walking backwards, parallel to the train tracks. He glanced up at the edge of the promenade above and then walked to the other side of the structure and repeated his upward stare.

"What are you thinking?" the detective asked.

"DC has installed thousands of security cameras in the city since 9/11. It's hard to find a place where *someone* isn't catching your face on video. There are none down here."

"Nothing to steal. No one to rob. No need for cameras," the detective said.

"A good place to kill someone."

"So far, there is no evidence anyone has been killed."

"How long have you been a detective?"

"Long enough."

"In your experience, how many times have you seen two relatives die on the same night, in two different locations? Common sense should be screaming at the podium."

"Unfortunately common sense doesn't provide evidence. It's far more likely that your sister-in-law's death and your nephew's overdose had something to do with drugs. If you can ignore the big fancy house and the nice neighborhood, drugs are statistically the most likely connection."

"I've seen enough down here. Let's see if we can find another way out."

"You can't scale walls?"

"No, I can. I don't want *you* to get hurt."

CHAPTER 6

—

Dan spent the late afternoon and evening giving and receiving condolences from relatives known and unknown. Aunts in Texas. A great uncle in Hawaii. Cousins on Long Island he didn't know existed. His sister-in-law's family was flying in from California in installments, the first batch on a red-eye taking off in six hours. He notified the university on the passing of his nephew, called the funeral home, and made arrangements for a wake. He contacted ServiceMaster to have his sister-in-law's house professionally cleaned, top to bottom. When he couldn't think of anyone else to call, he opened a half-filled bottle of Jack Daniels and had a shot. Followed by another. And another. Five drinks in, the photo albums found their way down from the bookshelf in the corner of Dan's cozy living room. He put on some music and whispered the lyrics to a Passenger song, *"My liver may be fucked, but my heart, she is honest."*

And then he wept.

When the bottle dripped dry, he went top shelf and opened a seventeen-year-old Ballantine. He poured it neat, held it in his hand while he drank, and set his empty glass on the coffee table when his head swooned. Through teary, bloodshot eyes he was hypnotized by the family photos spread across the sofa cushions and coffee table.

The Lord family tree had been pruned. The proud Irish lineage ended with him. He was the last Lord standing and, as grand as the title may have sounded when kings in castles ruled as far as the eye could see, he felt lonely.

Sleep came in spurts, as if the digital display of the clock on the nightstand was nudging him awake, poking him with regularity. He knocked the clock onto the floor and when that failed to alleviate the silent interruptions, he threw one of his pillows over the subtle red illumination. At six in the morning he gave up. "Today has to be better than yesterday," he said, sitting up, feet on the floor.

He shook his head, felt the effects of the evening's indulgence, and then dropped to the carpet and cranked out a hundred perfect push-ups. Push-ups that would make an old-school Marine salute in honor. Straight back, eyes slightly up. Chin and chest to the ground. When he finished, he performed an equal number of sit-ups. Exorcise through exercise. With sweat dripping from his brow, he shuffled to the kitchen, choked down some bread with Advil, showered, and pulled on jeans and a mid-weight sweater. An hour later he pulled into a visitor parking space on the American University campus.

He dodged students heading out the main entrance of the five-story Hughes dormitory and announced himself to the red-haired woman seated at the front desk.

"My name is Dan Lord. Conner Lord was my nephew. I'm here to collect some of his belongings."

The woman, in her mid-fifties, slid a three-ring binder in Dan's direction. "Sign in to the visitor's log and I'll need to see some ID."

Dan noted the gruffness of her tone and then put it down to dealing with unruly students who spent their waking hours trying to pull the wool over her eyes.

Dan flashed his driver's license to the woman named Ruth. "Your nephew was on the fifth floor. Room 513. Elevator to the fifth floor. Down the hall. South end."

"Thank you."

"You know, the DC police were here earlier in the day."

"The police?"

"Yes. A detective. A man."

Dan looked down at the visitor's log. "He didn't sign in?"

"A police badge doesn't require a signature."

"Do you need to escort me to the room?"

"No. My line of defense ends here at the door. I have a radio if I need legs for pursuit. This place isn't Fort Knox. It's a dorm.

There are a dozen emergency exits, windows with no screens on the first floor, fire escapes on the backside. It's impossible to keep track of four hundred students. Besides, you look honest. I have a built-in bullshit detector. Comes with two decades of dealing with students. Keeping an eye on a residence hall can be tricky. I spend most of my time trying to figure out who is sneaking in alcohol, who is selling weed, who is trying to get their pecker pulled in one of the lounges."

Dan smiled. "I'll remember not to bullshit you."

"I'm sorry for your loss."

"Did you know my nephew?"

"Knew the face. He usually said hi on his way out. But like I said, there are four hundred kids in this building. Sometimes it takes a while to learn all their names. I usually get there by the end of the fall semester."

"I don't doubt that."

The elevator doors opened and Dan parted a group of four girls in sweatshirts, short shorts, and flip-flops. He turned right, following the arrow for the south side of the building. Music played from nearly every room. Most of the doors were open to varying degrees. He eyed the numbers above the doorframes as he made his way down the coed hall. Each glance left and right provided insight into dorm life that Dan had last seen two decades ago. In the third room on the left, a boy slept on the floor. In the next room, a girl changed her clothes, her bare back exposed towards the hall. Further down the hall, he eyed a young man staring at a closed book on his desk while two sets of feet protruded from beneath a blanket in the loft bed above.

When he reached 513 he knocked on the open door.

"Yeah," a voice answered.

Dan stepped into the room. The cinderblock walls were painted institutional gray. Two loft beds with desks beneath them stood on opposite sides of the room, robbing the room of light and space, giving it a cave-like feel. An air conditioning unit filled the lower half of the window on the far side of the room.

"I'm Dan Lord. Conner's uncle."

A young man in baggy shorts stood from the wooden chair at the desk. He wore an American University sweatshirt with bleach stains around the hem. His attempt at facial hair resulted in bald spots along the jaw-line where his follicles weren't mature enough for the request to look older.

"Josh McKeen."

A blonde stepped from the bathroom and Josh introduced her. "This is Krista."

"I guess you heard the news?" Dan asked.

"Yeah, I heard," Josh said.

Krista ran her hand through Josh's hair in soothing strokes before adding, "I gotta go."

When the girl left the room, Dan sat on the unoccupied chair underneath his nephew's loft bed. The room was littered with electronic goodies: a cell phone, iPods, remote controllers, a flat screen TV, DVD player, video game consoles. Laptops. External hard drives. Digital Cameras. Flash drives.

"You guys are wired."

Josh looked around the room, not sure what to make of the statement.

"When I was in school we had a TV and a radio, and we barely studied. I don't know how your generation finds time to open the books with all your toys."

"We're multi-taskers. And a lot of the books are digital these days."

Dan looked around at the pictures on the wall, the clothes oozing from half-closed dresser drawers. "You mind if I ask you some questions?"

"No. Not at all."

"Was Conner into anything I need to know about?"

"Like?"

"The usual. Drugs. Drinking. Gambling. The kind of stuff that gets people into trouble."

"Not really. Me and Conner have been roommates for three months, most of the first semester. We were friends last year in a different dorm and we got along pretty well. We don't get in each other's stuff or in each other's faces. We drink beer together and watch sports. We're roommates. We're friends."

"You guys ever fight?"

"Sure, but nothing serious. Nothing physical. Occasionally we piss each other off—a wet towel on the bathroom floor. Someone dropping a deuce and not flushing. But Conner was my buddy. He had my back. I had his. That's all you can ask for in a roommate."

"What about drugs?"

"We smoked weed a few times."

Dan felt like he had been punched in the stomach. "Conner smoked weed?"

"A couple of times. But not here in the dorm. Never seen him do anything harder than that, but this is college and we are in DC; you can get anything you want." Josh held up his hand and extended two fingers. "Two calls, two calls."

"What do you mean?"

"Everything is two calls away. *Everything.*"

"You guys ever do heroin?"

"Jesus, no. You don't even see heroin. A lot of weed. A lot of ecstasy. Every once in a while you will see some magic mushrooms. You hear rumors about people doing meth and coke, but people try to hide that shit. Heroin? You go to prison for heroin. We're students but we're not crazy."

"Where were you on Monday night?"

"In the lounge. We were watching the football game. Chicago versus Green Bay."

"Can anyone vouch for you?"

"Half of the floor."

"And after the game?"

"I spent most of the night here, with Krista."

"Didn't go out?"

"Did you see her?"

Dan smirked.

"Conner left on Sunday morning. Early. Didn't see him after that. I figured he was at his girlfriend's or his mom's."

"Who's his girlfriend? Anyone steady?"

"Conner hooked up with a couple of chicks early in the semester, like we all do. Hell, there are more hoochie brothers here than anyone wants to admit."

"What's a hoochie brother?"

"You know, two guys who've banged the same girl. We call them hoochie brothers. And it's better to be the older brother than the younger brother, meaning that . . . well . . ."

"Yeah, I get the idea."

"Anyhow . . . Conner has been seeing a girl named Lindsay. Alpha Chi Omega. Nice girl. Real smart. A knockout. She came by last night after we got word from campus police. The floor held an emergency meeting and the university rolled out mental health counselors for anyone who wanted to talk. They handed out cards and gave direct numbers for the campus priest and rabbi. I have Lindsay's number if you want. Or you can try texting her."

"Send me her contact info."

"What's your number?" Josh opened his cell phone, punched in Dan's number, and sent the information.

"Does she live in this building?"

"No. She's at the Alpha Chi Omega sorority house. Other side of campus. Near Nebraska Avenue. There are about seven or eight houses over there. Kind of like American University's version of Greek Row, though it's unofficial and not sanctioned by the school. It's not much, but it's all we have."

"You say this girl Lindsay is a hottie, huh?"

"Smokin'. You'll see."

"Do you mind if I take a few of the things here?" Dan asked, motioning at the desk.

"No, not at all. Everything on the desk is Conner's. The backpack too. His computer isn't there. I assume he took it with him."

"What about his GPS? I didn't see it in his car."

Josh looked around, cocked his head and said. "I don't think I have ever seen him bring it to the room."

Dan scooped a variety of objects off the desk and put them in the backpack that was hanging on a hook under the loft bed. "I may be back for the rest of his things, or the university may box them up for me."

"I can box them up."

"I'm sure you have enough to deal with."

"I can handle it. The university is giving me a free ride for the first semester. All my grades are pass/fail and all my classes are pass. One of the perks when your roommate passes away."

"That's a hell of a way to get out of studying."

"Only works once."

"What's your GPA?"

"Three point six."

"So you weren't motivated to kill your roommate for the semester off."

"That's a no."

"Just thought I would check." Dan stood and threw the backpack strap over his shoulder. "What did the detective have to say?"

"What detective?"

"The one that was here this morning."

"There were no cops here as far as I know. I stayed at Krista's last night. I got here an hour ago."

—

Dan stopped by the front desk on his way out. "You said there was a detective here this morning?"

"That's right."

"A slightly built Asian guy?"

"No. Caucasian. About your size."

"Gun?"

"I don't recall a gun. He could have had one under the jacket."

"Did you see him leave?"

"No, now that you mention it. But I do have to use the bathroom on occasion."

Ruth thought for a minute. "We have a security camera running."

"I would love to see it."

"In the back," Ruth said, flicking her head over her shoulder, happy to add sleuthing to her morning duties.

Dan followed Ruth to a converted closet steps beyond the front desk. Two monitors sat on a metal shelf. Ruth took up position next to the open door, keeping one eye on her desk while she fiddled with the keyboard and monitors. "These are DVRs that run on twenty-four hour loops. The recordings are stored on a server for a week, and then they are dumped from the memory by campus police. Pretty high tech. Used to be all tapes. The building may be old, but the university likes to cover its ass."

"Can you show me the last two hours?"

"Just give me a second."

Ruth ran the DVR recording in reverse. A girl walked backwards out the door and Dan followed a few minutes later.

"That's you," Ruth said.

A rush of students walked out the door backwards and Ruth continued her commentary. "Those are students with nine o'clock classes coming back." She waited a few more minutes and the recording blipped. Then it showed another group of students walking backwards through the door and across the lobby."

"And that's the nine o'clock class students leaving the building."

"There is nothing in between."

"It appears to be missing."

—

The large Greek letters in the yards of the brick houses for a block near Nebraska Avenue provided every indication that Dan had arrived at Greek Row. Alpha Chi Omega was the third house on the right and the only one on the block that looked habitable. The fraternity next door had a sofa in the yard and another on the porch. The fresh coat of paint the fraternity applied every summer to spruce up the place was already under siege. Ten guys under a single roof aged a house like beer-drinking termites.

Dan approached the front porch of the Alpha Chi Omega sorority house and suddenly he felt his age. Memories of college life flooded back to him. Nights huddled around a keg in some yard, drinking out of red Solo cups, keeping one eye out for the police and the other out for a girl better looking than the one you were currently chatting up.

Dan knocked on the door and gazed at the Greek letters emblazoned on the ceiling of the porch. Under the letters the sorority's slogan—Real Strong Women—was painted in bold strokes. Or as bold as strokes can be when stenciled in light pink.

A young lady in pajamas and flip flops opened the door. *At least these students aren't killing their parents with expensive clothing bills,* Dan thought.

"Hi," Dan said to the black-haired, blue-eyed girl. He guessed she was of Hungarian descent, but kept his opinion to himself.

"Hi," the girl replied.

"My name is Dan Lord and I'm looking for a girl named Lindsay."

"We have two Lindsays, which one are you looking for?"

"I have no idea."

"What class do you teach? One Lindsay is a Psyche major, the other is International Affairs."

Dan brushed off his ego. If he needed further evidence he was no longer college-aged, the black-haired, blue-eyed junior had just provided it.

"I'm not a professor. Or a student," he quickly added. "My nephew passed away this weekend and I think he was seeing, or at least knew, Lindsay. Or one of the Lindsays."

"You're talking about Conner, right?"

"Yeah."

"That would be Lindsay Richer."

"She around?"

"Yeah, I think I heard her fire up the shower a little while ago. Come on in. She's been a mess since she got the news."

Dan followed the dark-haired girl into the living room. The room décor was a head-on collision of Ikea and Martha Stewart. "Have a seat, I'll get Lindsay."

Dan nodded and sat down on the edge of the sofa cushion.

"Man in the living room," the black-haired girl yelled loud enough to be heard next door. She looked at Dan. "House rules on weekdays. Now if someone comes dancing through the living room naked, you'll be innocent."

"Good rule," Dan replied as the girl bounded up the stairs. He turned his admiration to the array of magazines on the table, none of them fit for male consumption. Each cover offered its own sex secrets comingled with the recurring themes of how to catch your man cheating and tips to lose weight.

He heard footsteps above and a moment later a blond with wet hair wearing a white bathrobe came down the stairs.

Dan stood.

"Hi. I'm Lindsay."

"Lindsay Richer," Dan replied, showing that he'd been paying attention. "My name is Dan Lord. I'm Conner's uncle."

"He mentioned you," she said, tears welling up in her eyes. "I can't believe it." She looked like she had been crying, no small feat for someone who had just exited the shower.

"You want to grab a seat? Talk for a minute?"

Lindsay sat on the far end of the sofa and Dan returned to his seat a cushion away. Lindsay's hair was wet and she had yet to apply her daily cosmetic layering, but Josh McKeen had been right. She was a hottie. An angelic face. She reached for a tissue from the box on the coffee table and blew her nose.

"How well did you know Conner?"

"We've been dating for almost two months."

"Dating, dating?"

"Well, we weren't tennis partners, if that's your question."

"Fair enough. You mind if I interrogate you a little?" he asked.

"No. Go ahead," she said, blowing her nose again and then dabbing her eyes.

"Where was he on Sunday and Monday?"

"Sunday he said he was spending the day with his mother, helping out around the house. I don't know where he was on Monday."

"Did you talk to him?"

"I talked to him on Sunday. That was the last I heard from him."

"You usually talk to him every day?"

"Sure. Or at least a text or two."

"Did you hear where they found him?"

"Yeah. Under the Promenade in L'Enfant Plaza. Word travels fast."

"The police seem to think that it was a drug overdose, probably heroin." Dan paused. "Any thoughts on that?"

"Just one. It's not possible."

"Why do you say that?"

"I don't do drugs. I don't date guys who do drugs. I know Conner had smoked marijuana, but not since we started dating. I have a perfect 4.0 GPA. I'm planning on going to the Kennedy School of Government for my masters."

"Harvard."

"That's right."

"Was he involved with anything else that you're aware of? Something that would piss off the wrong person? Maybe an old boyfriend who was jealous?"

"No, nothing. You know, I don't throw the word love around too much. It's an abused word these days. But Conner was a good guy. A real good guy. And who knows where things would have gone between us. But every time he walked into the room my stomach did a tiny little summersault. Every time."

Dan paused as Lindsay wiped a tear away from her cheek. "Sorry," she said, her voice more faint.

"I've shed a few myself," Dan added. "I think something was going on with Conner I don't know about. I thought so before this morning, and I certainly think more strongly about it now that I have seen you. I'm pretty sure Conner wasn't under some bridge in Southeast DC shooting up. There are some people in life who keep you focused on the positive things. I get the feeling you were one of those for Conner. Call it a wild guess."

"Are you saying he was killed?"

"I don't know what happened, but I doubt what I've heard. Hell, I doubt what I have seen with my own eyes. Did you know Conner's mother also passed away this weekend in an apparent suicide? I don't believe in coincidences."

Lindsay started crying again. "That's horrible," she said between sniffles and those gasps of breath that come with substantial tears and lack of oxygen. A minute later she stopped crying and paused as if she had a secret to tell. "Conner . . . he was tough, you know."

"Yeah, I know."

"I mean, he was *tough*."

Dan looked into her eyes to convey something beyond words. "I *know*."

"We were at a party one night and this guy, a real jerk, wouldn't leave me alone. Conner asked him nicely a couple of times to move along, but the guy wouldn't listen. We decided to go a little while later, just to avoid a scene, and when we were leaving the house this guy and a friend of his, a bigger guy, blocked our way. Conner asked him once to move and another time to mind his own business . . . and you could just tell it was the last time he was asking."

Dan smiled.

"Sure enough this guy puts his foot on the doorframe and spews some movie-line bullshit like 'you can go but the girl stays here.' He went to poke Conner in the chest and before you could blink Conner had him pinned against the doorframe, his wrist bent behind his back. This guy's friend, the big guy, jumps in and hits Conner in the side of the face. Conner doesn't flinch. He twisted the wrist in his one hand, smashed the guy's face into the doorframe, elbowed the bigger guy in the nose, and then kicked out his knee. Then he grabbed my hand and walked through the door as if nothing happened."

Dan smiled again and reached into his pocket. "I'm going to be poking around on a few things. Here's my card. If you think of anything that may be helpful, let me know. If the police come to see you, I would be interested in what they ask. But that's up to you if you want to share or not."

"Sure, Ok."

"There is a service the day after tomorrow. St. Michaels. Ten o'clock. Burial at King David. Bring some tissues for me."

CHAPTER 7

—

Dan pushed the door open to the art gallery and jostled for position around four men in overalls. He dodged left as a massive slab of rock swung from an arrangement of pulleys, ropes and dollies. Neither the rock nor the men at work made any concessions for Dan interrupting the installation of what could best be described as a missing piece of Stonehenge.

The art gallery took up residence on the first floor of the only building on the small block, directly beneath Dan's sprawling, barren office. By default, the resident artist of the gallery downstairs was the only neighbor Dan had.

Dan peeked around the construction in progress and called out his neighbor's name. Lucia yelled from the back of the gallery and appeared a moment later, moving across the floor with a combination of grace and natural buoyancy. Mid-thirties, with a voluptuous body usually draped in a paint-covered smock, Lucia was the ideal neighbor. Cheerful and sweet. Helpful, without being nosy. She greeted Dan with a hug and a kiss on each cheek, her brown hair leaving a subtle trace of deliciousness on his shoulder as the embrace ended.

"How are you holding up?"

"As good as can be expected. Thanks for the flowers. Thanks for the food, too."

"I am sorry I missed the service. I was in San Francisco."

"I know. It's fine. The food was more than an adequate gesture."

"I didn't make it, but I knew where to deliver it. My family is still trying to come to grips with the reality that I don't cook. I guess when I'm fifty, single, and living an artist's lifestyle, maybe they'll take me seriously."

Dan changed the subject, nodding in the direction of the swinging slab of rock. "What are they making?"

"A desk. Italian marble."

"Good thing there isn't a basement, the desk might go through the floor."

"I was looking for something substantial. To make a statement."

"Business must be good."

"I can't complain. You want to see the latest and greatest?"

"Sure," Dan replied as Levi, an aging chocolate lab with thinning fur on his hindquarters, appeared from the back of the gallery. What his hips lacked in movement, his tail made up for with high-speed reckless abandon.

"There's my boy," Dan said, dropping to one knee so the dog could lick his face.

Behind the re-pointed brick wall of the main gallery, Dan took a tour of the artwork-in-progress in the studio. He stood under the lights and admired the oil on canvass, formulating his best guess as to the subject matter. "Two men climbing a mountain," Dan surmised.

"No," replied Lucia. "It's a woman on a beach."

"So there is, at least, a mountain or two."

Lucia shook her head.

Dan moved to the next work of art, a black and white rendering of what Dan could only guess to be a backroom painting accident. "I have no guess on this one."

"It is titled *Night Blind*."

Dan's eyes dropped to the already attached price tag and whistled. "That price will make you blind, regardless of the time of day. It's going to be hard to convince people of the starving artist lifestyle with that price tag."

"I didn't say anything about starving. Do I *look like* I'm starving?"

"I can't even hear that question," Dan said. He stooped to pet the dog again, wondering how people spent five figures on artwork that was open to interpretation.

"Can I take Levi out for a while? Maybe let him run in the park a little?"

"You know where the leash is," Lucia said.

Dan followed Lucia back into the front of the gallery where the large slab of rock was now resting on the three equally large supports.

"Looks like your walk with my dog is going to have to wait," Lucia said, pointing to the sidewalk in front of the gallery.

Dan looked out the front window and saw a young lady looking up at the metal numbers over the old doorway that led to Dan's second-floor office.

"A customer?" Dan said out loud.

"A novel idea," Lucia retorted.

"I'll take Levi out later."

—

Dan stepped from the gallery and startled his visitor as she pressed the button for the intercom.

"Can I help you?" Dan asked.

The young woman stepped away from the door and glanced down the street in each direction. There was plenty of midday foot traffic, well-dressed women strolling the cobbled brick, eyeing knick knacks that filled the stores of Old Town Alexandria.

"I'm looking for Dan Lord."

"You found him."

The young woman took another step back and Dan recognized his visitor was conscious of her space and the fact she was speaking to a stranger.

"My name is Sue Fine. I had an appointment for a job interview today."

Dan rolled his eyes, grimaced, and offered a greeting. "Shit."

"You forgot."

Dan grunted as he exhaled.

"It's OK. I can come another time," Sue said.

"No, no. It's my fault. Let's go upstairs." Dan swiped his security card in front of a wireless reader and then punched a five digit number into a key pad on the doorframe. He smiled at Sue as the outer door made an audible click.

The inside foyer, one large step from the sidewalk, stood at the foot of a long, solitary staircase. Both sides of the staircase were brick from floor to ceiling. Between the foyer and the first step was a large, thick plastic door. Sue noticed the closed circuit cameras in the foyer and in the staircase.

Dan pressed his hand against a pad on the left side of the wall and then used a high-security laser-cut key in a custom lock to pull the door open.

"You in the diamond business?" Sue asked, trying to break the silence as Dan went through his security protocols.

"Gold," Dan answered, gesturing for Sue to lead the way up the stairs.

"No, after you," Sue replied.

At the top of the staircase was another thick plastic door with the number 201 stenciled on it. Dan used two more keys and pushed the door open into his sprawling, sparsely furnished office. The main room was as wide as the entire floor. Two windows on the front of the room looked out over the bustling street scene below.

Dan walked around the office, flicking on the lights and turning on the radiator heat. As he moved about the room, he eyed his visitor without staring. *Brown hair with a reddish tint. Brown eyes. Athletic. Maybe five foot six. His eyes landed on her shoes and he adjusted her height for one inch heels. Dan guessed they were not her footwear of choice. Sandals, most likely, even in cool weather. He also imagined a tattoo on one of her legs. Maybe another on her shoulder blade. Nothing too grand, but definitely a stamp of independence somewhere.*

Dan's eyes met Sue's as the three-second window he allowed himself for measuring his guest expired. "I apologize for the mess. Deaths in the family have me a little behind in my housekeeping. Grab a seat," Dan said, gesturing towards a pair of wooden chairs on the other side of the lone desk.

"I can come back another time. It is no trouble, really."

"No, it's all right. I may need some help around here as it turns out. The timing is good."

Sue nodded and moved the chair so she had a partial view of the door. *Good instincts*, Dan thought. *Choose a seat where you can see the exit.* "I think I have your resume somewhere here," Dan said as he shuffled through a few folders on his desk. "I know I printed it out from the email you sent."

"I brought an extra copy, for your convenience," Sue responded, removing a resume from her leather shoulder bag and putting it on the corner of the desk.

Prepared, Dan thought to himself. *His second favorite attribute.* He perused the resume, absorbing Sue's life in one large chunk. He did many things quickly, but almost nothing as fast as he read.

"So you're studying Forensic Psychology at Marymount?"

"That's correct. Well, actually Forensic Psychology and Criminal Justice."

"The same double major combination as the last intern I hired. What do you think of the program?"

"I love it. As you know, the program started ten years ago with a dozen students and is now one of the largest on the East Coast. It's the only one in the DC area, so obviously it's popular for its proximity to the FBI, DEA, and Justice Department. We work on law enforcement issues, victim assistance, probation, and parole. Every aspect of the criminal justice system."

"Seems like it prepares those who are willing to study."

"The program has a lot of hands-on aspects. We actually work with the FBI and have on-site training exercises at the Bureau. A couple of weeks ago I was able to observe FBI interviews in progress from behind a two-way mirror."

"Anyone I would know?"

"It's all confidential, but if you read the newspaper you would recognize a name or two."

Respects confidentiality, Dan remarked to himself.

Sue continued. "We have ongoing investigative access to cold case files and associated investigative databases. Any student who helps close a cold case gets a five thousand dollar reward from the FBI, in addition to any other reward that may be outstanding. Not to mention it would virtually guarantee a job at the Bureau."

"I'm sure it would. So with all the potential glamour, why are you interested in a job here?"

"An internship. Professor Davis recommended you to me. He suggested I send you an email, introduce myself, and provide a resume."

"Is that all he said?"

"He told me you were a legal advisor, but I figured he meant more than he was letting on."

"Why do you say that?"

"In my experience, forensics professors are very exact, not surprising given forensics is an exact science. A certain lack of exactness led me to believe you may be more than a legal advisor."

"I see. If this interview works out, you will be the fourth intern I have hired from your program. Two of the previous interns were great. One was a train wreck. Just so we are on the same page, let me be blunt. What's the main reason you are here?"

"I have to fulfill an internship requirement in Criminal Justice and one of my professors told me you were someone who had hired interns in the past."

"You get an A for honesty. I will return the favor. Depending on what direction you are headed in your career, you may not get a lot of practical experience here. You may learn something about criminals, but the only forensics you are likely to practice will be on my dead body."

Dan noticed Sue stifle a laugh.

"You can laugh," Dan said. "It was a joke."

A small nasal blurt escaped. "I didn't really think I was going to see any bodies. I thought the job would give me insight into human behavior. Things that may help me in diagnosing a crime scene. A look at the criminal mind."

"A glance at the underbelly of humanity?"

"Yeah, something like that."

"Well, I don't want to be responsible for your therapy bills later, so tell me why I should hire you and, God forbid, why you wouldn't faint if you came into work and found my brains spread across the desk . . . for example."

"Nice example. In layman's terms it sounds like you are asking for my qualifications, beyond two years of forensic and criminal justice studies in grad school."

"That's a fair translation."

"I can type, answer the phones, use the computer, and send emails. I read two dozen newspapers a day. I'm a techno geek, meaning I'm connected all the time."

"Connected?"

"Texting. Tweeting. Facebooking. Email. Instagram."

"Can you use a camera?"

"I own a Cannon SLR."

"Parabolic mic?"

"Never needed to use one, but would love to try."

"Anything else?"

"I lost my parents when I was fifteen and went to court to become my own guardian when I was sixteen. I identified both of my parents' bodies. Your brains on the desk would bother you more than they would bother me."

"You smoke?"

"Is it a smoke-free office?"

"No. I only ask because I quit three years ago and don't need to have someone blowing smoke around the place. Paying clients, of course, can smoke all they want."

"I don't smoke, unless the situation calls for it."

"Like?"

"You never know. I can't sit here and say you will never see me smoke a cigarette. But I can sit here and tell you I'm not a smoker, nor do I intend to smoke, but you never know the circumstances."

"Good enough."

"I've smoked weed a few times."

"You buried your parents at fifteen. I'm willing to cut you some slack. Besides, I'm coming around to the opinion that everyone has tried it."

Sue glanced up at the pictures on the wall. Photos from exotic locations—deserts, mountains, crystal clear beaches. "What did you do before?"

"Before what?"

"Before you became a legal advisor. Private detective. Whatever it is you do."

Dan turned in his chair and looked at the pictures on the wall.

"Did you take them?" Sue prodded.

"Yeah. I spent half my life here in Washington and half of it wherever my father was stationed."

"Sounds cool."

"As for 'whatever it is that I do' . . . it is simple. I provide legal advice, for a fee, to discreet clientele. I am very selective. You won't find me in the yellow pages. I work by referral and I go after scum."

"Who determines what scum is?"

"Scum is self-identifiable. Like shit on a sidewalk, if you can excuse the crass imagery. You know what it is when you see it."

"The average person sees shit on the sidewalk and goes around it."

"Sometimes it needs to be stepped in. Or pushed to the side."

"Interesting analogy. Is there anyone you won't represent?"

"No one in intelligence and no one in the mob. They can solve their own problems."

"Seriously?"

"Seriously. Those two categories of people can make you disappear. I'm not afraid of confrontation. But the fight has to be fair."

"OK. No spies and no mobsters."

"As far as the job goes, I'm looking for someone who can run the office, run errands, and help me poke around a bit when it is needed. The pay is twenty dollars an hour. Twenty hours a week. If you go over twenty hours, the pay is still twenty dollars an hour. If you need time off, take time off. For school, whatever. Just let me know in advance. I expect you to be on time and I expect you to keep what you may see or hear to yourself. That's it."

"Sounds easy."

"Are you offended by foul language?"

"Hell, no," Sue answered.

"You're going to have to do better than that. I've been known to drop the occasional f-bomb combination and I don't want someone who is going to be upset when I do. But I try not to take the Lord's name in vain."

"'Fuck' is ok. 'God damn it' is out. Got it."

"I may need your help after hours from time to time."

"Are you looking for an excuse not to hire me?"

"No, why?"

"Because it feels like you are. And if you're looking for a reason not to hire me, I'm pretty sure you're going to find one."

Dan Lord rocked back in his chair and Sue mirrored his action, leaning back in hers.

"All right. Just so we have it clear: unusual hours, unsavory characters and undefined tasks."

"Understood."

"I was thinking you could start after the holidays."

"I was hoping I could talk you into hiring before the holidays. I could use the money."

Dan stared ahead in silence for a moment. "When can you start?"

"Tomorrow."

Dan scratched his chin. "The day after tomorrow. I'll set up the desk in the small room over there, first door in the hall. The bathroom is at the end of the hallway. There is a kitchenette opposite the bathroom. It's all you can drink coffee, and I don't have any decaf, so if you want some, buy some. Also, if you're around for lunch, I'll cover it."

"I may need you to fill out some forms. For credit at school."

"No problem. I'll get you a key and the entry codes to the office after I do a background check on you."

"A background check?"

"Yeah. You already told me you smoke pot, so the hard part is out of the way. It's just a run-of-the-mill background and credit check. I get the results in a couple of hours."

"You are cautious. I noticed the locks and closed circuit TV."

"The door downstairs on the street level is steel. It looks like an old wood door, but trust me, it is not. Multi-layer steel with a secret recipe in the middle. Well-lubricated, heavy-duty hinges. You could drive a car through it and the wall around it would collapse first. The doors at the bottom and top of the stairs are made of aluminum oxynitride, known as ALON. Very expensive and very effective.

It can stop a fifty-caliber round. It would certainly stop anything that can be carried up the staircase and aimed in this direction. By then, of course, I would have a few surprises. The staircase is not a location an intruder wants to spend any amount of time. At least, not while I'm upstairs on this side of the door."

Sue nodded, consuming the details.

"There's a motion detector attached to the CCTV at the top of the stairs. If anyone enters the staircase, the light comes on, and we can see that light through the door you just came through."

"Why so much security?"

"Occupational hazard."

"What about the windows?"

"The windows are also made from ALON, but the real security is in the lack of line-of-sight. The street in front is too narrow for a direct shot up to the second floor. There is a house across the street, owned by a former politician. From there, theoretically, someone could get a direct shot. But it's not likely, and like I said, the windows are made from the same bulletproof material. The building on this block and the one across the street are on the historical registry, so there is little chance of someone modifying the architecture."

Sue nodded her head with the flood of information.

Dan continued. "There's a room in the corner, just behind the top of the staircase. It is my gadget room. I know where everything is, so don't go getting cute and rearranging things."

"No housecleaning. Check."

"There is an art gallery downstairs. The woman's name is Lucia. It's an expensive gallery. All kinds of security equipment. For the life of me, I cannot figure out the prices on her art, but I do like my neighbor. On top of that, Lucia has a dog, Levi. Levi is my friend. Levi likes to bark. He is old and doesn't look like much these days, the kind of dog people walk past without thinking. But Levi and I have an understanding. I watch out for him. He watches out for me."

"I hope your partners get the same consideration."

"They do. And sometimes Levi takes his nap up here with me. If you don't like dogs, pretend you do. Get some Zrytec if you need it."

The phone on Dan's desk rang. He looked at Sue who looked at the phone and then back to him.

"You want me to step out?"

Dan thought for a second as the phone rang for the third time. "No. Stay."

Dan picked up the receiver. "Dan Lord."

"It's Cindy."

"Are you calling from a public phone?"

"Yes."

"Cindy, I'm going to put you on speaker. Is that ok?"

"Sure."

Dan hit the red button on the phone panel.

"How are things?"

"They're good. The divorce papers were filed by the court today. He also forfeited any visitation rights for the children. He agreed to the terms of alimony and I get a healthy percentage of the assets we acquired while we were married."

"That's super."

Cindy's voice choked and she cleared her throat. "I just wanted to say thank you for your help. I'm outside the bank right now and am going in to wire the money to the account number you gave me."

"You are very welcome. Let me know if your husband gives you any more trouble."

"I will. Thanks again."

"Good luck, Cindy." Dan hung up the phone and enjoyed the moment of victory. The reward for the risk.

"Interesting," Sue said, snapping Dan out of his high.

"It's a good day."

"Who was she?"

"The wife of someone prominent."

"So I take it you make your share of enemies."

"Does that scare you?"

Sue fidgeted in her chair.

"When I was sixteen I was in the wrong area of Baltimore, hanging out with people I shouldn't have been hanging out with. I ended up in a backroom with a guy who turned out to be a pimp of sorts. I told him too much, mentioned that I had lost my parents. Basically set myself up. A little while later, out came a knife. An hour after that I found myself locked into a sleazy rent-by-the-hour hotel room. A guy comes in the room a bit later, drinking a bottle of Jim Beam, and threw forty bucks on the bed. Told me what he was going to do to me. I played along. I stood at the dresser to take off my shoes and as the guy was undoing his belt, I pulled the drawer from the dresser and hit him in the side of the head. Nailed him in the temple. He went down. Hard. When the pimp came, I gave him the broken end of the Jim Beam bottle. Nothing really scares me."

"So, it definitely sounds like I need to run a criminal check on you."

"Self-defense," Sue said, standing.

"Be here at nine, the day after tomorrow."

Dan walked Sue down to the street level and watched as she reached her blue Honda Civic at a parking meter across the street. She sat down in the driver's seat, removed her shoes, and threw them into the back of the car. She slipped on a pair of sandals and, as she flipped her legs into the car, Dan caught a flash of a tattoo on the outside of her left leg.

CHAPTER 8

—

At night, the L'Enfant Promenade was a no-man's land, a desolate stretch of elevated road devoid of cars, devoid of life. The government buildings at L'Enfant Plaza, including the headquarters for the United States Postal Service, were dark. Even on the topside of the Promenade, the mean streets sprouted up from the working streets when the sun went down.

Dan walked up the promenade until he found the concrete staircase that led down to the train tracks. Fresh condoms were on the stairs, adding to the biohazard cesspool he had seen on his first visit. The concrete stairwell was well-guarded. Shoulder-high walls. No foot traffic. No one to hear a scream or a gunshot. The isolation confirmed to Dan why this place was chosen as his nephew's point of departure.

He made the turn on the landing and his neck snapped backwards as his eyes registered the end of a handgun in his face.

Instinctively, he raised his hands and backed up until he was against the wall of the staircase. "Easy," he said slowly and calmly.

"Wallet and car keys," the voice said in a cold tone. Dan's eyes focused on the man in front of him. Mid-twenties. Dredlocks. A torn T-shirt. Ratty jeans pulled down to the mid-portion of his butt, a belt the only thing keeping the pants off the ground.

"Ok. Sure," Dan said soothingly. "Do you want me to pull them out, or do you want to . . . ?"

The metal side of the gun crashed into Dan's head with a sickening clack. Warm blood trickled past his ear as he struggled to regain his posture. He continued speaking calmly through the cobwebs and throbs, supporting himself with the wall behind him. "I am unarmed. I'm reaching into my pocket slowly."

Dan pulled out his car keys and the man snatched them from his hand. The gun was still pointed at Dan's face at a distance too close for the both of them. "Wallet, motherfucker," the man repeated, glancing around.

Dan removed his wallet and the man reached for it with the same energy he had shown snatching the car keys. As the attacker moved for the wallet, Dan stepped *forward*, brushing the gun past his head with his right hand in one swift motion. He turned his body 180 degrees and put his left shoulder under the arm holding the gun. Both Dan and the assailant were now facing the same direction, the semi-automatic aimed harmlessly into the darkness. Dan reached up with both hands and pulled down on the mugger's wrist as the assailant tried to retract and re-aim his weapon. It was too late. The elbow of the assailant popped like a chicken wing, Dan's shoulder serving as the fulcrum. The gun hit the ground and the mugger let out a primal scream. Dan turned, stepped on the mugger's drooping pants at the crotch, and pushed his would-be assailant to the ground.

"You picked the wrong person," Dan said as he picked up the gun, ejected the magazine and the chambered bullet, and threw the gun over the side of the wall. Then he retrieved his keys and wallet from the concrete next to his assailant.

The mugger had turned from fierce to pathetic, sprawled on the ground, tripped by his pants, grabbing his damaged arm with his good one.

"Get up," Dan said.

"Fuck you."

Dan kicked in the direction of the mugger's balls through the tangled jeans stretched between his legs. "No, fuck you. Now get up." The man, cursing, drooling, and spitting through the pain, rose and moved backwards.

"Did you see a white kid around here Monday night?"

"Fuck you."

"You need some new vocabulary."

"Fuck you."

Dan grabbed the assailant's damaged elbow and squeezed. "Fuck who?"

"Aaaaarh. OK. OK. Fuck. No, I didn't see no white kid down here. White people don't come to this part of town at night."

"I may start."

"You're fucking crazy."

"What are you doing here?"

"I ain't white."

Dan squeezed the arm again. "That wasn't my question."

"I came down here to make a score."

"From who?"

The man with the dreadlocks looked over at the train tracks below. "Down there."

"What's his name?"

"Don't know and don't care." The man spit and gritted his teeth.

"Tonight is your lucky night. Get the hell out of here."

Dan watched as his assailant managed his way up the staircase and hobbled, elbow-in-hand, in the direction of Interstate 395. Once at a safe distance the man regained his bravado. "I'll get you, motherfucker. I'll get you."

"I doubt it," Dan whispered. He threw his leg over the same wall he had jumped from earlier with Detective Nguyen and landed in the abyss below the promenade.

—

"Hello," Dan announced soothingly as he approached the blue tarp tied to a promenade support column. The rusted underbelly of the promenade above provided protection from the elements. Privacy was another matter entirely. The angled slope of the tarp created a lean-to shelter, a changing area, a feeling of space. Defining one's own space in a world without walls, windows, or doors was a practice the homeless specialized in.

Light crept from the side of the angled tarp. A green sleeping bag was splayed on the ground. A worn lantern sat on a broken cinderblock. Dan moved closer and announced himself a second time. He bent at the waist as he approached, spreading his legs and taking small strides forward, ready to react, but keeping low enough to see under the tarp into the rudimentary campsite.

Another step forward and Dan could see through the sloping tarp to the darkness on the other side. No one was home. He looked around at the array of bottles. A Shiraz by Yellow Tail. A bottle of Grey Goose. A box of twenty-four mismatched microbeers. A half-finished bottle of scotch.

Someone was having a party.

"What the fuck you doin'?"

Dan stood and spun towards the voice.

The man staggered sideways. His dark pants and shirt made him almost invisible against the shadows of the night.

"Just looking," Dan said.

"Get outta here. It's *my* home," he said with an emphasis indicating it was a location that could be taken.

"I'm not interested in your spot."

"Then get outta here."

"I just want to talk."

"Get outta here."

"You celebrating?"

"Heellllll, no."

The man stumbled forward and a wave of stench accompanied him—alcohol, body odor, urine. Satan's smelling salts.

"You mind if I ask you a few questions? It'll only take a minute. Then I'll be gone."

"Fuck you."

Is it National 'Fuck You Day' and no one told me? Dan thought.

"I'll pay you for your time."

The man's staggering halted. "Hoowmmmuch?" he asked, the words slurring together.

"A hundred," Dan answered, removing a bill from his wallet and snapping it between his thumb and forefinger.

"Three questions," the man said, moving forward. "I'll give you three questions."

"Let's sit down."

Dan extended his hand, the money between his fingers, leading the man forward like a child feeding an animal at a petting zoo.

The man grabbed the money and stumbled again. Dan tried

to catch him as he reached the support column and gravity helped him to the ground. Unfazed, the man crawled under his tarp and got comfortable with his back against a large trash bag filled with all of his worldly possessions. Under the light from the lantern, Dan got his first good look at the man. His beard engulfed his face. His clothes were dirty, as if he had spent time habitually rolling about on his patch of God's earth. The man uncorked the top from the bottle of scotch and took a long, deep slug.

Dan cautiously sat on the ground outside the tarp. He felt safer with both of them nearer to the ground. People moved more slowly when they weren't standing. The man sealed the scotch bottle and dug through his trash bag of belongings. If you didn't count the occasional train passing fifteen feet away, the immediate surroundings were as quiet as a church during confessions. The melodic hum of the highway in the distance was the only sound. Depressing beyond words, but great if you were a light sleeper.

"Ok, question number one," the man said, taking enjoyment in announcing the statement like an inebriated game-show host. He leaned back against his trash bag and opened one of the beers from the box next to him.

"Were you here Monday night, around two in the morning?"

"Nooo," the man said, taking another swig of beer. "Question number twoooo . . ."

"How long have you been staying here, at this location?"

"Don't know. Moved here when the big snow fell."

Jesus. That was two years ago. Last winter had barely any snow, thanks to global warming, for those who believe in that sort of thing.

The man started humming a drunken version of the *Jeopardy* theme song, which faded into a repetitive loop before the man made a mistake and started over.

Dan waited for the song to end.

The homeless guy finished singing and licked his lips. "And now question number your final question," the homeless man butchered, becoming more drunk right before Dan's eyes.

"Where did you get all the booze?"

"Bought 'em."

The man took another drink, a more embracing one, and slurred something to himself.

"Thanks," Dan said, standing. He looked at the arrangement of alcohol, did a rough calculation of the cost, and then his face turned stern.

—

Dan reached his car and called Detective Nguyen.

"I went back to the promenade."

"Not recommended."

"You need to check on the homeless man with the camp under there. He probably knows something."

"Why do you say that?" Detective Nguyen asked.

"He isn't in any condition to talk at the moment but he has enough booze on site to get a sumo wrestling team drunk. Expensive booze. Not the type of brown paper bag crap that you would expect a homeless guy to have. And you know what that means."

"Sudden wealth."

"Either someone gave him money, or bought the booze for him. Either paid him not to be there on Monday night, or paid him to look the other way."

"Or maybe a relative stopped by and gave him some cash. A once-a-year thing. Who knows, maybe it's his birthday."

"Just check it out."

"I will. And I have an update for you. I checked your nephew's medical background. He did have multiple broken bones, most of them occurring during sports activities. A few trips to GU hospital. One each to GWU, Sibley, Holy Cross. The injuries were noted as accidents or sports-related. Child Protection Services did an inquiry and found nothing suspicious. So I guess your story checks out."

"Anything else in the medical history?"

"Besides an abnormally high number of fractures for such a young man there is nothing out of the ordinary."

"That's it?"

"That's it for the medical record. But I did run into another problem with your story."

"I'm not sure I like the sound of that."

"You won't. You said your sister-in-law called you at roughly two in the morning the night she died."

"That's right."

"There is no record of that phone call. There is no record of any phone call from your sister-in-law's phone. None from her house phone. None from her cell phone. None from your nephew's cell phone. Nada. Zippo."

"Did you check my phone records?"

"Yes."

"And . . . ?"

"Nothing. No call."

There was a long pause. "You still there?" the detective asked.

"Yeah, I'm here."

"I think we need to have another chat. You available tomorrow?"

"Give me a call. I have an appointment with an attorney in the morning, but after that I'm free. I'm not hiding from you."

"I hope not Mr. Lord. In light of your story about receiving a phone call from your sister-in-law—evidence for which there is no record—I'm planning to reopen her case. And you're at the top of my suspect list. Answer the phone when I call. Don't make me come find you. You'll like me a lot less than you do now."

Dan hung up the phone and thought for a moment. It is *National Fuck You Day.*

CHAPTER 9

—

Dan crossed the street at the intersection of River Road and Wisconsin Avenue, a block up from the UDC-Tenleytown Metro Station. College students ducked in and out the coffee shops and family-run restaurants nuzzled in the cracks and crevices of large office buildings. Development was choking out the city's character. Block-by-block, small shops were being overrun, consumed and digested by national chains with concrete façades and neon charm— Best Buy, Target, CVS.

Dan found 4501 Wisconsin without a map or checking his coordinates. A five-story, mid-nineties office building with a faux stone exterior. Inside, a lone security guard sat behind a large concrete desk with his head down, entertained by the sports page and the match-ups for the upcoming weekend.

"Pass through the metal detector," the oversized-guard said momentarily glancing up. "Keys, cell phone, and all metal objects in the basket and on the conveyor belt."

Dan did as told, ducked through the rectangular opening, and reacquired his objects on the other side of the inconvenience. He entered the octagonal lobby and looked for the directory, spotting the list of tenant names on the board near the elevators. The sunlight coming through the glass lobby illuminated the white lettering.

He put his finger on the suite number for the Parkson & Peterson law firm and rode the elevator to the top floor of the five-story building. Moments later he was seated in a book-filled office with a recently shined desk. The law firm's secretary, a bland woman in a beige dress who Dan imagined was as boring in other aspects of her life as she was in her fashion, offered him a coffee and then disappeared, shutting the door and leaving him alone in the office. A large map of DC hung on the wall, a historical replica with artificially browned edges to give the new art piece faux antique ambiance.

Moments later, Clyde Parkson opened the door and entered the room. The attorney had a smile fit for a toothpaste commercial. Huge white teeth, nearly oversized, filled his mouth and ran roughshod over other first impressions. His teeth flashed through his neatly trimmed goatee, like an animal revealing perfect fangs.

"Mr. Lord. Nice to meet you. My name is Clyde Parkson."

"Pleasure."

"May I extend my sincerest apologies to you and your loved ones. I truly, truly regret that we are meeting under such unfortunate circumstances."

Dan noticed the southern twang. Not too far south. Not too hick. North Carolina. Maybe Georgia. Definitely not a DC native. Clyde was wearing a dark pinstriped suit with shoes almost as polished as his teeth and the desk. His black hair was perfectly coiffed. His eyebrows waxed. The wireframe glasses on his nose were German, new, and expensive. The combined perfection of the outfit, teeth, hygiene, and demeanor left Dan wanting, at the least, to put the guy in a headlock and give him a noogie.

"Now, did you bring any documents with you?"

"Just what my sister-in-law's sister found in the house. She spent a few hours digging around and found copies of a will where you were listed as the attorney of record."

"Well, I'm glad your sister-in-law kept her records in a place where they could be found . . . to expedite the process."

"I imagine it would get done sooner or later."

"Sooner is always better, Mr. Lord."

"Call me Dan."

"I will. How about we start at the top, Dan? I'll give you a rundown of where we stand and where we need to go, and you just tell me when you have any questions."

"That's fine."

What transpired was more rambling than legal explanation.

"As you know, the death of a loved one, or two in your case, can be a traumatic experience. On top of the grief, there are many loose ends to tie up. Loved ones may be gone and with the Lord, but that doesn't keep Uncle Sam from reaching for his portion of the worldly possessions left behind. But rest assured that at Parkson & Peterson, we will do everything in our power to make sure the transition, at least on this side of the light, is a peaceful one. The financial and legal implications can be daunting."

"The probate process."

"I guess you are familiar with it then."

"My parents died a little over ten years ago."

"I see. Well, I'm sorry to hear that. Although it is little consolation, the second time serving as the executor of an estate may be a little easier."

"It's actually my third time," Dan corrected.

"I apologize for the assumption," Clyde Parkson added. "Well, then, let me cut to the chase, so to speak. We have the will and final testament of Victoria Lord, signed last September. In that will, it gives the value of her entire inheritance to her son, Conner. Obviously, God had his hand in that equation and your sister-in-law's sister is now the sole heir."

"I figured she might have written it that way."

"We have a pension from a previous employer, a 401k, and a home assessed for over nine hundred thousand dollars. Only twenty-two thousand remains on the mortgage balance. There is a stock portfolio with almost three-quarters of a million in it. There is another million in a term life insurance policy. It is likely that the life insurance policy is in limbo, pending the outcome of the investigation into her death. As you are aware, some life insurance does not pay out for a suicide. There is a common misconception that all life insurance doesn't pay for a suicide, but that is not true. Most policies do indeed pay for a suicide, just not within the first two years. At any rate, once that nasty little piece of business is concluded, we can make the final determination on the size of the estate."

"The death was initially ruled a suicide. I'm planning to meet with the detective in charge again to revisit a few facts on the case." Dan sounded agitated and the attorney seemed to pick up on the vibe.

"And I judge that you disagree with the initial ruling."

"It's irrelevant as to whether I agree. The ruling is what the ruling is."

"If the cause of death were virtually anything other than suicide, the estate could be worth considerably more. A million dollars more. It may be worth investigating. A million dollars is a lot of money."

"And of course you would get a cut."

"That is certainly not where I was intending to go with that conversation."

"What else do you need?" Dan asked.

"We need an inventory of the deceased's assets. Automobiles. Jewelry. Other properties. We need to confirm that all the potential heirs have been located."

"The entire family was here for the service."

"And did anyone express interest in the estate?"

"Just the sister. The sole heir."

"No one else?"

"My sister-in-law had one sibling. She was married to my brother. He passed away after my parents. He had one child. Conner. He also passed. There is nothing unusual in the progression of heirs."

"Are there any unexpected illegitimate children lurking in the weeds, so to speak?"

"If they're lurking out there, they've been lurking an awfully long time."

"Yes, yes. Just being thorough. It would be helpful to have copies of your sister-in-law's most recent tax statements. And if she has a safe deposit box, we should look into gaining access to make sure everything is accounted for."

"I should have that by the end of the week."

"Once that is done, we should be able to complete the probate on the estate. All outstanding debts will have to be paid, as well as any potential inheritance tax. If there is any tax to be paid, it is generally due . . ."

"Within nine months from the date of the death."

"You *have* done this before," Clyde Parkson said from his chair on the other side of the desk. "Well, as there is a single heir and a nice estate, your sister-in-law's sister stands to gain considerably. A financial windfall. Does this cause you any angst?"

"None. My mother came from money. When my parents passed away, both my brother and I received a rather large inheritance."

"Just asking. Sometimes people take the news of inheritance, or lack thereof, hard."

"All things being equal, I would rather have my family back."

"If you don't mind me asking, what was your brother's cause of death?"

"Cancer. Started as prostate and moved to his bones. It wasn't pretty."

"It never is. Prostate cancer is more aggressive when it is discovered in younger men . . . from what I gather."

"So they say."

"Well, I guess you have your marching orders. If you would get back in touch with us regarding your sister-in-law's latest tax information, as well as an inventory checklist, we will move forward. If you have issues gaining access to any safe deposit boxes, please contact this office."

"Anything else."

"Please let us know if you are contacted by any unforeseen potential heirs coming forth to stake a claim."

"I will."

"And let us know if the cause of death in your sister-in-law's case is going to change. There is a million dollars of life insurance to consider."

"The cause of death isn't likely to change without causing a few additional deaths," Dan muttered.

The attorney heard the comment, stood, and extended his hand. "Good day, Mr. Lord."

CHAPTER 10

—

Reed Temple stood next to the bare metal table in the tight white room. His jacket hung on the chair, the wrinkled top half of a tailor-made, single-breasted number he'd gotten in Bangkok while burning time on an assignment he could no longer recall. Reed Temple paced around the table, ran his fingers through his dark hair, and yearned for a cigarette, his pack of Marlboro's waiting in the car. No lighters were permitted in the building. Ditto for matches. And unless an employee was willing to munch through the business end of a cigarette to get their nicotine fix, security achieved their no-smoking goal without prohibiting the real target.

Reed Temple checked his watch. Three minutes late. Three minutes he would never get back. His patience ran naturally thin, a trait he inherited from his mother's side of the family. He had always been a doer. He still had faint memories of early childhood and his mother's voice floating out from the kitchen, shaking him from his daydreams, telling him "idle time is wasted time."

Fortunately, most of his time was absorbed by his hobbies and his job. In the middle, wedged neatly between interests and employment, was overlap. According to Reed Temple's grandfather, his love of his work made him one of the lucky ones. Combine work and a hobby and you have a happy man. Throw in football on Sunday afternoons and the occasional roll in the hay, and you were describing nirvana.

Reed Temple's current unofficial job description was running hundred-million-dollar programs with nonsensical names like "Cranberry" and "Low Tide." Wild-hair-up-the-ass ideas that got funded with unknowing taxpayer dollars and ended up on his "to-manage" list. For him, successful management was measured by two things: secrecy and status quo. Nothing else mattered. Secrecy gave him freedom. Maintaining status quo gave him a future. The number-one rule to government was not doing a job so efficiently you would eliminate yourself.

But he missed the field. He missed the overseas assignments. The glamour of drinking dirty water and rolling the dice at fly-laden food stalls. He wanted back out. He had seen enough of the States. Give him an hour and he would be gone. South America, Asia, even Africa, God forbid.

He had been sold on the domestic program management path as a fast-track up the political ladder. An express ticket to the seventh floor, the upper echelon of Langley. Or so he had been told. Three months into his assignment, he knew he had been lied to. Some of the blame rested squarely on his own shoulders. Wishful thinking. He was fully aware domestic clandestine assignments didn't officially exist within the Agency. What he came to realize was because they didn't exist, there was little interaction with management at HQ. The seventh floor, the people that made decisions and careers, didn't discuss domestic programs. Reed Temple had volunteered for a position based on incomplete intelligence. It was the most prudent lesson he had received since his training on the Farm. It hammered home a simple lesson he had forgotten. Trust no one, particularly those above you.

But the domestic assignments did have benefits. There was simplicity. He was given funding with no strings attached. From there, he simply had to point the ship in the right direction and not fuck it up. He was responsible for writing reports and ensuring evidence of his work remained on a secure server or locked in a filing cabinet at Langley or one of its sister buildings in Rosslyn, Springfield, or Vienna. The dark-windowed buildings with the American flags in the front but no names on the façades.

But he was now standing in an unpleasant square chamber because he had fucked it up. The evidence to that fuck up had been removed from under the promenade in L'Enfant Plaza. And he imagined what was coming next.

He stepped to the window and tapped his finger on the thick security glass lined with high-tech wire mesh designed to thwart eavesdropping. He looked out at the lunchtime traffic below, cars choking the road as they did in every nook and cranny of the DC area. *The masses who know nothing,* he thought. *Ignorance is bliss.* He couldn't remember the last time he experienced that kind of bliss. He could barely recall a time when he didn't know too much. And when you have done, seen, and heard too much, there was no putting the genie back in the bottle.

He paced around the table one more time and moved closer to the two-way mirror on the far wall. He stared at the material, looking at the glass as if he wished hard enough he would see through it. Through the charades. Through the bullshit shoveled by both sides. Just one small glimpse of truth.

He was told the person behind the two-way mirror was his boss. As far as he knew, they had never met. Names were names, titles were titles, and reality didn't interfere with either. For all he knew the two-way mirror was actually a no-way mirror. Such was the life he chose. A life of deception. Half of the job—and therefore half of life—was simply keeping your lies straight. And, of course, *not fucking it up.*

The speakers in the corners of the room crackled to life and Reed Temple stepped back. "We can get started now," the synthesized voice said from behind the glass. It was like taking orders from the automated voice on a customer service hotline. Not quite human. Not quite robotic. Reed Temple imagined he would recognize his superior's real voice if he heard it without the disguise. The cadence. The lack of any emotion. The careful grammatical precision. The selection of inspiring vernacular like teamwork and patriotism. Words his boss embraced. Words most people wouldn't be able to utter without someone questioning their sincerity.

"Mr. Temple, could you enlighten me on the current status of our situation?"

"How many are in the audience?"

There was a pause, silence, and then Reed Temple heard breathing escape from the speakers.

"I am alone."

Tisk, tisk. There are at least two of you. It doesn't take seconds to check with yourself.

"Please provide your update," the synthesized voice stated.

"The boy is dead, as is his mother."

"As previously reported. The mother's death has been designated as unnecessary collateral damage. Is there any *additional* information as to what transpired?"

"There was an emergency. Based on that emergency, there was fear the boy could have ended up in the public domain. Interaction with authorities."

"What could he have told them?"

"Everything."

"And none of it would have been verifiable."

"There was a sense of urgency we didn't foresee. We may not have had enough time for proper sterilization."

"The boy should have been transported to the university or dropped off in front of an emergency room. Regardless of how the boy was found, we would have had to sterilize."

"The university or a hospital would have required exposure to surveillance cameras, witnesses, medical professionals. Operationally, we did what we thought was best."

"Mr. Temple, need I remind you, we don't exist. Authorities cannot chase, charge, or convict ghosts. Who would the authorities pursue?"

Reed Temple leaned on the doorframe, the sole of one shoe on the wall. "There is an additional problem."

"What is it?"

"The mother made a call to a brother-in-law. The boy's uncle. Holds a private detective's license. Also has a law license. Both in Virginia. He arrived on the scene shortly before fire, rescue, and the police."

There was a long pause and more silence, as if the room had been put on mute. The synthesized voice boomed again as Temple walked back to the window. "What else do you know about the uncle?"

"He has an office in Alexandria. He is the younger brother of the deceased boy's father, who passed away five years ago. We are running additional parameters on him now."

"Anything else?"

There was another long pause.

"I would appreciate direction on how I should proceed," Temple said.

"With what?"

"The uncle, for starters."

"Stand down."

"With all due respect, if he is a private detective, or a lawyer, he will look into this."

"And he will only find smoke and mirrors. You don't know what I look like and I don't know your real name."

"Ignorance truly is bliss," Reed Temple said aloud, returning his thoughts to the people outside, trapped in their cars, encased in ignorance. "I understand the timing may not be perfect, but I would like to request re-assignment from domestic. I would like to return to the field. Practice the skills I have honed. Anything overseas."

"Clean up your mess, keep the Agency out of it, and I will work on approval for your request."

"And in the course of sterilization, what if the uncle gets lucky?"

"He cannot catch a cloud. There is nothing to tie us to anything. Walk away and there is no connection. You start playing with this man, and he might, indeed, get lucky. We don't need a self-fulfilling prophecy. Three deaths in the same family in under a week, in three separate locations, well, that could raise some red flags if anyone is paying attention. If the press picks it up, we'll be answering internal inquiries for months. Someone's ass will be testifying before Congress."

"What about the study?"

"Without the boy, the study portion of the program is canceled. There will be no additional funding regarding that pursuit."

"We can find a replacement."

"We already looked for a replacement."

"We can look again. I will look myself."

"Mr. Temple. You have always refused to embrace the odds on this study. This kid was one in seven billion. I will say it slowly one more time so there is no misunderstanding. The study is now closed. We had a once in a generation opportunity here and *you fucked it up*."

"And the rest of the program? Money has already been paid."

"The rest of the program is being evaluated in light of the current failure. The monetary concerns are inconsequential."

"There has been measurable progress on multiple fronts."

The voice was no longer listening. "Here are your orders. Clean up the mess with the boy without garnering any additional attention. Walk through the establishment of the entire study in reverse. Trace the boy's movements. Go through every meeting, transportation to the meetings, everything. All interactions, all locations, everything disappears. Understood?"

"Understood," Reed Temple replied. The intercom went silent and Temple could hear the automatic door lock click.

Understood, but too late.

CHAPTER 11

—

Dan parked his car on the west side of Idaho Street and walked across the wide expanse of sidewalk in front of Police Headquarters for District 2. The squat two-story building, with its plain red brick exterior, looked more like a school than a law enforcement establishment. Dan pushed through the large front doors and showed his ID to the white officer on crutches sitting behind the glass, manning the main security booth. Dan glanced through the thick translucent glass at the officer's bandaged ankle and wondered how the one-legged officer was going to keep the criminals in while keeping criminals out.

"I'm here to see Officer Nguyen."

"Detective Nguyen?"

"Yes."

The officer gave Dan a more focused, measuring stare. "Did you have an appointment?"

"Nothing concrete. I said I would stop by. He was working on a case involving some family members. I tried to reach him on the way over but he didn't answer."

"Have a seat," the hobbled officer said, leaning over in his stool and swiping the receiver off the phone next to him. Dan sat down in the small waiting area, wedging himself in between a man hiding under a hoodie and an inoperable TV sitting on a corner table.

Moments later, Officer Crutches tapped on the glass and Dan approached the security booth for the second time.

"Detective Wallace will be with you in a moment."

"I was here for Detective Nguyen."

"I heard you. Detective Nguyen isn't here. Detective Wallace is.

Here he comes now," the officer said, nodding in the direction of the other side of the room.

A heavy-set black male came bounding down the stairs and Officer Crutches pointed at Dan as if he were picking a fish out of a Chinese restaurant aquarium.

The officer extended his hand. "Detective Wallace."

"Good afternoon, Detective. I'm trying to reach Detective Nick Nguyen. He was working on a case involving my relatives. We were supposed to talk today."

"When was the last time you spoke to him?"

"Last night. Around eight or so." Dan felt the stare from Officer Crutches and noticed the red eyes and irritation of his newfound police detective acquaintance. His gut told him something was wrong. The detective confirmed his suspicion.

"Mr. Lord. Detective Nguyen was killed in the line of duty."

Dan recognized the emotion of a man in mourning. "I'm very sorry to hear that. I recently lost some people dear to me as well."

"Detective Nguyen was a good man."

"He seemed like it. I only met him a couple of times."

"I trained him. Worked with him. He was like my little brother. My Asian brother."

"I am truly sorry. What happened? An accident? He seemed like he was in good health."

"In the line of duty. That's the statement for now. Found him last night. Waiting for reports. Was on the news earlier today."

"I was away from the TV." Dan started the next sentence, stopped, and then started again. "I don't want to sound impersonal, but what's the protocol on cases he was working?"

"Depends."

"On what?"

"Type of case. Why don't you come upstairs and let's see what we've got."

Dan followed Detective Wallace up one flight of stairs and on the turn in the landing he heard the detective's knees creak. Dan estimated the detective's age at just over fifty, the few gray hairs more of a spoiler than the lines in his face.

On the second floor, Wallace led him through the maze of old wooden desks and chairs. He motioned for Dan to sit in an empty chair next to his desk. "Have a seat, don't touch anything, and I'll be right back."

—

Detective Wallace put his grieving in check as he walked through the cubicles and desks of the Robbery and Homicide Division. The floor was poignantly subdued, the normal chatter silenced by reflection. Detective Wallace sat his large black frame at Nguyen's desk and shook his head at the pile of papers. A stack of folders twenty high teetered precariously on the corner of the desk. Opened personal mail littered the workspace—a bill from the gas company on top of one from GEICO. A desktop calendar was hidden beneath the pile. A half-finished Diet Coke stood in front of the computer monitor. Detective Wallace reached for the stack of folders and flipped through the tabs until he eyed one simply labeled "Lord."

The detective looked at the report printed from the police system computer. He read quickly and tried to interpret the highlights of the case as seen through his colleague's eyes. In every word he saw fingerprints of his own tutelage, the deceased his protégé, his friend.

Vicky and Conner Lord. Vicky Lord found dead by her brother-in-law, Dan Lord. Cause of death an apparent suicide by hanging. Her son, Conner, was found dead the next morning from an apparent heroin overdose under the L'Enfant Promenade.

Wallace reread the last sentence and cursed. He read the sentence a third time and felt his face go flush. He peeked out from behind the folder and watched from across the room as Dan sat in the chair next to the detective's desk, looking up at the wall of information posted by the Robbery and Homicide division. Wallace stared intently at Dan as his visitor gazed at the wanted posters and framed accolades for exemplary detective work. *Cool as a cucumber*, Wallace thought.

Wallace turned his attention back to the report and read the half-dozen sticky notes pasted and taped to the inside cover of the manila folder. *Waiting for toxicology*. An arrow pointed downward. Written on the folder itself was Dan Lord's home, business, and cell phone number, in addition to his work address in Alexandria. Next to his name, circled in red ink, were two short handwritten sentences: "*Possible Suspect. Phone records missing.*" Detective Wallace paused and again glanced over at Dan before turning his attention back to the folder. "*Be careful*" and "*Military or martial arts background*" were scribbled at the bottom of the folder, both followed by large exclamation points.

"Uh-Oh," Wallace mumbled. He removed the computer printout from the manila folder and shoved it into a new empty folder, leaving the handwritten notes and Post-it opinions behind. He looked over the sea of desks and chairs and watched as Dan now sat motionless. *Be careful . . .*

Detective Wallace pushed himself out of the chair and stopped at the small refrigerator on the wall near the water fountain. He retrieved two bottles of water and weaved his way back to Dan, who was now eyeing Wallace.

"Water?" Detective Wallace asked, holding the bottle in front of Dan as he sat at his desk.

"Thanks," Dan replied. He took the bottle from the detective's massive hand, opened it, and drank half in two large gulps.

"I found a folder on Detective Nguyen's desk." Wallace opened the sanitized, abbreviated version of the folder and went over the highlights of the case. "Vicky and Conner Lord. A suicide and a drug overdose."

"Correct, but incorrect. Anything else?"

"That's it. A few of the other details, it seems, were provided by you. We are still waiting for toxicology. Do you have anything else to add?"

Dan looked at Detective Wallace's desk. "I am wondering if you have Detective Nguyen's notebook?"

"What notebook?"

Dan pointed at the notebook on Detective Wallace's desk. "His detective notebook. He took notes like he was a court reporter. And his notebook was the exact same as yours. Same blue cover with red trim. I don't imagine that is coincidence. Probably bought in bulk. Or purchased at the same time. Maybe a gift you both received."

Nguyen's written words again flashed across Detective Wallace's eyes. *Be careful.*

"We haven't found his notebook. Or his badge. His service weapon was found on scene. The magazine was full. We haven't determined if he kept one in the chamber, and if he did, whether or not it had been fired. We also located the likely murder weapon."

"Any suspects?"

"We are running ballistics and forensics."

"I hope you find him."

"Oh, we will. I will. If it is the last thing I do. Nick was like a brother to me."

"An Asian brother. I was listening, Detective."

"Can I get your contact information?"

"Isn't it in the file?" Dan asked.

Suspicious, Wallace thought. "Just being thorough."

"Give me a piece of paper and I'll write my contact info for you."

Detective Wallace handed Dan a piece of paper and a pen. As he wrote, Dan continued to talk. "Detective, I'm sure you're grieving, on top of being busy with all the shit this city has to offer, but I also lost two family members. And at the risk of sounding unsympathetic, there are things you need to know. I have reason to believe my sister-in-law and nephew probably died in manners inconsistent with the findings to date. Things just don't add up."

"Like what?"

"Religion, upbringing, financial security. Other things."

"Mr. Lord, I get it. No one wants to think that a family member killed themselves or died of a drug overdose. It makes us feel as if we failed them. I see it every day."

"This is different," Dan said, folding the paper and placing it on the detective's desk.

Detective Wallace spoke from the same detective rulebook that Detective Nguyen quoted from. "I can only work with evidence. I'll follow it where it leads. I promise to keep you in the loop. But the priority around here is going to be finding Detective Nguyen's killer. After that, his cases will be examined and reassigned according to need. Homicides will be examined first. Robberies next. Suicides and drug overdoses are down the list."

Dan Lord shook his head. "Then I guess I will have to find the truth myself."

"Mr. Lord, where were you last night around ten o'clock?"

"I was at Good Time Charlie."

"You with anyone?"

"Mr. Good Time himself."

"Well, Mr. Lord, I'll be in touch."

Dan stood and Detective Wallace mirrored his movement. "I'll let you know if I find anything," Wallace said.

"Thanks. I'll do the same. Expect me to call first."

The detective watched as Dan headed to the stairs and waved as he disappeared downward. As Dan hit the front door, the detective yanked opened his bottom desk drawer and pulled out a box of evidence gloves and a quick seal evidence bag. He dumped the pens from a coffee mug pen holder and poured the contents of the water bottle Dan Lord had touched into the mug. With gloved hands he carefully placed the empty water bottle into the evidence bag and sealed it closed.

Detective Wallace snatched the bag and propelled his oversized frame to the basement evidence collection area. The young, brown-haired forensic technician on duty snapped to attention when the seasoned detective barged into the room, nearly hyperventilating.

"Stop whatever you are doing and run the prints on this water bottle. There is nothing more important. I'll be upstairs at my desk. If I'm not there, act like a detective and find me."

Sweat appeared on the young man's brow, his twenty-something appearance suddenly looking more childlike. "Sure thing, Sarge. I should have something in an hour."

"No breaks, no emails, nothing until you give me an answer."

—

Sergeant Detective Wallace knocked on his captain's door and waited. Wallace looked through the glass as the captain paced around his desk, phone to his ear. The captain looked as if he had aged since earlier that morning, since he broke the news of Nguyen's death to the department. His gray hair looked more white. The lines on his face deeper.

The captain finished his phone call, cradled the receiver, and waved Detective Wallace in.

"I heard you at this morning's meeting, but I want to be assigned to Nick's case."

"I know you do and no you can't. You are too close. It is too personal."

"Captain, he was my partner."

"Exactly. And when emotions get involved, protocol has a way of being forgotten."

"Captain . . ."

"How long have we known each other, Earl?" the captain asked, using Detective Wallace's first name.

"Twenty years."

"Two decades. A long time."

"Too long to be treated like this."

"How many times since I've been captain have I let an officer or detective work a case they were involved in, or had family members involved in?"

"None."

"That is correct. None. And I am not starting now. Dietz and Noyes are the lead detectives on Nguyen's case. Support them anyway that you can. But I expect the support to be passive. Passive. Do you understand?"

"But I may have found something important. Nguyen was working on a case involving an apparent suicide and an overdose. One of the deceased was found in the same location Nguyen was."

"Great. Turn the evidence over to Dietz and Noyes."

Detective Wallace stood in silence.

"Understood?" the captain asked.

"Yes, sir."

—

Forty minutes later, Detective Wallace was at his desk, spinning an unopened pack of cigarettes. The cessation battle was raging and for the morning, Detective Wallace was victorious. When the phone on the desk rang, he pounced.

"Sarge, there are no prints on the bottle."

"You mean they don't show up in the system?"

"No, I mean there are no prints on the bottle at all."

Wallace cursed, stringing together a set of expletives colorful enough to garner attention from half of the detectives on duty. He finished the blush-generating outburst with a more mild, *"Son of a bitch!"* Spittle gathered in the corner of his lips.

"How can that be?" he gasped, almost foaming at the mouth.

"Well, either it was wiped down, or the man has no fingerprints."

Detective Wallace leaned back in his chair as the forensic technician waited for a response. *Be careful.* The words rolled around the detective's head. He could feel his blood pressure rising. His chest thumping. He looked down at his desk and reached for the paper Dan had written his contact info on. He slowly unfolded the paper, read it once, and cursed again. *"Motherfucker!"* The words reverberated around the room, ricocheting off the walls, trickling down the staircase.

Written in eloquent penmanship was the simple sentence: *If you wanted my prints, you should have just asked for them. Thanks for the water.*

Detective Wallace turned his attention back to the phone. "I want you to run prints in the database for Dan Lord. I will send you the contact information I have."

"Does he have a criminal past?"

"Not that I am aware of."

"The main database holds all criminal fingerprints and all recorded prints for military and government personnel. If his prints are in there, I will have something by the end of the day. If he is not in that database, we will have to go to plan B."

"Which is?"

"Getting access to civilian fingerprint databases for civilians without criminal records. Those are restricted access. You generally need a warrant. Case numbers. Approval from the Captain. You could also bypass procedures. Call in some favors. Play the fallen law enforcement officer card. See if anyone wants to help."

"Get me whatever you can find, any way you can get it."

"It could take some time."

"Just get it."

CHAPTER 12

—

Lindsay Richer finished her evening run, a five-mile jaunt starting at the gate of American University on Nebraska Avenue. She ran down MacArthur Boulevard, past the assortment of embassies and distinguished residences, through Georgetown and back uphill on Wisconsin Avenue. It was a run she had done three times a week without fail until Conner had died. She was now trying to get back into her routine, to move on.

The exercise was therapeutic. As much as the loss she felt for her boyfriend, she was sorting through the shock to her foundation. She missed him to be sure. Every couple she saw on campus reminded her of what she briefly had and what she knew, somewhere beyond the grief, she would have again. The pain was persistent, but it wasn't life-ending.

The shock was different.

It was the shock that jolts youth when they first discover how short life can be. How quickly it can be snuffed out. What Conner's death had taught her was to keep moving, because your last day can come as suddenly at nineteen as it can at sixty-five. Most young people just didn't think that way. It usually took a tragedy.

She did her post-run stretch on the porch of the Alpha Chi Omega house, her sweat drying in the late autumn air. A group of frat boys exited the house next door, waved to her and piled into an older-model Jeep Cherokee. She put her leg on the edge of the staircase, touched her head to her knee, and then bounded up the stairs.

She took off her sweatshirt and threw it on the pile of clothes in the hamper in the corner of her room. She sat on the bed and kicked off her shoes. When she looked up, she was staring at a picture of herself and Conner, wedged into the frame of the mirror over her dresser. She tried to smile but failed. She looked at the St. Christopher medal hanging on the other corner of the mirror, a gift from Conner.

She stood at her dresser and her eyes welled up. She opened her underwear drawer and in the corner was a memory box, a gift from her grandmother when she turned twelve. She put the box on the dresser and opened it slowly. She unfolded a single love letter from Conner, read it from beginning to end, and then folded it again. In the corner of the box was a folded napkin with torn edges. She unfolded the napkin and finally managed to smile, smirking at the numbers scribbled in permanent marker, the writing leaking through the layers of the napkin. She remembered back to when Conner had given the numbers to her. His cell phone number. His dorm number. His mother's house number. A number he listed as emergency. *He wasn't taking any chances*, she thought.

She removed her phone from the Velcro pocket on her running pants and called Conner's cell phone to listen to his voice recorded on the voicemail greeting. The service was still connected and she shed a tear as Conner said "You've reached Conner Lord. I'm unavailable to take your call at the moment, but if you leave a message I will get back to you as soon as I can."

She had listened to the message a dozen times since the funeral. Each time it hurt less. A step in the healing process.

She had also called the dorm number the first few days, but Conner's roommate erased it after the service. The voice of a dead guy on the answering machine was only cool for so long when you actually knew the person. Lindsay looked at the last number on the napkin and wondered if there was another recorded voicemail message, a last chance to hear the dead speak new words. Different words spoken by someone she cared about and someone she would never speak to again. She dialed the number labeled "emergency."

She shut her eyes as she waited.

—

Reed Temple passed through the security booth at the three-story gray octagonal building just down the hill from Tyson's Corner Mall. The unremarkable gray stone exterior of the building was in deep contrast to the gleaming flagships of Northrop Grumman and Lockheed Martin, the outlines of their respective corporate castles peeking out from behind the trees dotting Tyson's skyline.

Every commercial tenant in the zip code was paying two hundred dollars a square foot while charging Uncle Sam three hundred dollars an hour for contractors and engineers. The contractors and engineers, in turn, built the systems that Uncle Sugar bought with taxpayer money. They charged the government to employ their engineers to build systems they would in turn sell to the government. It was brilliant.

Tel Q Labs was the baby on the defense industry block. While Lockheed and Northrop Grumman cranked out fighter jets and tanks, Tel Q Labs was stocking their offices with PhDs, MDs, Harvard MBAs, and UPenn accountants.

It was no secret that for the past decade the CIA had been dabbling in private sector technology incubation. It had been splashed across the front page of the *Washington Post* and discussed over tea and biscuits on the BBC. NPR was the first media outlet to list the names of companies the CIA was interested in. The only questions that remained truly classified were which companies they already owned and which companies they were looking to purchase.

Tel Q Labs had spent the last five years trying to make it onto the list of companies under consideration, to make themselves attractive enough to be invited to the dance. After five years, a hundred sponsored dinners, and an unsanctioned trip to New Orleans, they succeeded. The success of the first government contract opened the door to a second contract. A second led to a third, and by the time a half-dozen contracts had been signed, Tel Q Labs was firmly on the radar of the intelligence and defense community as an innovative supplier of key defense services vital to national security. Or so the brochure read.

In the large scope of things, Tel Q Labs was little more than a few dozen highly motivated individuals backed by a series of deep pockets and angel investors disguised by LLCs and blind trusts. Tel Q Labs didn't build missiles or subs or have spy satellite launch capabilities. The only drone they offered was palm-size and was still flying test missions in a basement lab on US soil.

Tel Q Labs' specialty was on the personal level. The company used inventive nomenclature like Headcount Reduction Efficiency to give their personal brand of killing capabilities a certain statistical significance which could be embraced without sounding murderous. Smart ammunition, enhanced protection armor, advanced personal accessories. Dual-use items that were attractive to both intelligence and the DOD.

Tel Q Labs' timing was perfect. The defeat of long-standing enemies and the conquest of lesser countries had left the US without a state-sponsored adversary. And without an organized dark force with which to do battle, the US intelligence and defense communities were being forced to look beyond tanks, fighters, subs, and aircraft carriers. Real war, where the real money could be made, was being curtailed. Nothing rang the cash register like boots on the ground, and the lack of a defined enemy was crippling the defense industry business. Asymmetric warfare was different. Demand for drones was booming. Robotics was on the horizon. The use of technology on a smaller scale was finding itself very popular amidst shrinking budgets. Smaller monetary allocation for smaller toys.

Reed Temple took his Tel Q Labs' visitor pass to the third-level basement where his all-access privileges ended. He stood in front of the camera and put his palm against the wall-mounted reader. A light flashed and the reader mapped the unique pattern of the veins beneath the surface of his hand. While the scanner mapped the layout of the veins, another sensor checked for perspiration and a temperature on his palm. A moment later the door slid open.

"Thank you, Fujitsu," Temple whispered to himself, marveling at the borrowed technology being applied to personalized weapon grips.

Temple Reed walked into the large windowless floor without

fanfare. In the corner, a woman in a lab coat sat with her back to the door, looking through a high-powered microscope at the current version of the world's smallest hundred-terabyte solid-state drive.

Along the near wall, amidst multiple rows of newly arrived boxes, a massive mechanical exoskeleton lay in pieces on a large table. The skeletal outline of composite material rested on a large white sheet. Reconstructive surgery on the skeleton was in session and a large black man was moving from piece to piece, bolt to wrench, twisting and tightening, flexing and straightening. On the other side of the table, a white male with a military haircut checked the wiring between the exoskeleton's forearm and bicep.

Reed Temple approached the table and nodded to his two private-sector program leaders, Major and Ridge. "We need to talk. I just had my ass chewed out and I am going to return the favor. You're not going to like what I have to say."

Ridge, six feet and four inches of chiseled ex-marine, stood straight from his position over the exoskeleton and stretched his back. The scars on his massive black hands and thick neck were souvenirs from a seven-hour stint defending a position on a hilltop in Afghanistan with eight other marines. Temple knew the story well. Seven hours of hell. Blood. Screams. Piss. Shit. They'd endured shelling and ambushes throughout the night, asses dug into the earth so deep the worms were evacuating to make room. Blinding rain had intermittently pounded their position, torrents of water running through crevices in the ground and filling their foxhole. When air support had arrived at dawn, the enemy had been within twenty yards and Ridge had been firing his last magazine, his knife ready for action. Around him, eight team members had lain injured or dead. One of the survivors would never walk again. By the time the last bomb had dropped on the encroaching enemy and the dust had settled, Ridge's transformation was complete. A young man named Robert Williams, with limited combat experience, had gone to the top of the mountain to oversee a supply route. He came down the mountain with two names—Hero and Ridge. The last one had stuck.

Major's outward appearance was straight from the Army catalog for standard issue, military-grade, white male. Short, dirty blond hair. Dark blue eyes. Average height. Average weight. Wiry strong. The characteristics that made him malevolently above average were between his ears.

His first foreign post with the Army had been working with the Colombian government teaching anti-narcotic trafficking tactics in the jungles of South America. The war on drugs. It was a war that couldn't be won. After three years of burning coke labs and watching drug lords do business with impunity, Major had been assigned to DC. Two years later he was shipped to Iraq. Then to Afghanistan. In Colombia, he had witnessed the killings. The innocent and the guilty. The murderers and those trying to feed their families. But his government-issued weapon had missed out on direct action.

All that changed in Afghanistan. Major took to slaughter without conscience, and his grip on reality loosened. He slipped from soldier to self-appointed mercenary. His lifelong photography hobby blossomed into trophy shots with deceased Taliban and less-guilty Afghani locals. The new angle on his old hobby encouraged more ill behavior. He embraced a penchant for talking to his victims at length before he killed them, and an equally dishonorable habit of taking souvenirs from those he murdered. An ear here. A family heirloom there.

As Reed Temple examined the ankle joint on the exoskeleton on the table, Major looked over at Ridge and flicked his head in the direction of the glass-walled office in the corner. Inside the soundproof glass room, Reed Temple shut the door and the three men sat down at the round table. More boxes filled the corner of the room.

"Where are we with the site?"

Ridge sat at perfect attention with board-like posture but didn't speak.

Major had no such reservations. "We had a visitor. A white male, age approximately thirty-five to forty."

"Did we get an ID?"

"No. We followed the agreed upon protocol. Paid a local informant with a long record two hundred dollars to keep an eye on the location. He was given the order to obtain ID but was unable to do so."

"Was the informant armed?"

"Yes."

"Then what went wrong?"

Major nodded towards Ridge for an explanation. Eyes forward, Ridge provided a description as if there were a script in front of him. "The hired help pulled a gun on the visitor, who evidently took offense to having a firearm shoved in his face. The visitor disarmed our man, breaking his elbow in the process."

"What is the status on our hired help?"

Ridge looked back at Major who picked up the conversation. "Our hired help is currently residing a few hundred yards north of the Pennsylvania Avenue Bridge. He is properly weighted. He shouldn't resurface until the spring when the city does its annual *Keep the Anacostia River Clean* initiative."

Temple nodded quietly in approval. "The visitor was probably the uncle of the boy."

"Yes. We are assuming the same. Our hired help gave a similar description when he was debriefed. We didn't set eyes on the subject ourselves," Major said.

"Well, the uncle is turning out to be a little bit more than a lawyer or private detective, isn't he? Disarming a man with a gun at point blank range is not for novices."

"No, it is not," Major agreed.

"What else do you have?"

"The homeless subject who lives under the L'Enfant Promenade was paid to find somewhere else to live. As you can imagine, he chose not to follow these orders."

"Status."

"Missing."

"Outlook?"

"None, sir."

"And the police?"

"We had a complication," Major said, relishing his time at the mic. "The police filed their report on the dead boy. The site was checked once when the body was reported and then visited again by a detective and the uncle. The medical examiner records show they are waiting for the toxicology report on the deceased boy."

"And the complication?"

"The site was visited again, late last night, after the run-in with the uncle. It was the same detective. He caught us by surprise."

"And . . ."

"It was on the news this morning."

"Law enforcement is off limits."

"It was unavoidable. But not all hope is lost."

"Explain."

"We gave the police some assistance in locating a suitable suspect."

"Very well."

Major stood from his chair, retrieved a large cardboard box from the corner of the room and placed it on the table with the top off. He removed several items from the box and put them on the table for Temple to assess as he spoke.

"We have made progress eliminating our tracks. Most of the boxes you see here are from the other location. We took the GPS from the boy's car. No trace there. We removed his computer from the dorm room. No trace there."

Temple looked at the black laptop, opened the lid, and shut it again. "Was the hard drive destroyed?"

"Erased first then destroyed."

"Good."

"As for personal intelligence trails, there is no telling what he may have said to anyone. At this time, we have no indication that he spoke to anyone about our program. The uncle doesn't seem to know and it appears they were close."

On the table, a cell phone started to vibrate.

"Whose phone is that?" Temple asked.

"It's the boy's. The one we issued to him."

"Does someone want to tell me why the fuck it is still active? That thing should be scrap plastic by now."

All three men watched as the phone vibrated in position, moving clockwise slowly.

Reed Temple stared for another few seconds before he picked up the phone and pressed talk.

A voice on the other end of the phone answered. "Hello."

"Who is this?"

"Who is this?" a female's voice parroted.

There was a long pause, followed by, "Who were you trying to reach?"

"I was trying to reach Conner Lord."

"He's dead," Reed Temple said flatly.

"I know," the female responded. "My name is Lindsay. I was Connor's girlfriend. Who am I speaking with?"

There was another pause and Temple disconnected the call with the punch of his thumb. He looked around the table and sweat appeared on Ridge's brow. Temple squeezed the phone in his hand until his knuckles turned white. In one swift motion he stood and threw the phone against the far wall with as much velocity as he could. Pieces of plastic scattered across the floor.

"Our orders are to sterilize. I assume I don't need to walk you step-by-step through the process."

"No sir," Major and Ridge replied in unison.

"Clean up this mess and I will get support for the other products in the pipeline."

"What about the uncle?"

"Our orders are to stand down on the uncle until further notice. My superiors are concerned that three family members dying in the same week may get some play in the media. For now, sterilize."

Temple stood from the table and pointed at the broken cell phone on the floor. "And that fucking thing better not ring again."

Reed Temple walked out of the building in quick, strong strides.

—

In the basement, Major put Conner Lord's belongings back in the box as Ridge picked up the pieces of the broken phone.

"That was not a positive conversation," Ridge stated plainly.

"Don't let it concern you. We have a paid-in-full contract with the CIA in the name of national security with immunity protection. And if our work with the CIA is terminated, there are other interested parties for our work. The US is the number one exporter of weapons and ammunition in the world. We work for something far more powerful than the CIA."

"We do?"

"Yes. Corporate America."

CHAPTER 13

—

Dan stretched a twenty-five minute walk to forty. The air helped him think. But it didn't help him think he was wrong about his nephew or sister-in-law. His nose had always been good. Always. His gut rarely failed. He knew the planet was teeming with people who were far smarter than himself. Far more intelligent. Kids so bright they ended up in classrooms at MIT at sixteen. Kids who didn't understand their own intelligence, they just knew they could answer questions that stumped their high school teachers.

But Dan had a nose. A gut. He usually saw what was coming before it turned the corner. It was a watered-down version of a sixth sense, the capability of looking at the pieces of a puzzle and fitting them together to see the bigger picture. For him, it just happened. His grandmother had loved jigsaw puzzles. Dan's jigsaw puzzles were life, each piece a scene in his mind—a person on a street corner, an off-the-cuff comment made in passing. He paid attention to everything around him and the pieces just fell into place. Most of the world walked around in a state of reaction. He walked one step ahead. And that alone had kept him alive more times than he had the right for.

Dan walked away from Old Town Alexandria and the Potomac River, heading west down King Street and then turning right on Washington. He loved his city. Alexandria had it all. Million-dollar condos overlooking the river. Majestic townhouses built in the seventeen and eighteen hundreds on cobblestone streets still used by residential traffic. Twenty square blocks of housing projects so crime-ridden even the roaches ducked and weaved when entering. And every neighborhood in between.

Five blocks up Washington Street, Dan took a left and the neighborhood quickly transformed to lower-rent housing. The street was darker. The cars were dilapidated, former modes of transportation in need of various repairs. A missing wheel to the left. A broken windshield on the other side of the street.

He kept his eyes open and his head on a casual swivel. He noticed the group of young men on the porch across the street as they whispered and nodded in his direction. He felt a car drive slowly by, its occupants measuring him. He turned to make eye contact with the driver and the car accelerated to the next block and punched it through the corner, wheels spinning on the pavement. A hundred yards ahead, the sign of his destination peaked through the leaves of a leaning tree holding on to the final vestige of fall foliage.

Dan knocked on the door under the Bail Bondsman sign attached to the brick façade. He smiled upward at the security camera over the doorframe and waved. A faint buzzer buzzed in reply, and the door lock clicked. Dan stepped into the office of the converted two-story shotgun house. A client waiting area spread across what used to be a narrow living room. A small desk sat in the corner, littered with unorganized paper and unopened mail. A lone light in the corner illuminated half the room. A voice rang out from the former kitchen at the back of the house and Dan announced himself to the empty room, his voice echoing slightly. "It's Dan."

A head popped around the corner. "Come on back," the man said with a hint of franticness.

The kitchen at the back of the house was now a private room designed for playing cards, drinking, shit-kicking, and any number of illicit activities that could have its bail bondsman proprietor in need of his own services. The room was where real deals were completed—the front of the establishment reserved for official business. Never would the two mix company.

Steven Ricks went by "Striker," a moniker created from the combined bastardization of his first and last name. It was a name he'd been answering to for so long he couldn't remember who tagged him with it first. The use of the name infiltrated every corner of his life. Teachers, family members, and doctors alike adopted the name with equal enthusiasm.

Most bail bondsmen, Striker's brethren, ran their businesses from small establishments that encircled the nearest courthouse. Tiny offices that shone neon signs towards the steps of justice, close enough for relatives or friends of the indicted to fall from the courthouse stairs to the nearest bail bondsman's office.

Alexandria was different.

Four blocks from the water, the Alexandria Courthouse stood in the middle of property selling for a thousand dollars a square foot. It promoted a price on rent few bail bondsmen could cover bailing out local prostitutes. Most of the people Striker bailed out would have been flight risks, if not for the fact they didn't have money to run. He dredged the bottom of the criminal justice system and came up with enough small fish to keep himself in official business two miles from the courthouse. He bailed out the occasional whale and took chances on people with short records, but most of his income came from peripheral side-jobs. The legitimate side of the business was enough to keep the IRS from getting too suspicious. He had cash in bank accounts with fake names, in footlockers at various storage facilities, in a dozen safety deposit boxes across an equal number of states. Striker, as if the name alone was insufficient indication, was omitted from the list of invitees to most hobnobbing black-tie affairs. But he was at the top of the go-to list when it came to garnering information not available through normal channels.

Dan's type of people.

Dan stepped into the backroom. A circular poker table engulfed one quarter of the room. A bar stood on the left where the kitchen counters and cabinets once hung. A small sink had replaced a larger one where dishes had once been cleaned after dinner. In the far corner was the establishment's lone restroom.

Striker, skinny with curiously wide shoulders, had his back to Dan as he entered the room. His dark hair was cut short. He was wearing jeans and a blue button-down shirt.

"Dan, good to see you." Striker said, quickly zipping a black leather bag and putting it on the poker table. He flicked his head in the direction of the closed restroom door, just as the toilet flushed out of view.

A large white man exited the narrow door to the bathroom and cast a shadow on the poker table.

"Dan, this is Doyle."

Dan extended his hand and Doyle latched onto it in one of those greetings meant to prove who the Alpha dog was. Dan squeezed back, turned Doyle's wrist slightly, and then pushed his weight forward. Doyle felt the redirection in the grip, then the subtle pain, and he let go. "Serious grip," he complimented.

Striker emceed the introductions. "Doyle, Dan is an acquaintance of mine. He has done some surveillance and tracing for me in the past. I help him out from time to time. It works out."

Doyle nodded at Dan, and Striker continued.

"Doyle here is helping me track down a couple of bail skippers. And a few other things."

"Fugitive Recovery Agent," he said, giving his profession an image boost through improved nomenclature. Doyle stood six three, two-forty, with short blonde hair and a physique that made office workers slink away in shame when he entered the gym.

Dan nodded. "You Australian?"

"Did the accent give it away?"

"It's faint, but there."

"You ex-military?" Doyle asked.

"Why do you ask?"

"You have that look about you."

"What look is that?"

"A certain look. Aura. Someone carrying a secret. Delta, Recon, Ranger, SEAL. The quiet professional. An operator with a don't-fuck-with-me demeanor. You're also the right size. Not too big, but strong. Most professionally trained killers are average size."

"Most of the government-sanctioned killers."

"Most."

There was an awkward pause and then Dan took his turn. "And I am guessing you're probably ex-SAS. You've also been incarcerated for an extended period of time."

"Guilty as charged. Military. Prison. Been to both. Can't say I prefer one over the other."

"All right. That's enough reading each other's resumes," Striker interrupted.

Dan looked at Doyle and then back at Striker. "I need to talk," Dan said, hoping he could expedite the Australian's exit.

Doyle took the hint without missing a beat and picked up the leather bag from the poker table. He slapped Striker on the shoulder and nodded at Dan as he moved towards the back door. "Gentlemen," he said before leaving, the hinges on the old door squeaking in salutation.

Dan slid onto a padded wooden chair at the poker table and watched as Striker moved a small box from the table to a shelf behind the bar.

"You looking for info or work? I have a few things on the arrest reports that you may be interested in. A congressman from New York got arrested Saturday night for running a red light. Claimed he was in a hurry to see his ill child. Turns out the child was illegitimate and he was on his way to his mistress's house. So far, the story hasn't broken."

"If it breaks, I can't use it."

"Had a Fairfax County Council Member arrested for getting a blowjob on a GW Parkway overlook. Male prostitute with pink lipstick."

"Steve, I'm not here for work." The use of Striker's real name was enough for the bail bondsmen to know it wasn't business-as-usual.

Striker nodded. "I heard about your sister-in-law and nephew."

"Where did you hear?"

"Public channels. I recognized the name 'Lord,' of course. Then I asked around. That's tough, man. Real tough. First a brother, then a nephew. I know you were a father figure to the kid. A sister-in-law can go either way, really, but a brother a few years back and now a nephew, that is family blood. I am truly sorry."

"Thanks."

"Tell me what's cooking."

"I need to talk to tech support," he said being cryptic for someone's name he knew but was cautious to use.

"Tobias?"

So much for caution.

"Yeah. You know where I can find him?"

"Did you try?"

Dan tap-danced around the answer. "Skip tracing is getting easier every day. I make a call, pay a fee, and they can tell me the last time you bought a cup of coffee or pissed it out. Tobias is different. Skip-tracing him is a dead-end."

Striker ignored Dan's feign of ignorance. "How far did you get on your own?"

"I looked around. Tobias moved from that little shack in Del Ray."

"From what I know, that place wasn't his anyway."

"Well, he's not there."

"I checked my contact at the phone company and got nothing. My contact ran a list of everyone with high-bandwidth Internet lines, or multiple lines, established in the last year. T3 and above. Anything going residential. The list is long and I don't have time to do a line-by-line."

Striker joined Dan at a chair at the poker table and leaned back. "Yeah, man. Tobias's still around. Crazy as ever. Shit, crazier than ever."

"You know where he is?"

"Fuck. Yeah. I know how to find him. But it's not that simple. Last time I sent someone to see him he wasn't happy. He shut down my website. Cut off my cell phone service. Took over all my email accounts. Just went off the reservation. Didn't want me giving out any info on him. Didn't want me introducing anyone. Said he's working on retirement and doesn't want to spend his golden years in solitary confinement."

"Steve, I wouldn't ask if it weren't important."

Striker picked a cigarette from the pack lying on the poker table. He lit the white stick of joy with a Zippo lighter and flipped the top shut with a smooth motion of the thumb. He blew a large bluish white cloud into the air over the table and finished his thought aloud. "I'll give you the address, but you can't tell him I sent you."

"I'll tell him I found him through a source at the phone company.

Or the cable company. Chances are he is using a lot of bandwidth, whatever he's up to. He has to be paying someone for it. I'll tell him I found him that way. Just going through the list of bandwidth hogs."

"Pretty good cover story. It could work, theoretically. But it would take you forever to locate him that way."

"I don't have forever."

"Well, if we play it your way, I guess I'd only be giving you a shortcut to what you would find eventually anyway."

"Exactly."

"OK. I'll tell you where he is. But this is on you. Don't have this shit coming back to me. Tell him we had a falling out. Call me an asshole and a motherfucker if you have to. Spit on the ground at the mention of my name if it is called for."

"I appreciate it."

Striker took another long drag from his cigarette. "Anything else?"

"Yeah." Dan reached into his jacket pocket and put a rectangular chunk of military explosive C-4 on the table. "I'm finished with this. Can you get me some PETN?"

Striker swiped the C-4 off the table, reached behind him and slid it into another drawer on left side of the bar.

"PETN? Sure. I can get it. The man I need to talk to just left."

"Don't need to know that."

"You know, military-grade explosives were designed to blow shit up. Not many people bring it back unused."

"My money, my prerogative."

"Fair enough, man. Fair enough. PETN is the same price as the C-4. You bring it back unused, I return half the purchase price."

"I know the deal."

"For Tobias, well, you're going to owe me one."

Dan stood from the table. "Before this is over, I'm going to owe everyone."

CHAPTER 14

—

Good Time Charlie, off Route 50, just inside the Beltway on the Maryland side, was visible from a quarter mile. The LED bulbs that framed the roofline of the establishment twinkled just right. The brass fixtures near the entrance—the handrails and lamp posts—were lightly polished for a hint of class. The outside of the building attracted customers like insects drawn to light. The dark interior, the preponderance of royal burgundy carpeting and walnut paneled walls, gave it a sense of prestige. It was a place where secrets could be kept, right out in the open.

The main room of the restaurant was a well-heeled steakhouse which served—as Charlie the owner liked to claim—the best pieces of meat between New York and Texas. On the left side of the massive room, behind two large archways, was a bar that stretched the depth of the restaurant, the stash of alcohol running the gambit from Grey Goose to resurgent PBR. On the right side of the restaurant, behind massive doorways adorned with red velvet curtains, was a private party room that seated a hundred comfortably. The clientele at Good Time Charlie varied from pure-hearted meat-eaters to average johns looking for top-grade meat of a different nature.

Detective Wallace sat in his car in the parking lot and watched the first wave of carnivores disguised as tourists from Florida pull themselves up the three front steps under the awning entrance. For half an hour, Wallace observed and noted the extra-curricular activity of cars pulling behind the restaurant for what his detective mind quickly registered as illicit takeaway.

At seven, the beginning of the weekday dinner rush, Detective Wallace left his car in the far corner of the lot and walked through the front door. He nodded at the twenty-something hostess in a low-cut black dress and, after a quick surveillance, headed in the direction of the first archway leading to the bar. The bartender, replete with a bow tie, took his drink order and returned a moment later with a tonic water and lime. Wallace looked up and around at the line of TV screens surrounding the massive room.

"Nice set up," Wallace said to the bartender.

"Yeah, the owner is a sports fan. But he's also a steak fan, and the two don't necessarily agree."

"So he built a sports bar inside the restaurant, with the TVs out of direct view from the dinner customers."

"Something like that."

Wallace looked at the collection of photos on the wall above the shelves of liquor. Without being asked, the bartender answered his question.

"Twenty-four of the thirty-two NFL teams have eaten here. Good Time Charlie is sort of the de-facto restaurant of choice for most teams who come to town to play the Skins."

"No love for the local team?"

"We have players in here all the time. Every day of the week, practically. But eight times a year we have visiting teams, and they all have Good Time Charlie on their itinerary. Nothing makes a football player meaner than raw meat the night before a game."

"So they say." Detective Wallace took a sip of his virgin beverage and made eye contact with a woman seated at the bar by herself. His eyes scanned the room as he completed a 360 degree assessment with the help of his swivel bar stool. By the time he came to rest facing his drink and the bar, the woman several seats down had closed the distance.

"Good evening."

"Evening," Wallace responded.

"You looking for company?"

"No sugar. I'm just having a drink on my way home."

"My name's not Sugar. It's Ginger. Sugar may be sweet, but Ginger can be the spice of your life."

"Married."

"I can keep a secret."

"I prefer black women."

"Honey, I am black."

Wallace smiled at the woman's Irish white skin. She had dark shoulder length hair and fire hydrant red lipstick. "I prefer not to pay."

"We can call it a loan," she purred, licking the end of a straw.

"No offense, Ginger . . . thanks anyway."

The woman ran a strand of hair behind her ear, rotated her pearl earring once, put her hand on Detective Wallace's thigh and ran her nails up his slacks. Before his soldier could salute, Wallace removed his badge from his pocket and flashed it below the level of the bar. "This can go two ways. I can run you in or you can have a few drinks and answer my questions."

"Nice try," Ginger answered. "That's a DC badge. This is Prince Georges County."

"You know your badges."

"I've seen them on the dressers of a few customers."

"How about I call in the PG County cops and we shut the place down for drugs being sold out of the back, prostitution in the front? Not sure that would be good for business."

"Not much of a choice there. Though I prefer money when I get fucked."

"What happened to the classy, sophisticated woman who was here a moment ago? The one who came over for a free drink and some fine conversation?"

"I didn't get my free drink."

Wallace motioned for the bartender and pointed at his bar mate. The bartender nodded and disappeared without asking what Ginger was drinking. *Definitely a regular*, Wallace thought.

"How many nights a week you work here?"

"None of your business."

"Doesn't seem like you want to take the easy route."

The woman looked away and sighed. "Two or three nights a week. I have class on Thursday nights. Take care of my mother when I have free time. When business is slow, I work as a psychic. A strong connection to the otherworld runs in the family."

"A student, a saint, and a psychic."

"Broke."

"How come you didn't see that coming?"

"Asshole."

"Life ain't fair. Who you work for?"

"No one."

"How many girls work this place?"

"A few. We have it covered most nights of the week."

The bartender paused on his way down the bar and slipped a drink in front of Ginger. "Everything OK, here?"

"Everything is fine," Wallace answered before waiting for the bartender to saunter off.

"What's the house's cut?"

"What do you mean?"

"Come on. Don't let my youthful appearance fool you. I've been around the block."

Ginger glanced over at the bartender who was mixing drinks ten feet away. "The house gets ten percent."

"How do they know what you charge?"

"It's a deal."

"You mean you service a john who knows the owner, and they report back the going rate."

"You have been around, Officer."

"Detective. Any rough stuff? Anyone laying hands on you?"

"Plenty of people laying their hands on me. Nothing rough."

Wallace handed Ginger his card. "You run into trouble, you let me know. I'll sort it out for you. Jurisdiction or not."

"I can handle it. It's not as bad as it sounds. I am independent. No manager. I work in a nice environment and pay a small fee for having that safety."

"Thanks, Ginger."

"Don't get me in trouble."

"I'm after something bigger than a blowjob or a steak dinner. Be safe."

"You too, Detective. If you want to have your palm read, let me know."

Detective Wallace winked at Ginger, turned, and raised his badge to the bartender. "I need to see the owner."

"Let me see if he's in."

—

Charlie Springs, all five foot six of him, popped out from a side door that melted into the wood-paneled wall. He looked at the bartender who pointed his nose in Detective Wallace's direction.

Charlie approached the detective who stood and towered over the owner of the eponymously named establishment. He motioned for Detective Wallace to join him at a secluded table in the corner.

"Detective Wallace, DC Metropolitan Police."

"Good evening, Officer. Charlie Springs. How can I help you?"

"I'm checking on the alibi of one of your customers."

"I have a lot of customers."

"I can see that. Nice place. Seems to be doing good business. Never been here before."

"Well, there is no reason you would have been here for work, seeing it is not in your jurisdiction."

"I can gather evidence anywhere it leads."

"Yes sir, you can. Can't really arrest me without assistance from law enforcement within the jurisdiction. Unless you witness the commission of a crime. But you are always welcome for dinner. Bring the missus. Dinner on the house."

"Very generous of you."

"We try to support law enforcement anyway that we can."

"I see business is good. Full house of patrons, working girls in the front, drugs going out the rear. Probably a bookie somewhere in the works. Maybe the bartender."

"I don't know anything about it."

"I'm sure you don't. I'm equally sure you don't want the DEA and ICE to stop by for a meal and haul away half your staff. Those guys are federal, by the way. They aren't handicapped by jurisdiction. I could also have uniformed DC Metro put this on their places of establishments to visit on their way home. The DC line is not far down the street. Not sure how all of that would be for business."

"How can I help you, Detective Wallace?"

"Dan Lord. You recognize the name?"

"Yes, I do."

"Can you tell me if he was here two nights ago?"

"Let me think. Yes, he was. Had a couple of drinks at the bar."

"Did he pay with a credit card?"

"He always pays cash."

"Always?"

"Yes. Dan is a character. Suspicious by nature."

"Anything illegal?"

"Nope. I mean, he will drop a fifty on a football pool, but Dan is both a character and a man of character."

"And yet, he hangs out here?"

"From time to time. He likes steak."

"How did you two meet?"

"He helped me out of a sticky situation a few years back."

"Legal advice?"

"Something like that."

"You run security video."

"Sure do. Cameras in every room except the bathrooms."

"You have the tape for the other night? Proof Dan was here?"

"I am sure I don't. The camera runs on a twenty-four-hour loop. Unless there is a holiday, an onsite injury, or we think someone is stealing from the till."

"So you have no evidence Dan was here the night before last?"

"Talk to the staff. Ask around. I will sit right here at this table. Won't talk to a soul. See what the employees say."

Detective Wallace pulled out his detective notebook. "This is how this game is going to be played. You provide the names of available witnesses. You, Ginger, and the bartender will grab a seat in the corner and be quiet. I want the young lady at the front door to gather everyone on the list of witnesses and bring them in here, as a group. Line them up. They will stand along the wall and I will question each of them in turn."

"Pretty specific instructions."

"Necessary. I can't have corroboration among the witnesses and

I think that you, the bartender, and Ginger would attest to each other being at the first lunar landing if it served you. The young lady at the front of the restaurant is too young to know anything. She is the one who is going to get the witnesses and bring them out here."

"As you like, Detective."

An hour later, Detective Wallace had burned through nine witnesses and twice as many pages of his detective's notebook.

He stood from his table and approached Good Time Charlie, the bartender, and Ginger.

"Your employees can get back to work."

Charlie nodded at the bartender and Ginger and they quietly exited the table.

"Satisfied?" Charlie asked.

"Not the adjective I would use."

"You know you're wasting your time."

"Why is that?"

"If Dan wanted to get away with a crime, he would."

"Not the kind of endorsement you want to convey to an officer of the law."

"Look, Dan is a good man, unless you piss him off."

"And then what?"

"Then, look out."

The detective shut his detective notebook and stared Good Time Charlie in the eyes.

"If I find out you're lying, I will bring all the forces at my disposal down on this little place of yours. I am old. Approaching retirement. I have a long list of favors to call in. You won't like me if I do. I got you on drugs and prostitution and I was only here an hour."

"You ran the show. You got to interview witnesses without any intervention. They didn't have the chance to talk amongst themselves. No opportunity for one person to warn the next person about the type of questions that were coming. You got clean testimony. You can't say I didn't cooperate."

"How long before you call Dan and tell him I was here."

"I won't. But it doesn't matter."

"Why not?"

"Because if you're here, then he already knew you would be coming."

CHAPTER 15

—

Dan pulled off Route 66 and merged into the traffic on Route 7 going west. He turned at the second light into Pimmit Hills, a sea of box houses built when subdivisions were in their infancy, a time when streets were streets, houses were houses, and neighborhoods were neighborhoods without fancy titles like Sugar Run Heights.

Dan's eyes scanned left to right, from house to house, as the neighborhood changed from shabby one-story houses to two-story colonials and back to shabby again. At the end of the road, Dan turned right on a gravel driveway just beyond an all brick mailbox constructed to withstand the impact of a baseball bat swung from a moving vehicle—a dying form of teenage entertainment. Dan inched slowly down the driveway, assessing the area. A group of high school kids were playing three-on-three basketball on a distant blacktop to the left, music wafting from an unseen source.

The driveway curved around two large oaks and a Sears and Roebucks bungalow peaked out from the shadows. The house was tucked between the sprawling Pimmit Hills neighborhood and the retaining wall for the Dulles Toll Road in the property's backyard. Dan stepped from the driver's seat and the steady hum of cars from the highway could be overheard, drowning out the four-letter din from the basketball court.

The two-story wooden house was worn, the front porch flirting with neglect. The boards on the front steps sagged, seventy years of use taking their toll one foot at a time. What had been a modern marvel of the mail-order era, the bungalow was now the first house to have its candy inspected by parents on Halloween—for the kids with brass ones large enough to make it to the door.

Dan knocked on the screen door and a moment later the curtain covering the main window of the living room moved. A pair of hands disappeared from the edge of the glass as Dan tried to peek inside.

"Not taking visitor's today," a voice yelled from the confines of the house.

"Tobias, it'll only take a minute."

Tobias, binary wizard dressed in jeans and a white t-shirt, paced on the small carpet runner on the other side of the door. He mumbled to himself, his hands moving wildly, his words slipping between whispers and overstated grandeur.

After a moment of verbal self-debate, Tobias pulled the old front door open, leaving a beat-up screen door between the two men.

"Dan Lord," Tobias said, indicating that dementia wasn't one of his ailments. His shoulder length dark hair was wet, the mop still dripping on his shoulders. His face was shaven. His feet bare. Small sprouts of hair pushed out from his ears.

"Tobias. Good to see you."

"Not if you're trying not to be seen."

"Can we talk for a few minutes?"

Tobias leaned on the frame on the other side of the door and eyed Dan through the dirty screen. "How long has it been?"

"Almost a year."

"How is the little project I programmed for you?"

"I know we tested it and it worked, but I haven't had real-world verification yet."

"I am confident it will work. So confident, in fact, I used it for myself."

"Then we will both see."

Tobias nodded his head in a small rapid burst. "I wasn't sure you'd still be alive."

Here we go, Dan thought. "There were moments I didn't either."

"Then you are a lucky one."

"Can I come in?" Dan asked through the door. "I need your help."

Tobias opened the door and looked in both directions.

"I'm alone," Dan said, close enough to smell Tobias's deodorant, and thankful he was wearing some.

"Enter, enter," Tobias groaned as if he had just made the most difficult decision of the year.

Dan followed Tobias into the house. The homeowner flicked his hand subtly and Dan took his cue to sit on the couch.

Tobias started to ramble, pacing back and forth on the other side of a shin-high coffee table. "You know I'm up to 213. Needless to say, thirteen is a particularly bad count. Two hundred and thirteen dead. None of them were my fault."

"I'm sure they weren't."

"My painter died last week. I told him to keep to himself but the man loved to talk. Had a weak bladder to boot. Always coming in the house to use the can. Always wanted to talk. I warned him, best I could, but you know people these days just don't listen."

"Some of us have that problem."

"Painter was almost finished with the house, too. Only had the front left."

"I can find someone to finish it for you. Free of charge. And I'll make sure they don't talk to you."

"I'd rather pay. You get a better job when you pay."

"Who else did you lose?" Dan asked out of morbid curiosity. He figured the sooner he could get the gruesome conversation out of the way, the quicker he could get down to business.

"I lost my favorite cashier at the grocery store. I tried to go to different cashiers, to mix it up, spread the risk, but apparently it was one conversation too many. Problem is, I shop at night and there aren't that many cashiers working the graveyard shift."

"I'm sure there was no connection."

"I have a new postman. He seems to be playing by the rules. I told him not to talk to me, and that seems just fine with him. Some people just can't keep quiet."

Dan nodded. "Some people don't listen and some can't keep quiet."

"I lost my dentist. I came down with a few periodontal issues and needed a couple of root canals. Spent a week in and out of his office and one Sunday morning they found him floating face down in his pool, his dog barking like mad from the diving board at the deep end."

"That's awful," Dan said. He had forgotten how mesmerizing a meeting with Dr. Death Count could be. He watched and waited in amazement as Tobias, a wet-haired ball of energy in jeans and a t-shirt plowed through his ongoing body count.

"I lost an aunt and uncle in a house fire. Lost two second cousins during a family reunion when a bolt of lightning hit the party tent they were standing under. What are the chances of that?"

"Pretty rare for adults to die in a house fire, unless they are elderly. And it's rare that anyone gets killed by lightning. Only seventy people per year in the US, give or take."

"Did I tell you I lost one of my roommates from college in a sky-diving accident? Another was shot in Tijuana."

"Risky behavior, especially visiting Tijuana."

"My first fiancée drowned in the bathtub after hitting her head. My wife died of a sudden aneurism."

"I recall you mentioning both of those before. I'm sorry for your losses."

"It's my curse, I tell you. Everyone who gets close to me dies."

"I don't believe in curses."

"Just the same, I'm giving you fair warning. The countdown has begun and every minute you are here is another minute the Grim Reaper has to zero in on your location."

"You are absolved of all responsibility."

"OK. OK. So, what does Striker want?"

"I'm not working for Striker this time. I'm working for myself."

"Striker didn't send you?"

"No. We, uh, had a falling out. I'm not sure I will ever work with that prick again."

"Hmm. Then how did you find me?"

Dan delivered his packaged response. "You have a lot of bandwidth for a residence."

Tobias flipped a wad of wet hair over the top of his head and considered the statement. "I suppose, if you knew what you were looking for, you could *eventually* find me that way. Otherwise, I am pretty far off the grid. I have solar panels in the back of the house. They provide forty percent of the power I need. I have generators in the basement that run on ethanol. Not the cheapest option, but storm-proof and government proof. Geothermal heating as well. I have a generator running on natural gas and another on propane. Spreading things around to remain below the radar."

"Government proofing?"

"The government can monitor everything based on power consumption. And believe me they do. This old place still has a working well, which I run through a filter system. By all appearances, I'm just an average middle-aged guy, living a quiet life doing computer work."

Dan was lucky. His visit dovetailed perfectly into two of Tobias's greatest fears. Death and conspiracy. "I could use your help. I need your help. I lost my nephew and sister-in-law recently. I think there is more to it than what the authorities are telling me."

Tobias moved towards the window and peeked out the front blinds. "Solving crimes is not my area of expertise."

"I'm looking for a phone number."

Tobias began a slow slide into ego-mode, a chest-thumping personality who was as arrogant as his Dr. Death Count counterpart was crazy. "Phone numbers are easy. Frankly, I'm surprised you need help."

"I'm looking for a phone number that doesn't exist."

Tobias twirled and looked Dan in the eyes. "You have my attention."

"The night my nephew and sister-in-law were killed, I received a phone call to my landline at home. That call, according to the police, never existed."

"And you believe *the police*? By law, the police are permitted to tell you any untruth they want to aid an investigation. By law. They can legally lie to you. Until they get to the courtroom. Then they lie, but it is illegal. Hell, lies are more prevalent in a courtroom than lawyers or criminals."

"Can you help me determine if the police are lying?"

"Did you try your other connections?"

"I did."

"I'm insulted you didn't come to me first."

"I am here now. My contacts confirmed there is no record of a call to my home on the night in question."

Tobias paused and ran his finger in a circle on his temple. "You want my help, here are the rules. First, the meter is running. Going rate is a thousand dollars an hour. That is a one, followed by three zeros. Those are US dollars, not Guyanese dollars. Second, everything you see and hear remains confidential. Third, and most importantly to you, fuck with me, and I will make your life very uncomfortable until I have extracted what I determine to be an appropriate amount of revenge. Curse-proof or not. You fuck with me, you will never again have a working phone, get money from an ATM, use a credit card."

"I get the picture."

"OK. Good. Good. So, you need a trace on a call without a call record."

"Can you do it?"

"You still living in Alexandria?"

"Yep."

"Is the home landline Verizon?"

"Yes."

"Let's go upstairs and see what we can do." Tobias tossed his head to the side and Dan followed him up a narrow staircase to an office on the second floor. The room had a slanted ceiling that sloped downward to the left, following the roof angle of the 1920's bungalow. The walls were lined with racks of computers and servers. A desk stretched the length of the far wall, topped with a multitude of computer screens in various sizes. A small sofa sat along the other wall, under the narrowing roofline.

Dan motioned towards the sofa. "Is this where you daydream the latest schemes to fleece the deserving and unknowing?"

"Yes. Have a seat."

Tobias sat down in a wheeled office chair and pushed himself down the length of the desktop with one shove of his legs. The chair came to rest in front of a keyboard near the largest monitor in the room.

"Nice space."

"A thousand processors in this room. Over a hundred teraflops in total computing capacity. A thousand terabytes of data storage across the hall."

"Serious numbers. What's on the agenda?"

Tobias mumbled to himself and then raised his voice. "Working on retirement. Got a few things cooking. Been spending some time on the gambling front. Working on perfecting spyware that allows me to see the hands of other players in most of the large online poker communities."

"Trying to get into the Tournament of Champions, or just making more enemies?"

"Enemies of the righteous. Internet gambling is illegal in the US. Most of the online gambling sites are run from Central America. But the computers and servers, well, most of them are sitting on an Indian reservation in Canada."

"Canadian Indians?"

"Completely autonomous Indians. Their own nation. Their own police. Their own government."

"And they have taken to online gambling?"

"Like fish to water. Nothing new for the Indians. They were fucked out of everything else. Left them with alcohol and gambling, and if that wasn't bad enough, they don't have the enzyme to breakdown alcohol. Lots of Indian tribes running casinos, but these Canadian Indians are different. They don't have casinos. They just host the computers for online gambling sites."

"Let me guess, Indians know more about getting fucked than they do about computer security."

"I always said you were smart, Dan."

"Just trying to pay attention."

"Anyhow, I've been working on some really slick code. But it's a matter of finding the right asshole to fleece. I mean, with my software I can outplay any number of US citizens gambling online and there would be no recourse. What are they going to do, go to the cops? That's like a drug dealer complaining someone stole their stash. Besides, believe it or not, I'm not into fucking over innocent people."

"A man of principle."

"Yes. As a result of my principles, I have to spend precious time vetting other players at the poker table. Background work. Make sure I'm not about to tilt the table in my favor at the expense of a recently laid off father of three who is just trying to make ends meet. The guy probably shouldn't be gambling, but shit happens. I get it. Now, the son of a billionaire with a dozen martinis in his veins indicted for running over a young couple in his Ferrari . . . well, that is a different story. He could stand to lose a few dollars to finance my retirement."

"Not worried someone is going to track you down?"

"They would have to go through Estonia, Poland, the Ukraine, and Belize. I am bounced off so many servers, I can't keep them straight. Spoofed IP addresses thrown in for fun. On top of that, they would have to find the people I pay to make cash withdrawals at the end of a very long paper trail of fake names and companies. And they would have to get one of these non-US citizens, who are making a very good salary, to turn in their very generous yet equally unknown employer. It doesn't really keep me up at night."

Dan imagined wads of cash stashed behind the drywall of the old bungalow. The attic awash in currency and precious metals.

"What else do you have?"

"The most accurate computer program for picking winning football games in the history of sport. Professional football only at this point, but I am looking to take the program and apply it to other sports."

"I can't imagine the odds makers would be too happy about that."

"They will be if I sell it to them."

"Vegas cornered that market shortly after the first casino opened in 1906."

"No one has any software even close to this. I have the historical data for every professional game ever played. Home team, visitor, favorite, underdog. I know how far each team traveled to get to each game and by what means of transportation. For every hundred miles the visiting team has to travel, their expected score drops by two tenths of a point. I have injury reports by position. I have data on the referee teams and their tendencies, and I keep track of how far each referee has to travel for a game. I have the weather at kick-off for every game and another variable for the weather at halftime. I have the type of field and variables for how the field conditions change with weather and humidity. I know how much moisture is retained by various models of artificial turf, and how that equates to the footwear of various teams. I have the attendance records, the average decibel of the crowd per location per attendance, which by the way was not easy to get, particularly for the stadiums that have been decommissioned, so to speak. I have taken into account time-zone changes, arriving and departing airports. Local food. Prostitution and drinking ordinances."

"Prostitution and drinking laws?"

"Absolutely. For example, if Las Vegas had its own football team, they would hold a distinct 0.4 additional point advantage due to the increased likelihood that the visiting team would partake, at least to some extent, in the all night boozing and strip shows."

"So you are assuming the home team is more immune to the local temptations."

"Maybe not immune, but perhaps they get their fill of sin during the week."

"How accurate are you?"

"I have a statistically significant advantage. On average, my spread is one point closer than the best bean counters in Vegas can do."

"That's worth millions."

"It is worth billions."

"A lot of data crunching."

"The computer power here is just a fraction of what I have at my disposal. I've installed thousands of Trojan horses on unsuspecting, unsecured computers around the country. Mainly people who leave their computers on and connected. I borrow their computers during the day, when most people aren't home. Nothing malicious. Just using their CPUs when the owners aren't."

Dan changed the subject. "How are you with unlisted phone numbers?"

Tobias grunted.

He pounded on some keys and the screen directly in front of him went blank. He entered code onto the black screen, looked over at Dan as he typed, and then hit the enter key.

"Time of the call?" he asked over his shoulder.

"Two in the morning. Last Monday night."

"Tuesday, then."

"Correct, Tuesday."

"Address and phone number the call was made to?"

Dan recited it slowly as Tobias typed. The screen filled with columns of numbers and every call made to Dan's home phone in the last five years.

"They started keeping all records after 9/11. Everything you do is monitored on some level."

"You mean everything *can* be monitored."

"I stand corrected. As you know, all phone records reside in databases at the phone company. By law, the phone company has to maintain these records. In legal proceedings and investigations, the phone company provides these records to law enforcement. They also use this data to create invoices, monitor usage, to develop marketing plans. And then, of course, at the far end of the spectrum, this information is being crunched by the NSA for terrorist threats."

Dan scanned the screen as Tobias zoomed through the list.

"Good, it's not there," Tobias said.

"Why is that good?"

"Well, it narrows down the options, which can be helpful."

"What address was the call made from?"

"I assume it was made from my sister's house via a cell phone. Her phone records are also clean, according to the police. She lives in Northwest DC."

"Address?"

Dan provided the address and Tobias's fingers danced.

"Yes, there is no record of a call from her home either. Once again, that is helpful."

"Your definition of helpful differs from mine."

"A couple of things can explain a phone call that doesn't exist. The first and most obvious is that it has been erased from the database. This, I imagine could be done by a handful of people at the phone company. In your case, you are talking about a call to your house landline, so deleting that record would very likely have to be an intentional act. There are probably some controls on the people who could write to or delete from the database."

"So someone on the inside or someone like you, on the outside, with the skills to infiltrate the system and delete evidence."

"Yes. And that too is useful information."

"What are the other possibilities?"

Tobias sighed. "After 9/11 the NSA and CIA saw the vulnerability of the current phone system. Anyone who made a call in the DC or New York area on that September morning remembers the phone networks were overloaded. Landlines worked in some cases, but cell phones were inundated with a volume of calls the system could never handle, nor was ever designed to handle."

"And?"

"Even the CIA was impacted. People working for the most powerful spy agency on earth couldn't make calls from their cell phones. The CIA had two choices. One was to provide the phone carriers with all CIA phone numbers and those phone numbers would take precedence on the network should there be another incident of national security. This plan would have been the easiest route, except that the CIA and NSA refused to give a list of phone numbers to the phone company. Many of the local law enforcement agencies readily agreed. So the next time there is an emergency situation, the calls made by police officers and response teams will take priority and their calls will go through the system. The average Joe will be screwed. Well, you, not me."

"So the CIA and NSA and others did not agree to give their phone list to the phone company."

"No, they did not. The CIA and NSA built their own wireless network. In high-strike-probability locations. Washington, New York, Los Angeles, San Francisco, Boston. The NSA acquired, or appropriated, a narrow sliver of the wireless spectrum for these proprietary network endeavors. Sometimes they attached their equipment to existing cell towers and in other cases they put up their own cell towers on government-owned buildings."

"A private network . . ."

"With no public records of calls."

"And if this number came through this network?"

"Beyond my domain. Wouldn't even try to poke around if I thought I could. Don't need that type of attention."

"Any other good news?"

"Let's stick with the likely scenario. Let's assume the call was deleted from the database. Let's also assume that the call came from a cell phone."

"Why do we assume that?"

"I could be wrong, but I'm guessing we're dealing with professionals. What professional is going to use a landline? Landlines require interaction with the phone company. Real phone company employees come to real addresses to hook up landlines. If you have nefarious intentions, who is going to go through that?"

"No one."

"Correct. Secondly, from a pragmatic standpoint, if the call originated on a cell phone, and the record no longer exists in the central database, we can still get the data via another route."

"How?"

"Even if a cell phone number is deleted in the central database, the record of a mobile call will still exist at the physical cell tower. Phone companies install hard drives on every cell tower and that hard drive stores the records of all calls that come through that tower. It is a failsafe. Required by law."

"Let's take a look."

"It's not *that* easy. First, there are a couple of dozen cell towers in the DC area. Run by different companies. AT&T, Verizon, T-Mobile, Sprint. All of these companies have different cell tower hard drives. Some of these companies may lease space on the same phys-ical tower, but their local hard drives would not be shared. So right off the bat, I have to get access to the hard drives of five or six differ-ent companies in several dozen cell tower locations. That requires time, which for you means money. I currently do not have access to every cell tower. Never needed it before."

"Just an issue of time and money."

"Exactly. And once I locate the cell towers and the hard drives, and break the security of the hard drive, I still have to decipher the data."

"How is that?"

"The data stored on the hard-drive at the tower is raw data. Nothing but zeros and ones. I have to figure out the algorithm for translating the ones and zeros into meaningful information. Hu-man readable information. That will also take time as every com-pany probably has their own protocol and formats for translating this data."

"How soon do you think you can get an answer?"

"Depends on the level of encryption of the hard drives. Given enough time and processing power, any encryption can be broken."

"So, if you take all those dummy computers you have out there and combine it with all the computing power in this house, and you focus it on this task, you can do it."

"Yes, but as I mentioned, the meter would be running and the going rate is a thousand dollars an hour."

"Ouch."

"And that is my discounted rate for people I like."

"Work fast."

CHAPTER 16

—

Detective Wallace looked for the entrance to the underbelly of the L'Enfant Promenade for ten minutes. He found the staircase that led downward to the adjacent street and examined the wall from where Dan Lord and Detective Nguyen had ambled into the abyss, one using a stack of pallets, the other employing nothing but gravity. Neither of those routes would end favorably for a detective in his early-fifties with two bad knees and thirty extra pounds.

He followed the outside wall of the train tracks down the street for two blocks until it disappeared into a tunnel under a newly re-claimed piece of real estate a block from the Mandarin Oriental. Detective Wallace looked up at the silhouette of the hotel as he moved towards it, an isolated oasis on the wrong side of the tracks. But when you have enough money to stay at the Mandarin, you have enough money to hire a driver to chauffer you to the brighter side of town.

Entering the hotel, Wallace, dressed in black slacks and a black sweater, flashed his badge at the receptionist and motioned for him to move to the unoccupied end of the check-in counter.

"How can I help you, Officer?" the perfectly groomed white male employee asked.

"My name is Detective Wallace. I'm investigating recent crimi-nal activity by the railroad tracks."

"You mean the murders?"

"Who said anything about murder?"

The receptionist lowered his voice a notch. "We hear things."

"I know the tracks run under the street out front and under the Promenade a couple of blocks down, but do you have access to the tracks themselves, from the building?"

The receptionist looked around and dropped his voice even further. "Second floor of the basement. Near the laundry facilities. Just past the employee locker room. There is an access door directly to the tracks."

Detective Wallace looked down at the receptionist's fingers. The yellow stain between his pointer and middle fingers hinted at a reason for the intel provided. "The unofficial smoking lounge for employees?"

The receptionist glanced sheepishly at his hands.

Wallace smiled. "Been smoking for thirty years, myself. On and off. Last week, I broke down and gave electric cigarettes a whirl."

"How did you like them?" the receptionist asked. "I was considering them."

"They work. Just not like the real thing."

"Nothing ever is," the receptionist replied with exasperation.

"Can you show me the basement?"

"Follow me."

The receptionist led Wallace across the crescent-shaped marble foyer, under the crystal chandelier, and down a flight of burgundy carpeted stairs. They followed a short hall to the right, took another flight of stairs down, and pushed through a large set of double doors. They passed through the cramped laundry facility and the plethora of Latina maids folding a never-ending supply of linens. The stench of bleach invaded Wallace's nose. Another short passage led to the back door.

"Here you go," the receptionist said, opening the steel fire door and inviting Wallace to an area of trampled ground that was level with the train tracks. Wallace looked at the impromptu smokers' lounge. Large plywood planks served as the floor. A group of folding chairs nicked from a conference room huddled to one side. A heavy bulb above the door illuminated the space. A hundred yards to the left, sunlight seemed to flicker with temptation. To the right, light danced intermittently as the tracks disappeared and reappeared as they went under the Promenade.

"Paradise," the receptionist interrupted.

"You ever walk down here?"

"Uh, scary," the receptionist answered with rising intonation. "No way."

"You ever see anyone who shouldn't be down here?"

"Hard to say. We have three hundred employees. We do try to keep the door shut and locked so the homeless don't wander in. Found a few dozen sheets running out the door one afternoon. Looked like a bunch of ghosts."

"Security cameras."

"Yep," the receptionist said, pointing upward.

"I may be back to look at the footage."

"Where are you going?

"For a stroll."

"Well, be careful. It isn't Disneyland down here."

Detective Wallace unholstered his gun and checked the chamber. Then he reached in his pocket, pulled out a cigarette, and lit it. He inhaled deeply, blew the smoke into the air, and responded. "Don't worry. No one is going to mistake me for Mickey fucking Mouse."

—

The area under the Promenade had seen more action in the last week than in the previous decade. The homeless camp was gone, trampled clay ground the only indication of a previous permanent settlement. The discovery of Conner Lord and Detective Nguyen in this location had led to a cleanup of the area. All of the debris was taken as possible evidence, garbage bags of discarded crap that were still being filtered through, piece by piece. If anything was overlooked in the removal of Conner Lord's body, it would not be overlooked in Detective Nguyen's subsequent death. The police knew how to take care of their own.

Wallace looked up at the rusting joints of the promenade infrastructure and a tear dropped from his right eye and trickled down his face. *Someone is going to pay. And I don't care what I have to do. There are no more rules.*

—

Dr. Lewis, the medical examiner, was finished with Nguyen's body. Detective Wallace walked in without any warning or announcement.

"Talk to me, Doctor."

"Detective Wallace. I can't tell you how sorry I am. Nick was a good guy. One of my favorite officers."

"One of mine, too."

"You missed the analysis. I gave the captain and two other detectives the run down this morning. On top of the updates from yesterday."

"You mind giving *me* the rundown?"

"The captain asked if I would inform him of any additional inquiries."

"I am officially *not* working the case."

"Oh, I see."

"Problem with that?"

"No, Detective."

"Then let's get to it."

"You want to see the body?"

"Yes."

"It's not pretty."

"I think I can handle it."

The ME led Wallace to the wall and pulled on the stainless-steel handle. Detective Nguyen's body rolled out for display, inch by inch.

"Gunshot wound to the chest and the head."

"What caliber?"

"A .45. Hollow point."

"That rules out most gang bangers. The nine millimeter is the preferred caliber for most criminals in this city. Usually gives them more shots, which they need because they don't spend time on the range. And the bullets are cheaper."

"Yes, Detective. Most gunshot wounds I see are nine millimeter."

"Which came first, the shot to the head or to the chest?"

"The shots were virtually simultaneous. Within a second of

each other at most. Very accurate. Chest first. Head second. Both perfect shots, if you can excuse the expression being used under these circumstances."

"Double tapped. Professional. Someone with military training. Maybe law enforcement."

"I can only speak to the wounds. Either shot would have been fatal."

"Other evidence?"

"The detective's personal belongings are back at the station, I believe, but they were carefully categorized by yours truly. I went through everything three times. With the naked eye, the aided eye, and under high-resolution microscope. All documented. All photographed."

"And?"

"Detective Nguyen was always well dressed, and the night of his death was no different, from a fashion perspective. He was wearing dark gray wool slacks bought within the past year, a new clothing line from Nordstrom's. The shirt was from Joseph A. Banks Clothier, as was his tie. His socks were from Target. Same brand I usually buy. He had on ECCO straight-lace shoes. Pretty comfortable, a little on the expensive side."

"Detectives splurge on shoes. We need something with traction and support. And they have to look reasonable with most clothes."

"As you know, his gun, badge, and detective notebook were not with the body. His car keys and his wallet were on his person when he was found."

"Not a robbery."

"Didn't even take his watch."

"Anything else?"

"He had a fair amount of grayish clay on his shoes, as well as some on the back of his clothing."

Wallace looked down at his own shoes. "Something like that?"

The Medical Examiner bent at the waist and stared intently at Wallace's black shoes. "That would be consistent with the clay found on his shoes and person."

"Not surprising."

"We are putting the toxicology through as we speak. Primary indication is that alcohol was not a factor. But I don't recall Nguyen as a drinker."

"On occasion."

"You would know better than I."

Detective Wallace pulled out a business card and handed it to Dr. Lewis, a man he had spoken with hundreds of times. "Call me on my cell if you find anything that could be helpful."

"There was something else I thought about after your captain left."

"What's that?"

"You know we had another body earlier from the same location. A college student."

"What about it?"

"I am just curious. Two bodies found in the same location. One has clay on his shoes. The other doesn't. And then we have you. The tie-breaker."

Detective Wallace looked down again at his feet. "I will make a note of it."

"Just thought I would mention it."

CHAPTER 17

—

Dan had made three calls to Lindsay and left three messages. By mid-afternoon he decided he had waited long enough for a reply.

He weaved through the afternoon traffic on Massachusetts Avenue, took a side street, and parallel parked with inches to spare off each bumper.

He exited the car and immediately his eyes fell on the crowd of college students engulfing the sidewalk thirty yards away. He subconsciously found himself picking up his pace, his eyes glued to the gathering. Before he could see the tears, he felt the somberness on Greek Row, the weight of tragedy sucking the life out of a block of houses usually full of verve. The hugs told him it was condolences. Ten yards from the edge of the Alpha Chi Omega property line he was certain someone was dead. His gut told him it was a blonde with an angel face.

Dan approached the sidewalk and scanned the faces in the yard. Dozens of girls in sorority solidarity, their Greek letters plastered across their chests. On the porch, he saw a face he recognized. He excused himself as he cut through the crowd around an influx of fraternity brothers from next door offering open arms and shoulders to cry on.

The girl on the porch recognized Dan as he climbed the short staircase to the sweeping brick front porch of the house.

"My name is Dan Lord. We met last week."

"I remember," the girl said. Her leg was on the chair, her knee pulled near her face as if to hide in plain sight.

Dan started to ask a question and his own instincts were intersected by the girl's.

"Lindsay was killed by a car on MacArthur Boulevard. Out for her daily run."

Dan sat on the wall of the porch, processing his thoughts, the flood of possibilities. "When?"

"This morning. Usually she runs in the evening, but lately has been running before class."

That is four. Four innocent dead people, Dan said to himself. "I'm so sorry."

The girl's eyes were red. Worn from tissues and rubs against her sleeve. "Me too."

"Would you mind if I took a look around her room?"

"For what?"

"I'm not sure."

"I guess," the girl said, standing. Dan followed her into the house and up the stairs. They turned left at the landing and followed the hall to the last room on the right.

Dan took one look around the neat room and a quick glance out the window overlooking the back yard. "Any chance she had her cell phone with her?"

"I don't know. I assume she did. I guess the police would know."

Dan poked around and looked at the dresser. His eyes were drawn like magnets to a picture of his nephew and Lindsay, still wedged in between the edge of the mirror over the dresser. "Mind if I take this?"

"I don't mind. Lindsay's parents may want it."

"I'll make a copy and bring it back."

"Yeah, sure."

Dan opened the drawer on the left and felt embarrassed by the girl's lingerie. He removed a memory box from the small drawer and placed it on the desk. He looked at the girl he was with, she shrugged her shoulders, and Dan opened the box. A letter from his nephew to his girlfriend was on the top and Dan read the first two sentences before his eyes watered. Hoping the tears wouldn't roll down his cheek he folded the letter and placed it to the side. An old folded napkin with ratty edges stared up at him. He slowly opened the delicate paper and then mumbled, "Son of a bitch."

"Something interesting?"

"Helpful, maybe."

"Can I ask a question?"

"Anything you want?"

"You think she was killed?"

"Why would you say that?"

"Because she told me you thought Conner was killed. That he didn't overdose."

"She told you that?"

"There aren't many secrets in this house. The walls aren't very thick."

"Then to answer your question, yes, I don't think Conner overdosed."

"And Lindsay?"

"Probably not."

"I have a question for you. What is it exactly that you do for a living?"

"I make things right."

"Is that what you're doing here?"

"You can bet your life on it."

There was a long silence. "I hope I don't have to."

—

Dan Lord sat in his car and stared at the tattered paper in his hand. His nephew's handwriting captured in a two-ply napkin from Scottie.

"All right, Conner." Dan said aloud. "Lead me to them." *Then God have mercy.*

He punched the buttons on his cell for the number marked emergency on the napkin. An automated voice reply whispered in his ear. *"This number is not in service . . ."*

"Shit," Dan said aloud, slamming his hand into the steering wheel. He hung up, dug around in his wallet for a business card, and then dialed another number.

"Detective Wallace," the baritone voice answered, reverberating over the din of the Robbery and Homicide division.

"Hi Detective, this is Dan Lord."

"Dan Lord," the detective repeated mockingly.

"Sorry about the fingerprints."

"You mean the lack of fingerprints."

"All you had to do was ask."

"You ready to come in and discuss Detective Nguyen's death? I assume you know he was also found under the promenade."

"Are you telling me it's suspicious when a police officer dies down there, but not so much for a rich white kid?"

"I am saying there are fingerprints on the gun found on the scene of Nuygen's death and I would like to compare them to yours."

"I assume you checked my alibi?"

"I checked. Nine witnesses. All of them said you were there."

"Then I guess you don't have enough evidence to bring me in for questioning. Otherwise, we wouldn't be having this conversation over the phone."

"Just dotting my i's and crossing my t's. Don't want to have any procedural inconsistencies. Can't have you slipping free on a technicality."

"You're wasting time, Detective."

"Maybe. And then maybe I'm talking to a serial killer who is leaving a trail of bodies behind. Someone who likes playing cat and mouse with the police. You wouldn't be the first."

"Follow the evidence, Detective Wallace."

"Count on it."

"Speaking of a trail of bodies . . . a student from American University was struck by a vehicle this morning on MacArthur Boulevard. Hit and run. The girl didn't survive."

Wallace sighed and considered whether to answer. "What do you care?"

"There might be a connection to Detective Nguyen's murder."

Wallace paused then spoke. "Accident reconstruction was out there earlier. They found the car already."

"They found the car?"

"Yep. The vehicle was dumped at the end of the road, just off

Nebraska where the old railroad trestle crosses over the canal and the bike path."

"Not exactly off the beaten path."

"You know the area?"

"I've mountain biked through there a couple of times. The parking lot is at the end of the service road, but it's only, what, fifty yards from the nearest house?"

"Sounds about right. Haven't been down there in a while myself. Maybe two years."

"What else can you tell me?"

"I shouldn't be telling you anything."

"Lighten up, Detective. I'm on your side."

"No, you are on your side."

"Then trust me. Our sides are after the same thing."

"The only thing I'm interested in is finding Detective Nguyen's killer."

"I think the same person is behind both our losses. What else can you tell me about the stolen car and the hit-and-run?"

"The vehicle was reported missing *after* we found it. Stolen off Georgia Avenue near Catholic University. Total time from theft to abandonment was less than two hours. Probably some kids who stole a car, hit the girl, and then panicked."

"I doubt it."

"Why do I get the feeling you are going to complicate things?"

"I have a guess. Was the car incinerated?"

Detective Wallace shut his eyes and rubbed his thumb across his brow. "Burned almost to the frame." The detective paused. "How would you know that?"

"Because that's what I would've done."

"Professionals?" Detective Wallace asked.

Dan was already gone.

CHAPTER 18

—

Sue Fine stood from her desk as soon as she heard the door chime. She exited the small office off the hall as Dan threw his jacket on an empty client chair in front of his desk.

"Anything you need help with?" Sue asked.

"Did anyone call?"

"Two calls. One from a woman with a slight accent who wouldn't leave her name. The other from a male who also wouldn't leave his name, but did oddly enough say he had some information for you. He said to bring your checkbook. He said that would be enough for you to figure it out."

"Thank you," Dan said, settling in behind his computer screen.

Sue stood on the other side of the desk, waiting.

"Yes?" Dan asked.

"You know, it's not really my place, or in my character, to disparage my boss, but answering two phone calls a day is not my idea of a good day on the job. I know you're working on something and I think I can help. If you let me."

"Probably not a good idea on this one. I don't pay you enough for what I am doing."

"What exactly are you doing?"

"Chasing ghosts."

"Your specialty, if you ask me. You are a ghost chasing ghosts."

Dan leaned back in his chair. "Did you make any progress on the George Becker case?"

"Followed him on Tuesday. After work, he spent two hours driving in Route 66 traffic to Warrenton. Then he spent an hour and a half watching a Thanksgiving play at a local elementary school.

After the play, Mr. Becker spent a few minutes with Pocahontas and her mother and then left. I'm doing a rundown on the students at the school to see if I can find out who Pocahontas is."

"The girl is his daughter," Dan said definitively. "Did you get pictures?"

"Good ones. There was no sneaking around. Everyone in the audience had cameras."

"Illegitimate kid. That should be good enough. One of the more common cases."

"Good enough for what?"

"Good enough to get paid by the person who wanted to know. Anything else?"

Sue paused.

"Yes?" Dan asked.

"How about we make a deal?"

"A deal?"

"A test, really. If you're impressed, you let me help you chase ghosts."

Dan glanced at his computer screen as an email pinged in his inbox. "I'm intrigued."

"I'll start with you."

"Me?"

"Sure. Let me see what I can find out about you. If you're not moved by my research, I will go back to manning the endless phone calls."

Dan ignored the warning signs rumbling through his stomach. "OK. I'll sign up for the experiment."

"Good. You want to learn what I found out so far?"

"Getting a little ahead of yourself?"

"Being proactive."

"Impress me. It better be good."

"Let me get my folder."

Shit, a folder?

Sue returned a minute later and assumed her standing position in front of Dan's desk.

"You were born in 1974. The day Nixon resigned from office."

"The first politician I ran out of town."

"You weren't here. You were born in Chile to American parents. Your father was a geologist. Worked for some big oil companies. Traveled all around the world. Your mother taught English as a Second Language. She taught out of US embassies as your father dragged you around the planet. Africa, Asia, Central Asia, South America."

Sue paused and pointed to a picture of Dan's mother on the wall. In the photo she was surrounded by fifty school-aged children, her face the lone Caucasian in a sea of African smiles and headdresses.

"Your mother's family made money in aluminum and industrial packaging. Patented several processes used in canning. Very well-known in certain industrial circles. Still a very lucrative business."

"My mother didn't care about money."

"Based on tax records, your father made good money."

"Oil companies pay good money to people who can tell them where to drill."

"You had an older brother named David. He was four years older than you. Died five years ago from cancer. Your sister-in-law and nephew both recently passed away. Your sister-in-law's death was reported as a suicide. The toxicology report is still outstanding on your nephew."

Dan nodded.

"You have spotty school records here in the US. Your freshman and half of your senior year of high school were here in DC, well, Virginia, at Washington and Lee. No record of your sophomore or junior years until I found a reference in your college application. You graduated from UVA in three years with a 3.6 GPA. Interestingly enough, you had As in every class except those in which you failed. All As. Three Fs."

"Some classes just weren't worth sitting through."

"After college you vanished from the system again. Probably overseas taking pictures," Sue said, glancing around again at the photographs on the wall.

Dan didn't move.

"Then you reappeared. Attended law school, also at UVA. You

passed the bar, then disappeared again. Five years of nothing. Completely blank history. Then you resurfaced and passed the Foreign Service Exam, both the written and the oral. But you chose not to pursue that field. Your application indicated you speak four languages other than English."

"I can get by in a few others."

"You have been self-employed for the last few years, but you've worked a variety of odd jobs as well. You drove a delivery truck for six months."

Dan rocked back in his chair. "You can learn a lot about a location, a city, its population, by doing deliveries."

"You have a clean record. Your fingerprints are not in any standard criminal database."

"Did you dust my office?"

"I had to have something to do," Sue said smiling. "I also obtained your tax returns for the last several years. And that is where things got interesting."

Dan tried to conceal being perturbed. "Go on."

"Well, I know you own this place. And the place downstairs. In fact, you own this half of the block, under a real estate trust. You bought the buildings in 2001, before the housing boom, which was before the housing bust. Based on the purchase price, it must have been a dive."

"It needed work."

"The art gallery downstairs pays you rent, but something less than what you could really charge. Almost at a discount. I can imagine there is a reason for that."

"Using imagination now?"

"If I didn't know better, I would say that you chose this place primarily for its location. Street front. All brick façade. No windows on three sides. A well-controlled stairwell. A walled-off alley in the back."

"Yes," Dan offered, stumbling a little.

"I still haven't figured out exactly where you live. I mean, this office is listed as your official address. It does have a shower and a kitchen, and it is zoned for both residential and commercial, but that doesn't answer where you put your head down at night."

"I don't sleep."

"Maybe not."

"And you got all this information how?"

"FBI. Local law enforcement. IRS. County real estate documents. Interpol. I have access to all of these through the cold case program at Marymount University. They can't expect us to solve old cases without access to the information. As for the rent you charge, I asked Lucia downstairs."

"I should have known."

"Anything else I need to know about you?"

"No."

"Good. Oh, and by the way, I also figured out who called the other day. The woman named Cindy. You took the call when I was here for my interview. I ran a check on the local county court systems for divorce filings on that day. Only two came up with the name Cindy. Cindy Lei, a manicurist in Prince Georges County, and a Cindy McMichael in the district. McMichael is married to Judge Terrance J. McMichael. I am guessing . . ."

"I guess if I don't give you work, you are going to keep digging around in my past. That, I could do without."

"Just tell me when to stop."

Dan sighed. "You study forensics and criminal justice, correct?"

"Yes."

"What do you know about death?"

—

"I'm so excited to be meeting one of your close associates," Sue said, pulling out a notebook.

Dan turned the car down the long driveway. "Temper your enthusiasm. This guy is a little unusual. He may throw us *both* off the property."

"Everyone has whacky friends."

"Let's stick with 'acquaintance' on this one. Tobias doesn't have any friends. Literally. It's a long story."

"I've moved past excited right into intrigued."

"Here are the rules. Better yet, let's just go ahead and call them standard operating procedures for any and all future endeavors. You, as my employee, are my responsibility. If at any time I determine it's in your best interest to vacate, then you vacate. No questions asked." Dan handed the car keys to Sue. "If I tell you to leave, you leave. I don't care where you go. Get in the car and drive. Don't worry about me."

Sue looked down at the key ring.

"Be alert," Dan said, getting out of the car. As they approached the front porch, he announced himself to the house, loud enough to be heard down the driveway.

The old porch squeaked under the weight of his foot, and before Dan knocked, Tobias yanked the interior wood door open. Sue jumped. The dark silhouette of Tobias came into focus through the still-locked screen door. Dan noted the partial concealment of an object in Tobias's left hand.

"Who's your friend, Dan?"

"Employee," Dan corrected. Dan motioned towards Sue with a nod of the head and an upturned palm. "This is Sue Fine. Sue, this is Tobias."

"And why is she here?"

"Nice to meet you," Sue said through the screen. "I think we spoke on the phone earlier."

"Dan, you know how I feel about visitors."

"You'll like her. I promise. Besides, she is handling my accounting and is in charge of paying you."

Tobias raised a piece of bread to his lips, took a bite and began to chew.

"Can we come in?" Dan asked. "Please."

Tobias pushed the door open and the hinges protested in a metal-on-metal screech.

"Did you warn her?" Tobias asked, struggling with the emotion of having two guests at the same time.

"Warn me about what?" Sue asked.

Dan hemmed as the movement of the three stalled in the open foyer. "Tobias has an issue with people."

"What kind of issue?" Sue asked.

"An inordinate number of people he knows have died. He believes it's a curse."

Sue looked at Tobias and tried not to laugh.

Tobias picked up on her reaction. "Go ahead, laugh at the devil. Consider this your warning. If something happens to you, it will not be on my conscience."

"Understood," Sue answered, biting her lip.

Tobias looked at Dan. "Another cousin called over the weekend. Was dead by Tuesday. Carbon monoxide poisoning."

"So that's 214?"

"Good memory."

"Two hundred fourteen people?" Sue asked.

"Indeed, 214. Everyone I know, everyone I get close to, well . . . It started when I lost my brothers in a car accident, my mom to cancer, and my father to a heart attack."

"Those are three of the top killers in the US," Sue replied. "Hardly unusual."

"Where did you find her?" Tobias asked.

"She's a forensics student. Death is her thing."

"Ahh. A shared interest. Well, Ms. Forensics, shall we have a civil discussion over tea?"

"That would be great," Sue responded.

Dan followed the two into the kitchen and sat at the large wooden table in the corner as Tobias and Sue danced through a routine that would make a CDC specialist proud.

"The number four cause of death is pneumonia," Sue cited.

Tobias responded. "Not in the US. In the US, lower respiratory disease is number four. Pneumonia has its own place at number seven. Stroke rounds out the top five."

"Not in 2010. There was an anomaly that year."

"Stick to the data from the most recent year."

"Diabetes, suicides, and septicemia are also in the top ten."

"Malaria, if you go worldwide."

"Mosquitoes, if you limit it to deaths caused by insects."

"Spiders, if you include arachnids."

"Jellyfish, if you move to marine animals."

"Invertebrates."

"Still an animal."

The verbal jousting lasted until the tea kettle mercifully served as the bell to end the round.

"I do like her," Tobias announced as he topped off Dan's cup.

"She's all right. Nothing to write home about."

"She knows her death."

"I would imagine that is quite a compliment in some circles. Probably would give an undertaker a hard-on."

"You're just jealous," Sue added. She raised her cup which Tobias quickly toasted with the edge of his own.

"Tobias, let me ask this question while you are in such a cheery mood, and while our death specialist is here. Did you ever think that most people just don't bother counting all the people they know who have died. Maybe you are only unusual in that you count?" Dan asked.

"I considered it. I even developed some code to run those scenarios."

"And . . ."

"The likelihood of someone my age knowing 214 people who have died is one in seven million."

"Based on?"

"Based on my demographic. White, non-military personnel living in an urban area with a murder rate of five per hundred thousand. I took into account the incidence of disease, as well."

"Impressive, statistically speaking," Sue chimed. "Did you consider the likelihood of disease within a subset of family genes?"

"I also took into account the cause of death of family members for three generations."

"OK, OK," Dan said. "I hate to break up this celebration of killer inflictions, but I have a number."

"You have a number?" Tobias asked.

"A phone number," Dan answered, holding up the old napkin he had taken from Lindsay Richer's dresser drawer in the sorority house.

"Then I guess we will have to call it a tie. The reason I called earlier—and left a message with little Miss Death here—is because at 4:17 this morning, I hit on the number that called your house. The call from the phone that doesn't exist. For those interested in accounting, the bill to locate the mystery number passed six figures this morning. I take cash or a cashier's check. Some of these phone companies are employing 516-bit encryption on their cell tower hard drives. It was not elementary. That is a lot of possible combinations to surf through."

"Bit power," Dan added looking at Sue.

Tobias picked up the conversation. "516 bit encryption equals possible combinations numbering in the millions of millions. Imagine a number with over fifty commas," Tobias said. "A number so large there is no useful name for it, but it represents a lot of possibilities. It is represented by the number two, to the 516th power."

"I get it," Sue said.

"There are forty-seven towers within the Beltway. Split between the five major cell carriers and four lesser carriers. Each company had their own security and firewalls to bypass. I have been running crypto-breaking code non-stop since your last visit," Tobias said.

"Then let's go upstairs and compare numbers," Dan said.

Sue and Dan followed Tobias upstairs and through the doorway to the left. Sue gasped when she saw the array of computer equipment.

"I was secretly hoping for that reaction. I don't get too many visitors."

"None that live to tell about it," Dan added.

"Sit down on the sofa there. Give me the phone number you found."

Dan handed the folded napkin to Tobias and the computer wizard held the worn paper between his pointer finger and thumb. "It has seen better days."

"Haven't we all."

Tobias shrugged his shoulders in agreement and sat down. He started typing on multiple keyboards and moved from monitor to monitor, pounding code at a feverish pace. He interjected intermittently and Dan was not sure if he should respond. "You know the Rolling Stones and U2 announced summer tours. I need to free up some resources so I can obtain the required number of tickets for re-sale."

"I would love to see the Stones," Sue added.

"Maybe we can go," Tobias responded. "If I can find the time."

Behind Tobias's back Dan scowled at Sue and shook his head.

"OK, let me show you what I found," Tobias said. "I am running the query again so you can see the results as I did. And it does look like the number I found on the cell tower hard drives is the same as the one written here on the napkin."

"So based on the napkin evidence, we can assume the mystery number was a cell phone that my nephew owned."

"Yes. Well, we were running on the assumption it was the phone your sister-in-law called from on the night of her death. With the napkin evidence, we now know it was likely a phone your nephew possessed and that your sister-in-law merely used it on the night in question."

"What can you tell me about the number?"

"On the screen, I have the detailed history of calls involving the mystery phone. We have one ping for that number in DC. Two in DC. Three in DC. One in Tysons. One in Alexandria. Two more in DC. Two more in DC. Another two in DC. Almost all the calls made on your nephew's phone are to an encrypted number which is represented on the screen by ten fives: 555-555-5555."

"They use that number in movies."

"Frequently. It is completely fictitious. The real phone number has been replaced with ten fives. Not the best news for us, but not a complete waste of time, either."

Dan stared over Tobias's shoulder as data ran down the screen, too fast for him to decipher. He watched as the data scrolled and Tobias pointed out relevant information. A minute later the scrolling stopped and the cursor held its position on the bottom of the screen and blinked.

"Well, in total, your nephew's secret cell phone was only used a handful of times. We have sixteen calls in total. Thirteen of those calls were outgoing to the same encrypted number, represented by all fives. The sole incoming call to that phone was the last one made. It came from a cell tower near American University and terminated at a cell tower in Tysons. It was made two days ago. After your nephew was deceased."

"That is the call that got Lindsay Richer killed."

"Should I know her?"

"No. And it wasn't your fault."

"All of the calls were found on Verizon towers, so Verizon is the carrier for your nephew's phone. The cell tower with the majority of the phone records is located on a building on Chesapeake Street, Northwest DC. The building leases a twenty-six-foot tower on the roof. If you look at the list of calls from this phone, there has been one call per month to 555-555-5555. Thirteen in total."

"What else can you tell me about the calls to 555?"

"I have evidence a call was made, but the real number was manipulated and encrypted before it was stored on the cell tower's hard drive. I have a start and end time for the thirteen calls, so I can see that a phone call took place. In fact, except for the phone number itself, it appears the data for the calls is legitimate."

"What about the call to my house?"

"Of the fifteen outgoing calls, we do indeed have one that was made from your nephew's mystery phone to your home number on the night your sister-in-law died."

"At least I'm not crazy."

"Hardly enough evidence to clear your mental state."

"Did my sister-in-law call 911?"

"She did. Records indicate the call was terminated upon reaching the tower on Chesapeake Street."

"Which did she call first?"

"911."

"How much time between the time she called 911 and the time she called my house?"

"Two minutes."

"What the hell was she doing for two minutes?"

"That I cannot answer. But based on these logs, she was not

talking to 911. As I said, the call reached the cell tower and was terminated."

"So, we have the phone number for my nephew's mysterious cell phone. It has fifteen outgoing calls, one to my home, one to 911, and thirteen to 555-555-5555."

"Correct. Those thirteen calls to the number represented by all fives were very regular. One per month. Usually in the first week of the month. We can see that all of those calls were completely handled by the cell tower on Chesapeake Street. That cell tower never passed those calls to another tower, at least not to any cell tower in the greater metropolitan DC area."

"So you can see when the number was called, the duration of the call, and whether or not the call was handed off to another cell tower in the DC area, but you cannot provide the number, beyond the ten fives."

"That is correct."

"Did you check to see if that 555 number is used elsewhere? Maybe there are calls from other phones outside of the beltway made to that same number."

"At a thousand dollars an hour, I was sticking to the work you asked for. You wanted to know if I could find a missing phone call made to your house. I did. You didn't ask me about the numbers called by your nephew's mysterious cell phone or anything else further upstream."

"Fair enough," Dan said. "You know, the fact that most of the calls came through the same tower in Northwest DC is not surprising. That area was my nephew's backyard. That is where he went to school. Where he grew up. Where his mother lived."

"You are missing the important part of the equation. The interesting tidbit of the logs is that the destination number of those calls—the recipient of those calls—was also within the same cell phone area. All of the thirteen calls started and ended within a very defined geographical area. Whoever answered the 555 number when your nephew called was close."

"So, it's a landline?"

"No. The calls from your nephew's phone to that number were

received by the cell tower but were not passed to a landline. It was very likely a fixed location cell number."

"How does that work? Sue asked.

"Landlines are going the way of the dodo. Cell phones are the ubiquitous choice for communication. Fax machines can now employ cellular technology. You can control the systems in your home through your cell phone. Ditto for security alarms. So in looking at the 555 number, the only evidence I have of this number is in the Chesapeake tower location. If it is not a landline, it has to be a fixed location cell phone. Or a cell number that never ventures out of the footprint of the Chesapeake tower."

Tobias waited for Dan to stop pacing.

Dan paused at the window and spoke over his shoulder. "Can you print out the metadata elements you do have for all the calls made on that phone, outgoing and incoming? And can you print the physical address of the cell tower on Chesapeake Street where the calls originated and terminated?"

Tobias tapped on the keys and a printer came to life in the far corner. Dan retrieved the paper and came back to Tobias's chair.

"What is the coverage area for that cell tower?"

"Give me a second."

Sue was mesmerized as Tobias pulled up a map of DC and several dozen cell towers populated their respective locations throughout the city with overlapping concentric circles.

"The footprint of a cell-tower is not perfect," Tobias added. "There are a lot of factors. Other buildings, elevation, capacity, height of the tower, technology components, weather. The size of the cell tower footprint can vary."

Dan glanced at Sue who hadn't blinked. He watched as Tobias focused on the cell tower address and a bright red circle appeared, estimating the tower's coverage area. Tobias then overlaid the red circle onto a DC metropolitan map. He leaned back in his chair and smiled at his own work. "Thirteen of the calls were made to and received by a phone or location within that red circle."

"What is the area, size-wise, more or less?"

"A mile and a half in diameter."

"And we can't triangulate on a more defined location for a phone call?"

"No. We could triangulate a position if a cell phone was actively in use, or if the cell phone had its location services turned on. But without that, regardless of what you see in the movies, triangulating a phone call after the fact is impossible."

"Probably won't matter anyway."

"Maybe. I mean, if these guys are pros, they know how to cover their tracks."

"And that may be good news."

"Can you tell me how long it would take to check if anyone else called this 555 number, from any landline, from any carrier?"

"I can run a few tests to give you an idea of the cost. I'll start while you buy lunch."

—

Lunch was comprised of a run to Tippy Tacos, a no-nonsense establishment at the end of a long-in-the-tooth strip mall near Merrifield. It was the first time Dan had ever been in public with Tobias and it would hopefully be the last. There is nothing like a backseat driver who sees death at every intersection, possible dismemberment with every passing car.

Back at his house, with a pound of rice & beans in his stomach, Tobias sat down in front of the computer and pulled up a blank screen.

"Houston, we have a problem."

"Let me guess, there are no records of anyone else calling 555-555-5555."

"Worse. It no longer exists." Tobias cursed like a sailor in a port city bar and pulled a second keyboard from the far end of the table. He began typing code, one hand working each keyboard, his head on a swivel between monitors.

"These guys are indeed professionals."

"Please tell me you are not going to say it is a good thing."

"Nope. You still have the printout with the date and times of the calls from the tower in Chesapeake Street?"

"Yeah, why?"

"You are going to need it. All the records have been erased. All records on the cell tower. A hundred hours of work just vanished. All you have is the piece of paper."

Dan pulled the paper from the pocket of his urban hiker pants and paced.

"OK. Let's see if we can use these guys' strength as their weakness."

"What do you have in mind?" Tobias asked.

"Well, if you wanted to get rid of a cell phone, you would just get rid of it. Throw the phone away. Get rid of the fax machine. Change security systems. Destroy whatever is using the cell phone technology and the related number."

"Sure. That would be the normal route for normal people."

"Well, if you could just discard the phone, system, or machine using the cell phone, then why would these guys be racing to delete a record of a phone call, better yet, an encrypted phone call?"

"Because they are hiding something other than the phone number."

"Exactly. I think I am done searching for something hidden. It's time to change tactics. Time to look for something I know doesn't exist."

—

Dan stood by the car and waited until Sue sat in the passenger seat. He took a deep breath and checked the surroundings. He glanced up and waved at Tobias who was peeking out from behind the curtain on the second floor. Dan took a deep breath, exhaled slowly, and pulled the door handle.

"What do we do next?" Sue asked.

"There is no 'we.' Your work-study program is officially over. I'll sign whatever you need to show your university you completed your requirement. I'll give you full credit for whatever time you need. I'll sign your time sheets, and hell, I'll pay you for the rest of the school semester. Just let me know what you are reporting to the university and I'll support it."

"That's bullshit."

"Excuse me?"

"You heard me. You could have gotten rid of me anytime. You are just using today as an excuse."

"Today was the tipping point."

"Today was not the tipping point for you. I watched you in there. I saw your reaction. You weren't surprised by anything you saw. You already knew the CIA, or whatever other agency designation you pick, was involved in this ghost chase of yours."

Damn, I hate good intuition on everyone but myself. "I suspected it."

"So what changed in Tobias's house?"

Dan was stumped. Sue was right.

Sue continued. "We didn't just pass a tipping point. A point of convenience maybe. A point where you could say to me, 'Things are about to get dangerous.'"

"Well they are."

"They already were. In fact, I should be pissed. If you knew you were involved in something dangerous, you should have told me earlier. We didn't have to go through the charade of some great discovery that suddenly made things dangerous. They were dangerous before and they are dangerous now."

"Now I remember why I am single."

"This is not a joke."

"No, it is not. Are you aware there are at least four dead bodies? My nephew, his mother, his girlfriend, and a police officer?"

"I am aware."

"And do you have any idea who could kill four people, especially a police officer, and get away with it?"

"Professionals."

"Let me tell you what a professional is. A professional is someone who can put a bullet in your head and then have dinner. Someone who can take a single mother and string her up in her own closet and watch her twitch with her last breath. Someone who can kill a young man just starting out in life and run over his girlfriend in broad daylight with no witnesses."

Dan released a primordial yell and punched the ceiling of the car. The veins in his neck pulsed and his eyes watered. He looked at Sue, whose expression hadn't changed. "You have any next of kin? Any brothers? Cousins? Anyone? Anyone who is going to miss you if you get yourself killed?"

"No, Dan. I am just like you. Alone."

CHAPTER 19

—

Dan and Sue parked between Third and East Capitol, three blocks behind the Rotunda. The neighborhood was still dark, streetlights illuminating the sidewalk in patches. Capitol Hill, the neighborhood, was the original heart of the now political district. Running behind the Capitol and the Supreme Court and pinched between Independence and Constitution Avenues, Capitol Hill— before it became a political lair—had been home to the working class and immigrants. Blistered hands that had built the Capitol stone by stone. The eclectic mix of craftsmen who toiled at the largest munitions plant in the late-nineteenth century world, just down "the hill" on the banks of the Anacostia.

Today's Capitol Hill was a mix of million-dollar row houses, small businesses, and the burned-out remains of part-time crack shacks. Most of the shacks had been bought during the housing boom, later to be reclaimed by public funds, and ultimately returned to their former abandoned glory. The real estate was now on its third upswing in a decade. Living on Capitol Hill was hit or miss. A trip to the neighborhood market was just as likely to end in a conversation with a congressman as it was a mugging. *Real America*, down the street from those who made the laws for it.

Dan walked behind Sue as they ambled down the narrow brick sidewalk.

"Thanks for letting me stay on with you," Sue said over her shoulder.

"Don't thank me. It's against my better judgment."

"I wrote and signed a waiver of liability last night. You could have signed it this morning. It exonerates you of any injury, illness, accident, death, or dismemberment that I may incur as a result of my semester-long, credit-generating, real-work experience internship—of sorts."

Dan changed the subject. "You know, at the peak of immigrant labor in the city, this street used to be a horse track."

"So the horseshit never really cleared the air," Sue said.

Dan laughed as he fought to avert his eyes from Sue's silhouette in the passing light of the street lamp.

"You feel safe back there?" Sue asked.

"I feel better with you in my sights, and with the two guns I'm illegally carrying within the DC city limits."

"I feel better with you back there."

"I'd feel better if there were someone covering my back with a couple of illegal firearms, too."

"Teach me how to shoot."

"We'll see."

"You any good?"

"You could say that."

"Where did you learn?"

"From a neighbor. The first gun I fired was an M40. It's a marine sniper rifle."

"And . . . ?"

"Turn left at the next corner."

The Supreme Court stood on First Street—its final resting place decided after a decade-long game of Marco Polo. The Supreme Court, its need determined long before its location, originally met in New York and then bounced around the country like a traveling carnival. New York, Philly, Washington. From a committee room to a senate chamber to a tavern down the street. In 1935 the cornerstone was laid on its current location and the nine men and women who determine the supreme law of the land had a place to hang their gowns.

Dan and Sue approached the Supreme Court building from the same direction as the lantern-run tavern where the justices of yesteryear made their cases and drank their share of them in the process.

Dan nodded forward and Sue looked up to see the line of people snaking down the massive steps. Bodies wrapped in warm clothing. Small makeshift tents and sleeping bags splayed on the ground. Flashlights flickered on waiting faces and their belongings. In the darkness, before most of the world stirred from their beds, people were camped out on the steps of the highest court in the land as if waiting for a Black Friday sale at Walmart. Sue pointed at the police on horseback at the foot of the Court.

"Yes, the Capitol Police still use horses. They have a stable in Rock Creek Park." Dan reached the bottom of the stairs and turned upward next to the meandering line. On the fourth step, the first voice of rebellion yelled out. "Back of the line."

It was followed by another voice, "No cutting, asshole."

Ahhh. A local, Dan thought.

The police officer on horseback whistled and Dan and Sue retreated back to the first step. "At 8:30 we allow for swapping of places, but there is no cutting in line and no swapping before then."

"I just need to have a quick word with someone in line and then we'll be gone. Two minutes."

The cop looked down at Dan. Sue was staring into the eye of the massive horse. "Two minutes," the officer agreed. "I will be watching you from here."

The horse moved back as if he understood the conversation and Dan and Sue again started to climb the marble stairs. Sue watched with curiosity as Dan peaked under hooded sweatshirts and examined exposed faces popping from sleeping bags. He whispered the name of the person he was looking for under his breath and then gradually raised the volume.

Nearing the front end of the line, Dan had used a minute of their allotted time.

"Jerry Jacobs," Dan yelled, looking upward.

"Why don't you just use the phone?"

"Because he doesn't want any phone records. I usually contact him via pay phone."

"Now that's convenient."

Dan yelled again for Jerry, and two steps from the top a face popped out from beneath a black hoodie. Jerry pulled the head-phones from his ears. A wool army blanket draped from his waist to his knees. A stash of newspapers was wedged into one armpit.

"Dan Lord," Jerry said. The two exchanged an elaborate hand-shake that was more for show than for reason. "Who's the girl?"

"My assistant, Sue."

"Since when do you have a partner?"

"Been busy. Needed some help."

"You always are."

Dan turned towards Sue. "Jerry here works in the Office of the Clerk at the DC Circuit Court. He has access to public information in a more expedient fashion than I do."

"He does your dirty work."

Jerry jumped in. "SShhhhh. Don't say dirty. I deal with public information. Public. It's just that Dan here can't wait for public in-formation to be officially public."

Dan nodded. "I was hoping I would find you here."

"At two hundred bucks an hour, where else would I be?" Jerry motioned downward towards two acquaintances huddled on the ground under a red blanket. "Two hundred a piece."

Sue looked at Dan for an explanation.

"Lawyers, and others who can afford to, pay people to wait in line for them. It's officially unsanctioned, but accepted. Just another shortcut in a city that lives on loopholes. Anyone who wants to lis-ten to the entire argument before the Supreme Court has to wait in line. If you only want to hear a few minutes, usually done as part of a tour of DC, you stand in the other line. It's much shorter."

Dan turned back to Jerry. "Who's on the docket?"

"Lewis and Leaven. A revisit of automatic weapons and the sec-ond amendment."

Dan felt the weight of his weapons, one in the small of his back, the other on his ankle. "Appropriate. How much longer are you here?"

"Doors open at eight thirty. Whoever I'm holding a spot for needs to be here by then. Have to be at work by nine."

Sue interrupted. "You haven't met the person who hired you?

How are you going to know them when you see them?"

"He'll be the person with a thousand dollars in his hand."

"Each," a voice rained out from beneath the red blanket.

Dan glanced down the stairs at the police officer who was still watching him. "I need your help looking into something."

Dan reached into his jacket pocket and pulled out a copy of the paper from Tobias's house. He handed the map of the cell coverage area and the physical address of the cell tower on Chesapeake Street.

"I need to find property ownership records for addresses in this circle."

"Man, you can do that online."

"You can't if the files have been deleted."

Jerry rolled his eyes. "What do you want me to do?"

"I need you to look at the hard copies on file at the courthouse. I need you to check the physical paper files on properties located in the red circles. Then I need you to see if there is anything online. I am looking for properties that are not online but have a paper record."

"That won't be easy."

"I need it done for every address in the red circle." Dan pointed at the map.

Jerry looked at the address and the circle. He turned the map once, turned it back, and got his bearings. "Shit, Dan. That is a highly populated area. The University of DC. American University. Rich. Poor. Condos. A ton of apartments. It will take time."

"I don't have time. I'll make it worth your while. Recruit some help. I'll pay you double what you are making here."

"Triple," a voice boomed from the blanket.

"Dan, if you need this now, I will have to take time off from work. I do have a job you know. I have to use sick leave. That ultimately costs money. And if I am going to have to dig around online, I need a new laptop. Mine got swiped a few days ago."

"OK. You're hired. You and your friends. Triple what you are making. Six hundred an hour, per person. And three new laptops. I don't want any excuses."

Jerry felt like he should have asked for more. "You got it."

"No Happy Hours until it's done. I catch you out on the town, any of my bouncer friends tell me they saw Jerry bellied up to the bar hitting on some GW student, and you and I will have words. And no smoking weed until you are done, either. I can't afford something being overlooked."

"Hey, that's uncool. I don't smoke dope," a voice called out from under the blanket.

Jerry grabbed Dan by the elbow and pulled him close.

"What are you into? You look nervous and I've never seen you nervous. Quite frankly, it upsets me."

"Just get me the information."

"A needle in a haystack."

"At eighteen hundred dollars an hour and three new laptops for you and your friends, you won't find a better job."

"Let me call in sick."

CHAPTER 20

—

Detective Wallace sat in the forensics office in the basement of Police District 2. The forensic analyst left with the task of locating Dan Lord's fingerprints was organizing his information, preparing for a presentation of his findings. Wallace was seated across the desk from the young man with a clear complexion and brown hair. The analyst finished making three short stacks of folders, cleared his throat, and began.

"The individual you asked me to find is definitely unusual. I spent a week calling in favors. Breaking some rules. Breaking a few laws."

"For a good cause. Welcome to real police work."

"Easier to say when you are a bit closer to retirement than I am. I barfed twice yesterday from the stress."

"If anyone gets you in trouble, tell them I forced you to do it. I have a long list of people who don't like me, including a Senator and an unknown terrorist organization. Tell them I made you do it. They would much rather have my balls on a platter than yours."

The forensic analyst looked down at his crotch.

"No offense," Wallace added. "I am sure your balls are attractive."

"Thanks. And I am not complaining about the work. Just providing some background."

"You stuck your neck out, I get it."

"More precisely, I stuck my neck out and I got nothing."

"Nothing?"

"Not exactly nothing. More than nothing. But nothing. The suspect is a chameleon."

"Explain."

"Well, he does not have a criminal record that I could find. And he definitely has not worked for the US government, or the US military."

"Are you sure? Detective Nguyen thought perhaps he had a military background."

"I am confident in the results I got back. There are no prints in the military database for a Dan Lord fitting the description you provided. There were two Daniel Lords who were killed in the line of duty in World War II. One in France. One in the Pacific on some island I have never heard of. But unless your guy is in his nineties, neither of those is him."

"I agree. Continue."

"You told me this guy was a private detective in Virginia. All private detectives have to be fingerprinted. Those fingerprints are checked against the criminal database before the person can get a license. Dan Lord passed that inspection—as you would expect given I couldn't find prints for him in the criminal database. Virginia, fortunately, is one of the few states that also keeps an electronic copy of those fingerprints on file after the application is processed."

"So you found some prints?"

"Don't you want to know what it cost me?"

"Not really."

"I am going to tell you anyway. Turns out that Sherry Williams, who handles the fingerprinting for private detective licensing in the Alexandria courthouse, lives in DC. She has a parking issue. And when I say parking issue, I mean that she can't seem to read the parking signs. She has over thirty outstanding parking tickets and has been booted a dozen times. For a copy of Dan Lord's prints, I had to make those parking tickets disappear. In order to make those tickets disappear, I had to agree to a date with Olga's sister."

"Olga in parking enforcement?"

"Yes."

"I hope her sister is better looking than she is."

"So do I." The forensic technician slid a photocopy of the prints to Detective Wallace.

"So these are his prints?"

"Those are printouts of his electronic record. But not exactly."

"Contrary to what you may think, I assure you I am not into riddles."

The forensic analysts nodded. "Dan Lord also has an active conceal and carry permit. This, too, required a background check and fingerprinting. Getting access to this information required another favor regarding a cousin of someone charged with indecent exposure in Georgetown at two in the morning. To make that charge go away, I am now taking a Boy Scout troop to a Washington Wizards game. It is a long story."

The forensic technician sighed and then slid another set of prints across the desk. "As you can see with the naked eye, the electronic prints on file are not the same."

"WTF?"

"Indeed."

"This story is not going to have a happy ending, is it?"

"No, it is not. The third print was obtained from the Virginia Bar Association application. All applicants taking the bar and applying for a law license in Virginia are required to undergo the standard background check—with fingerprinting." The forensic technician slid the third set of prints across the desk. "And I cannot tell you what I had to agree to in order to get those prints."

"Dressing up in heels and running the DC Drag Queen race?"

"Not far from it."

Detective Wallace looked at all three prints in turn. "So this guy leaves us a water bottle with no prints and then leaves three different prints for three different civilian applications?"

"Yes. And those applications are not trivial. We are not talking about taking an electricity bill to the DMV to get an ID. Those applications require multiple forms of government issued ID, in addition to the prints."

"So how did he do it?"

"I have no idea."

"Whose prints are we looking at?"

"I don't know. But you are dealing with someone who may require more care than usual."

"I guess I'm going to have to get a print another way."

"How is that?"

"Old school detective work."

"Good luck. Oh, and by the way, none of those three prints match the prints found on the gun that killed Detective Nguyen."

"Of course they don't."

CHAPTER 21

—

Dan looked at his cell phone and didn't recognize the number. "Dan Lord, here."

"Dan, it's Jerry. I got something for you. Can you meet?"

"Where are you?"

"Rosslyn."

"How about Common Grounds in Clarendon?"

"That place is a maze."

"I'll meet you upstairs in the far back room. Overlooking the church parking lot. Last time I was there, the room was painted blaze orange. Make yourself comfortable."

"In an hour?"

"That should be perfect."

—

Dan carried his coffee up the worn linoleum stairs and meandered to the back of the second floor of the coffee shop. The establishment had once been a large family house, the myriad bedrooms now converted to individually themed rooms. The orange room, as Dan called it, was dedicated to surfing, and various posters of monster waves combined with a large mural to provide the necessary décor. A Hang Ten sign hung on the wall over the door to the toilet in the corner. Dan stepped into the room and Jerry the clerk waved from a large, worn leather sofa, an accordion file folder of information in his lap. Dan sat next to the sofa in a gold wingback chair with torn seams.

"Tell me what you found."

"Man, you better have the money. Took us two days. Up most of the night. Three dudes. Working our asses off. Copying shit. Digging around. Lying to people. Burning favors at the courthouse for after-hours access."

"I'll pay you. And don't talk to me about calling in favors."

"We looked at everything in that red circle of yours, except for the dorms and most of the University property," Jerry said, looking around suspiciously.

"And . . . ?" Dan said, snapping his fingers to focus Jerry's attention.

"Right. It was two hundred and some square blocks, by the way. Which is a shitload of property records. A shitload of property owners. Buildings with multiple owners, trusts. If it's residential, each condo on each floor has a different owner."

"I get it. A shitload."

"We went street by street. Building by building. And we were finding nothing. I mean nothing concrete. All records are online for DC. All records have been electronic for at least the last five years. But the information is not perfect. People screw up. Bits of information can be missing. Some properties don't have online sales information. Some properties don't have information for assessments. Some properties don't have accurate survey and plat information. Some don't have information on taxes paid. All this information comes from different sources but is presented online in a single property search. And don't get me started on REITs, which opens up another can of worms."

"Get to the good part."

Jerry took a sip of his coffee and looked around again. "Of all the properties we looked at, only one property didn't have all of the above. No sales data, no tax data, no land survey data. Nothing online. As if the address didn't exist in the online records. I mean, there is the possibility one or two records could be missing, but for *all* of them to be missing . . . ?"

"Only one property had no records?"

"One. It only exists in the real world. There are no online records at all."

"What's the address . . . ?"

Jerry pushed the folder in Dan's direction and took another drink from his tenth coffee in as many hours. Dan glanced at Jerry's shaking hands and pulled out the stack of paper. He started reading from the top, flipping the pages over as he went. Jerry watched as Dan's eyes moved rapidly from line to line.

Then Dan looked up.

"Silver Star."

"Exactly," Jerry stated proudly. "A company named Silver Star owns the property. It has no online records. It has no tenants. The only way you would know this property existed is if you went looking for the physical record."

Dan looked up at Jerry and said something to make his court connection sweat. "This building exists. I know the address. It's on Wisconsin Avenue. I was there last week."

"I don't want to know anymore."

CHAPTER 22

—

Dan pulled up to the curb on Wisconsin Avenue, took a couple of quarters from the ashtray of his car, and shoved them into the parking meter. He surveilled the building from afar with a walk on the opposite side of the street. At Guapo's Restaurant he crossed four lanes of traffic and headed back downhill. He moved slowly, using the reflection in the windows of various shops and storefronts to keep the building in his periphery while remaining inconspicuous. Methodically, he examined the building from all sides, absorbing the details of the glass-and-rock façade. On his second pass in front of the building he pushed on the revolving door. It didn't budge.

He shaded his eyes from the sun and touched his nose against the glass window of the lobby. Gone were the security booth and the desk he had passed by. The floor was barren. The directory on the far wall where he had checked his sister-in-law's attorney's location was void of names. The empty floor glistened with moisture. Dan felt a momentary pang of failure. His instincts had failed him. He had been catfished. Hook, line, and sinker. By a fake lawyer of all things. *Clyde Parkson, Esquire, my ass.*

Dan looked up again at the outside of the building and then back at the wet floor of the lobby. And then he smiled with the prospect of redemption.

He stepped back from the door, casually walked to the corner and turned down the alley beside the building. He tugged on the fire doors and peeked into spotless Dumpsters.

In the far corner of the alley, Dan smiled again. The white van with the large magnet on the door that read "Capital Cleaners" glistened like a mirage in the desert.

Dan sent messages on his phone, checked in with Sue, and waited for an hour on an old wooden bench before a six-person cleaning crew poured from a locked backed door. He sprang from his seat as the women in bright yellow attire walked empty-handed from the building to the white van.

"Good afternoon," Dan said in Spanish. "Who is in charge?" he asked with perfect pronunciation.

Five of the women quickly disappeared to the other side of the van and Dan was left facing the shortest, most elder of the cleaning crew.

"I am in charge," the fortysomething woman stated, her gold left incisor glistening.

Dan jumpstarted the Spanish corner of his brain and his comfort with the language returned with each conjugated verb, with each dusted off piece of vocabulary.

"My name is Dan. Where are you from?"

"I am from Virginia."

"Where were you born?"

"I was born in Virginia."

"No, you were born in Guatemala. Judging by the accent, probably somewhere near Antigua."

The cleaning woman stepped back and her mouth gaped. "Are you the police?"

"No."

"Immigration?"

"No."

"Then I don't have to talk to you."

Dan pulled out a thousand dollars and extended his hand. "You can answer my questions, get paid, and forget me, or you can deal with immigration after I give them a call."

The woman looked back towards the large van. The five other maids inside were watching the proceedings, their faces pressed against the window.

"What do you want to know?"

"How long have you been cleaning this building?"

"A year."

"Anyone in it?"

"The building is empty. It is very easy to clean."

"How do you get into the building?"

"I call a number and give them a security code. They open the door via the phone."

"Have you ever seen anyone in this building?"

"No, but there are cameras on each floor and they are watching."

"How do you know?"

"Because when you walk in front of them, a little red light comes on."

Dan thought back to his visit to Clyde Parkson and tried to remember seeing the cameras. "How many offices do you clean?"

"There are five floors. Two offices on every floor. There is also a basement area."

"Six floors."

"Yes, but we don't go into the basement."

"Do you have keys?"

"No, the doors to the offices are open. Except in the basement."

"What about the trash?"

"Sometimes there is a little trash. Usually, none. We were told not to take any trash with us. We bag the trash and our cleaning rags when we are done and leave it in a utility closet on the first floor. We dust. Vacuum. Clean the toilets."

"What is the phone number you call to enter the building?"

The woman paused and looked at the other ladies in the van.

Dan peeled another thousand dollars from his pocket. "I don't want the security code. I just want the number you call."

The cleaning lady gave Dan the number and Dan's hand momentarily shook with adrenaline. As Dan turned away, the prized phone number in hand, the cleaning woman with the gold incisor added a final thought. "We were told today is the last day we are cleaning this building."

—

Sue walked into the blaze orange room and sat down next to Dan. She had on a beret, black boots, a short skirt with tights, sunglasses, and a large backpack.

"How do I look?"

"Almost like a grad student."

"Funny."

"Did you pick up a couple of phones?"

"Yeah. I grabbed a few from your storage room. You have boxes of them. All unused. Hundreds probably."

"I purchased a few when Circuit City went out of business."

"A few?"

"OK. All of them in the DC area I could get a hold of. Some drug dealers beat me to the store in Southeast DC. Everyone wants disposable phones but the authorities are making it harder and harder to get them. Those are a cheap Chinese model called GoodBuy. Funny name, but they work well enough. The only thing that matters is they can't be traced back to me."

"Well, you have the mother lode."

"I figure enough for the next ten years or so."

"You could always sell them."

"There's a thought."

"You know, it's not my place, but you seem to be on a spending spree. A thousand dollars an hour here, a thousand an hour there. I only mention it because I don't see clients coming in the door with any money. That equation just can't work out over the long haul."

"I am aware of the current financial situation."

"Just thought I would be the voice of reason."

"I threw reason out the window when I hired you, and again when I kept you on."

"So what's the plan?"

Dan ran through the details of what Jerry the clerk dug up in his offline record search at the courthouse. He then explained both of his trips to the Wisconsin Avenue building and his previous run-in with the person purporting to be Clyde Parkson, as well as today's meeting with the cleaning crew.

"Holy shit. You *are* a detective. You found the building and the phone number and you know what the guy looks like—the man who impersonated the attorney."

"Actually, the only thing I can be certain of is that he is white and a little taller than I am. The rest can be imitated. Hair, teeth, outfit, goatee, accent. I know because I have done it myself many times. Though there is something about him I imagine transcends all of his disguises. Or maybe he didn't alter one of these description markers. Or can't. Or won't."

"So you can't identify him?"

"That's why we are here."

"I thought we were here for role-playing. Old man picks up college student in local coffee shop."

"I am not old."

"You know what I mean."

"I chose this location for a couple of reasons. This building has ten different rooms on the second floor alone. It's a maze. It's the perfect place for surveillance. Or counter surveillance."

"Who are we surveilling?"

"Whoever comes when we turn on one of those throwaway phones and start making calls. Did you bring your computer?"

"Yep."

"I want you to sit over there in the corner, in the big chair, and act like a student. Write a paper. Put on headphones. Play with your cell phone. Act distracted. Like you have ADHD. Keep your eye on the door. When someone comes in looking for the phone, text me."

Sue looked around the room.

Dan continued. "There are four other people in this room. Others could come at any moment. There are probably another twenty-five people in the other rooms on this floor. The first floor is packed as usual."

"Are you trying to make me less nervous?"

"A little. The crowd is good for safety. No one is going to kill you here with all these witnesses. They'd probably drug or otherwise incapacitate you, then call a fake ambulance, and take you out that way."

"That is not making me feel better."

"They wouldn't get far. I'll be watching the front door from the deli across the street. Are you comfortable with the graduate student persona?"

"I'm ready."

"OK. I am going to dial the number the cleaning crew calls to enter the building on Wisconsin Avenue. I assume it is the same number my nephew called thirteen times. Obviously, it was used to access the building in some fashion. Ready?"

"Ready."

Dan picked up one of the prepaid phones, turned on the location services, and checked the signal strength. He punched the phone number and put it to his ear. To his surprise, a female voice answered on the second ring. "Security code, please."

"Yes. My name is Conner Lord," Dan said.

"Security code, please."

"I forgot my security code. My name is Conner Lord. I dial this number the first week of every month for access to the building."

"Just a moment."

Dan raised his eyebrows and waited. A moment later the voice returned.

"You have the wrong number."

"Are you sure?"

Click.

"Now what?" Sue asked.

"If I am correct, then in, say, about fifteen minutes someone will enter the room with some sort of electronic device and search for the phone."

"But you hung up? How are they going to find you? I thought they can only triangulate on an active signal."

"That is correct. And I have a plan for that." Dan dialed the customer service line for COX cable. After bouncing through two voice menu selections he was in the customer service queue, listening to light jazz. The voice recording stated the company was *experiencing higher than normal call volume and wait times would be longer than usual.*

Dan kept the phone on and slipped it under the sofa on the ragged carpet. "That should do it. The phone is live. Location services are activated. I am on hold with the cable company. The customer service wait time is forty-seven minutes. That should provide plenty of time."

"And what do I do?"

"Go to the chair in the far corner. Act inconspicuous. When someone comes to look for the phone, you text me as soon as it is clear to do so."

"Easy."

Dan looked at his watch. "Gotta go. Keep your head down. Don't make eye contact. Use your disguise. Blend in."

—

Dan sat in a window seat at Sam's Corner Deli, twenty yards from the front of the coffee shop. Before the lady behind the counter could deliver his salami on rye, a burgundy sedan double parked next to a delivery van on Wilson Boulevard. A white male with a short haircut jumped from the driver's side, throwing some credentials on the dash of the car. A large black male with an imposing physique slipped smoothly from the passenger door.

Who do we have here? Dan said to himself. He depressed the shutter button on his SLR camera, the lens of the expensive black equipment protruding from under a copy of the *Post*. By the time the two guys reached the front door of the coffee shop, Dan had snapped over two dozen photos.

Minutes later his phone vibrated with a text message from Sue. *Two men. One white. One black and very large.*

On their way out of the coffee shop, Dan zoomed in for another twenty photos. He moved from his window seat, camera in hand, finger depressed. He stretched to get a photo of the car's license plate as he moved towards the door of the deli, camera in full motion. The incoming lunch crowd ended his paparazzi effort. Between the delivery truck, the angle of the car, and the lunch time regulars, the burgundy sedan escaped without showing its license plate.

—

Dan pulled a bottle of Gentleman Jack from the desk drawer and filled the two paper cups on his desk. Sue was at the printer, collecting printouts of the photographs he had taken of his two suspects. When Sue sat down, Dan picked up his cup.

"To a successful day of detective work."

Sue grabbed her cup. "What makes it successful?"

"The same thing that makes everything successful—we survived."

The shots went down the hatch and Sue spread the photos across the desk.

"So what happened inside the coffee shop?" Dan asked.

"Exactly what you thought would happen. Two guys showed up. One of them had a handheld device with an earpiece. It was obviously pretty accurate. They walked into the orange-colored room, took one circle around the couch, turned over the cushions, and then looked on the floor underneath. They were in the room less than a minute. They took the phone with them."

"Did they check you out?"

"Not really. And I wasn't looking up."

"Did one of them seem like they were in charge?"

"Maybe the white guy. But the black guy was so large, I couldn't imagine him following any order he didn't want to follow."

"Who do you think they are?"

"Ebony and Ivory."

"Seriously."

"Ex-military. Beyond that, I am not sure."

"You think Tobias would know?"

"I think Tobias could find out, but he won't. When those phone numbers disappeared from the cell tower hard drives after he ran his queries for us, I think he got, shall we say, 'spooked.' The only thing Tobias wants is to be paid and to move on with his plans for retirement."

"Are you worried about him?"

"Not really. He knows how to disappear. And he has the means. He knows the risk of what he does. Thus, he charges accordingly for that risk."

"So how do we find the guys in the pictures?"

"I'm working on that."

"Are you sure the white guy isn't the attorney you met at the building on Wisconsin Avenue? You said you may not be able to identify him."

"He's not tall enough. Height—particularly for men—is one of the parameters difficult to alter. Heels are obvious on a man. Ditto for hats. A combination of lifts inside the shoes and a baseball cap may provide an inch or two of discrepancy that is not too obvious. Otherwise, it is tough for a man to hide his height."

"You know anyone else who can help identify them?"

"I know someone who has access to military records, but he is out of the country. And of course, even if he were around, we would have to go through thousands of photos."

"That would take forever."

"Indeed. My attorney friend, Clyde Parkson, is another story. I am reasonably confident he is not military."

"Someone in intelligence?"

"Very likely. One with a high-level security clearance and a big set of balls."

"What makes you say that?"

"If I am right, he has orchestrated the killing of four Americans on American soil. That is a very big no-no."

"So how do you find him?"

"I call in another favor."

—

In the basement of the Octagon building in Tysons, an agitated Reed Temple watched as Ridge wrapped the last strap to his lower left leg and stood. The exoskeleton looked like scaffolding for the body, an outer frame of space-age composite bone layered over real flesh and blood.

"How does it feel?" Major asked.

"Effortless," Ridge replied.

"Then give it a test drive."

Ridge started easy with lunges and deep knee bends. The hinges on the exoskeleton slid smoothly and silently.

"Any resistance?"

"None. It's like I'm not even using my own muscles."

Reed Temple grinned. "So it works as designed?"

Major responded. "Indeed. The exoskeleton picks up the user's body movements as they occur. There are hundreds of sensors in various locations and several microchips with backup redundancy. The microchips process the data in real time and translate it into exoskeleton movement. The exoskeleton assists the user's own muscles with the task it is performing, supplying power to the user's intended movement. Pretty awesome, really. And of course there are all kinds of practical applications if you are concerned with non-military scenarios. Physical assistance for the elderly. For the paralyzed. Once the sensors can accurately read brainwaves, the system will bypass the body's muscle movement, or lack thereof, entirely."

"I am only concerned with the military application."

"Imagine a team of special forces parachuting behind enemy lines and strapping on these skeletons. Preliminary estimates indicate that a team of special forces soldiers could cover one hundred miles a day on foot, in total silence, without exertion. Add body armor and you are talking about a truly dominating force. With the added strength assistance of the exoskeleton, we could load additional gear. Biohazard suits. Radiation protection. Scuba gear. Anything you can imagine."

"How strong is it?"

Major turned to Ridge. "You ready to lift some weights?"

Ridge smiled and walked to the corner of the concrete-walled room. The large barbell on the floor had six forty-five pound plates on each side.

"We have been testing it with just under six hundred pounds," Major said.

Ridge bent over and lifted the weight to his waist as if beginning a clean-and-jerk routine. He held the weight at belt height for a full minute before setting it down.

Ridge provided his assessment as Major and Reed whispered to each other. "Hurts the hands a little. My body can support the weight, no problem, but a barbell requires grip and the exoskeleton does not currently assist well enough with that."

"We are working on it. Try a squat."

Ridge moved two feet to his left and stood under a weighted bar that was shoulder height.

"Six hundred again?" Reed Temple asked.

"Affirmative."

Ridge bent slightly to position the weight on his shoulders and then flexed his own muscles to stand. The bar bent on each end, the weight pushing the limits of the steel. Ridge began doing deep knee squats. Once again, he was smiling during what would have otherwise been crushing exertion. "I can do this all day long."

"Try the treadmill," Reed Temple said.

Ridge followed orders and moved to the treadmill, the large bar still arching in its position. With the bar resting on his shoulders, Ridge freed one hand and pressed the start button. Seconds later, the treadmill, with Ridge and an additional six hundred pounds, came to life. For ten minutes Ridge ran on the treadmill, six hundred pounds on his shoulders, the bar bouncing gently with the natural rhythm of the running motion.

"Jesus. Look at that. He's hardly sweating."

"I know," Major said. "A thing of beauty."

"Can't say the same for the treadmill. I think the engine is burning."

"I smell it. I'll turn it off. I think we have seen enough."

Ridge dismounted, returned the weights to the rack, and joined Reed Temple and Major in the corner.

Major was holding up a throwaway phone in a zipped bag.

"That is the phone?" Temple asked.

"Yes."

"Did you see who put it there?"

"No. It was obviously a plant. A ruse at our expense. It is a low-quality, throwaway Chinese model. Goes by the name of GoodBuy."

"I am sure the uncle was behind this," Reed Temple replied.

"Probably. We were in and out in a few minutes, but the location had some complexities. If it was a stakeout, then I am sure we were captured in photos."

"Which means we have all been seen."

Major replied. "We have all been seen, but Ridge and I were not benefitted by a disguise. You were the hunter. We were the hunted."

"Any prints on the phone?"

"Two sets of prints. It would be easy enough to match with the uncle through typical surveillance and dusting."

"Easy enough? Didn't we try this with the DC police already?"

"Yes. We provided a gun—a murder weapon—with the uncle's prints to the police."

"Obviously, there was a hiccup."

"According to the now deceased mugger-for-hire, the uncle's prints should have been on the gun used to kill the police detective. The hired help indicated that during the confrontation on the stairs of the promenade, the uncle possessed the gun, held it, dismantled it, and threw it over the wall. That is where we found it, and where it was used on the Asian detective when he surprised us. The weapon was white gloved. We left the gun five feet from the detective's body. We can't do the police's job. We gave them the evidence. We can't force them to use it."

"We better figure out something. The uncle is on to us. I'm not sure how, but he is making progress. He is becoming a potentially serious hazard to operations and career longevity."

Major smiled. "We were told not to kill the uncle. Does that still stand?"

"For now."

"What about other collateral damage?"

"Not my concern, as long as it doesn't come back to us."

Major held up the bag and eyed the phone before smiling even wider. "Christmas may have come early. We just need to decide where to hide the present."

CHAPTER 23

—

Dan parked in front of Prospect House, a massive white condominium in Rosslyn. The fourteen-story building had been constructed in the seventies and was the proud owner of one the finest views in the DC area, if not the entire East Coast. The front of Prospect House conjured little envy. The west façade peeked down on sprawling blocks of low-rise apartment buildings that ran down the still-affordable side of Route 50 between the Potomac and Courthouse. Low-rent Latino strongholds mingled with swanky townhouses and blocks of squat brick apartment buildings heavy with military and student clientele. It was a prime example of real estate owners embracing their middle class tenants until they received an offer too good to refuse, finally forcing the under-financed to locations further afield.

The east-facing side of Prospect House was another matter entirely. Balconies and two-story windows perched over the Iwo Jima Memorial, in perfect alignment with the Mall on the other side of the Potomac. The Lincoln Memorial and the Washington Monument stood at attention. The Capitol, over three miles away, was the cherry on the visual sundae. Dan's date for the evening lived on the top floor of residences, on the sexy side of the building.

Dan walked through the glass doors of the lobby and approached the front desk. "I'm here to see Haley Falls. Apartment 1212."

The man behind the desk did a quick measure of Dan and nodded in the direction of the intercom on the lobby wall. "Punch in the name."

Dan ran through the names and found Haley's number. The speaker crackled after a quiet beep.

"I'm in the lobby."

"I'll be down in five."

Haley Falls strolled from the elevator in a leather skirt and a tight-fitting white sweater that left little to Dan's imagination, other than the question of whether it was the chilly air or his mere presence.

Dan opened his arm and Haley, a leggy brunette, walked into his embrace. The man behind the desk looked up and then eyed the monitor on the desk, scanning the feeds from the other security cameras.

"You up for a walk?" Dan asked.

Haley looked down at her red heels. "How far are we going?"

"Two blocks."

"The Quarterdeck?"

Dan winked.

"I'm wearing a white sweater."

"I will get you a bib."

Haley Falls, formerly known as Lena Pavlovna, whispered a curse in Russian, her rusty native tongue.

—

The Quarterdeck was an Arlington institution. Nestled on the corner of two residential streets that ran along the north side of Fort Myers and Arlington Cemetery, the Quarterdeck wasn't on the tourist maps. The faux 7-11 next door, with which the Quarterdeck shared its parking spaces, had been there nearly as long as the seafood and crab shack. Rumor hinted there was once a strip club in the back, but any patron old enough to have firsthand knowledge wasn't talking. As men get older and wiser, they learn wives never forget. And there was no sense in dredging up suspicion from decades ago.

Dan and Haley stood in line on the back deck for a couple of minutes before the waitress led them inside to a quiet corner. The waitress plopped down a stack of newspapers, a pair of wooden mallets, and a scratched-up laminated menu. "Y'all having crabs?" she asked, the presumption already made.

"And two beers," Dan added.

Haley Falls waited until the waitress walked away. "I got a call about you. Ginger was out at Good Time Charlie and a DC detective was asking questions about you. A lot of questions."

"Good old Ginger. Always keeping her ear to the ground."

"She is a good friend. And she always liked you. What about the detective?"

"I figured he would ask around."

"Are you in trouble?"

"Not yet, but I am working on it."

The waitress dropped two light beers off on the table without breaking stride.

"I should have asked for the best American beer in the house."

"It's a crab shack."

"I'm trying to balance snobbery without drinking piss-water."

"You take a woman to a crab shack, you have to lower your expectations."

"Isn't the saying you can take a woman out of a crab shack but you can't take the crabs out of . . ."

"Careful."

Dan made a quick toast in Russian. "To another year alive."

The crabs came, steaming hot, and the wooden mallets were put to work, bits of shell rocketing from the table onto the worn tile floor. Beer mixed with crab meat dipped in butter sprinkled with Old Bay. When they were finished, Haley and Dan pushed their chairs against the wall and sat parallel to the table.

"A whole meal and you didn't ask for a single favor," Haley said. "It must be important."

"Are you saying I can't have dinner with a friend without something in it for me?"

"No, I'm saying you were never much for small talk, so the last hour must have killed you."

"You have no idea. Seventy-two minutes of crabs and chit-chat. I deserve a star."

"We shall see," Haley said, slugging her beer with a flip of her hair.

Dan noticed Haley's radiant skin and perfect brown hair. Her smile warmed the table. Smiling himself, Dan finally succumbed. "I have a favor to ask."

Haley looked at her watch. "Seventy-three minutes."

"Eighty-eight minutes since we left your front door."

"But who is counting?"

"I need help from one of your girls."

"Dan, darling. *Women*."

"Women then."

"What kind of help?"

Dan looked around the room and lowered his voice amidst the din of crabs being pounded by hammers. "I'm looking for a particular kind of customer."

"Someone with a little foot fetish?"

"No. Someone with certain knowledge of the intelligence variety."

Haley sighed and swigged another mouthful from her beer. The room was emptying, the mix of office workers and neighborhood couples heading home for the evening. "What about the Dan Lord rule book? No spooks was at the top of the list, if I remember correctly."

"Good memory. No spies, no mafia. Those are my rules."

"I also recall you touting that those rules keep you alive."

"They have."

"So if you have rules that keep you alive, and those rules state you are not to do business with intelligence personnel or members of organized crime, what are we discussing?"

"This time it's personal."

"Conner?"

"Yeah."

"His death was not an accident?"

"It is currently labeled as an overdose. The official test results have not come back yet."

"I don't know, Dan. You have rules. I have rules too. Rules that will keep *me* alive. A woman has to think about her future."

"I'll make it up to you."

"Yes, you will. For starters, the next time I need a check on one of my *girls*, or a client, you'll do it gratis."

"The next five times."

"Ten," Haley added.

"Russian negotiation tactics?"

"The first rule of negotiation is that nothing is agreed to until everything is agreed to."

"Then I will stop talking before I owe a debt I can't repay."

"What exactly are you looking for?"

"Someone who can be compromised. Someone who has been around the block. I don't want some wet-behind-the-ears rookie. I'm not looking for a desk-jockey. I'm not looking for a computer whiz. I already have one of those charging me more than I can afford. I'm interested in someone long in the tooth. Someone with real experience."

Haley cursed in Russian and then switched back to English. "Jesus, Dan. You are not ordering from a catalog."

"We've done this drill before."

"Not with this type of clientele."

Dan lifted his beer and drained his bottle. "I'm trying to find a ghost. I need someone who can help me find someone without a name. Can you help?"

"I have a client in mind, though it is hard to say for certain. Remember *my* first rule: people are generally full of shit. Cab drivers claim they were once doctors in their home country. Office workers who have trouble ambling up the stairs claim they are former athletes. High school dropouts claim they have PhDs from Harvard."

"Politicians who claim to be honest."

"Exactly."

"So what about this client makes him more believable than the rest? Why is he not a liar?"

"This client talks in his sleep. I haven't met anyone who lies in their sleep. Yet."

"Brilliant."

"You have to come up with a plan that doesn't implicate me or my employee. And if you compromise this guy and he stops seeing one of my employees, you are going to need to pay for the lost income. Regular customers are becoming rarer. This guy has been a regular for a long time."

"How much compensation?"

"The going rate for services is three hundred an hour. So if this guy has weekly appointments, you are looking at somewhere in the neighborhood of seven thousand for, say, six months of compensation."

"Not a problem. What else can you tell me about the client? Married? Potentially angry wife?"

Haley just smiled.

"Nothing else?"

"Be prepared. That is all I can say. Remember, there is a reason you have your rules."

Haley took a slow sip of her beer and then ran her finger around the edge of the glass bottle neck. "You want to come back? Have a nightcap?"

Dan felt a tingle below his waist—an old tingle but one without complications.

"Is that part of the deal?"

"No Dan, not with you. Paybacks, favors—those were never part of the equation when it came to you."

"I might not have my A-game. I have a lot on my mind."

"I'll take your B-game."

"I'll get the check."

"I'll make a call and get you the latest information on your spy."

—

Dan put his shoes on in the living room, overlooking the flickering lights of the city and the illuminated National Mall.

"Great view," Dan said aloud.

Haley was in the kitchen wearing only her sweater, talking on the phone. She stopped at the kitchen counter to scribble on a piece of paper then walked into the living room, her long legs and exposed derrière shining in the reflection of the glass wall.

"Another great view," Dan added as Haley ended her phone call.

"Thanks, Dan." She handed him the piece of paper. "Here is the address and the time."

"Standing weekly meeting?"

"Regular as clockwork."

"Thanks, Haley."

She bent over and kissed him on the neck. "Walk me down to my car. I have to go into the city. Have an employee issue to straighten out."

"One of your girls get busted?"

"Not yet. And I was hoping to keep it that way."

CHAPTER 24

—

Detective Wallace kept a running tab of murder scenes—no small feat in a city averaging a murder a day since the advent of crack. With twenty-five years on the force, he had processed over four hundred murder scenes. Some locations were hotbeds. Recurring supply for the morgues. The five years he spent in the lawless blocks that ran from little Trinidad to Catholic University revealed widely accepted drop-zones for those on the wrong end of a drug deal. Pull your car down one of the narrow backstreets, push the door open, and roll the body to the curb. No fuss, no muss.

Wallace had seen the city grow meaner, more callous. Where the narcotics trade had once been the most risky extracurricular activity in the city, a mere accidental shoulder bump with a stranger was now likely to end with an upward tick on the city's body count.

The alley behind the Ritz Carlton residence was a murderous first for the detective. The broad stretch of clean concrete was immaculate, less for the dead woman between the spotless Dumpsters that were emptied twice a day to keep away the rats. The Ritz could afford the extra garbage pickup. It couldn't afford not to.

A squad car blocked each end of the alley and Detective Wallace could feel the stares from the Ritz Carlton guests in their windows above. The manager of the hotel, a squat man in a tailored suit, had spoken with the first officer on the scene and begged, nearly wept, for expediency in processing the scene. Dead bodies did even less for hotel ambiance than rats.

A white uniformed police officer stood behind Detective Wallace as he kneeled, processing the scene. The officer took turns taking notes for the detective and eyeing the alley for rubberneckers.

Detective Wallace spoke over his shoulder without taking his eyes off the victim.

"White female. Mid-thirties. Leather skirt and white sweater still intact and unmolested. Looks like strangulation. Ligature marks on the neck. Dead maybe five hours, but the coroner will be able to give a more exact time."

"The coroner is on the way. He had a busy night."

"Not in this section of town," Detective Wallace replied, opening the small red purse next to the deceased's hand. "Any surveillance cameras?"

"We have one above the back entrance, but we're doing a canvass for horizontal views from ATMs and other establishments."

"What does the back entrance camera show us?"

"Not much. The back door is used by staff. The camera is focused on the doorway. Probably theft prevention. There are three other fire doors, one-way exits with alarms. None are reported to have been accessed."

Detective Wallace opened the purse with his latex-gloved hands. He placed the contents of the small bag one-by-one on the concrete next to the body and described the inventory as the officer continued to take notes. "One red lipstick. L'Oreal. A folding hairbrush. A Samsung cell phone. A pair of sunglasses, still in their case. A set of keys. A car key to a BMW, three keys that look like house keys, and one key that probably fits a post box, meaning she likely lives in an apartment building."

Wallace unsnapped the women's matching red pocketbook. He read the driver's license and paused as he always did when a name came with the body, when the dead took back a moment of life to tell the detective who they were. "Haley Falls, resident of Arlington County. Lives at Prospect House, unit 1212."

"So, you were right about the keys being to an apartment building."

"She's a considerate victim. I'm used to working without an ID."

"A considerate victim would have let you sleep in."

Detective Wallace continued with the inventory of the

pocketbook. "Three hundred and forty-two dollars in cash. Five credit cards and a check card."

"A cell-phone, credit cards, and over three hundred in cash?"

"Not a robbery, unless the perp got caught with his pants down and had to run." Detective Wallace turned the purse upside down and shook it gently.

The white detective donned latex gloves and turned on the Samsung phone. "Detective Wallace, you are going to need to check this out," he said, holding out his hand.

Detective Wallace negotiated with his knees to get vertical before looking at the screen of the Samsung cell phone. He read the black text message on the pale blue screen to his associate. *Dan Lord murdered me.*

"What is that?"

"It appears to be an unsent text message."

"So the girl types in a message and doesn't send it to anyone?"

"That is my guess. Who is Dan Lord?"

"Nguyen was working on a case involving his family members. And including this young woman here, that makes five bodies."

"A serial killer?" the white detective asked.

"This guy is clever enough to be anything he wants."

"Why wouldn't she just call 911? Why bother with the text?"

"Maybe she couldn't speak. Damage to the neck."

"It fits with strangulation."

"Take a look around and see if there is anything else," Wallace said, bagging the evidence.

A moment later, the white detective yelled out from a prone position on the ground, next to a large Dumpster. His arm was outstretched, beyond view, under the dark nastiness of the Dumpster's shadow. "I got something." He grunted once and pulled out another cell phone, holding it by the small antenna.

"What is it?

"A cell phone. Some company I have never heard of. GoodBuy. Maybe a throwaway. A disposable."

"Bag it and take it back for prints."

CHAPTER 25

—

The Central Detention Facility, known more commonly as the DC Jail, sits on D Street in Southeast Washington, a few hundred yards from the outer parking lot of the old RFK stadium. Its anonymous brick façade could easily be mistaken for a college lecture hall or a corporate office building from any office park in the country. With a maximum capacity of thirty-eight hundred, the criminals ruling the neighboring blocks of old row houses outnumbered the inmates four to one.

Detective Wallace pushed Dan through the main doors, holding on to Dan's handcuffed wrists. He moved his grip to Dan's elbow and steered his suspect to the registration desk. Beyond a glass wall, a female officer shuffled papers, moving pages from a pile on the left to an equal pile on the right, pausing briefly on each page long enough to hit it with a rubber stamp.

"Detective Earl Wallace, Sergeant. 2nd District," Wallace said, flashing his badge.

"Good evening, Detective. You know the routine," the female officer stated, shoving a clipboard with an attached form through the slot in the security glass.

Detective Wallace nodded. He filled in the form with one hand still holding Dan's arm. Moments later, Dan lost his cell phone, wallet, keys, and belt. Dan watched as his belongings disappeared into a large plastic envelope which was sealed, marked, and signed.

Wallace steered Dan through a doorway metal detector, followed by a more thorough handheld wand scan. The security shakedown was followed unceremoniously by fashion mug shots.

With remnants of flash still in his eyes, Dan was shuffled down a narrow corridor.

"Have we had enough fun yet?" Dan asked, wrists now cuffed in front of his body.

"Wait until the rectal exam," Detective Wallace replied.

"I am entitled to a phone call," Dan said as the detective gleefully pushed him towards a sign on the wall that read "Fingerprinting."

"Patience. You haven't even been processed yet."

At the fingerprinting station, Wallace uncuffed Dan's wrists. A large corrections officer with a crowd control baton stood at attention at the end of the table.

"I will admit I've been looking forward to this. Let me see your hands, palms up."

Dan did as he was told and Wallace bent over to examine his fingertips. "You have rough hands. Almost like a carpenter. Knuckles like a boxer."

"There's more to the opposable thumb than holding the remote control."

"Like killing a pretty woman and leaving her in an alley?"

"I have never killed a woman."

Wallace looked at Dan with curiosity. "You can put your hands down."

Dan once again did as he was told and then looked down to assess the fingerprinting station.

"This is how it works. The machine before you is called a LiveScan. You put your fingers on the scanner, one at a time, until the light turns green. Do not remove your finger until the light turns green. We will start on your right hand and then move to the left. Every finger in order, starting with your pointer. Thumbs are last. This is probably a bit different than the last time you were printed."

"Anything else?"

Wallace grunted. "This method of fingerprinting is faster and more accurate than traditional means."

"And if the bullshit charges you are filing don't stick, you legally have to delete the file."

"Let's cross that bridge when we get to it."

"We will cross that bridge as soon as I get my phone call."

Wallace grunted again and reached for Dan's wrist. Five minutes later the fingerprinting process was complete. Wallace gently pushed Dan away from the fingerprinting station and nudged him in the direction of a bank of elevators. "Keep moving. Towards the elevator. We are going up."

Dan stepped in the elevator and watched Wallace press the button for the fifth floor.

"The fifth floor, eh?"

"Makes a breakout difficult. Freedom isn't so free when it is fifty feet below. You would also have to break through reinforced glass and somehow squeeze out a very narrow window. Unless you lose some weight, I don't see it happening."

The elevator door opened and Wallace pushed Dan to the left. The cinderblock walls breathed monotony. Boredom. Wallace knocked on the third metal door on the right side of the hall and then pushed it open.

"Welcome to our discussion chamber."

"I think these were called interrogation rooms before it became unpopular nomenclature. I mean, with all the water, the towels, people being hung upside down until proven guilty . . ."

"Sit down."

Dan shuffled around the small room and took a seat on the far side of the table. The cuffs dug into his wrists and he grimaced briefly before finding a comfortable position.

Detective Wallace sat in the empty chair on the opposite side of the table, facing Dan. "This conversation is being recorded."

"It may not be much of a conversation," Dan replied.

"Tell me, where were you last night?"

"Had dinner with a friend and then went home."

"Who was this friend?"

"Haley Falls."

"So you admit to being with her."

"Yes."

"And do you know her current whereabouts?"

"The morgue. Why, are you looking for her?"

"Do you have a problem with authority, Dan?"

"Let me know when some arrives."

"You don't believe in the easy way, do you?"

"I don't believe there *is* an easy way."

"You ever been to prison, Dan? Because that is where you are heading."

"Here is the situation, from my seat. Haley Falls was found dead. You found evidence at the scene that somehow linked me to her. You did some investigating, probably talked to the doorman at her apartment. He told you we went out. Probably led you down the street to the Quarterdeck where you probably had a nice conversation with the waitress. She told you I was there and that I was with Haley. You are now following the tried-and-true assumption that the last person seen with a dead person is responsible for their death. In eighty-five percent of cases you would be correct."

The detective scribbled in his notebook. "Just to be clear, you admit you were with Ms. Falls the night she died, and you admit you were the last one to see her alive."

"No. I admit Ms. Falls is a friend of mine and that we had dinner. Then we went back to her place. Later, I left. She was leaving too. I put her in her car and then got in mine. There should be video of my car on Route 110 near the Pentagon, then again in front of that brick building on the corner of Washington Street that houses an office of the DIA. The building with the underground parking entrance manned by two guys with automatic weapons. You should also have my image in the camera at the bank next to the IHOP in Old Town. Another camera and a digital entry stamp at the Union Street parking garage. That will provide a lot of evidence for someone who was supposed to be elsewhere killing a friend, in public, when I could have just done it in her apartment."

"So, back to the question. You were the last one to see her alive."

"No. Whoever killed her was the last one to see her alive. And that wasn't me."

"Haley Falls seems to think it was you."

"Based on what?"

"An unsent message that was typed into her cell phone."

"That is convenient."

"Actually, inconvenient for you. Considerably inconvenient."

Dan's mind began to replay the last twenty-four hours, the evening with Haley unfolding slowly in his mind and then speeding forward as if he hit a button on the remote control.

"Why did you have dinner with Ms. Falls?" Wallace asked.

"Because she's an old friend."

"How do you know each other?"

"I was once hired to find her."

"Find her? How?"

"It was a private investigation. I was hired by her family to locate her. I found her, alive and well I might add, and we became friends. She told me she didn't want to be found and she was not interested in being reunited with her family."

"And?"

"We were friends after that. She changed her name, relocated a couple of times, and created a new life."

"Were you romantically involved?"

"Once again you are playing the odds. Most murders are committed by loved ones, relatives, friends, and boyfriends."

"So you can do the probability calculation."

"Two strikes against me."

"So you were romantically involved."

"On occasion."

"Was last night one of the occasions?"

"A gentleman shouldn't kiss and tell."

"When I picked you up, you already knew she had passed away. How did you know?"

"I have friends in low places."

Wallace stood and walked around the room once. He yawned and rubbed his face with his palms. "Things can go one of two ways here."

"Detective, things can go one of one way here. I want my phone call."

"Your phone call?"

"Yes. Ten digits I am going to start reciting over and over until you provide a phone."

"Childish, don't you think, Mr. Lord?"

"Any more childish than playing Sesame Street as an interrogation technique? Worked in Guantanamo on some members of Al-Qaeda."

"You are a piece of work."

"As are you, Detective. Senator John Day seems to have issues with you. And then there was the subway incident, which I believe you had your hand in."

"You do your homework."

"I try. What do you say we save some time and you just let me out of here? Or you can give me my phone call and you can watch me walk out of here. Either way, if you want to find out what happened to Haley Falls, or my sister-in-law, or my nephew, or that poor student from American University, and likely Detective Nguyen, feel free to follow me. In fact, you can sign up for an email update."

"You are a prick."

"A prick with no time."

"You are going to find some time."

Dan started reciting a ten-digit number out loud and Detective Wallace shook his head.

"You are going to have to do better than that."

"In DC, you can hold me for forty-eight hours until I see a judge. Then you have to officially charge me or release me."

"You want to spend forty-eight hours here?"

"I'll take my phone call now. I will be out before I need a nap."

Detective Wallace disappeared and reappeared ten minutes later. "Stand up. We are moving. You can have your phone call. I have arranged for your accommodations."

Detective Wallace led Dan down the hall to a small cubicle. An old phone was affixed to the cinderblock wall. The cord to the phone was short, forcing Dan to lean over to hear the dial tone. "Do you mind?" Dan asked, hinting at his desire for some privacy.

Detective Wallace stepped back several paces and waited for Dan to finish his call, which he did through whispers. When he was done, Dan looked over and smiled.

"All finished, Dan?"

"Tick tock."

Detective Wallace re-cuffed Dan's wrists and led him through a manned security door and down another long hall with matching gray interior. At the end of the hall they stepped into an open foyer. A security control booth peered out from behind thick security glass. Closed circuit cameras hung from the ceiling in every corner. A traditional jail door, replete with bars, blocked the far exit. An older guard with a starched uniform and no sense of humor was standing at attention near the barred door. Wallace nodded at the elder corrections officer.

A voice boomed from behind the security booth window. "Put him in the last cell on the left, Detective."

The old guard opened the barred door and Wallace escorted Dan to the destination cell and unlocked his handcuffs.

"I'll be out in an hour. You can start counting."

"A lot can happen in an hour," the detective said, pulling the cell door open for him to enter.

—

Moments later, in the glass security booth, Detective Wallace stood behind the head guard, looking over his shoulder at the closed circuit monitor.

"You could get me in trouble with this," the guard stated.

"Relax. This is a suspect in the killing of a fellow officer. I will take full responsibility."

"Are you going to pay my pension if they fire me?"

"Tell them I pulled a gun on you. Now, what's your response time from here?"

"I hit this button," the security control officer said gesturing towards a red circle on the dash in front of him, "and four guards will expedite their support of the senior guard at the door. Response time is less than twenty seconds."

"That should be fast enough."

"Only takes a second to kill someone."

Detective Wallace ignored the statement. "Who do we have in

the cell?"

"Three assaults, one with a deadly weapon. Two attempted murders. Both with guns. A carjacker. A drug dealer who tried to run over a non-paying client. A guy who allegedly beat his cousin to death with a tire iron. The last two are repeat felony drug dealers. "

Detective Wallace nodded. "Keep your eyes on the screen and your hand on the alarm button."

—

Dan found half a butt cheek worth of space at the end of the bench along the far wall. It was the seat closest to the toilet and the odorous aroma was the prime reason for the location's vacancy. He looked around the cell, his new roommates falling into silence. Dan switched his mind into assessment mode. Ten males. All black. One stoned. One asleep. Three who didn't seem to care about his presence. The remaining five appeared to care deeply about the intrusion and were rising from their seats.

As if on cue, one of the inmates Dan had designated as trouble invaded his real estate near the open toilet. Dan processed the information. The man had him by two inches and forty pounds. Thick arms meant time in the gym. Thick arms also meant slower reflexes. Only genetic freaks could gain both mass and speed, and most of them were in professional football, not a cell at the DC correctional facility.

"Stand up," the man said, crossing his arms in front of Dan. The massive forearms were covered in black ink, the original artwork lost in a sea of pictures, letters and ideas applied hodgepodge over the years with prison ink and needles.

Dan looked up. The man frowned downward. Dan responded. "No disrespect intended, but I suggest you move on."

"Move on? Shiiit, motherfucker. Where we movin' to?"

"I'm not looking for trouble."

"I said, 'stand up.'"

"And I said, 'move on.' I could use the exercise and you aren't up for it."

The man started a deep choking laugh and the air in the cell became charged. Spittle gathered in the corner of his lips. The dozing man on the bench next to Dan opened his eyes, stood, and staggered to the other side of the cell. Dan took the extra space and got comfortable. Two other men stood and took position behind their lead dog.

The standing perp announced his first movement while simultaneously calling Dan something that rhymed with "itch," but was less scratchy. The man's arms unfolded from their crossed position and Dan saw the punch coming in slow motion. He moved his head to the right far enough to avoid the punch, raised his foot and powered it forward. Dan's foot drove the man's knee backwards as the man moved forward and the ligaments snapped. The man reacted and his attention fell to his joint, the pain reaching his brain. Dan reached up and pulled down on his neck, slamming the man's head into the bench next to him.

The two guys behind the injured man rushed forward and Dan shot from his seat, staying low and moving past the high punches that were coming fast. *Amateurs.* The first wave of punches missed and Dan was behind the two who were turning to refocus on their target. Dan took out a second knee, this time from the side, and followed that with an elbow to the temple as he spun 180 degrees. Three down.

"Are you finished?" Dan asked as two more men stood. The first man took up a boxer's stance and began throwing jabs. Dan blocked the punches, keeping his feet moving as the two remaining men tried to flank him.

"Fuck you, man," the man standing in the rear said, raging forward past his boxing partner.

Dan dropped his center of gravity and drove his waist into the charging man's upper thigh. He simultaneously reached up and grabbed the flesh of the man's pectoral, ripping both shirt and skin. He pulled the chunk of muscle downward and the resulting flip sent the man's feet towards the ceiling before he crashed to the concrete floor, head first.

The boxer caught Dan with a hook to the left eyebrow, and Dan flinched and arched backward as an uppercut just missed its target. Dan blocked the next two punches as blood trickled into his left eye obscuring his vision. As the boxer continued his methodical approach, Dan glanced down at the second knee victim who was now on all fours trying to regain vertical positioning. Dan used the back of the man as a platform, jumping high enough to deliver a knee directly to the face of the boxer who was ill-prepared for an impact propelled by the strongest muscle group in the body. Dan landed on his feet as the boxer's eyes rolled into his head.

"Like I said, I am not looking for trouble."

Dan glanced around at the carnage and wiped the blood from his brow. The stoned prisoner looked up at Dan from the bench, his eyes bloodshot. "You're bleeding."

"I wasn't looking for trouble."

"Found you anyway."

Dan stepped to the toilet area and unfurled a wad of toilet paper. He patted his bleeding eyebrow and the toilet paper turned crimson.

—

"Jesus," the guard in the security booth said to Detective Wallace. "What the hell was that?"

"A lot of knees. One elbow. Some kind of gravity-inducing throw."

"How did you know?"

"I didn't know. But I needed to find out. Get someone in there. Tend to the injured."

"What are you going to do with him?"

"Get him his own accommodations."

—

Detective Wallace slid open the small window in the cell door and peeked into solitary confinement. Dan was lying on his side, eyes open, staring in the direction of the stainless-steel toilet in the corner. Wallace rattled the keys and Dan rolled over on the thin mattress, shifting his weight on the concrete slab that extended from the wall.

Detective Wallace pushed on the cell door and stood at the

entrance with a guard on each side. One of the guards gripped a Taser. The other held an unholstered can of pepper spray. The men were at full attention, ready to unleash legal retribution for any resistance Dan may offer.

Wallace barked commands. "Please stand up, Dan. Hands on your head. Turn around and face the far wall. Cuffs are going back on."

Dan complied as Detective Wallace slipped on the cuffs and steered him out of the room and down another cinderblock hallway. Detective Wallace gripped Dan's elbow and could feel a strength that belied Dan's size. Wallace flanked Dan as the four men traveled down the hall. At the elevator door, the detective gently pulled on Dan's arm to indicate they were stopping. All four men boarded the elevator and Wallace held Dan's arm, keeping his prisoner facing the back of the elevator. When the door opened, Wallace again pulled on Dan's bound wrists. Moments later, the detective nudged Dan through the door of another interrogation room. Wallace directed Dan to the metal chair on the far side of the table in the middle of the room. Standing next to the chair, he uncuffed Dan's hands and moved them to the front of his body. He glanced at the dried blood on Dan's shirt and reattached the cuffs. He motioned for Dan to sit and Wallace stepped back towards the door, never taking his eyes off his suspect.

In the hallway, Detective Wallace turned towards a red-haired woman in her late forties and extended his hand.

"Detective Earl Wallace."

"Cathy Bailey. Assistant District Attorney."

"Pleasure."

"Is he good to go?"

"He's all yours."

"You want me to go in with you?"

"No thank you, Officer."

"Are you sure? He has the potential to be dangerous."

"Is that why he has dried blood on his shirt and appears to have an injury over his eye?"

"There was a scuffle. It happens. This place lacks men of character."

The assistant DA looked Detective Wallace over from head to toe and Wallace felt himself blush. After the silent slap on the wrist, the assistant DA continued. "Stand guard at the door. No one behind the glass. Attorney-client privilege."

"Yes, ma'am."

—

Assistant District Attorney Cathy Bailey stepped into the room and the door shut behind her with a resounding click.

Dan looked up, recognized the face, and smiled.

"You are Dan Lord?"

"Yes."

"My name is Cathy Bailey. Assistant District Attorney for the District of Columbia."

"I recognize you. Your face, at least. Your stockings are different from the knee high, red lace numbers you were wearing in the picture I saw of you. And of course, you're wearing the rest of your clothes, not decorating the room with them. The panties on the bedpost were priceless, by the way."

The assistant DA walked around the table as she spoke. "I was sent here on behalf of Judge McMichael, whom you called. I have reviewed your case and the DA's office has chosen not to pursue your arraignment based on currently available evidence. You are free to leave."

Dan was about to stand and the assistant DA gently pushed his shoulder down, forcing him back into his seat. "However, should the facts of the case change," she continued, "should the authorities have further evidence linking you to any of the cases under investigation, your situation will be revisited."

Dan suppressed a smirk. "Thank you."

"You are welcome."

"May I stand now?"

"I am not finished. Judge McMichael would like you to know that this is a one-time deal. The two of you are now even. The slate is clean. He knows who you are. Any further interaction between the two of you will be through normal channels and under normal circumstances, meaning he is a judge and if you should ever find your way into his court, you are . . . what is the legal term I am looking for?"

"Fucked."

"Yes, fucked."

"And I am sure you had nothing to do with this deal. Photographs of you knocking boots with Judge McMichael doesn't threaten you in any way?"

"I saw the photos. They could be anyone. Besides, the man has filed for divorce. We are consenting adults."

"You are an assistant District Attorney who is banging a judge presiding over cases in your jurisdiction. I believe that is called a conflict of interest. And to be clear, the judge's ex-wife filed for divorce. The judge did not. So please tell the judge I am still in contact with his ex-wife and that portion of our arrangement is still intact. Also, please tell the detective outside I would like to have a sketch artist for an hour."

The assistant DA nodded silently. "Now you can stand."

"Thank you," Dan said, moving his chair out and stretching his still cuffed arms upward.

The assistant DA finished another lap around the table slowly. Dan continued to stretch. "The judge wanted me to pass one more message to you."

"What's that?"

The assistant DA's knee hit Dan's testicles with the punch of a mule kick and Dan crumbled onto the table, bent over, and then fell to the floor.

"That is from both of us."

—

The assistant DA exited the room and Detective Wallace peered in the doorway to see Dan in the fetal position near the leg of the table.

The assistant DA looked back at Dan and then locked eyes with Detective Wallace. "He is free to leave. He's requesting the services of a sketch artist before he departs. I suggest you supply it. When he is done, return his belongings and show him the door."

CHAPTER 26

—

Motel Fifty had lost its name, the last knuckle on its grip on the past and the glory days of decades prior. The seventies had been a heyday—free sex, drugs, and political conversation in the buff for anyone with the wherewithal to pull into the modest parking lot and find the party in one of the rooms. But everything gave up the ghost eventually, and Motel Fifty had hung on longer than any reasonable hippie from back in the day could have expected. Surviving in the shadows of high-rise apartments and office buildings that had sprouted up in the Arlington corridor between Ballston and Rosslyn, most of the yuppies who now called that particular stretch of land home had never heard of Motel Fifty. For the patrons of yesteryear, the new name, Iwo Jima Motel, was an insult to patriotism.

Dan sat in the driver's seat while Sue took aim with the camera.

"OK. Let's run through a few things. How long in advance do you stakeout a location?"

"Depends."

"On what?"

"The surroundings."

"What do these surroundings tell you?"

Sue turned her head over each shoulder. "For surveillance, it sucks."

"Why?"

"Well, the parking lot is U-shaped, surrounded on three sides by the motel. All the doors and windows for the motel rooms face the parking lot."

"Which can be a benefit."

"Sure. Probably not going to miss anyone coming or going, but if they're paying attention, they aren't likely to miss you either."

"All true. Good. What else?"

"Behind us we have the relentless flow of Route 50. Good for an escape route, I guess."

"Potentially good as a diversion as well."

"I don't follow."

"The human eye is drawn towards movement. So if we're sitting in a still car, with movement behind us, it is likely we'll be overlooked for movement in the scenery to our rear."

"I hadn't thought of that."

"Which is why I mentioned it. What about surveillance cameras? How many are there?"

Sue looked around, eyes darting. "I count two, one on each end of the building."

"There are six," Dan replied. "The two you saw, another on the light post to the right, and three more on the apartment on the hill behind the motel, though it may be too far to render detailed images."

Sue counted all the cameras with her own eyes. "Well, there is nothing wrong with your eyesight."

"Are you saying there is something wrong with the rest of me?"

Sue put the digital SLR camera to her eye to stifle her response. Dan watched as the lens zoomed and focused.

"What are you doing now?"

"Just getting used to the equipment."

"You should get acquainted with the equipment before the mission."

"Standard operating procedure?"

"Common sense. You don't want to be sitting in a parked car with a camera to your eye any longer than absolutely necessary. And you sure as hell don't want to try to get comfortable with a firearm when the time comes for you to use it."

Sue acknowledged the statement and then continued her observations. "You know, with this camera I can see into the apartments beyond the hotel pretty clearly. This parking lot, on the other hand, is so close to the motel rooms we could use one of those ten dollar instant cameras from 7-11."

"It's not an ideal location. In a perfect world, we would be in one of the rooms, shooting through the blinds. But the layout of the motel doesn't allow it. The suspect could get a room on the same side, hell, even in the next room, and we wouldn't have a clear shot."

"A hotel room *would* be better," Sue said before realizing how it sounded.

Dan looked at Sue and then glanced away. "Keep your eyes open. Ten minutes until showtime."

"What are we looking for?"

"A single individual checking into a room. Followed by a second individual arriving by car, knocking, and then entering the same room. And I have twenty bucks that says the first person seems a little suspicious."

"Let's up the ante another twenty bucks and I say that same someone will be wearing a wedding ring."

"I'm not touching that bet."

—

The first car arrived at precisely two. A man with a brimmed hat and beige jacket moved quickly from his car to the motel office. A minute later he climbed the external stairs, disappeared for a split second as the staircase turned, and the reappeared on the balcony that surrounded the establishment. Without looking around, the man slipped the card key into the door of the first room near the corner.

"I didn't get a good shot," Sue said. "He didn't look in this direction."

"Almost like he knew we were here," Dan replied somberly.

"They rent rooms by the hour?"

"Depends on management," Dan said, before breaking off the conversation. "Check it out."

A scene unfolded through the car's windshield. A taxi with DC tags pulled into the far corner of the parking lot, away from the motel office. A bleached blonde popped from the back seat and paid the driver.

"Why do guys always go for blondes?" Sue asked, flipping her brown hair before snapping successive pictures in action mode.

"Not always. Sometimes we can't choose," Dan replied, nodding back in the direction of the cab.

A brunette appeared from the far door and Sue let out a small gasp. "Are you kidding me? It is a Wednesday afternoon. Does anyone work these days?"

"Two of them *are* working," Dan corrected.

Sue continued depressing the shutter button as the women climbed the external staircase and entered the same room the man had entered minutes before. The door shut and Sue set the camera in her lap. "Now what?"

"We give them five minutes."

"Why five?"

"Long enough to get down to business, but not so long as they might finish. These girls get paid by the hour, but the customer can only do what he can do."

"It should be a once-and-done rule."

"A once-and-done rule?"

"You get one shot. Once your gun is unloaded, the transaction is complete."

"But there are two girls."

"Fair point," Sue conceded. "One shot per girl."

"The guy probably popped a couple Viagra on the ride over. Wants to get his money's worth."

"Men are pigs."

"Not all men. And those who are, well, are just victims of their DNA. Men are like gorillas, bred to have a harem and to spread their seed to as many flowers as they can, so to speak."

"Pigs."

"Within society and its rules, men could be classified as pigs. But from an evolutionary standpoint, we are just doing what we're programmed to do."

"That's bullshit. If I had a dollar for every man who blamed their lack of fidelity on faulty hard-wiring, I would be a rich woman."

"So young, yet so cynical."

Dan checked his watch and scanned the parking lot. Sue kept her eye on the door through the lens of the camera.

"Time to go. This is how it works. We are going up the same stairs everyone else went up. The stairs are in the corner and, luckily, close to the room if an expedient exit is required."

"Is an expedient exit a possibility?"

"Anything is possible. At no time are you to get between me and the john. Is that understood?"

"Why?"

"Because I said so. I am your line of defense. That line should not be breached. You remain behind me and take pictures. If I have to use your name, I will call you Betty. You can call me Bob."

"Betty and Bob," Sue confirmed.

"Here is your situational reminder. If there is trouble and I tell you to get the hell out of here, you will not argue. Come down to the car, get in, and drive away. I don't care where you drive. There will be no questions asked."

"All right," Sue said, sounding concerned and annoyed at the same time.

Dan lowered the driver's window and left the key in the ignition. "Ready?"

"Hell yeah."

—

Sue followed Dan up the stairs and stopped at the corner on the edge of the second floor. Dan flashed his palm for Sue to stop and headed down the exterior balcony to the first door. He knocked loudly once and then pushed open the unlocked door.

The blonde from the cab was standing in front of the mirror, primping, lipstick in hand, lips pouting, breast exposed. She flashed a look of surprise, her mouth open but muted. Beyond the blonde, the brunette straddled the man on the bed. Startled, the man swiftly pushed the brunette off his midsection and the woman bounced once on the mattress and thudded gently against the wall. Dan could hear Sue taking pictures to his rear.

The man on the bed lunged for his pants, which were hanging over the edge of a wooden chair. Dan stepped further into the room and kicked over the chair.

Sue entered deeper into the room, snapping photos like a paparazzi. The blonde escaped into the bathroom and fumbled with her blouse. The brunette gathered her clothes from the foot of the bed and stood facing the corner of the room away from the camera. Her fingers danced through snaps, zippers, and lace.

The man rolled from the bed, naked, soldier at half-mast, and threw a left elbow. Dan stepped back a few inches and the second hardest bone in the body flew by harmlessly. Dan kicked the back of the man's leg and the man went down in a pile of flapping flesh onto the floor.

"Relax," Dan said.

"Fuck you," the man replied, grappling at Dan has he stumbled to stand. Dan grasped an outreached hand and twisted the thumb back and upward. The man rose to his tiptoes. They were now face-to-face, one with a distinct situational advantage.

"Are you Alex?

The man grimaced, his weight at the mercy of Dan's grip, his thumb stretched to its natural limit.

"Yes, and you are?"

"Trouble, for you. If I don't hear what I want."

The blond exited the bathroom as presentable as an office secretary on her lunch break. The brunette turned away from the corner, her display of professional speed dressing complete.

Dan looked over at the women near the dresser. "Ladies, if you don't mind, Alex and I have some business to attend to."

The women gathered their pocketbooks from the dresser and Sue moved from her position in the doorway, edging into the room in the direction of Dan, keeping her boss between her and the man in the nude. Over his shoulder, Sue continued to take pictures until Dan said, "I think you have enough."

Dan nodded at the women as they silently slipped out the door.

Dan changed his grip on the man's thumb, moving to manipulate the wrist. He kicked the man's pants off the floor and onto the bed. He noticed a wedding ring on the man's finger and motioned towards Sue. "Looks like you would have won your bet."

Dan released his grip on the man's hand and pushed him onto the bed, next to his pants.

"It's not what it looks like," Alex said.

"I'm sure it's not. But I'm not so sure your wife will see it that way."

"My wife?"

"For starters."

"What do you want?"

"I need your help. And obviously, you need mine."

Alex muttered something under his breath and Dan's eyes widened.

"*You speak Russian?*" Dan asked in Russian with a Muscovy accent.

"*I am Russian,*" the man replied in his native tongue.

Dan felt the air rush from his lungs. "Russian?" Dan asked, switching back to English.

"Yes, asshole," Alex answered.

A silence fell over the room. Dan stared hard at the man for a moment. The man's barrel chest heaved, his blue eyes measuring. "Betty, you need to leave," Dan said.

Sue didn't move.

"Betty, you need to leave," Dan repeated.

Again Sue didn't move.

Alex interrupted. "Young lady. I think the gentleman is referring to you by a cover name. You are Betty. I think he would like you to leave."

Dan didn't flinch. "Leave now. I will catch up with you later."

"I assure you, the girl is in no danger in this room," Alex said coolly.

"Out," Dan said forcefully, and Sue hurriedly exited.

Dan stepped back towards the dresser and reached back for the man's wallet without taking his eyes off the target seated on the bed. He pulled the license from the wallet and held it up between himself and Alex, looking back and forth at the man and the photo. "Alexander Stoyovich."

"Not who you were expecting, I take it," Alex said somewhat gleefully, pants still lying next to him on the bed.

"Maybe, maybe not."

"A fishing expedition, perhaps," Alex said, more relaxed.

Dan's mind raced back to Haley and the conversation they'd had—before the throes of passion, the heated clutches of lust intensified by the illumination of the city lights in the distance.

"Perhaps you would care to share a drink?" Alex asked, motioning towards the round table near the wall. A vodka bottle was open, three glasses neatly arranged near the center of the table.

"Put on your pants, then stand, then move," Dan said. "Slowly."

Alex did as he was told. "In the chair," Dan ordered as he stepped towards the man's rear.

Alex sat.

"Arms straight out," Dan said. From his vantage point behind his target, he looked at both of Alex's arms briefly. "Left arm across your chest."

Alex again followed orders and Dan quickly pulled several zip ties from his pocket. He grabbed Alex's left hand and attached it to the right armrest of the chair, crossing Alex's arm across his body.

Dan stepped back and moved deliberately to the chair on the other side of the table. He positioned the chair far enough from the table to react quickly to anything his new comrade may try.

Dan poured a glass of vodka for Alex and motioned for him to drink first.

"You don't trust me?"

"I see lipstick on one of the glasses here, but not on the other two. There were two women here, one of them with thick red lipstick, so it is possible that someone hasn't been partying. I'm just being cautious."

Alex downed the large shot of vodka with his free right hand. "You are not a professional."

"I'm sorry?" Dan asked, pouring another shot for Alex and one for himself. He swapped glasses with Alex and gave the man one of the other two on the table.

"You have been trained, but you are not operations. Not officially sanctioned."

Dan nudged the edge of the large shot glass with his finger. "How can you be sure?"

"Nothing is for certain in this life. Probably not in the next life either," Alex replied, sliding his glass towards his side of the table. "You move as someone who has been trained. Yet you lack the air of a clandestine operative. You pay attention. Make the suspect drink first, then use the suspect's glass as your own in case the other glass has been compromised. The use of zip ties, which you applied to my dominate hand."

"There was a faint tan line on the right wrist, and few people wear watches on their dominate hand."

"A basic trick of the trade."

Dan raised his glass and gave a traditional Russian toast.

Alex responded in kind and both men downed their glasses.

"The girls work for you?" Alex asked.

"No. They don't."

"But they knew you were coming. The blonde left the door unlocked. Very sloppy on my part."

"She knew I was coming. But I have never met her before."

"I think I'm going to have to take this up with the girls' management."

"The girls are sole proprietors now. Their employer is dead. Passed away earlier this week."

"And she was a friend?"

"Yes."

"And the reason you speak Russian?"

"No, I knew Russian before I met her."

Alex nodded towards the vodka bottle on the table and Dan filled two more glasses.

"To your friend, and a fellow Russian," Alex said, pouring the vodka into his mouth.

"You work for the Russian embassy?" Dan asked.

"And if I said yes . . . ?"

"Then perhaps you can still help."

"Why would I help you? You just ruined my afternoon. My only true enjoyment all week. Afternoon vodka and female entertainment."

"Perhaps we can help each other."

"What are you looking for?"

"Information."

"On what?"

"Let's say intelligence-related information."

"Ha. You barge into my room, chase out my entertainment, and then think I'm going to turn over information on my country? Certainly you cannot expect me to hand over intelligence without some form of reciprocation?"

Dan filled both glasses with another round of vodka. "Who said anything about *your* country?"

Alex leaned back in his chair, as far as his restraints would let him. Then he began to laugh, his hairy chest bouncing up and down with each bellow.

"Now you are the one with his pants on the floor!" The laughing reached a crescendo and Dan almost thought it was an act. "I see. I see. It is all clear to me. Yes! You came here based on information that you would find an intelligence officer in a compromising situation. But you didn't know you would find a *Russian* intelligence officer."

Alexander began laughing harder, which turned into deep-rooted gasps.

"That is correct," Dan said, relenting.

Alexander downed another shot and motioned for a refill. "You know, many years ago, on my first tour of duty here in DC, before your country allowed us to build our Embassy on the highest spot in the entire city, I met another American with a request similar to yours."

"Really?"

"Yes. She was a high school student."

"I can hardly wait for the punch line."

"There is no joke, so there is no punch line. We received a letter from a high school student who was doing a report on the CIA. This girl was trying to find information on the Agency, and well, before the Internet and FOIA requests, this information was hard to come by. It was quite a surprise, I must say, the request from this girl. We sent an agent out to follow her for a few days, to verify that she was indeed just a high school student doing a report. Her mother was a housewife and her father was an architect for Fairfax County Public Schools. I met with my supervisors at the time, we went over the letter and decided to help the girl out. To have a little fun with our adversaries."

"About a month later, the girl sent us an article from her school paper. Prominently displayed on the front page of the school paper was her article on the CIA, complete with the stats we had provided. The general structure of the organization. The major subgroups. The estimated number of employees. The annual budget. Square foot of the headquarters. Associated buildings.

"We all had a laugh. It was good for business. I mean, there was no real harm being done. The CIA had to know that we knew this information, or at least that we could make an educated guess."

"A good story."

"Indeed." Alexander caressed the shot glass with his free hand. "This is not about my country?"

"No. This is personal."

"Personal with the CIA?"

"Yes."

"You realize the CIA is not a person."

"I am aware of this."

"How does a person who is not in intelligence get involved with the CIA?"

"I lost someone very close to me. I have reason to believe the CIA is involved."

"Tell me more."

"I have told you enough already."

"I will decide when you have told me enough," Alex said, gaining confidence and growing more at ease. "You want information, you provide information." Alex raised his chin and slightly flicked his middle finger against the side of his throat, indicating he wanted more vodka. Dan filled the glass.

"Now, tell me who did you lose?"

"My nephew."

Alex looked at Dan, approximated his age, and did the math. "A teenager?"

"Yes."

"How old was he, exactly?"

"A sophomore in college. Nineteen."

"Where was he killed?"

"Here in DC. It was made to look like an accident."

"Hmmmm. The Central Intelligence Agency involved in the killing of a nineteen-year-old US citizen on US soil . . ." Alex stared off into space and hummed to himself. A moment later his mind returned. "And what leads you to believe the CIA is involved?"

"A missing phone call."

"Phone systems are imperfect. In Russia, outside the large cities, more often than not."

Dan didn't reply.

Alex continued. "There is something else to your story. Something you don't want to tell me."

Dan paused and slowly rotated the shot glass on the table in a circle. "My nephew was rare."

Alex closed his eyes and hummed the opening of a traditional Russian song. He opened his eyes slowly at the end of the first verse. "Your nephew . . . this young man . . . I have two questions about him."

"Shoot."

"I am without my weapon."

"Funny. Ask your questions."

"My first question is this: How rare was he? How rare was this nephew of yours?"

"Exceptionally."

"Unquantifiably rare?"

"Some have said."

"And should he have already been dead?"

Dan froze. "Sorry?"

"Statistically speaking, had he exceeded his life expectancy?"

Dan swallowed. "That is my understanding. But there is no way you could have known that."

"Ha! Americans! You think you have a monopoly on knowledge and good ideas."

"I'll try to keep that in mind."

"Let me offer you some advice. Free advice. I want nothing in return. Perhaps you should focus on celebrating your nephew's life, not being consumed by his death. I doubt I will outlive my life expectancy. And given your mere presence here, and your inquiry, I highly doubt you will outlive yours."

"I will celebrate my nephew's life when I am done with the task at hand."

Alex stared intently at Dan, who returned the glare. Alex spoke first. "There is something enjoyable about watching your enemy writhe in agony, even if it is not at your own hand."

"Then you will help?"

"It is not in my best interest to provide direct assistance."

"What if your wife were to find out what transpired here in this hotel with your pay-by-the-hour friends?"

"My dear comrade. My wife passed away many, many years ago. Before you started to shave. My only wife now is a cover wife, and my only marriage is to my country. I can retire at any moment. There is nothing you can threaten me with here."

"You said you cannot not directly help," Dan said, changing tactics, carefully reading the agent and repeating his choice of words.

Alex stared at the light coming through the crack in the curtains. "I have spent most of my life recruiting Americans to spy on America. It is not hard. Particularly if you can identify an American without religion. Atheists are fertile soil. Agnostics even work in most cases. No fear of retribution. No fear of hell. Not scared by damnation. They are only concerned with this life. Money. Power. Thrills."

"I am looking for revenge."

"What else do you know about the people you pursue?"

"I know one of them is white. My height. Maybe a little taller. Well dressed. Perfect teeth, hair, shoes."

"You have met him."

"Yes."

"Let me see the sketch."

"How do you know I have a drawing?" Dan asked, his hand

subconsciously moving slowly towards the envelope in his cargo pants pocket.

"Experience."

Dan removed the envelope and pulled out the sketch. He placed it on the table and took another shot of vodka. Alex stared at the drawing intently, slowly digesting the possibilities of the face on the paper. He mentally removed the glasses and shaved the goatee. He altered the hair color and imagined smaller teeth. "Appearances can be changed."

"Indeed. But he cannot alter everything. And regardless of what he looks like, he cannot discard his core. This guy likes order. He is anal. His dress, hygiene, demeanor."

"You are describing half of the espionage world. Order keeps agents alive."

"I will know him when I see him."

"And all you need is to know who he is."

"Or where he is."

Alex thought hard. "Very well. I know someone who can help your particular situation. But you are going to have to work for it. I am not going to just hand everything over to you on a silver platter. You want to play the espionage game, time to lose your training wheels. Everyone you are playing this game with has a head start."

"So I am learning."

"And another thing. This person you are going to meet, he will not come cheap. He will cost you. As he costs us."

"How do I reach this person?"

"Pen and paper."

Dan glanced around the room and retrieved a small motel pad and pen by the phone on the dresser.

"Ready?"

"Yes."

"His name is Benny. He works at Langley. HQ. On weekends and some weeknights, he can be reached in the trailer in the rear parking lot next to the Sears in Seven Corners. He can point you in the right direction. Be sure to ask him about his skydiving adventure. It was most insightful."

Dan scribbled.

Alex smiled ear to ear. "But before we go, one more drink. To your enemies' enemies!" Both men threw their drinks back.

Dan stood, the liquor robbing him of some sharpness. "I assume you will be able to get out of your constraints," Dan said, moving towards the door without taking his eyes off Alex.

"I will be free before you reach your car," Alex replied. "But I may sit here for a while. I have the room for another hour. Maybe there is a European hockey game on cable."

"Goodbye, Alex."

"Good luck."

CHAPTER 27

—

Dan drove through Bailey's Crossroads, once home to a circus as designated by a small historical sign in the parking lot between Old Navy and Office Depot. Bailey's Crossroads, a simple intersection in a former life, had long since been replaced with a concrete overpass and an octopus of on-ramps. The stables for the circus animals were now a string of funky strip-mall shops hosting a selection of ethnic restaurants unseen outside of Brooklyn. As Dan drove, hundreds of hopeful but illegal immigrants swallowed the land around the Culmore Post Office, the threshold to the neighboring sea of brick apartments unsafe for US citizens without employment opportunities to offer.

A mile up the road from Bailey's Crossroads was Seven Corners, a transportation nightmare evident by name alone. A handful of cities in the US sport intersections named "five corners," and as insulting as they are to commuters' sensibility, the intermingling of five roads was *almost* understandable. But when the discussion of Seven Corners crept into a department of transportation development meeting decades ago, a group of presumably hung-over men were rumored to have just nodded in agreement. Seven intersecting pieces of multi-lane asphalt at a single point wasn't *that* many.

Dan's eyes darted between the merging and unmerging lanes of traffic. Dozens of pedestrians, some with strollers, added to the skills challenge. Dan turned left on Patrick Henry Drive and then took the service road between a closed bank and a black-and-white office building designed in the seventies and now begging for an update. Signs for a travel agency and nail salon, long since shuttered, clung to the façade. A banner indicating twenty thousand square feet of available leasing space flapped from the top floor.

Behind the building, and adjacent to the backend of the Sear's parking lot, Dan found the first clue indicating he was on the right path. A white van with a hand-done paint job spelled out a single word, emblazoned down the side of the vehicle in red and blue. An arrow pointing towards the back of the lot was the final piece of directional guidance.

Dan drove towards an old brown trailer and parked near a half-dozen other cars at the edge of the lot.

The roof of the trailer was covered in pine needles. Leaves were matted to the roof, the first stage of decomposition underway. Near the front door of the trailer stood an inoperable barber's pole. An unplugged orange extension cord disappeared behind a piece of plywood on the skirt on the trailer.

Dan opened the door and the barber shop paused for one full beat before resuming its natural atmosphere. Six cushioned chairs with metal frames lined the wall. To the right, a silver-haired senior citizen read a fishing magazine. In the far corner another man napped, his head nodding slightly, a shallow, throaty breath escaping with each exhale. Dan grabbed a seat to the left of the door. Another man in a green sweatshirt stood and walked to the magazine rack, expertly pulling a *Playboy* from the back of the top shelf where it was hidden from view for those not in the know. *A real barber shop*, Dan thought.

The lone barber finished with the patron in the chair and slapped the open leather seat with his apron. "Who's next?" The sleeping man in the corner sprung to life and filled the chair. The departing patron peeled off two twenty dollar bills and slipped them to the barber, whispering into the barber's ear as the register opened and closed. As the patron left, the barber grabbed a pencil and put a single mark on a small notebook near the register.

Dan read through *Car and Driver* while he waited for the fishing enthusiast and boob aficionado to get their haircuts. When *Playboy* left, Dan stood.

Benny the barber greeted the newcomer to his establishment. "Haven't seen you here before."

"Haven't been in here before."

"That would explain it."

"You know your pole isn't working," Dan added.

"Don't tell anyone. My wife might find out."

"I meant your barber pole."

"There's a short in the cord. The whole electrical system in this place needs to be updated. To fix the pole, I need someone young to crawl under the trailer and sort it out."

"I hope you mean someone younger than I am."

"Age is all a matter of perspective."

"Forget I mentioned it."

Benny the barber, sixty-five years old with only a strip of hair running around his head horizontally, prepared Dan for his haircut. He organized his scissors, thinning shears, and collar guard. He quickly washed his hands in the sink. "How do you like it cut?"

"A little off the top and over the ears."

Benny tightened the apron around Dan's neck and tugged. He pulled out his scissors, ran his comb through a thicket of hair and lopped off a small chunk. "You know the history of the barber pole?"

"Didn't know it had a history."

"Everything has a history. The red stripe on the barber pole represents blood, or more specifically blood-letting. Back in the day, barbers used to do more than just cut hair. Used to do a little bit of surgery, a little bit of blood-letting. Kept leeches in a bowl. Over time, as medicine evolved, or was invented, we were excused from our extra duties and focused on cutting hair. But the white and red on the pole represents blood and bandages. Back in the day, the bandages drying outside were an advertisement of sorts. Of course, the representation of blood is better than hanging actual blood-soaked towels in front of the shop."

"How long you been in the business?"

"Been a barber for forty years. There's not much I haven't heard about. Customers tell me things they wouldn't tell their psychologist. Haven't been surprised by a conversation, well, since can't remember when."

Hang on to that thought, Dan mused. "How's business?"

"I should be retired, but I am working more than ever."

"Recession-proof employment, I would think."

"True and false. A man can only go so long between cuts. Eventually we all start to look shaggy. Unless you permanently solve that problem through natural hair follicle reduction, as I have done. The trouble with being a barber these days is different. Used to be that a bad back, a stooped posture, and sore feet were your main worries. Nowadays, old guys like me, we are being replaced by Asian women who charge half of what we charge. Six, eight, ten of these women will work in a barbershop. Hell, they'll live together too. You get a haircut and a massage. Probably more if you ask for it."

"You mean I'm not getting a massage today?"

"No. And the competition also means I have to cut more heads to make the same income. Been working weekends and nights, off and on."

Fifteen minutes later the conversation lulled as Benny the barber spun Dan in his chair and showed him the results. "Looks good. Looks like you've done it before."

"I figure I've given between twenty and thirty thousand haircuts over the last forty years."

"You are good with math."

"I do all right."

"Are the numbers being kind to you?"

Benny looked up into the mirror as he undid the apron around Dan's neck. Dan smiled in the reflection.

"Not sure what you mean."

"Well, two of the last three patrons handed you forty bucks. Being that a haircut is only fifteen, according to the sign over the register, it seems a little steep. Even with a tip."

"They didn't pay last time and were covering their tab."

"Maybe. Maybe. But then again, maybe you are running numbers. College football. Pros. You take the bets, maybe hand them off, but you get a cut."

"I think you misunderstood what occurred."

"And I think you have misunderstood my intention. How much is a three-game parlay."

"A three-game what?"

"A three-game parlay. NFL only. I have a hundred to spend."

Benny the barber went to the door to the trailer and locked the knob. He turned around and Dan had moved from his chair, flanking the barber.

"Grab a seat," Dan said. "Alex the Russian sent me. We are going to have a chat."

Benny eyed his scissors next to the sink on the counter behind the chair.

"No chance," Dan said flatly. "Have a seat."

Benny moved slowly and flopped into his own chair.

"Tell me about Alex the Russian."

"I think I saw a character by that name on TV. In a cartoon. He drives around town in a car that doesn't work very well, eats a lot of caviar, and drinks vodka straight from the bottle."

"No, he is a Russian intelligence officer and he told me you could provide certain information for a fee. You want to hear the recording of the conversation?"

Benny's pupils tightened slightly and that was all the confirmation Dan needed.

"You can talk to me, or I can turn your traitor ass in. Make myself a hero."

"Hypothetically speaking, you could turn me in anyway. After you get what you want."

"Possibly. That is a conversation I have every week with assholes like you. I'll tell you what I tell them—it is a chance you'll have to take."

"Maybe. But, if you *only* wanted to turn me in, you already would have. So what else do you want?"

"Just a little off-the-record discussion on someone I'm looking for."

"Go ahead. Ask whatever you have in mind. It doesn't mean I will answer. For all I know, *you* could be a foreign agent."

"I can tell you the score of every Super Bowl since 1978 and can tell you where I was when I watched it. No foreign agent would bother with that info."

"Super Bowl sixteen. You have five seconds."

"Played in 1981. 49ers vs. Miami. 49ers won 26-21. Joe Montana was the MVP of the game. The game was played in the Pontiac Silverdome, Pontiac, Michigan. I watched the game in Cape Town, South Africa. Kickoff was 1:20 a.m."

"Proves nothing."

"How long have you worked at the CIA?"

Benny didn't reply.

"Let's not make this difficult. Alex said you work at Langley. At HQ. A little confusing at first, I must admit. But I watched you in here while I sat over there reading my magazine. You are a barber. No question about it. It could be a cover, but I don't think so. Maybe a cover for a day. But not for forty years. You have calluses on your fingers. You can't stand up straight. Neck bends forward. You wield those professional-grade scissors on automatic pilot. You have put in the time behind the chair. Swept mountains of hair. So the way I figure it, you are a barber. But you also work at the CIA."

"I am contractually bound to silence. I can't discuss where I work."

"How about being bound to a cell? No windows."

"You know, as you get older, you will find the thought of prison is not as repulsive as it was when you were younger. Not a federal prison anyway. Free retirement. Room and board covered."

"I'll take freedom. And as much as it revolts me to say this, I'm willing to pay you for information. Certainly if you accept payment from a Russian, you would accept payment from an American for the same information."

A low groan, resembling a deflating balloon, escaped Benny's lips. His face slowly grimaced.

Dan pushed forward. "I can have the FBI here in a half an hour. You can try out your theory on the beauty of a federal penitentiary by the end of the year."

"If I did sell information, it would be expensive. I would doubt you could afford it."

"My expenses *are* soaring lately. And I need information today. What is the downside for you? Prison today or payment in, say, a week."

Benny stared downward and for a moment Dan thought the barber was going to cry. "I did it for the money. I didn't mean to betray my country."

"Well, you did. And you are going to do it one more time for the money. If you need to feel better about yourself, know that I will use the information to bring some form of redemption to our nation's clandestine services."

Benny took a deep breath before spilling the beans. "I have been working there for twelve years. Before that I worked at the Department of Energy. Prior to that a few private shops here and there. Usually some dingy corner of space next to the shoe shine guy. Same thing at Langley. I work in the basement. I'm not sure what floor."

"You're not sure?"

"No windows, much like prison. Inside the building, I take a service elevator that has no numbers on the buttons. I press the third button from the bottom, on the right hand side. The elevator moves at variable speeds. The variable speed of the elevator makes it difficult to figure how many floors up or down you have moved."

"I assume the elevator eventually opens."

"Yes. There is a camera in the elevator. Once I step out of the elevator, I am contained. I have a two-seat shop on a floor with plain white walls and a light blue tile floor. There is a bathroom at the end of the hall and an emergency staircase, which I have never used. There is another camera and guard on the floor."

"So you are a civilian employee."

"Correct. I am not employed by the CIA. I merely work in the building, providing a service for their employees."

"And you run numbers."

"Let's assume I did."

"Do you get polygraphed?"

"Every year."

"How do you pass? Gambling is a red flag."

"I had a retired FBI agent as a customer for years. He was a polygraph operator. Over the years, we talked about how to beat the machine."

"Rumor has it lots of people have beat the machine. Aldrich Ames. Karl Koecher. Ana Belen Montes. Leandro Aragoncillo."

"Yes, they have. Rule number one for passing a polygraph is to build rapport with the examiner. It calms you down. The second rule is to remember that the exam is only eighty percent accurate. That's why it's not admissible in court. People who are really nervous fail the test every time. Most people confess to things they shouldn't confess to. That, by the way, is the true magic of the polygraph. Belief that it will catch you and acting as if it will."

"So how did you meet Alex?"

"He walked through that door, just like you."

"And?"

"He asked some questions about one of my clients who had just left. I assume he had been following him."

"Did you know the customer?"

"I knew him from Langley. His face anyway. People at work don't tell me their names. They don't tell each other their names. These employees, they have multiple cover identities. They have their real name, their main work name, another name if they are using government credit cards, another name if they are working overseas. Another name if they are signing contracts. They have so many fucking names they don't know who they are working for. Add compartmentalization to that, and you get the idea. You could work with someone for a decade and never know you are working with them. Hell, I imagine there are cases of people reporting to themselves."

"So Alex came in and asked you about a customer of yours."

"I told him I couldn't help him."

"And then came the money?"

"He showed up a week later. Started spewing what he knew about me. He knew where I worked. Wanted to establish a business relationship, as he put it. Handed me a brown bag full of unmarked hundreds and fifties. I figured, what the hell, I don't know anything. I'm not in intelligence. Figured I would get paid for telling him nothing."

"And . . ."

"Once a month he would come to this shop around closing. He usually had a bunch of photos with him. He would ask me questions like 'Do you recognize this person?' 'Have you ever cut this guy's hair?' 'When was the last time you saw this person.' 'Has this person ever placed a bet with you?' Sometimes he would have multiple photos. He would ask if I ever saw certain people together."

"Anything else?"

"Most of the photos were from people in their cars. Face shots."

"Did he tell you what he was doing?"

"No, but it was pretty obvious. He was trying to figure out who was who. Data collection for identification purposes."

"And he wanted the gamblers because those were the people susceptible to blackmail."

"Not just the gamblers, though he did find particular interest in them."

"How many people did he ask about?"

"Thousands."

"Jesus."

"He was quite proficient."

"So it seems. Did you get paid the same amount every month?"

"Usually. On rare occasions he would bring extra. Tell me some of the information was particularly helpful."

"Can you help me find someone at the CIA?"

"Depends. Who are you looking for?"

Dan pulled out the sketch of Clyde Parkson. "Do you recognize him?"

"Not off hand."

"Look again. Imagine him without the glasses. Without the goatee. With crooked teeth. With no teeth."

Benny looked harder at the photo. "Not really. I don't know everyone. I mean, there are tens of thousands of people who work at Langley. Just count the parking spaces."

Dan looked at Benny and tried to assess whether or not the barber was lying. His human attempt at polygraph was no better than the electronic version being used at Langley. Benny the barber was stoic. His face unchanged. Dan noted perspiration beginning to soak the fabric near the barber's armpits.

"You have to consider that maybe Alex knows something I don't. Russians love to play games."

"Alex also used the word 'game.'"

"It's all a game. It's very real, don't get me wrong, but to the people playing, it is a game."

"Alex told me to ask you about your skydiving adventure."

"I see."

"Says you went with your son."

"I did."

"Where?"

"Manassas Regional Airport. It was one of those day courses. Spend a few hours in the classroom then they fly you up to thirteen thousand feet and you jump out of the plane in tandem with an instructor."

"And?"

"I almost shit myself. Tried to scream but nothing came out. Twisted my ankle on the landing. Never again. Told my son I would do it on my sixty-fifth birthday, if I lived that long. I did and I did. There is nothing else on my bucket list."

"When was this?"

"May the fifth. My sixty-fifth birthday."

"Cinco de Mayo. A good birthday. But I don't understand why that story is relevant to Alex."

"It was what occurred after the jump. The skydiving hangar is next to one of the private jet hangars. Quite by chance, on the day I celebrated my birth by risking death, I saw several Langley employees disembark from a private jet in front of one of these private jet terminals. I memorized the tail number of the jet, and that information Alex found very interesting."

"I bet he did. What kind of airplane?"

"A small jet. Nothing too big flies out of Manassas. It probably was a twelve-seater. Not much bigger for sure. Twin jets. Beige stripe on the plane."

"Anything else?"

"I got caught gawking a little."

"How is that?"

"Saw some of the people leaving on the other side of the terminal as we left. Two of the people who got off the plane locked eyes
with me in a way that gave me goose bumps. I wasn't breaking any
law or anything, so I wasn't too worried, but the glance was noted
and uncomfortable. I kept my feet moving. Walked to my son's car.
Got the hell out of there."

"Was the guy in the sketch one of the people on the plane?"

"No."

"You sure."

"Pretty sure. Nothing wrong with my vision."

"Do you remember the tail number on that plane?"

"Yes, I memorized it. And if you bring me ten thousand dollars
I will give it to you."

—

In the government-issue sedan parked in the Sears parking lot,
Reed Temple lowered the small pair of binoculars. He turned to
Major in the passenger seat. "Remind me again, why is this guy not
in jail?"

"We can't answer that," Major replied, glancing at Ridge in the
rear seat on the driver's side. "We pinned evidence of two murders
on him and he walked out of the DC correctional facility in a little
over an hour."

"He knows someone," Temple said flatly.

"Who?"

"I'm looking into it. This is a person with virtually no background and the ability to extricate himself from custody in less
time than it takes me to have a proper lunch. If I didn't know any
better, I would say he is in the intelligence field."

"Suggestions?"

"Terminate him."

"What about your superiors?" Major asked.

"I was considering a change of employer. Maybe joining the private sector. Do some consulting. I hear the money is good."

"The money is very good," Major agreed.

"Get it done. Set it up clean, run it clean."

"Yes, sir. Any preferences on method?"

"No."

"Freedom is good. Keeps the alternatives open."

"How long will it take you?"

"We should be able to devise and execute an appropriate head-count reduction alternative in twenty-four hours. Thirty-six at the most. It is our specialty, after all."

Reed Temple stroked his chin. "I think we could all use a haircut."

—

Benny the barber swept the floor a final time, his nerves rattled from Dan's visit. He finagled the large pile of hair into the dustpan with the bristles of the broom and emptied the contents into an open-top rubber trashcan.

Major knocked on the locked door and Benny replied, "Closed for the night," through the unopened blinds in the trailer window. Benny turned his attention to the till and opened the cash register drawer to count the take for the evening. The thick stack of twenties was welcomed. He counted the pile twice, removed a few off the top and put them in his wallet. He placed his wallet on the old table top next to the register and did a quick calculation in his head. He nodded several times and smiled with the realization that this evening's work was enough to cover a quarter of the monthly rent. The electric bill was an additional modest sum, covered mostly by tips. He would claim forty dollars on his income taxes. Cash only services had their advantage.

With more concentration, Benny ran his fingers across the tick marks on his small bookie notepad, each tick representing the wagers placed by customers. He tried to commit most of the bets to memory, translating his shorthand into meaningful information in his head. It was an exercise in prudence—keeping track of bets without recording explicit details that could lead to incarceration.

Engrossed by his favorite moment of the workday, Benny didn't notice the door lock being expertly picked until Ridge's shoulders cleared the door frame on his way into the trailer. Major pocketed his lock picking set as he followed Ridge across the threshold. Reed Temple brought up the rear, closing the door behind him with an authoritative thud and reconfirming the sealed exit with an additional tug on the knob.

Benny looked down at the doorknob, unsure of what had just occurred. He looked up at Ridge and over at Major as the ex-military professionals moved to opposite sides of the barber. Reed Temple stood in front of the closed door, his eyes meeting Benny's.

"Sorry gentlemen, I am closed. You can come back tomorrow evening."

"We are not here for haircuts," Major replied.

"What can I help you with?"

Reed Temple commandeered the conversation. "Have a seat," he replied, motioning for the barber to once again sit in his own chair. Benny complied, lowering himself slowly onto the old leather seat. "We want to know about the last customer who was here. The gentleman with the fresh wound above the left eyebrow."

"He was a walk-in. I have never seen him before. I don't know anything about him."

"How did he like it cut?"

"He asked for a little off the edges."

"You took your time for just a trim."

Benny the barber tried to wish away the sweat beads forming on his forehead. The moisture in his pits from the conversation with Dan had already started to spread, soaking a larger area of his shirt. He was feeling guilty and he understood where that emotion would lead if he couldn't rein it in.

"I gave him a trim. He was a talker. It may have taken longer than usual, but he was the last cut of the night and a potential new client. I didn't want to be rude. My livelihood depends on repeat customers."

"What did you talk about?"

"Nothing. Small talk. The history of the barber pole."

"You said he was a talker, and yet you talked about nothing . . ."

"Nothing important." Benny could feel the perspiration on his neck, dripping down the small of his back. Ridge and Major moved to the rear of the barber chair, pawing through the barber's tools of the trade that littered the counter area near the sink.

"Do I know you?" Reed Temple asked, squinting at the barber.

"I don't think so."

"You look nervous. We don't mean to make you nervous."

"Three guys coming through a closed door when you are counting the day's cash would make anyone nervous."

Reed Temple nodded. "The hours of operation on the door claim you are here in the evening and weekends. You don't work during the week?"

Reed Temple casually picked up Benny's wallet off the table next to the register and started flipping through his credit cards and IDs.

Benny's perspiration broke its remaining containment and a deluge of sweat poured out. The barber wiped at his forehead with his open palm and dried his hand on the leg of his pants. "I work at another location. It's common for barbers to work at multiple shops."

Reed Temple held up an ID card identifying Benny the barber as a contract civilian employee for a well-known building in Langley. He flipped the card between his fingers like a magician and stopped with the ID photo facing Benny, the barber's own picture reflecting in his pupils. Benny's face turned ashen, adding to the sheen of sweat to combine for an unhealthy complexion.

"Ben Stenger."

"My friends call me Benny."

"Well, Benny. I'm going to give you one more opportunity to tell me about your last customer."

Benny the barber stammered, regained composure, and then spoke, spittle gathering in the corner of his mouth, his throat becoming dry.

"He was interested in wagering on football games."

"Are you a bookie, Benny?"

"I facilitate bets and get a cut."

"What else did he want?"

"That was it."

Reed Temple stepped forward and grabbed Benny's wrist. Benny tried to stand and Ridge's large hands came down on his shoulders with crushing strength, holding Benny firmly in his chair. Reed Temple closed his eyes and counted to ten.

"Your pulse is racing."

"Wouldn't yours?" Benny replied, glancing at the large paws digging into the flesh on his shoulders.

"Last chance, Benny. Last chance before something bad happens."

Tears welled in Benny's eyes. "OK. OK. He was looking for information on an airplane. An airplane at Manassas Airport. I told him to come back with ten thousand dollars and I would give him the tail number."

Reed Temple stared into Benny's eyes. The barber's wet shirt was glued to his chest, sweat permeating every thread of the fabric.

"Don't you feel better?" Reed Temple asked. "The relief of getting that off your chest."

Benny didn't respond.

Reed Temple nodded at Major, who was at the small sink to the rear of the barber's chair. Major pulled the plunger to the closed position and slowly turned on an equal amount of warm and cold water. The water pooled in the bottom of the sink and began its slow rise upward.

"Benny, I can understand how three strange men entering your shop at closing time would cause you angst. To alleviate your anxiety, I am going to step out and leave you with my associates."

Benny the barber turned just as Ridge's massive forearm moved over his head and around his throat.

"I'll be in the car," Reed Temple said to Major as he exited the trailer, closing the door behind him. Ridge rotated the barber chair, using Benny's neck as a lever. When the chair stopped spinning, he was looking up at Major, his face a partial reflection in the mirror. Major turned the handles on the faucets and the water stopped flowing, the water level an inch below the edge of the sink. Major picked up a pair of worn scissors and rapidly opened and shut them with his thumb and middle finger.

"Nice scissors."

"Expensive, too," the barber said. "You can have them."

Major slipped them into his pocket and smiled. "I was planning on keeping them." Major moved over to the far side of the counter and picked up a hair dryer. He slowly moved from the far end of the counter to the sink and plugged the hair dryer into the socket over the mirror.

"You really need to be careful at work," Major said, turning the hair dryer on and then flicking it off. Sharp objects. Water. Electrical equipment."

Moments later, the lights in the trailer flickered off and Ridge and Major walked out the front door of trailer, locking the door behind them and wiping the knob.

CHAPTER 28

—

Dan squinted at the light in the art studio and rang the buzzer on the front door. A heavy rain translated into light weeknight street traffic. The slickened cobbled brick sidewalk hosted a few fast-moving locals and a smattering of leisurely tourist on their way to no place in particular. The air had turned cooler and Dan saw his breath for the first time this season.

Dan pressed the door buzzer for a second time and Lucia finished adding an entry into her leather-bound accounting journal. She stood and stretched behind her massive stone desk and then walked to the front door of the gallery. Levi the dog raised his head as Lucia passed by.

Dan waved through the glass as Lucia smiled and pulled the left half of the double door open. She was dressed in a white painter's smock, the colors from the day's trial-and-error with cubism dried to her sleeve. She looked at Dan's face and immediately winced at the wound hiding in his eyebrow.

"Come on in. You look like hell."

"I feel better than I look."

"What happened?"

"I had a run-in with some criminals. Or criminals-to-be."

Lucia stood on her toes and touched the skin just above Dan's eyebrow. "You probably need stitches, if you want it to heal properly."

"I don't care enough."

"You might later, and by then it will be too late."

"I think it makes me look tougher."

"I think it shows you are slow."

"Ouch."

"Call it like I see it."

Dan looked over Lucia's shoulder at the large new painting on the wall. Streaks of colors rained across the canvas diagonally, as if the brilliance of autumn leaves had been smudged across the wall.

"Foliage?"

"Shooting stars."

Wrong again.

"You are starting to hurt my feelings. You haven't guessed one right yet," Lucia added.

"You still arranging things in the gallery?"

"Just a little. Moving some of the smaller pieces to the back of the shop so that customers will be forced to pass the more expensive, larger pieces."

"Thinking like a businesswoman."

"Read it in a magazine."

Dan pointed to a smaller painting on a corner table. "I think I have a shot at deciphering that one. It is clearly a dock of some sort."

"A fishing dock. I was experimenting with realism."

"I have been experimenting with that my whole life."

"We have an art show this weekend down the street at the Torpedo Factory. You should stop by."

"I may just do that."

"Oh, you got a package. It's on the other side of the door. Someone dropped it off late this afternoon. That front door of yours confuses more people."

"A little confusion is good," Dan added. "Where is Levi?"

"I don't know. He was here."

"Levi," Dan yelled. Three sharp barks in succession brought the hair on Dan's neck to attention.

Dan peered around the corner and found Levi sitting at attention. Levi looked up at Dan, raised his paw, and put it on the package that had been delivered to the shop. He barked three more times in succession. Dan's bowels loosened and then time stood still.

Somewhere between hurling his body at Lucia and crashing onto the floor on the other side of the mammoth stone desk, the front of the gallery disappeared into a million shards of flying glass. Shrapnel ricocheted off the walls and smoke filled the room, drifting out the newly opened front entrance. Dan looked down at Lucia's crumpled body. Her chest heaved. Blood trickled from her left ear. Dan tried to stand, stumbled, and then succumbed to the darkness.

CHAPTER 29

—

Dan turned his head away from the bright ceiling lights as the neurons in his brain relearned their connections as part of the healing process. A deafening ring persisted in his ear, intermittent with a skull-thumping pulse that was threatening his sanity. The nicks and scrapes on his exposed flesh had been bandaged, the blood coagulated. Dan cranked his neck the other direction and found the dangling remote control to the hospital bed. He raised himself to a seated position and squinted at the wall-mounted TV.

Gradually, he moved his feet over the edge of the mattress and pulled back the curtain dividing the double-occupancy room. The next bed was empty. He tugged the curtain room divider to the wall, exposing the bathroom on the far side of the room. A streak of pain emanated from behind his right eye and Dan fumbled for the call button on the remote. Moments later a nurse appeared.

"I need more pain reliever."

"You are already at full dose. 800 mg of Ibuprofen. You refused stronger medication earlier, though I doubt you would remember."

"I usually take 800 mg of Advil after the gym."

"Well you shouldn't," the nurse replied. "It's rough on the kidneys." She grabbed the penlight and moved to Dan's bedside. "Turn this way. Look straight ahead."

Dan stared forward as the penlight flashed back and forth in front of his eyes like blinding windshield wipers.

"You have a concussion. You took quite a blow to the back of the head. You will have a lump and some discomfort for a while. But all things being equal, you are lucky. It could have turned out a lot worse."

"What time is it?"

"Early. Just after four in the morning."

"How was the woman who was brought in with me?"

"She will be fine."

Dan let out a sigh of relief.

"The police and fire chief want to speak with you. They have been waiting."

"I am sure they have."

"You want to talk to them now? I think they headed to the cafeteria, but I can have them paged. Or I can hold them off for a few hours. My medical prerogative."

"I'll take a couple hours of rest. Hold them off with a whip and a chair if you have to."

As the door shut behind the nurse, Dan pulled his butt off the mattress and stood. The loose-fitting hospital gown clung to his neck in a square knot. He looked under the hospital bed and removed the plastic bag from the shelf rack beneath the mattress. He poured the contents onto the wrinkled white sheets, fishing out his cell phone, keys, wallet, and pants. A mix of burnt wood, dust, and fire extinguisher spray wafted out of the bag.

Dan pulled on his pants and filled his pockets with his necessities. He located his shoes and flipped through the sheets looking for his socks. Ears still ringing, he didn't hear the two men enter the room until he glimpsed them in his peripheral vision. The first man to enter was older, more distinguished. Well-groomed and well-accessorized. An expensive suit to go with expensive leather shoes. Dark hair. Dark eyes. The second man was stuffed into a leather coat with no collar or visible indication of a neck.

"Dan Lord?"

"Depends on who's asking."

"Joseph Cellini."

Dan located his socks, sat down on the edge of bed, and pulled them on. "The name sounds familiar, but I can't picture the face." Dan dropped his shoes on the floor and jammed his feet into them. "And if you don't mind, I am in a hurry."

The man with the leather jacket was slowly working his way

to his right and Dan registered he was being flanked. He eyed both men and sent a request to his brain for a database search on his visitors.

"I am Lucia's father," Joseph Cellini replied, without elaboration.

Dan's thumping cranium digested the second part of the introduction. He had done a complete background check when Lucia had moved in and signed the lease, but the name Cellini was not in his memory banks.

"What was the last name?"

"Cellini."

"Lucia's last name is Messi."

"Her last name is Cellini. As far as *you* know, her last name is Messi."

Dan thought about the answer and his concussed mind chugged through the possibilities.

"How is she? The nurse mentioned she would be OK."

"She's going to make it. A broken arm, bruises. Things she will overcome. Injuries that will pass. Lucia tells me you tackled her before some kind of explosion tore the gallery apart."

"I did."

"You mind telling me you how you knew the place was about to blow?"

"Long story."

Joe Cellini nodded at his accomplice and the massive leatherneck took several steps back towards the door. He grabbed one of the two guest chairs in the room and wedged it between the edge of the doorframe and the wall.

"How about you tell me just the same," Cellini continued, hands together in front of him, fingers wringing.

The man's pose jarred Dan's subconscious mind and his brain generated a delayed response to the silent inquiry made moments before. "*Joey* Cellini."

The man in the suit nodded slightly. "I call myself Joseph. Sometimes Joe. The media bestowed the Joey moniker on me, in honor of all Sicilian first names ending in a 'y.'"

"Yeah, you guys definitely get a bad rap when it comes to names."

"So now you know who I am. And in turn I want to know a few things about you."

"Dan Lord. I have an office upstairs from Lucia's art gallery. I own the property."

"I'm aware you're the landlord. I'm curious about the bomb. More specifically, why you suspected there was one and who the fuck would try to kill you and hurt my little girl."

Uh-oh, Dan thought. "I had reason to believe there were explosives. Levi told me."

"The dog?"

"Is there another Levi?"

The massive leather jacket moved back in the direction of Dan with his own hand extended. Joseph Cellini waved him off with a flick of his wrist.

"Start explaining."

"I took the dog for walks on occasion. I usually watched the dog when Lucia was out of town or doing an exhibit. I liked the dog."

"You fucking my daughter?" Joey Cellini asked abruptly.

I would but I am not, Dan thought. "That is a 'no' on the daughter-screwing. The reason Levi alerted me is because I trained the dog to smell explosives."

"That old mutt?"

"He is old, but he isn't a mutt. Wasn't a mutt." A brief wave of sadness was washed away by a larger dose of piss and vinegar over Levi's demise.

"Any reason a normal person would teach an old mutt to smell for explosives?"

"The store was out of milk bones and I hate chew toys. Especially those squeaky ones."

"Danno, may I call you Danno?"

"No, you may not. Danno is reserved for only one person."

"Boyfriend?"

"Cute."

"Danno. I have a good sense of humor. Thick skin. My friend here, well, he is less jovial, shall we say."

"You looking to join the list of people trying to kill me?"

"I want an answer to the question. Why in the fuck would you teach an old mutt to smell explosives?"

"Well, if I didn't teach Levi to smell explosives, then you would be talking to a corpse right now. I mean, it seemed like a good idea when it first occurred to me, and now it seems like it was an even better idea."

"There are a lot of ways to die, Mr. Lord. Why would you think someone is going to blow you up?"

"I've made a few enemies."

"You're a lawyer, of course you have."

"I prefer legal consultant or legal advisor."

"OK. So instead of someone running you over with their SUV or—I don't know—maybe shooting you in the back of the head, you thought someone would take the time to get their hands on explosives, build a bomb, and kill you that way? And not only did you think it, you trained a dog to help you defend against it? Help me understand."

"It was an accident. An unplanned discovery. I took Levi for a walk one day. I usually take him a couple times a week."

"So you say."

"One day we're down by the river front, in the park, and Levi walks right up to this kid sitting in the grass, resting his arm on his backpack. He looks like he's waiting for someone, or maybe just hanging out. I don't think much about it until Levi walks up beside him and sits. Almost as if the dog was at attention. Then he lets out three crisp barks, scrapes his paw on the ground, and lies down. At first I ignored it, but then Levi wouldn't budge. He just sat there next to this kid with the backpack, barking and scratching at the ground with his paw. About this time, the kid starts breaking out in a sweat. He looks real uncomfortable. I figure maybe he doesn't like dogs. I try to reassure the kid Levi doesn't bite and I reach down to grab Levi by the collar and that is when I get my first big whiff of weed."

"A drug-smelling mutt."

"Exactly."

"My daughter owns a drug-smelling dog?"

"Make you nervous?"

"Careful, Danno."

"So, after this incident, I figure our mutt Levi had a history. I mean, Lucia got him from the pound so who knows where he really came from. Maybe his owner was an old cop who died. Maybe the dog didn't like the way he was being treated at home and ran away. There are a million possibilities. I called the animal shelter and they said Levi was found in Old Town with nothing but a dog tag with his name on it. At any rate, one thing was certain. Levi smelled something and was trained to respond."

"So how do you make the jump to explosives?"

"I figure, who knows what this dog was trained to do. So I bought some gun powder and sure enough Levi goes ape shit. After that, I got my hands on more formal explosives."

"How do you get your hands on explosives?"

"This is the USA. It's all made right here. Certainly you know how easy it is to come by."

Joseph Cellini ignored the implication. "Go on."

"That is pretty much it as far as Levi is concerned. I'm going to miss that dog."

"What is it exactly you do that would attract this kind of enemy?"

"I can't divulge that information."

"The fuck you can't. Let me tell you exactly what is going to happen. You are going to tell me everything I need to know about who could have possibly bombed my daughter's art studio. I want a list of suspects. I want names and addresses. If you can't figure out a likely suspect, then I want a list of all your clients and I will have my people go through the list and find suspects myself."

"Not going to happen. My files are very confidential. They are privileged information. And they are all right here," Dan replied raising a finger to his temple.

Joseph Cellini ignored Dan's rebuttal.

"Then, after you give me the names, you and I are going to talk money. I lost a lot of investment cash in that art gallery."

"The place is insured."

"Only if you can collect."

"What are you getting at? Didn't pay your bills?"

"Let me tell you a few things, smart guy. Number one, explosions are covered by insurance when some part of the house or building—like a water heater—blows up. When you start talking about bombs, well, that is a different story. Someone taking offense to your legal advisory skills and trying to remove your head with a special delivery may not qualify for an insurance claim. And then there is the matter of the investment money I have lost in the gallery."

"I'm listening."

"My daughter—God love her—always wanted to be an artist."

"She is an artist."

"Have you seen her work?"

"Yeah."

"What do you think?"

Dan became uncomfortable. "Art is not really my thing."

"It's awful. I know it. You know it. I look at some of these paintings and I don't see anything. Just colors. Shit, sometimes I can barely even see that."

That much we agree on, Dan thought. "They seem to be selling."

Cellini paused and looked back at the closed door. "They are selling because I am buying."

"You are buying your daughter's artwork?"

"Well, not under my real name. I pay to have others buy the art. I mean, it's not like I can buy it all and put it on the walls at my house. I have buyers who pose as art dealers and connoisseurs. People who are willing and able to do me a favor and buy artwork at top dollar from an artist in DC."

"Oh."

"Right. And one of the major calculations for insurance claims is . . ."

". . . fair-market value."

"And you can see where that may be trouble for insurance."

"Hard to determine fair-market value when the market is manipulated by one buyer. Probably even harder to collect an insurance claim for a man with your, uh, history. Not to mention it would raise some money laundering questions."

"You are a smart guy. I have customers who have ordered and paid for some of that artwork. I have a daughter who was almost killed. I spent enough money on renovations for that art gallery to buy a mansion. And I am going to have to sign another big check to fix it up again. I only think it's fair that the person responsible be held accountable. After all, they injured my daughter. They almost killed my only child."

Dan nodded. He didn't want to, but he understood.

"Maybe we can sit down and decide on some level of financial compensation. Maybe once we find the guys who tried to blow you up, they will feel compelled to agree with a reasonable monetary settlement. To right the wrong they have done. If not, then it is on you."

"Me? I was almost killed as well."

"You or the people responsible. Makes no difference."

"I can tell you this—the people who bombed the art gallery are not going to be around long enough to help out financially."

Dan and Joseph Cellini exchanged a long, deep stare. Dan looked away first, but not until he had seen a flicker of recognition in Cellini's eyes. A look of recognition indicating Cellini understood Dan was anything but just a lawyer.

Dan pulled the tattered t-shirt from the plastic bag. He shed the loose-hanging gown and stuck his head through the neck hole of his shirt.

"I will let you know when I find the guys you are looking for," Dan replied. "As for a financial settlement, I am a little pinched at the moment."

Joseph Cellini nodded at his side kick. Mr. Neckless stepped forward and grabbed Dan's shoulder. Dan stepped to the side, raised his right hand and trapped the big mitt against his own shoulder. In one fluid motion he brought his other hand over the arm he now controlled. He felt the bones, muscles, and tendons tighten. Mr. Neckless groaned and Dan drove him to the floor using his shoulder as the fulcrum. Dan looked over at Cellini.

"Let me see what I can find."

"I'm in town through this weekend. Before I head back, I want names and addresses and a way to get reimbursed. I don't care where the money comes from."

"I'll put you on the list." As the words rolled around in his concussed mind, Dan saw a potential solution to half his problems.

—

Dan muttered to himself as he walked through the sea of chairs and benches in the emergency waiting room. *The mafia. There goes another rule.* His head pulsated and he sat down in a worn brown chair just as the sliding glass doors to the emergency room opened. Dan watched as a team of paramedics pushed an accident victim across the tile floor on a large stretcher. Blood-soaked sheets dripped from a plethora of braces and tubes, the human subject hiding beneath the pile of life-saving paraphernalia. Dan made a phone call, spoke quietly for a minute, nodded several times, and then hung up.

As the commotion in the emergency waiting room quieted, Dan rubbed his temples and stood again, testing his internal gyroscope. Satisfied with his condition, he went outside, put one foot on a wooden bench, and made another call. Sue answered on the third ring.

"Where are you? You OK?" Dan asked.

"Yeah. Good thing I wasn't working late last night. I am here in the hospital. In the surgical waiting area on the north side of the first floor. I tried to get in to see you but the nurse's station wouldn't budge on visiting hours."

"I'm surprised that stopped you."

"It didn't. But the Alexandria police officer near the elevator in the hall was a little more persistent about honoring visiting hours."

"Apparently they only allow family members and *family members.*"

"What does that mean?"

"Nothing. Forget it. How did the office building look?"

"It needs some remodeling. It was all over the news. A dozen fire trucks and enough rescue equipment for a mass shooting. They shut down the block."

"How about the second floor?"

"Seemed OK. I figure the bullet-proof glass and all that other jazz you claim you have probably helped."

"Maybe. But nothing is bomb-proof. The bomb wasn't trying to take out the building. It was targeted and I was the intended victim. Very likely a cell phone detonated device. They were most certainly watching from outside."

"What is our next move?"

"Get your car. Drive around the block a few times and see if anyone is following you. I will meet you in the circle in front of the emergency room entrance. It's going to be a quick pickup. Just throw open the door and keep your foot off the brake."

"Dukes of Hazard style?"

"No, they slid over the hood."

"Where are we going?"

"To see a doctor."

"But you're already at the hospital."

"I am at the wrong one."

CHAPTER 30

—

Sue pulled into the Yorktown Shopping Center parking lot at the intersection of the Gallows Road and Route 50. The morning crowd of prescription fillers snaked down the aisle in the CVS next to the Staples and the half-dozen little restaurants crammed into the nooks and crannies of the sprawling concrete layout. Dan pointed at the small fire lane in front of a Thai restaurant.

"Drop me off here and keep moving. Take laps around the parking lot until you see me at the curb."

"Will do."

Dan exited the car as rain began to fall. He disappeared around the corner near an ice cream shop and returned a few minutes later. He stood at the curb and scanned his environment.

Sue pulled over. Dan opened the door and handed a bouquet of flowers to his driver.

"You shouldn't have."

"I didn't. They aren't for you."

"You could have humored me for a minute."

"I'm trying to keep you alive."

"Can't do both?"

Dan patted the plastic CVS bag in his lap. "I did get you a few things. Toothbrush. Change of underwear."

"Nothing screams flattery like drugstore gifts."

A few blocks south of Gallows road, Dan directed Sue to turn into a narrow entrance next to a three-story concrete parking garage on the premises of Fairfax Hospital. A gate arm blocked the entrance and Sue stopped the car and read the sign through the windshield. "It says 'Physician Parking Only.'"

"I know."

Sue watched as Dan jumped out of the car and pushed the gate arm into the air. The bright yellow fiberglass deterrent rose without protest. Dan waved Sue through the entrance and then jumped back in the car.

"I get the feeling you've done that before."

"Once or twice. The gate has been broken for years. Lucky they haven't fixed it."

"I'm not sure I want to know how you know that."

"I'm not sure I want to tell you."

Sue pulled into the middle aisle of the parking garage and parked between a Mercedes Benz and a Lexus. They both got out of the car and Dan grabbed the flowers and the plastic shopping bag. He pulled out a new plain blue t-shirt and a pair of dark gray cargo pants with myriad pockets—the finest clothes CVS offered—and quickly dressed in the parking garage between the cars. He balled up his tattered, blood stained, odorous, bombed-out attire and threw it in the trunk.

"Is the car safe here?" Sue asked.

"They don't require a parking permit. You need a badge to get the through the gate."

"Unless you know the gate is broken."

"Yeah."

"Are you going to share what you have in mind?"

"Just follow my lead. Hold my arm. Put those flowers in your other hand. Smile and nod at the security guard as we go in."

A taxi cab with an expectant mother and panicked husband pulled into the semi-circle drive in front of the red brick building as Dan and Sue walked through the large automatic doors. The security guard at the podium on the right nodded to Sue who smiled and nodded back. Dan never looked over.

"Tight security."

"They don't really check IDs once the sun is up."

"Something to do with vampires?"

"Probably labor union rules."

They veered left through the waiting room, sofas stuffed with families. Pacing husbands wearing tracks in the floor.

Dan walked directly across the room and picked-up the courtesy phone on the far wall. "We're here," he said into the phone, followed by "thanks."

Minutes later, a blonde woman in light green scrubs approached Dan and Sue loitering near the coffee stand in the corner of the lobby. Her shoulder length blonde hair framed her high cheekbones. Stethoscopes hung around her neck. Her white doctor's coat fell to her knees. The toes of her clogs were stained with some unidentifiable liquid in the process of drying.

The doctor never broke pace as she approached, opening her arms as Dan stepped forward to meet her. Sue noted the duration of the hug, the intimacy of the bodies, and women's intuition told her everything she needed to know. "What have you gotten yourself into?" the doctor asked, stepping back to eye Dan and then Sue.

"It has to do with Conner," Dan said, shamelessly tugging heart strings.

Dan stared into the doctor's face as she provided her initial medical assessment of the man she once loved. "Cut over the eye. Bruises. Multiple smaller lacerations."

"Got in a fight and survived a bombing," Dan replied.

"Some things never change."

"Indeed. You still look beautiful."

The doctor turned and extended her hand in the direction of Sue. "April Cathright."

"Nice to meet you. I think these flowers are for you," Sue said, transferring ownership.

"Thank you."

"You're welcome. You look young to be a doctor."

"And you look young to be dating a forty-year-old man."

Dr. Cathright glanced over at Dan to see him wince.

"Ouch," he replied.

"We're not dating. I work for him. Sort of an internship," Sue said.

"It all starts somewhere. But that's a conversation for later. Let's go. Follow me."

Sue and Dan followed Dr. Cathright as her heels stepped on

the pink path in the gray tile floor. At the door of a secure elevator, the doctor swiped her badge, waved at the closed circuit camera in the corner of the ceiling, and pressed the button for the fourth floor. A minute later, the party of three stepped onto the labor and delivery floor of Fairfax Hospital. Two pregnant women in matching flowered gowns waddled by, grunting through a conversation about contractions and breathing methods.

Dr. Cathright walked her guests past the first nurses' station and turned down a short hall. Her ID badge ushered them through another set of security doors and past a dual set of cameras, one on each wall. Down another hall, her magical pass provided access to yet a longer hallway where unoccupied gurneys and wheelchairs lined the right side.

"Should I be leaving breadcrumbs?" Sue asked.

"Wouldn't help. Even if you knew how to get out, you can't without a badge," Dan replied.

At the end of the hall, Dr. Cathright stopped at a pair of locked swinging doors. She stepped to the wall, punched a five-digit code into a panel, and the large doors swung inward. Another hall, an additional door, and a final swipe of the badge left the three standing shoulder-to-shoulder in a small foyer. Three identical doors lined each side of the wall. An open bathroom was in the corner, providing a glimpse of a shower and toilet in the reflection of a dimly lit mirror. Dr. Cathright went to the door on the far left, pushed a combination of numbers on the lock, and pushed the door open.

"Here we are. Welcome."

Sue approached the open door cautiously, not sure what to expect. She popped her head in first, determined it was safe, and then entered. There was a full-size bed, a metal desk with two chairs, and a reclining lounge chair. On the far side of the room, a wall-mounted TV with a DVD player clung to faded yellow paint. The computer on the metal desk was on, the screen illuminated with graphs and charts, moving and flashing in different colors.

"There isn't much space in here, but we can share what we have."

"Come again?" Sue asked.

Before Dr. Cathright could answer, the screen on her computer began flashing red. The small black pager clipped to her waist simultaneously erupted in a mind-melting array of notes.

"That's my patient. I gotta go. Emergency C-section. I will be back in an hour or so, provided there are no complications."

"We'll be here," Dan said, finding a seat in the recliner. "Before you leave can you log me into the computer network? I need medical records and Internet access."

"My user name is my first initial and last name. My password is my date of birth, followed by my zip code. If you can remember them, the computer is all yours."

Dan winked. "Thanks."

Dr. April Cathright flashed her own magnificent pearly whites, flipped a strand of hair behind her ear, and then left.

Sue sat on the edge of the bed. "What the hell are we doing here?"

"It's safe. In fact, outside of a safe house with armed guards, a security system, and maybe a few dogs on the perimeter, this is one of the safest locations on the East Coast. Multiple security doors, multiple cameras, multiple guards and numerous safeguards."

"I noticed. Where are we exactly?"

"You are in one of the call rooms for the OB/GYN doctors on duty at Fairfax Hospital. This labor and delivery ward is the fifth busiest in the country. But most people don't even know these physician call rooms exist. And if you do know they exist, you wouldn't know how to find them. There are no signs pointing you in this direction. You can't exit the floor without a badge. Not without setting off alarms and generating a very serious response."

"What's up with the security?"

"Prevents kidnapping."

"Seriously?"

"Yes. A newborn was taken from this building a few years ago. After that, the hospital wisely decided they would do whatever was necessary to ensure there would not be a repeat incident. Now all babies have RFID chips attached to their umbilical cord. Scanners monitor their locations at all times. On top of that, all the locks and doors limit the movement of adults. Eyes on the infants. Eyes on those who could take them. Pretty brilliant, really."

"There are no windows in these rooms."

"Even safer. Good for sleeping. Emergency rooms and labor and delivery wards are always open. They are staffed twenty-four hours a day including Christmas, Hanukkah, and Kwanza. These medical professionals don't sleep regular hours. They drop, sleep for two hours, then wake up and perform surgery."

"Never thought about it. So we are locked in a room in the middle of the hospital?"

"I wouldn't say we are locked in. We are here voluntarily."

"Speak for yourself."

"It's safe. That is my main concern. For you."

Sue smirked. "So, who is Doctor April Cathright?"

"She is a friend."

"More than a friend, I imagine."

"In a previous life."

"It is only a previous life if you leave it behind. We are here. For her, maybe it's not a previous life."

Dan grunted and moved to the chair in front of the computer. He patted the empty seat next to him and Sue moved from the bed.

"What are we doing?"

"Checking on a few things."

Dan minimized the flashing lights associated with heartbeats and contractions and then clicked on the icon for the Fairfax Inova network. He nailed Dr. Cathright's birthday on his third attempt. "Here we are."

"What are we looking for?"

"An airplane."

"What kind?"

"Jet. Landed at Manassas Regional Airport on May the fifth of this year. Cinco de Mayo.

"What is the tail number?"

"I don't have one. I didn't have the money to buy that information. The asking price was ten grand. I was hoping I could find the information myself. After all, finding information is an intricate part of my job description."

"Don't take this the wrong way, but I am not sure which you are burning through faster—money or friends."

"I am running out of both."

Sue nodded, her eyebrows furled.

Dan continued. "OK. Pay attention. Maybe you'll learn something about public information channels. Who knows, I may be able to write down a truthful tidbit on your internship evaluation form for once."

"Funny."

"The thing about looking for planes is that they are all registered. Like automobiles and boats. Systematically, the government does a good job of keeping track of these."

"Probably because people have to pay taxes on them."

"Exactly. For planes, they also need to have registration information for things like filing flight plans, as well as for less glamorous undertakings such as sifting through the wreckage of downed aircraft. All planes are registered. All parts are registered to that plane. All parts are tracked back to the manufacturer, the day they were created, and who was working the assembly line that day. Zero defect tolerance."

"Imagine the possibilities if they made everything so carefully."

"The FAA website maintains information on every airport in the country. All flight plans. So all we have to do is go to the FAA page for Manassas Regional Airport and search for jets that landed at the airport on May the fifth."

"Why are we interested in jets that landed?"

"Because that's what the barber said."

"But of course," Sue responded, watching Dan type.

Dan pointed to the screen. "Here are the flight plans for all the airplanes that landed that day. Forty-two in total. Most of them small personal aircraft. A lot of Cessna. None of them were jets."

"It would be easier with a tail number."

"Don't get distracted by what we don't have."

"OK, we *have* nothing, if you like the sound of that better."

"I am undeterred. In fact, if this plane really had CIA personnel on board, as the barber indicated, I would imagine they don't have to file a flight plan."

"Probably not."

"But they do need gas. And they do house the plane somewhere. So there is a chance the plan resides on site at the airport. All planes must be registered with an airstrip and all the planes maintained on airport premises have paperwork filed with the FAA."

"People can find out anything these days."

"If you are willing to get dirty," Dan added.

"Most people already are dirty."

"Now you're coming around to my side." Dan put his finger on the screen. "There are 120 aircraft registered at Manassas Regional Airport."

"A big number."

"But manageable. For the airplanes registered at Manassas Regional Airport, I can now access their information and get granular information on all of the registered airplanes for that location. The type of aircraft. The seating configuration. The number of toilets. Who owns each plane."

"Wow."

"So if we only look at jets, we have a total of eleven that are registered with Manassas Airport, listing the airport as their home location. Eleven out of 120. Of those eleven jets, we are now going to look at who owns them."

"I'm getting nervous."

"That is the adrenaline of the hunt. It is one of the perks of the job."

"I was beginning to wonder if there were perks. I see mostly downside."

"Sometimes, I agree . . . If we go back to the eleven jets, we see that one of the planes is owned by Amgen. One is owned by Alcatel. Capital One has a plane. Northrup Grumman and Orbital Sciences each have a plane. Oscar winning actress Mary Streaker has a private jet. The AOL founders each have one. Then you have planes owned by companies you have never heard of: Spearhead Tech. Joost. Silver Star."

Dan paused.

"We know that name," Sue said.

"Yes we do. That is the same name as the company that shows up on the sales transaction for the property on Wisconsin Avenue. The owner of the mystery property."

"A multi-faceted company."

"A front company could be anything. And it could have multiple uses. There was a big story last year about front companies being used for tax evasion. Did you know there is a single building in the Cayman Islands serving as the official registered address for over five thousand companies? It doesn't take much to be a front company. A name and some documentation. You can open an LLC online in about ten minutes. Try it sometime."

"So you think this plane is the one you are looking for?"

"This is the plane the barber saw on his birthday. I think this plane does not have to file flight plans. I think the tail number you see there is the one the barber wanted $10,000 for."

"Can you check the flight history again, now that you have the tail number?"

"I can." Dan typed on the computer and the results flashed on the screen.

"Nothing. As you would expect. The airplane has no flight history. It doesn't show up in the flight records for the airport for the day in question and it doesn't have any flight information for any other day."

"What does that mean?"

"It means, ostensibly, there is a plane parked at the airport that has never flown. It also means the barber was telling the truth about the airplane he saw. But I am no closer to finding my attorney friend Clyde Parkson."

"Why don't you stop looking for him? Seems to me if you stand still long enough, he is going to find you."

"The winner of a battle is, in part, pre-determined by preparation. A planned offensive position is always better than an impromptu defensive one."

"So, what's next?"

"Sometimes you have to take a step back to move forward."

—

Dr. April Cathright returned to the room ninety minutes later. "How are we getting along?"

"Good," Sue answered from the recliner. Dan was on the bed, eyes closed.

"Move over. Nap time," April said. Dan scooted over on the bed, pushing his shoulder against the wall.

"How long are you on duty?" Dan asked, eyes staring at the ceiling.

"Seventy-two hours. I am covering the residents through tomorrow night and then I am on call with my own practice the following thirty-six hours. You are safe until then. No one will even know you are here. I'll bring food and water from the doctor's lounge. Toilet is in the foyer. Just pop your head out the door and see if anyone is there. There are six doors in the foyer. Six doctors all sleeping different rotations. No one will ask you questions because you just plain can't be here by accident. And if someone does ask, just say you are my cousin."

April Cathright peeled off her jacket and slid on top of the covers next to Dan.

"I accessed the computer network."

"You remembered my birthday?"

"Took three tries."

"Did you find what you were looking for?"

"Half of it. I have a question for you."

"I am not going to like this, am I?" Dr. Cathright responded.

"Can you change the information on medical files?"

"Not for closed files. Anything open, I can make changes to. But I cannot go back and change a patient's file from last year, for example. I can only add addendums. Everything is electronic now."

"So you can only addend, but you cannot change the original diagnosis."

"Exactly, if we could change the original information, every doctor would have a one hundred percent successful diagnosis rate. Just go back in, change the medical record, and the file would show you are always correct."

"What about making a record disappear? Who could do that?"

"No one. A completely corrupted database, maybe. Why do you ask?"

"Because I just checked my own medical history."

"And?"

"I don't have one. Nothing. Zippo. I have been to this hospital at least three times in the last ten years. And they don't have anything on me."

"Jesus, Dan. What have you gotten yourself into?"

"I'm not sure exactly, which makes extraction a little more problematic."

Dan pondered his missing medical files before his mind wandered to darker thoughts—the bomb, the mafia showing up in his hospital room, his nephew, his neighbor Lucia, his four-legged friend Levi. He reigned in the focus on his losses and turned his attention to problem-solving.

Dr. Cathright's pager started blaring a barely recognizable version of "Country Roads" and she threw her feet onto the floor and muttered, "I'll be back."

Sue waited for the door to shut. "You ask a lot from the people you know."

"Not all of them. She knows I'm in trouble. I have never brought my work anywhere near April. Ever. She understands. Without me saying anything, she understands. You only get a handful of people like that in your life."

"I'm not so sure she understands."

"She's smart enough to understand. She is a doctor—an OB-GYN. That means she practices medicine all day at the office, she delivers babies at all hours of the night, and performs surgery in between. People may stumble into medicine and find themselves working as a shrink, but people don't stumble into a surgical field. She is a hell of a lot smarter than I am. She knows exactly what is going on."

"And you repay these favors?"

"All of them. Twofold."

"Well, if you survive this mess, you are going to be very busy."

—

Dr. Cathright returned fifteen minutes later.

Dan stood and swiped Sue's keychain off the desk and reached for the doorknob. Sue interrupted him first. "Where are you going?"

"To run some errands. Find the people on the plane. Resolve this."

"You are going to need help," Sue added.

"No, I am going to need your car," Dan replied, jingling Sue's keys in his hand.

"Sure. Take it," Sue said, offended.

"Thanks. My main goal here is to keep you safe. Don't use your phone, even though reception in these rooms is awful. Stay off the grid. You have seventy-two hours of safety here. After that, we are both in real trouble."

"You know we are going to talk about you while you are gone," Sue said. "I'm going to grill Dr. Cathright here. I am going to ask her everything I can think of."

Dan looked at Sue and then locked eyes with Dr. Cathright. "Tell her anything you want. I trust her."

"Must have hurt to say that."

"More than I imagined it would."

CHAPTER 31

—

Sue pulled her leg up to her chest and wrapped her arms around it, leaning back into the recliner as Dr. Cathright lay on the bed.

"Dan gave me the green light to ask you about him. I have more than a few questions."

"You have more questions than I have answers."

"What's he like?"

"More than anyone I have ever met, what you see is what you get."

"I'm not sure what I see. I've only been working with him for a short time. I don't get the feeling the last week has been indicative of normal, or any version of normal."

"There may not be a normal with Dan."

"Honestly, at first I thought he was a little crazy. Someone in deep mourning who could probably benefit from depression medication. He was obsessed with clearing the names of his nephew and sister-in-law. Consumed with finding who was responsible for their deaths. I wasn't sure what to believe. I thought maybe he was wishing for a bad guy, hoping there was one, so he could validate a reason for his relatives' deaths. So he could prove their deaths were beyond a drug overdose and a suicide."

"And now?"

"I see someone who is relentless. Someone who has a long line of people—friends, acquaintances—whatever you want to call them, who are willing to help him."

"He has charm. He is honest. He helps people who are in trouble. He has good karma."

"He also hangs out with marginal characters. Hackers. Call girls."

"You mean Haley Falls?"

"You know her?"

"I know about her. I don't think Haley Falls was a call girl. I think she was a madam."

"Do you have any idea how that sounds?"

"Crazy, probably. But no more crazy than a bomb blowing up the art gallery beneath his office. A drug-sniffing dog. With Dan, you get honest, and you get crazy. But that's from an outside perspective. Dan spent so much time overseas during his formative years, he isn't like you and me. I think when you grow up all over the world, your definition of crazy changes. Or maybe your definition of normal widens."

"Maybe. He is a little paranoid. And secretive. I asked him where he lived once and I never got an answer. He has a car, but he doesn't drive it to work. He never talks about commuting, which, let's face it, in this town, is a popular conversation. His official address, the one on his driver's license, is his office. But I know he has a house because he mentioned it."

"So you're not sleeping with him?" Dr. Cathright asked.

"No. He is my boss."

"And you work in his office?"

"Yep. The one with all the security. The cameras. The locks. The special bulletproof glass."

"He likes his security. He says he has made some enemies."

"Like federal judges. Politicians. Powerful people."

"I never wanted to know, so I never asked. I knew if asked, he would tell me. And some things you can't unhear. Unknow. Unlearn."

"Is he wealthy?"

"When Dan's parents passed away, Dan and his brother received some inheritance."

"How much?"

"I don't know, exactly. A couple of million between them is my guess. Life changing but not enough to buy an island and retire. Enough to allow him to do whatever he does."

"I only mention it because he has spent a hell of a lot of money the last week or so."

"His prerogative. After his parents died, Dan decided he was going to do something meaningful. He had graduated from law school and had passed the bar. Already he was disenchanted with the legal profession. The way he put it, it seemed like the job was predicated on preying on others. A job that was always performed at someone else's expense."

"So he quit?"

"Before he really got started. He took his money and bought some property in Alexandria."

"I found some real estate records with his name on them. He owns the entire office building. Two floors. The gallery downstairs. It's the whole side of a small block."

"He owns more than that. He also bought the old Stonewall Jackson House. Built in the 1850s and on the historical registry. Dan bought it through a trust. A half acre right in the middle of Old Town Alexandria. He used his inheritance to purchase it as well as refurbish the residence and the grounds. He lets the Alexandria Historical Society use the place in exchange for maintaining the house and for tax purposes. Dan has full access whenever he wants, but he rarely goes in the main house. He took me in one night. Showed me around."

Dr. Cathright blushed and Sue noticed.

"The public can take tours of the property once a week. Historically, the house was used for lodging and rumor has it Woodrow Wilson enjoyed staying there. Dan lives on the property, but not in the main residence."

"He bought a historical house through a trust and he doesn't live there?"

"He lives in the carriage house behind the main residence."

"Once again, the only adjective I can come up with is crazy."

"For you and I, maybe."

"What is it like?"

"Beautiful. The carriage house is a couple thousand square feet. Completely renovated. Gorgeous views of a garden. On a fabulous piece of property that is professionally maintained. When Dan sells that property, I will know he's in financial trouble. Until then . . ."

"How far from the office is this house?"

"Down the sealed-off alley in the back. Through an old cast-iron door in a brick wall. He can walk from his house to work without going onto a public street."

"What about his car?"

"He parks in the Union Street public parking garage. Pays for a spot. Monthly rental. Open twenty-four hours a day."

"So this guy who grew up all over the world lives a hundred yards from where he works?"

"He does."

"Crazy. What else?"

"He speaks a few languages. I could never pin him down on an exact number. His French is native level. His Spanish is flawless. I have heard him speak Russian and he seems to do it fluently, though I don't speak any Russian so I can't really tell you. He speaks Thai. Some Farsi. Portuguese."

"Jesus."

"And he can fight."

"And lose."

"Not very often. He learned how to fight as a kid overseas. Started out innocently enough, or so he says. Says he was practicing some karate forms he had seen on a video and an ex-special forces soldier working security detail at some embassy invited him to train. Started showing him things. Kill and maim techniques, as Dan put it. As Dan bounced around from country to country, he moved from teacher to teacher. His family would arrive at a new destination and Dan would be practicing with the marines and diplomatic security personnel before he unpacked. He joined local dojos wherever he went. Trained in a bunch of martial arts and learned to fight with knives, sticks, and swords. Evidently, he had a reputation for being quite a handful as a teenager."

"Interesting. But a little childish for a grown man."

"Not if people are trying to kill you."

Sue nodded.

Dr. Cathright yawned and turned away. "Anything else you want to know?"

Sue parsed through the thousand questions flashing across the screen in her mind. She settled on a less personal one. "You ever meet this nephew of his?"

"Conner? Yes."

"What's so special about him?"

Dr. Cathright fell silent, closed her eyes, and began to snore.

CHAPTER 32

—

Bent at the waist, looking backwards through her legs, the woman thrust her hips to the music. With her hair dusting the floor of the stage, she smiled at the barrel-chested Russian. When the song changed, she stood, spun, and threw one leg around the silver pole in the middle of the stage. Alex loosened his grip on the wad of cash in his hand and the dancer swooped in for another payment. The Russian had already financed three dances and was looking for an invite into the VIP room. On the house.

Like every good establishment where the bills are paid with dis-robing booty, there were two main factors determining the success of the business. First, the place needed waitresses who were quick enough to fill drink orders before a patron realized a Bud Light cost fifteen bucks. Secondly, the dancers needed to smile. They stripped everything else. It was the only thing they had left.

Good Guys held residence in the second to last row house on upper Wisconsin Avenue, a block from Glover Park and adjacent to the Naval Observatory. The Observatory—an outdated scientific agency that had since moved its working bits to other parts of the country—was now home to the vice president of the United States. Rumor had it there was a secret path from the residence to the alley behind the club.

Next door to Good Guys, heading downhill towards the Poto-mac, was a sushi restaurant. The location of the sushi restaurant—with the strip club next door—was the butt of running jokes for customers of both establishments with regard to unwanted odors. While the owners of both businesses pointed fingers at one an-other during the summer months when the scent was strongest, the true culprit was two-hundred-year-old sewers that ran through Georgetown.

—

Dan walked into the bar and the bouncer stepped away from his stool to block the doorway. Dan flashed his driver's license and located Alex by the time the bouncer read his date of birth.

Dan scanned the room as he approached the black t-shirt and jeans bartender on the midday shift behind the bar. "A bottle of Standard Vodka. And two shot glasses."

"Two hundred dollars," the tattooed bartender responded, reaching into an unopened cabinet behind the bar. Dan peeled off a stack of twenties and put them on the counter. He grabbed the glasses and bottle and turned into a topless waitress buzzing by with a tray lifted above her head. The waitress performed a pirouette and Dan admired her rabbit-tailed derriere in addition to her balance.

A moment later, Dan slipped into the empty upholstered chair next to Alex. They were both facing the stage, within sweat-dripping distance. Dan put the bottle and the glasses on the table. The dancer was focused on Alex, providing a full view of the goods and a lesson in centrifugal force.

"I wondered if this was where you were heading," Dan asked.

"You followed me."

"I did."

"You've come to ruin another form of entertainment?" Alex asked without looking over.

"To share some drinks."

"I am technically working."

Dan pointed to the beer bottle on the table.

"Beer does not count," Alex retorted, his eyes on the stage.

"At least you didn't come far."

"It is 703 paces from the rear entrance of the Russian Embassy to this table. More or less."

"More or less," Dan repeated sarcastically. He poured two glasses of Standard and held one in the air for Alex. "To your health," he offered in Russian.

"To *our* health." Alex took a sip, licked his lips, and put the glass on the table. "You know your barber is dead."

"Yes, I know."

"Frankly, I'm surprised you're still alive."

"I'm a little surprised you're still breathing as well."

"Me? I am Russian. I am official. There are rules. In the intelligence world, you don't kill another operative unless you have reason. Merely indentifying a counter operative is one thing. This alone makes the operative ineffective. Once a cover is blown, well, it is time for a career change. Killing one? This is not good business. Kill one and you will lose one of your own."

"What about the barber? He was not a professional."

"I did not kill the barber. My guess is the same people who tried to kill you, got to him. Loose lips sink ships, I believe is the saying."

"But you have talked to me. Probably told me things you shouldn't have."

"I have told you nothing about what is sacred to *me*. My allegiance is to my country. My fellow countrymen. Mother Russia. Have I betrayed those?"

"No."

"Exactly. No, I have not. Nor would I ever. What I told you, well, it was not professional per se, but it was calculated. Perhaps I would get a slap on the wrist, but nothing more. Besides, at my age, I am in the position where I do more of the slapping, rather than being the one who is slapped."

Dan filled both glasses again.

"You did not find what you were looking for?" Alex asked.

"I learned there is a plane being used out of the Manassas Airport. It has no flight records. No history. I know the size of the plane. The make of the plane. Yet, it still doesn't help me find my man."

"If you wait long enough, your man will find you. Just stop running."

"You are the second person to suggest that. You know there is a tactical disadvantage to that strategy."

"Indeed."

"I have questions for you."

"As do I, for you. Tell me about your trip to the barber."

"He was not helpful."

"But yet, he told me the same story he told you. And the information he provided me was useful. Very useful, in fact."

"Maybe he withheld the good part when he told the story to me."

"Possible, but unlikely. At least not intentionally."

"Why?"

"Because I'm quite sure the barber did not recognize the good part."

"How could that be?"

Alex took the full shot glass, nodded to Dan, and poured it through his lips. "As I said, you are not an operative. You are not in operations. You are not a spy. You are something in between. You fight better than a spy. My wrist still hurts from our encounter in the motel room. But what you do not do is spy better than a spy. Quite simply, I listen better than you."

"I still need your help."

"Why should I help you?"

"Because you tried to help me before. Whatever that reason was, it is still valid."

"Your failure is not a motivating excuse."

"But you offered to help for a reason. You knew more."

"And once again, you show you are something more than citizen Joe."

"The average Joe."

"Ahh. Even after all these years, sometimes those stupid idioms catch me."

"Go on."

Alex smiled. "You are learning. When someone is talking, or willing to talk, you listen."

Dan nodded.

"As we mentioned before, the barber provided us with information we deemed useful from time to time. He was good with faces, remarkable actually. We used him to verify faces, identities.

Generally speaking, when people come to a barber shop, they are coming to get their real hair cut. And of course, we have a good idea who is a CIA analyst and who works in human resources for the agency. I, as you can imagine, am only interested in operatives. Or identifying operatives. And I will use whatever information we can get."

"And there was something more than his ability to remember faces and identify a toupee."

"Indeed. As you are aware, our barber friend ran numbers."

"A standard flipping opportunity."

"People at the CIA should not gamble, but they do. The barber cut thousands of peoples' hair at the agency. But if you are an average Joe and you can't get to the barber during the work week and, let's say, your barber had hours elsewhere on Saturday or Sunday or on a weeknight, you might go and get your haircut at an off-site location."

"And you might learn there is an opportunity to make some bets . . ."

"Standard flipping opportunities, as you put it. Low-level stuff, but not without reward. You find a gambler, you find a drinker. You follow him and you find a stripper. A call girl. You try to determine what he knows that could be useful to you, or what he doesn't know that could also be useful to you."

"And the barber helped you identify those who were gambling."

"In some cases. He didn't know many names, but he was very good with faces."

"And you provided photos to aid the cause. How did you get them?"

"Leg work. Unglamorous, nose to the grindstone, diligence. There are tens of thousands of employees at the CIA. We have photographs of a majority of them."

"How?"

"For many, many years there was only a primary, single entrance into the CIA. Now, there are two, plus an additional entrance for deliveries, but it is still a strategic bottleneck failure for your spy agency."

"You staked out the CIA?"

"Didn't have to. The CIA is on Route 123. A vast majority of cars entering the CIA come from either North 123 or South 123. There is no way around that."

"Don't tell me that Russian spies drive up and down the road taking pictures of all the cars and drivers."

"No. There is a gas station just north of the CIA at the intersection of Kirby road. One of the mechanics was a Russian by birth. He worked there for twenty years. We set up cameras in his car bay at the service station. Took pictures every day for two decades. It was very helpful. Until he passed away."

"Incredible."

"On the south side of the CIA on Route 123 there is a 7-11. That establishment was owned by a Russian. Also now deceased."

"So you rigged up both places to take pictures."

"Yes. And then technology improved. Cameras became smaller. Easier to hide. Easier to control remotely. We don't need to have the fixed location photography that we once did."

"So you take pictures and use them how?"

"Imagine for yourself. Let's say you think John Smith is a spy. You know he works at Langley. You follow him. Let's say John Smith gets his hair cut every few weeks. Let's say he doesn't show up for six months. We can then assume he is an operative. Analysts do not disappear for months at a time. Analysts also do not typically arrive at work in the middle of the night. We directed additional scrutiny to any vehicle that arrived at HQ at unusual hours. The CIA does not allow remote access to most of its computer systems for security reasons. A system that is not online cannot be hacked remotely. That means if you are in the intelligence field and you need information, you physically have be on the premises. As it is with life, you prevent A, but open the door to B. We cannot hack their systems remotely, but we can identify those people who have to come in to use their secure systems. We assume people arriving at three in the morning are not going back to the office because they forgot their house key."

"That is a lot of work to identify someone."

"Yes, it is. But, technology has made many things easier. For example, CIA employees on the operations side have a very limited electronic footprint. They are not permitted to have Facebook accounts. Their use of private email is limited. So if there are questions as to the legitimacy of a foreign diplomat, check the Internet. If there is no information, you have found someone in the intelligence side of the house. Legitimate State Department employees do not have the same restrictions. In fact, they typically have a large electronic footprint given that friends and family are located in all corners of the globe."

"A lot of work."

"Every country uses the same tricks. Overseas, if you want to find the spy within an embassy, just look for the employees who work the longest hours. Most Foreign Service officers clock out at five. Those Foreign Service officers who are spies work much longer. They have to perform their cover jobs first, and then their spy jobs. Or vice versa. Either way, they have a heavier workload."

Dan nodded his head, thought back to his years overseas, and said, "clever."

"Basic info. The key is getting the info without being discovered. Transportation is another weak point for espionage operatives. Have you ever seen those shuttle buses that pick people up from the metro?"

"Of course."

"Well, a small number of those shuttle buses check IDs when people get on the bus. That is a red flag. If you follow one of those buses and they drop people off at a building with a lot of cameras and no name on the façade, you have a second red flag. With those two pieces of information alone, you can pinpoint a location where some form of intelligence gathering is taking place."

"Benny the barber said you showed him thousands of photos."

"I personally have categorized somewhere in the neighborhood of five thousand personnel that work at Langley HQ. Another thousand at foreign embassies."

"Unbelievable."

"Not really."

"So do you know who my guy is?"

"When I sent you to Benny, I wasn't leading you to a person. Not exactly. I told you that you would have to work for the answer."

"You were leading me to the plane."

"No. I was leading you to the answer."

"My patience is wearing thin."

"And my glass is empty."

Dan filled Alex's glass. "Who am I looking for?"

"Did you ask the barber about skydiving?"

"Yes. The barber's son wanted to go skydiving for the barber's sixty-fifth birthday. Cinco de Mayo. I checked it out. I found the plane."

"Owned by a front company."

"Yes."

"The plane is not important. What else did the barber mention about his skydiving adventure?"

"After they finished sky diving, he saw people from Langley getting off a jet. A twelve-seater. Twin engine. Beige stripe."

"And then what?"

"He said he thought he was recognized."

Alex watched as Dan's anticipation rose. He slowly poured himself another shot and took a sniff, his nose near the rim of the glass.

"And did you ask the barber any further questions at this point?"

"No."

"You weren't curious as to how these people got to the airport, or how they got home?"

Dan's thoughts came to a screeching halt. He shut his eyes and shook his head.

Alex leaned forward in his chair. "Yes. The answer you seek was not about an airplane. It was about a car. For some reason, a CIA operative was driving a personal car to a private terminal at a public airport. Why? We may never know. Perhaps ego. Perhaps the person was late. Perhaps there was a mechanical malfunction of another vehicle. For whatever reason, a CIA employee drove their personal car, a very identifiable car as it turns out, and they just happened to be seen by a civilian employee."

"And that led you to discover something."

"That led us to a relatively big fish."

"And . . ."

"It is the big fish you are looking for."

"What does the big fish have to do with my nephew?"

"Everything."

"I want the person responsible."

"And I am providing a means for that. The first time we met, when I asked you those questions about your nephew, it was not random. I was trying to see if I could indeed help you. Do you remember what I asked you?"

"You asked me if my nephew was rare?"

"Yes, unquantifiably rare. Don't you find this to be an interesting question? What could it mean? Mathematically speaking."

"That there are only a handful of similar people in the US."

"No. Not in the United States. In *the world*." Alex started to raise his glass and stopped. "Out of this small handful of people, this tiny population, three of them are Russian. Russian Jews. Ashkenazi Jews from Saratov."

"The Americans tried to reach them," Dan said, beating Alex to the conclusion.

"Yes. Our spies followed them. They entered Russia. They went to the outskirts of the Saratov and they started asking questions at the synagogue. They were looking for other children similar to your nephew."

"Did they find them?"

"They would have. But we interceded."

"Did you apprehend them?"

"No, we followed them."

"And the first step in identifying and following these American spies was a car from the Manassas Regional Airport."

"Correct."

"So all I need is the car?"

"All you need is to find a gray BMW M5. Model year 2010. Virginia tags."

"Thank you."

"Now, I have another question for you."

"Sure."

"How did the call girl know I was someone who could help you?"

"She said you talked in your sleep."

"Ahh. I should have imagined. My wife mentioned that once. I think it's something that has gotten worse as I have aged. My own countrymen would have killed me in the 1980s had they known."

"They still might," a heavy baritone voice interjected over Dan and Alex's shoulder.

Dan and Alex turned to see Detective Wallace pulling up a chair.

"Oh, good. The police," Dan said.

"I think this is my excuse to return to work," Alex replied, moving slowly to stand.

Detective Wallace flashed his badge and ordered Alex back in his seat. The barrel-chested Russian bellowed a lung-racking laugh and slowly reached into his pocket. He pulled out his diplomatic passport and handed it to Detective Wallace. "I am an official representative of the Russian Federation. I have committed no crime, and if I had, you would be able to do nothing about it."

Detective Wallace flipped through the passport in the dim light of the club while an old song by Usher pulsed from the speakers. He took one last look at the photo and compared it to Alex, then handed the document back to its rightful owner. "Have a good day."

Alex nodded at Dan and walked towards the daylight squeezing through the frame of the front door.

"Detective Wallace."

"Dan Lord. The man without fingerprints."

"You've been following me?"

"Since you stopped by to take a look at the remains of the art gallery beneath your office. Quite a mess. I figured you would show up to see it for yourself, sooner or later. From there I followed you."

"A little out of your jurisdiction."

"I can stake out any location I wish."

"Including strip clubs?"

"Seems like a good place to find you. You don't seem to discriminate in the company you keep. Strippers. Call girls. District Attorneys. Russian diplomats."

"I've even been seen with an ornery old detective who threw me in a cell full of convicts."

"I think we are even. Sorry about the eye."

"We aren't even. I didn't try to kill you. Yet."

"No, but you did thwart my investigation. An investigation that is important to me and my colleagues. To a mother and a father. To a sister."

"Then you can help me."

"How?"

"I need to find a gray BMW M5. Year 2010. Virginia tags."

Detective Wallace looked up at the gyrating entertainment and then over his shoulder at the club entrance. His eyes fell to the table and the bottle standing in the middle. "You drinking?"

"You want to join me?"

Detective Wallace glanced around at the barflies hidden in the shadows, the strippers shaking their assets. "Nothing more depressing than a strip club during daylight hours."

Dan shrugged his shoulders.

"Make it a bourbon."

Dan raised his finger at the waitress who shuffled over. He whispered the order into her ear and she disappeared and returned a few minutes later, gently placing the glass on the table. "Drinks for law enforcement are on the house," she winked, wiggling her bunny tail before vanishing again to the far side of the club.

Detective Wallace picked up his drink and touched his glass to Dan's. He slowly tilted his head back, tasting the drink, admiring the streaks on the inside of the glass as he lowered it back to the table.

"A man who enjoys good bourbon," Dan admired.

"My father told me if you aren't enjoying the taste, then you probably shouldn't be drinking it."

"Not sure the Russians agree with that."

"What do you want with this car?"

"It may lead me to the man responsible for killing your partner."

"The killer is driving around in a gray BMW M5?"

"Someone is. And I need to find them."

Detective Wallace reached down for his glass, took another slow sip, and then reached in his pocket. He pulled a twenty out of his money clip and raised it between his fingers. The dancer on stage shifted her full attention to Wallace, bits and goodies gyrating as she closed in. Wallace shook his head and simply handed her the cash.

"I like you, Detective. Help me out. I'll make it worth your while."

"Before I help you, tell me what you have on the gray BMW."

"Nothing. Hearsay."

"I'm going to need more than that."

"I don't have the time or the whiteboard diagram I need to explain it."

"You are aware I am still a police officer. For the information you want, I have to go to the station. I can run license plates from my car. But you don't have a license plate number, so I have to run a query on the DMV database for all gray BMW 5 series. That, I have to do from the station. Especially for an out-of-state tag, of which Virginia is one. And, even that I can't do legally without a case number."

"Detective Nguyen's death must have a case number."

"It does, but I'm not working the case."

"You mean you are not allowed to be working the case."

"Is there a difference?"

"Yes. If you're not allowed to be working the case and you still are, then I like you even more."

"It's called loyalty."

"That is what friends do. Loyal friends are hard to find."

Dan pulled another twenty from his wallet and removed a tattered business card. He held out the twenty for the dancer and then turned to the detective. "I assume you still have my number. But just in case," Dan said, threadbare business card in hand.

Detective Wallace patted his detective's notebook in his chest pocket. "I have your information."

The two men shook hands.

"Did we just smoke a peace pipe?" Dan asked.

"I think we did. But don't confuse that with a post-coital ciga-rette. I'm still a detective. I'm still on the job."

—

Detective Wallace walked up Wisconsin Avenue and danced his way across the four lanes of traffic to the large square building on the hill. He looked above at the cameras perched on the secu-rity wall, certain his every move was being watched. And his every move was getting harder with every passing year. *I have to lose some weight,* he thought, marching onward and upward, step by step up the natural incline to one of the highest points in the city. At the large metal gate, adorned with bars and bollards thick enough to stop a runaway rig, Detective Wallace turned the corner on the sidewalk. The large square building stared down at him as if daring him to pursue his line of questioning. A young, fit, uniformed man stepped from a large concrete block security booth onto the bricked pavement on the public side of the gate.

"The embassy's visitor's entrance is to the rear. Off Tunlaw."

Detective Wallace pulled his badge and politely handed it to the security officer. "I know my badge has no jurisdiction on the other side of that wall. I only ask that you make a phone call on my behalf. I would like to speak with Alexander Stoyovich. I met him down the street a few moments ago. We have a mutual friend."

The security guard examined the police badge, nodded, and stepped back into the security booth, leaving the door open. A sec-ond man sat on a stool in the booth, both hands on a large auto-matic weapon with the safety off. The young man with the police badge in his hand picked up the phone and proceeded to have a brief conversation in Russian. He hung up, made another call, and then stepped from the booth to hand the badge back to Detective Wallace.

"Please wait here. The person you requested to see will be down momentarily."

CHAPTER 33

—

Gary Raven's forearms melted into his oversized wrists. A real life Popeye with tattoos and scars. His hands and feet were mangled. Pieces of anatomy that no longer resembled any diagram in any medical book. For a living, he wielded a welding torch and cranked oversized wrenches. For his passion, he ran the dojo upstairs, directly over his car conversion shop. In a former life he had been a diplomatic security officer, a private body guard, and a home and office security specialist with a penchant for creating safe rooms and ultra-secure residences.

Dan walked into the second-floor dojo and Gary Raven rose from the wooden chair behind the wooden desk near the door. A shelf of trophies and photos sat perched on the wall.

"Dan Lord, it has been a while. You here to practice?" Gary Raven asked, eyeballing the cut above Dan's eye.

"Not today, Sensei."

"I think I surrendered that title the last time we fought."

Dan smiled. "I cheated."

"Let's say you didn't follow the rules."

"I was fighting. You were practicing."

"I heard about your business. Guess all that security you paid for worked out."

"You did a good job. It worked as designed. The bomb was small. Meant for me. Not meant for collateral damage."

"So they were close. And they were watching."

"Probably still watching," Dan said.

Gary Raven shrugged his shoulders unconcerned with the possibility of a threat looming outside. "Sure you don't want to spar?

This is my Friday noon class. Open mat. Only black belts. I have a few students who may give you a run for your money."

Dan looked around the dojo and inhaled deeply. The smell gave him peace. It transported him to other places, to past friends. There was something about the permeation of sweat in the mats. A hundred dojos in twenty countries with the exact same scent. It became part of the makeup of the dojo, the experience. It was absorbed into the walls, sucked into the heavy bags hanging in the corner.

Dan spoke. "I'm here on business. I need a car."

"That's a first."

"And probably a last."

"What are you looking for?"

"Something special."

"Five minutes with my new third-degree black belt and you can have anything you want."

"Are you blackmailing me, Sensei?"

"Offering my assistance."

Dan thought for a moment. He looked down at his attire. He was still wearing his CVS cargo pants and t-shirt ensemble. His old shoes were blackened. He couldn't say a quick spar would ruin his outfit. He casually rubbed the back of his head and felt the pronounced knot. He made a quick mental note to keep his skull off the mat.

"Five minutes or until someone taps out," Dan relented.

"This kid is a tornado and you aren't getting any younger."

"He'll be done in less than one. Then I want my car."

"We'll see."

"What's his specialty?"

"Everything," Gary Raven said, smiling broadly. The teacher walked across the mat to the group of young men practicing various routines on each other.

Dan removed his shoes and bowed on the mat. He performed a few standing stretches, touched his toes, and tilted his neck from left to right.

The half-dozen students in the dojo lined up along the far wall, sitting on their knees under hooks on the wall that supported various weapons ranging from knives to wooden swords. Dan's competition stepped on the mat and bowed in Dan's direction. Dan returned the formality and then began his assessment.

A third-degree black belt, likely in his early twenties. A fairly high rank for someone so young, meaning he has to have some natural talent. The young man with the buzz cut did a roll on the mat as part warm-up and part intimidation. *He's wearing a double-weave jacket, which means he likes to grapple. He has on karate pants, allowing more room for kicks.* The student did a flying axe kick and then rolled to the center of the mat. *Nice form. But it won't help you.*

Gary Raven stepped to the center of the mat. "Five minutes. It is over when either person taps out, or when I decide I have seen enough."

Both Dan and the young student bowed at the teacher and then again at each other. The teacher stepped away and the two men began circling each other.

The student made the first move and came in low for Dan's knees in a lightning-fast take down attempt. Dan responded with simultaneous blows to both sides of the exposed neck. Not hard enough to cause damage, but hard enough to know he could. The young man rolled his neck and shook his head to remedy the effects of the concussive blows. Dan let the young man stand and his opponent wasted no time in his second attempt at the knees. Dan rolled over the back of his opponent, using his opponent's rear side as a platform. With Dan's legs no longer in their previous location, the student grasped at air before meeting the floor for a second time.

Again on his feet, the student changed tactics and fired off a series of straight kicks and punches. Dan intercepted the onslaught and countered with smacks to the face with the open palms and the backs of his hands. The smacks landed with more sound effect than impact and for the first time the student realized he was being toyed with. Low kicks came next and Dan blocked them with his own legs, raising his shins and meeting the young man's feet in painful collisions.

The young man grunted in frustration and Dan knew the final assault was next.

His opponent disappeared into a whirl of punches and kicks, high and low. Backfist. Elbow. Waiting for the knockout attempt, Dan bent his knees just as the opponent launched his spinning back kick. Dan moved under his opponent, grabbed the man's groin through the karate uniform, and threw him into a painful fall, head and shoulder crashing into the mat, his balls squeezed in Dan's left hand. Within a second of impact, Dan had the man's elbow in an extended arm bar, his heel on the young man's carotid. Seven seconds later, the man succumbed to unconsciousness.

"He didn't tap," Dan said, rising off the mat.

"He never does," Sensei replied.

"Bad habit."

"Skill he has. Wisdom cannot be hurried."

Dan looked over at the seated students who were stunned at what they had just witnessed. A middle-aged man walking in and besting the top martial artist in the dojo.

Sensei took the opportunity to drive home an educational lesson. "And that is why you don't fuck around with people you don't know. Martial arts are for defense. You never know if someone is going to have a weapon, friends, or if they are just plain more trouble than you are capable of dealing with."

"You owe me a car," Dan said, turning to walk off the mat.

—

Behind the dojo, on the first floor, Dan waited for Gary Raven to open the lock. "I have three cars in for customization," Gary said, stepping through a large metal gray door into a spotless mechanic garage. The garage room had six bays and a center repair area with thirty feet of immaculate concrete flooring. There were four cars in the shop. Three were nearly identical black four-door sedans. The oddball of the group was a black Mercedes SUV. "You said three cars."

"The SUV is the company demo vehicle."

"And I can have any color as long as it's black," Dan replied.

"Just like Henry Ford and the Model T." Gary Raven pointed at the SUV in the nearest bay. "You can have the company car for as long as you need it."

"Does it have the usual accoutrements?"

"Bulletproof glass. Bombproof undercarriage. Run-flat tires. Has a higher-than-normal ground clearance in case you have to go over a curb or two. It also has a few other technical advances. Hell, even the headrests are bulletproof."

"Perfect."

"And this baby has been tested. I have shot at it myself. I even sat behind the wheel while a prospective client threw a grenade under it."

"That is a hell of a way to guarantee your work."

"Bet your ass," Gary Raven said, slapping Dan on the shoulder. "Get it?"

"Yeah."

Gary Raven turned serious. "Why do you need it?"

"Being cautious."

"You are always cautious, but you've never asked for one of my cars."

"I have thought about it, for what it is worth."

Dan walked around the car parked in the second automotive bay. The doors were missing. The windshield had been removed. New pieces ready for assembly were neatly stacked on foam in the corner. Dan noticed the diplomatic tags in the license plate frames.

"Whose car is that?"

"French Embassy."

"How long is it in for?"

"Until I finish."

"Another favor. Let me borrow the tags. I'll bring them back when I return the car."

Gary Raven rubbed his chin and then stepped to the toolset on the work counter and picked up a screwdriver.

Dan's cell phone started to ring and he fished it out of his cargo pants as Gary Raven removed the tags.

"Dan, it's April."

"What's up, Doc?"

"She is gone."

"What do you mean, *gone?*"

"Sue is gone. I stepped out for a delivery on a woman with twins and when I came back the room was empty."

"Did you check the bathroom?"

"Of course."

"The other call rooms? Maybe she got confused when she came out of the bathroom. The rooms do look similar."

"I checked all the call rooms."

"Shit."

"What do you want me to do?"

"Let me know if . . ." Click.

Dan looked down at his phone. The display indicated the call was terminated at the thirty second mark. The phone vibrated again in his hand and a text message filled the screen. Dan read the text and shook his head slowly in disbelief. `Time to pay your bills, Dan. This phone will begin working again when I get my money. Sorry, rules are rules . . . Tobias.`

Dan whispered vulgarities as Gary approached, two diplomatic license plates in hand.

"Who was that?"

"Sensei, I wouldn't know where to begin."

"Here are your tags. Bring them back in pristine condition or don't bring them back at all. I can always report them as stolen. I can't so easily explain how they got damaged without the car getting damaged. You know, these diplomatic tags are hot commodities. A free pass to shenanigans. They are also expensive. Special reflective paint. Rumor has it they contain a traceable wire mesh. Return them in perfect condition or throw them in the Potomac."

Raven handed him the keys to the demo car. Dan reached into his pocket, removed Sue's car keys, and tossed them into the air. Raven snatched them in one smooth motion.

As Raven examined the key ring, Dan explained. "Those keys are to the car in front of the dojo. A Honda Civic. It's not mine. It belongs to a girl who has been interning with me. I'll be back for it later."

"Sure thing."

Dan walked to the demo SUV and opened the five-hundred-pound door. He slipped behind the wheel, inserted the Mercedes Benz key and started the ignition. Raven nodded at Dan through the windshield and pushed the red button on the vertical support beam. The large garage door behind the car opened. Dan flicked the door locks and checked the mirrors before rolling down the driver's side window. "I have another automotive question for you."

"What's that?"

"How many gray BMW M5s do you think there are in Virginia?"

"What year?"

"2010?"

"A handful at the most. BMW only sold eight thousand or so BMW M5s between 2005 and 2010."

"That would equal about 1,600 each year."

"That's about right. But I am pretty sure they offered them in black, gray, white, and burgundy."

"So maybe four or five hundred gray ones for the year 2010 . . ."

"Something like that. And that number is for the entire US. For Virginia, you have to figure ten, maybe fifteen."

"You know your cars."

"The BMW M5 is a good car for security modifications. We've seen a few of them in the shop. It has a lot of horsepower so it can handle all the extra weight that comes with armor plating."

"I'm not sure that is good news."

CHAPTER 34

—

Dan drove his security-laden Mercedes SUV up Glebe Road from Ballston. The car handled like a drunken pachyderm. Weighing in at nearly eight thousand pounds, its pavement-crushing heft was twice that of a normal vehicle its size. Armor plating, reinforced framing, and two-inch glass added weight. The diplomatic tags were an added stroke of insurance. Police in most jurisdictions around DC didn't bother cars with diplomatic tags. Red lights, speed limits, and double yellow lines were all optional driving suggestions for those with diplomatic immunity. For the police, only the most egregious disregard for rule-of-law would justify pulling over a car with diplomatic tags.

Dan crossed Lee Highway, drove two blocks, and pulled into the main campus of Marymount University on the right. He maneuvered the car into a tight spot and the brakes worked overtime to stop the mass of metal before hitting the concrete curb.

Dan jumped from the vehicle and ignored the sign stating the spot required a parking decal. A minute later he entered the four-story all-brick Gailhac Hall and bounded up the steps of the wide staircase two at a time. On the third floor, he read the names of the faculty members on each door, walking briskly down the hall at a pace rarely seen in academia. The fifth door on the right read Professor Davis, PhD. Professor of Forensics. He looked at the class schedule taped to the door frame, checked the old-school clock on the wall, and headed for the listed classroom in the basement.

Dan peeked through the glass window in the wood door and watched as Professor Davis practiced perfect penmanship on the large whiteboard in the class. A class of approximately twenty graduate students sat smattered about in three rows of stadium seating. The students methodically copied their professor's pontifications on fingerprint matching, typing the information presented on the whiteboard into the laptops in front of them, forever transforming the class coursework into digitally stored files.

Dan waited for a pause and when Professor Davis posed a question to a startled class body, he slipped in the back door unnoticed. His anonymity lasted one heartbeat before Professor Davis identified his acquaintance in the back of the room. "Ladies and gentlemen, we have a visitor. Does anyone want to impress him with the answer to the question at hand? It is a fifty-fifty question. Doesn't get any easier than that."

The students glanced over at Dan as they contemplated whether to answer. "What was the question?" Dan asked.

"The question is whether or not identical twins have identical fingerprints."

Dan glanced around at the students before answering the question himself. "They do not."

"Indeed," Professor Davis said before excusing himself. "Ladies and gentlemen, I will be back in one minute. Pardon the interruption."

Dan met the professor on the side wall, halfway down the small set of stairs.

Professor Davis extended his hand and then chided his visitor. "You could call in advance. Or even stop by during office hours."

"No phone. No time. I need the files you have on Sue Fine. I can't get into my office at the moment and most of the information I had on her was there."

Professor Davis eyed Dan with concern. "The files on whom?"

"My intern for the semester. Sue Fine. I think she may be in trouble."

"I don't have a student by that name. And the internship program has been moved to the spring semester."

Dan's stomach turned and a wave of nausea washed over him.

CHAPTER 35

—

Dan covered the six miles from Marymount to Pimmit Hills in the time it took "Hotel California" to play from start to finish on the radio. He gunned the heavy engine through the neighborhood streets, hit the gravel driveway without braking, and stopped the armored car on the other side of a small moving van in front of Tobias's bungalow. The back door on the orange twenty-footer was raised and the contents of Tobias's house were stacked from the floor to ceiling.

"Tobias," Dan called out calmly, not wanting to startle a spooked man with mental inconsistencies. He knocked on the side of the moving truck as he approached the cab and then turned towards the bungalow. The front door was open and as he reached the front step of the house he rapped gently on one of the porch columns. He slowly raised his voice and Tobias stumbled forward seconds later with a box full of multi-color computer cables. The spaghetti configuration of the wires told Dan all he needed about the expediency of Tobias's impending departure.

"Oh good. You got my message," Tobias said.

"You disabled my phone."

"Couldn't be certain you were even using that phone. I know you have a stash of prepaid throwaways. But just to make sure I got your attention, I also terminated Internet access at your office."

"Can't use my office at the moment. Can't get to my pre-paid phones."

"I heard about your little problem with exploding packages. Thought I had lost another acquaintance to be honest. Even raised a beer in your name and nodded to your memory. Then the news said there were no casualties."

"Disappointed, I am sure."

"Hard to get paid by a dead man. As you know, retirement is the only thing on my mind. And I'm too poor to retire, too old to start a legitimate career, and too rich to explain where all the money I do have came from. The only solution is to take as much as I can and get out of here."

"Where you headed?"

"You could probably guess based on our previous conversation. Not sure how long it will take me to get there."

"Moving is not a bad idea. In fact, I may be right behind you."

"Not much choice. Our little search for the mystery phone number likely put this location on the map. And not a map I want to be on. I can't risk it. Where is your sidekick? You know I liked her more than I like you."

"On that topic, we may have an additional problem. I'm not exactly sure where she is."

"Did you take her to the mall and lose her?"

"No, the hospital. And as it turns out, she is not who she said she was, either."

"If that means what I think it means, it's a good thing I'm leaving."

"Sorry for the trouble."

"I don't mind the trouble if I get paid. Did you bring my money?"

"No. But I have something better than that."

"Better than money?"

"Better than the amount I owe you. I brought you a proposition for retirement. Potentially enough money that you will never have to unpack this truck. Just drive it out into the country and set it on fire. Walk away. Vanish."

Tobias set the box in his arms down on the front porch. "You now have my attention."

"Time to put your money where your mouth is. You know that football program you have. I need the football picks for this Sunday. All the professional games. What team wins. What team is going to cover. Whatever you can lock down."

"Sixteen games in a weekend. How many do you need?"

"How many does Vegas get correct in a given week?"

"On average, ten. Five away teams. Five underdogs."

"I need you to beat Vegas. Convincingly beat Vegas. And I don't have time for a long winded explanation of your data points. I need a list of your picks. And then I need you to prepare some sort of sales pitch."

"Is that all?"

"No, actually, that is not all. Turn my phone back on and give me a number where I can reach you."

Tobias grunted and motioned his hand for Dan to follow him into the house. A lone laptop sat on the counter in the pass-through between the living room and the kitchen. A small portable wireless printer sat on the narrow counter near the wall outlet. Tobias opened the lid on the computer, swiped his finger in the built-in fingerprint reader, and then pounded on the keys for a moment.

Dan felt his phone vibrate in his pocket. "It's on. Now, print out this week's winners."

Dan opened the phone and called Dr. Cathright. April answered on the third ring.

Tobias paused to eavesdrop on Dan's conversation and Dan waved his hand in a rolling motion to get Tobias back to work.

"Hey Doc, it's me again. I had some phone issues to straighten out."

Tobias glanced at Dan with the evil eye and rubbed his fingers together in the universal sign for money.

Dan turned away and pressed the phone to his ear. "Any word on Sue?"

"I don't know where she is, but I know how she got out of the hospital. She swiped the badge from one of the doctor's coats while they were taking a shower. She dropped the stolen badge off with security on her way out the front door. She told the guard on duty she found the badge on the floor in the lobby. Security brought the badge back upstairs a while ago."

"Clever girl."

"But she still needed a passcode to exit through the main doors on this floor."

"93765," Dan replied.

"You little cheat."

"Prudence. You know I don't like being trapped. And if I watched you punch in the code, then she probably did too."

"Nice friends."

"Oh, it gets better than that. I'll fill you in on the details later."

"Be careful, Dan."

"I'm always careful."

Dan hung up the phone as Tobias handed him a printout. "Those are the spreads for the sixteen NFL games this weekend. And I wrote down a phone number where I can be reached."

"How do you feel about these picks?"

"I don't feel anything about them. I trust numbers. It's not like I have a chicken in the backyard and make picks based on where it defecates. I have put more work into that program than anything I have ever done."

"Good enough for me."

"Now when exactly am I going to get my money?"

Dan stared intently at Tobias. "Listen carefully. Keep your crazy side in check, stick by the phone number you just gave me, and you can walk away into a very happy sunset. Clear your schedule for Sunday. Make yourself available. And don't screw with my phone until then."

CHAPTER 36

—

Spies Like Us was a surveillance store hidden on an alley behind an outdated Vietnamese restaurant. Three blocks from the Clarendon Metro Station—and enough drinking establishments to host a rugby championship—the development of the surrounding area did not bode well for a renewal of the shop's current lease. The shadow of burgeoning condo developments—starting at half a million for a studio—now reached the jet black door with the blue neon sign above the doorway.

Spies Like Us embraced the essence of the clandestine community. No store front, no window shopping. A door, a small sign, and fifteen hundred square feet of aisles packed floor to ceiling. Most of the customers were on the fringe. Private detectives looking for surveillance assistance. Wannabe spies looking for toys. The occasional voyeur looking, well, to get a better look. On more than one occasion Dan found himself at a locked front door during business hours, voices on the inside indicating the shop was open only to certain members of the public.

Dan parked the SUV with diplomatic immunity in the alley and looked both ways as he exited the vehicle. He estimated twenty yards of empty space in front of the car and another twenty yards behind. Enough space to get the eight thousand pound behemoth up to ramming speed, if an expeditious getaway was in order. Five feet on either side of the car was sufficiently tight to keep other vehicles from pinning him in while simultaneously putting a stranglehold on potential through traffic. Satisfied with the security of the location, Dan slipped through the front door of the shop.

The man behind the counter with wild, curly hair and a

matching beard nodded in Dan's direction. Dan returned his standard greeting. As a private detective with an affinity for gadgets, Dan was a regular. In most establishments there would have been a personal relationship between the customer and the shop owner. When you drop fifty grand in a small business over a couple of years, the owner tends to want to know your name, remember your birthday, put you on a mailing list, offer you a drink. Spies Like Us did not. Despite clocking a hundred visits and doling out a stack of cash several inches high, Dan and the man behind the counter were stuck on the relationship equivalent of first base. Questions were asked, answers were given, and solutions and options were presented. Neither man elaborated. Dan always paid cash. Never offered his name. Skipped the chitchat.

Dan's eyes locked with the owner as he approached the counter. The man with the wild hair pushed aside a velvet-lined tray of wrist watches.

"Can I help you?" he asked with stoicism that hid evidence of any previous encounter.

"I'm looking for a remote camera I can use to monitor traffic flow at a high volume location."

"Will the camera be mounted indoors or outdoors?"

"Outdoors."

"Under an eave or in the open?"

"Exposed to the elements."

"Distance requirements?"

"Up to a half-mile."

"Remote control access of the camera?"

"Yes."

"Service life?"

"Let's say a week, for sure."

The man released a subtle "Hmm . . . Any size limitations?"

"No size requirements, but smaller is better. The camera will be hidden in plain sight and needs to be installed with very limited set-up time."

"Hiding a camera in plain sight requires an understanding of the environment for appropriate camouflage."

"The camera will be placed roadside. Major thoroughfare."

"Infiltration and exfiltration of the camera done by vehicle?"

Dan looked at the man with intrigue. "Yes."

"One-man job?"

"At this point."

The man behind the counter stroked his beard and for the first time Dan noticed a faint military ensign tattoo peeking from the sleeve of his t-shirt.

"Let me summarize. Correct me if necessary at any point. You will be in a vehicle. You will need to stop and exit the vehicle. You will set up the camera, in a matter of seconds, and return to the vehicle, leaving the camera without anyone knowing you left said equipment behind. The camera will have to function, remotely, with sufficient memory to last a week."

"Yes."

"I'm just spit-balling here, but it sounds like you may be trying to take pictures of the entrance and exit behaviors of a secure location. An intelligence installation, perhaps?"

Dan tried not to act surprised and failed. The relationship with the shopkeeper had just taken a large step forward. They had left first base, the initial kiss behind them. As they closed in on second, the shopkeeper was looking to cop a feel.

"I may have just what you're looking for," the shop owner continued.

The man stepped into the back of the shop, disappearing behind a plywood wall divider separating the front half of the store from the shelves of miscellaneous inventory in the rear. Dan heard a rattle of metal, a box hitting the floor, and the sound of breaking glass. Moments later the shop owner returned with a product brochure replete with a photograph and a diagram.

Dan looked at the diagram and then at the photograph of a gray stone about the size of a softball. "A camera disguised as a stone?"

"Field-tested and proven."

"Is it heavy?"

"Doesn't do any good to make a fake rock with incorrect weight parameters."

The man ran his finger over a small list of attributes written down the side of the product brochure. "It weighs just under seven pounds."

Dan took his time reading through the small print of the product specs as the shop owner made his pitch.

"It meets your requirements. Most people don't give rocks a second look. They don't view them as trash. Most people with custodial responsibilities don't bother to remove them when they are cleaning up an area. Rocks are heavy. The most prevalent danger to a rock is someone moving it either intentionally or accidentally. That would obviously upset your camera view. The US intelligence agency was recently discovered to have used a rock with a camera in it to keep an eye on sensitive locations in Moscow. It was quite successful for many years."

"What is the range for controlling the camera?"

"Virtually unlimited. The signal is cellular. You can program it to sync with your smart phone or computer. Just like a babysitter camera. It has focusing capability. It has a thirty-two gigabyte solid-state drive, but you can also save images and video to your computer."

"That should work."

"Problem is that I'm sold out. We had six of them earlier in the week. One lucky customer bought them all. I can have replacements in forty-eight hours."

"How much?"

"Fourteen hundred even. I'll knock a hundred off because I am out of stock."

"I'll be back for it on Monday morning."

"It will be here."

Dan looked down at the watches lying across the display counter. Various brands with various makes. Rubber, gold, titanium, black chrome.

"You need a watch?" the shop owner asked, picking up a platinum watch with an oversized face. He held the watch to his lips, opened his mouth, and exhaled onto the quartz face before wiping it with a cloth.

Dan replied. "I have a couple of watches at home already. I find myself wearing them less and less."

The shop owner snapped the round bevel off the face of the watch and pulled, extending his hands in opposite directions. A wire unfurled with a quiet tick, tick, tick. "Do any of your current watches have one of these?"

Dan looked at the piano wire pulled taut across his field of vision. "A garrote?"

"Get it around the neck, hold tight, count to ten, and then on to the next guy."

Dan felt another surge in the relationship between himself and the shop owner. As a couple, clothes were coming off and mouths were probing.

"What else do you have?" Dan asked, picking up a thick black chrome watch with a heavy rubber band.

The shop keeper with the wild hair smiled for the first time that Dan could remember. "What do you need it to do?"

—

Dan stepped from the store minutes later and looked down the alley in both directions. He checked the time on his new watch and smiled briefly at his acquisition. He pressed the remote on the keychain for the car and walked around to the driver's side with his head on a swivel. Dusk was on the horizon and as Dan reached the driver's door he thought he heard footsteps. Door still closed, he turned 180 degrees and saw nothing. He inhaled deeply through his nose and listened intently as the air escaped his lungs in a long, slow exhalation. He thought he caught a faint whiff of aftershave and unsuccessfully attempted to peer through the dark tinted windows into the back seat of the SUV. His spidey sense tingled again and he froze. He moved his eyes from left to right and then upward at the roofline of the buildings on either side of the car. He squinted at the condos on the horizon, and then opened the driver's door.

He put one foot into the car and before he could lift his second foot from the ground, he felt a sharp, brief pain in his lower leg. His eyes snapped downward and thought he saw the flash of a hand disappear beneath the vehicle. Dan reached for his leg and then fought to control his limbs. His head swooned and he dropped the keys in his hand and fell sideways across the front seat. Fighting for consciousness and losing control of his muscles, Dan watched in horror as Clyde Parkson pulled himself from beneath the vehicle, a hypodermic needle in his hand. Through increasing fog, Dan's eyes fluttered as Clyde Parkson put the cap on the empty syringe and slipped it into his breast pocket. The man in the suit casually glanced around and then shoved Dan's crippled body into the passenger seat.

Dan's eyes opened as the door shut. He watched as Clyde Parkson checked his sightlines in the mirrors and hummed quietly to himself. Dan blinked a final time and remained conscious just long enough to see Clyde Parkson flash his white teeth in an ear-to-ear grin.

CHAPTER 37

—

The ski mask with closed eyeholes that was pulled over Dan's face was as unsettling as the end of the handgun barrel bumping into his ribs from the left rear. Dan's head throbbed and his body ached, but being vertical and moving under his own power was infinitely more advantageous than being unconscious on his back with no muscle control.

He could feel his hands were tied at the wrist in front of his body with zip ties. He tugged on the restraints to gauge their strength and felt the gun stab him in the ribs. He imagined the gun was racked, a finger on the trigger guard. The hand grasping Dan's arm tightened and pulled him to the left. Dan felt the ground beneath his feet change from a hard surface to soft and back to hard. A few steps later he felt gravel under his feet and then was steered back to another hard surface. Dan's mind sifted through the options. *A stone pathway. An old driveway. A garden walkway.*

The next surface was noticeably more slippery and Dan narrowed his likely location to a few blocks of Georgetown or Old Town Alexandria. Nothing had the same feeling as old wet cobblestone.

He strained to listen through the ski mask as he was led up two short stairs. A brief pause. A turning doorknob. He concentrated on the sound of the door hinges as they protested. He registered the modest increase in temperature as he stepped inside. The sounds of the outside world—the faint hum of cars, the rain falling steadily—all vanished. The floor squeaked under his feet as he was pushed forward. He again noted the difference in his footing as he changed from hardwood floors to carpet and back to hardwood.

"Stairs down," Clyde Parkson said, pulling on Dan's arm briefly.

Dan paused, wondering if he were about to be thrown into some unseen abyss. Never to be seen again.

He stepped forward and down, not taking the weight off his back foot until his front foot found firm footing on what he assumed to be the first of many stairs. He continued the measured gait downward and the man behind him moved the gun from his back to the side of his head. A few steps later Dan was on flat ground. He inhaled deeply through the ski mask and vaguely registered musty, cooler air.

He heard other voices as he was steered across another floor. The surface beneath his feet was neither stone nor wood, somewhere between rough and smooth. Then Dan realized where he was. His momentary elation was squelched with a firm shove into an old wooden chair. Dan felt the seat rock and then settle onto the chair's four legs. Each of Dan's ankles were quickly strapped to the front legs of the chair, another zip tie restraint around the top of each calf, just below the knee. The zip ties on his hands were cut and his hands were moved behind him and restrained again.

With an upward tug of the ski mask, light blasted Dan's eyes and the charade ended.

Dan squinted at the two incandescent bulbs hanging from separate wooden support beams in the ceiling. His eyes moved around his environment, immediately conducting an inventory of a room he knew well. An early 1800s cellar with an earth floor in the main residence of the Stonewall Jackson House. Within fifty yards of his very own bed. Another hundred yards from his office.

His eyes focused on the two men standing at an old wooden table on the right hand side of the room. *Ebony and Ivory*, he thought. Dan's heart rate involuntarily quickened at the assortment of needles, guns, knives, and zip-tie restraints on the table.

The man Dan knew as Clyde Parkson threw an empty syringe on the table with the other tools of torment. He pulled Dan's cell phone from his pocket and opened the screen before snapping it shut again. He turned off the ringer and tossed it in the mix. Dan noted the thick rope on the far end of the table, still coiled in its packaging. A red gasoline can rested on the ground at the foot of the table.

Think quick, Dan told himself. His eyes darted more rapidly. In the far corner of the room, nearest the house and the stairs he had just come down, was the old coal closet, the earthen floor at the threshold of the door still stained black from decades of use in a previous life. In the nearer corner on the right was the old well. The dank scent of mold and mildew still wafted through the wood cover. The small brick wall around the base of the well showed moss near the seams in the centuries-old mortar.

Dan's mind raced through potential weapons. On his last visit to the cellar there had been a shovel in the coal bin, a prop to show tour guests and history buffs the utilitarian functionality and strength requirements of the old heating system. Dan moved his eyes upward and looked at the thick beams that ran in parallel across the ceiling. He scanned for loose boards, exposed nails, dangling wires, committing each possibility to memory and prioritizing which ones he could reach most easily.

Dan cranked his neck all the way to the left and he grimaced. Sue was seated slightly behind him, restrained in her own chair. There was blood on her lip. Her right eye was swollen shut. The reddish-purple flesh gruesomely on display. A thick strip of duct tape ran around her head horizontally. The thick gray adhesive matted her hair to her ears and ran completely across her mouth. Her hands were bound in front of her, on her lap. In turn, the zip ties that held her wrists were affixed around the belt on her jeans, like a prisoner in transport. She turned her neck towards Dan and mumbled something unintelligible through the tape across her mouth.

Dan looked up as the man he knew as Clyde Parkson smiled down at him.

"You like beating up on women?" Dan asked.

"I don't. But Major here has an infatuation with it. Ridge, on the other hand, has no emotional attachment or ideological affiliation. He simply does things for money. Doesn't talk much. Follows orders. A perfect soldier."

"There is no need to use names, even nicknames," Major replied.

"Oh, I don't see the harm in it," Clyde Parkson responded slowly.

"It provides a level of conviction that you won't let Dan here walk out the door with that knowledge."

"So we have Ridge and Major," Dan echoed. "Ebony and Ivory. And what is your name? I think we all know it is not Clyde Parkson."

"For the next couple of hours, you can call me Reed Temple. By the end of the evening, I will jettison that identity for another."

"I liked you more when you were an attorney. And I typically hate lawyers."

"Oh, I think you are going to like me even less in a few minutes."

"I must say you were pretty convincing as an attorney. You obviously rehearsed. I see your teeth were real. I assumed the hair was fake. Wasn't sure about the faint southern accent."

"Nice place you have here," Reed Temple said, looking around, ignoring the assessment of his previous disguise. "Of course when most people buy a house like this, they tend to live in it."

"The carriage house is smaller. Less upkeep. And there are tax advantages to the historical residence." Dan flicked his head in the direction of Sue who was fully conscious and listening. "Why the girl? She has nothing to do with this."

Sue shook her head and grunted.

"She was my insurance policy. At first, I thought I would simply use her to get to your attention. Now, well, I have other plans. A murder-suicide."

"You mean a murder-murder. I don't think either of us is going the suicide route."

"Semantics. Murder-suicide. Murder-murder."

"It does explain the choice of location. People are far more likely to commit suicide in a familiar location. So for my part in the murder-suicide fantasy you have in mind, this location would make sense. Not so much for a murder-murder, though."

Reed Temple nodded. "That's right. No one is going to question a man who kills himself in his own home. Especially one who is mourning the death of his last living immediate family members. But regardless of semantics, when we are done here, authorities will have a hard time proving anything definitively."

Dan tried to stall and changed the subject. "Temple, was it? Let me ask you a few questions while I have your attention. After all, you will be moving on with a new identity in short order."

Reed Temple pulled his cell phone from his jacket pocket and checked the time. "I have a few moments. What can I help you understand?"

"Did you kill my nephew?"

"Your nephew was already dying. I simply changed the direction of his death."

"Did you shoot him full of heroin? Drag him under an underpass? Leave him to die?"

"Your nephew was a group effort. As you know, he had unique capabilities that made subduing him potentially difficult. Took all three of us to do it without causing undue injury. But yes, the injection, the overdose, I delivered it."

"Manly of you. I guess you have a thing for needles."

"It is simply my job."

Dan choked back a sudden flood of emotions, his mind returning to his nephew. His last moments, alone, enduring the horror of physical restraint. Physical violation. Helplessness. Dan shook his head, hoping the welling tears would not break the confines of his eyes. "Which one of you killed the police detective?"

Reed Temple nodded perceptibly in the direction of Major. Major's posture straightened and he stepped forward to speak. "Based on ballistics and fingerprints, you killed him, Mr. Lord."

"That was a good effort," Dan replied. "But you couldn't shake my alibi. Good thing I needed a drink that night."

"Forgive us for our failure," Reed Temple added.

"Do we have any bomb makers in the room?" Dan asked. Major pointed to his own chest. "Right here. I made the bomb. I set the charge. Ridge here was the trigger."

Reed interjected again. "We are still not sure how you managed to escape the blast."

"I had help from a canine friend."

Major locked eyes with Reed Temple who shrugged his shoulders unknowingly.

"Which one of you strung my sister-in-law up in the closet?"

Neither Reed Temple nor Major moved. Dan's eye's bounced off each man's face before landing on Ridge, who stood still, half-standing, backside resting on the old wooden table.

Dan focused his eyes on Ridge's, squinting to see the large man's pupils. "It would probably take someone your size to pull that off. Getting a belt around someone's neck and lifting them off the ground without wounds to both the victim and perpetrator would not be easy. Hell, even you probably needed help."

Ridge refused to respond.

"OK. No one manly enough to answer that question. I can understand that. After all, there is nothing manly about killing a defenseless woman in her own bedroom. I don't think I would confess to that, either. Anyone want to confess to killing Haley Falls?"

Reed Temple approached Dan with a slow gait. He took one lap around Sue and Dan, running his hands over their shoulders as he passed. Dan shifted his weight in the chair and felt the old frame rock in response. He pulled on his wrists without success.

Reed Temple checked his phone again and cleared his throat. "Q and A is over. But in the interest of being fair, yes, I killed that whore friend of yours. Did you a favor if you ask me. You should know better than to be hanging out with trash. Women like that will give you a bad reputation."

"I'm sure she would have said the same about you."

"But she can't now, can she?"

"Asshole," Dan said pulling on his wrists until the restraints cut his skin.

"You know, Dan, I was under orders to let you be. Not to intrude. To let sleeping dogs lie, as it were. But you just kept digging. Kept poking around. Kept sticking your nose into places you shouldn't have."

"I do have that problem."

"Yes, you do, and this time it killed innocent people. And it is going to kill you and your intern here."

"Actually, she is not my intern," Dan said, glancing over at Sue whose eyes opened wide in a look of betrayal. "I'm not sure who she is," Dan added, focusing on Reed Temple's face to measure any reaction to Dan's admission.

Dan watched intently as Temple reached into his suit pants pocket and pulled out the car keys to Dan's security-laden Mercedes SUV. Temple jingled the keys slightly as he stepped forward. Dan strained to listen as Temple leaned into Sue and whispered directly into her ear. "I know exactly who you are. But it will be less messy if I pretend I don't." Sue thrashed and yelled something unintelligible into the duct tape over her mouth.

"Are we keeping secrets, now? I thought we were having a forthright conversation," Dan said.

Reed Temple checked the time again and then wrung his hands. "You will have to excuse me. I have a business meeting to attend. I will be taking your car, Dan. Those diplomatic tags can be a godsend when it comes to parking . . . So without further ado . . ."

"What's the rush, Temple? Not man enough to shoot me yourself?"

"Outsourcing is the American way."

"Pussy. Go ahead. I'll take care of these guys and meet up with you later."

"I appreciate your spunk. But you are in an earthen cellar with no windows, in a very big house, on a very large lot. It is also raining outside. Sound will not travel far." Reed Temple walked to the table and moved his hand across the tools and weapons. "Scream if you must. But make it a good one. I now leave you in the very capable hands of Major and Ridge here. Enjoy." He blew a kiss in the direction of Dan and Sue before heading towards the stairs. "Call me when you are done with them," he yelled down as he reached the top of the staircase.

Dan listened and looked upward as the floorboards above creaked with the weight of Reed's steps. He felt both relief and failure as Reed Temple pulled the front door shut with a resounding thud.

Major let the echo of the door run its course before coming to animated life. He walked deliberately across the room and pulled the duct tape off of Sue's mouth, uprooting a wad of hair in the procedure. Sue spit and tried to swallow. She coughed, gagged, and then finally spoke through raspy vocal chords. "You're an asshole," she said.

"The two of you share the same vocabulary," Major replied, amused.

"Fuck you," Dan and Sue said simultaneously.

Major walked back over to the table and looked down at the options at his disposal.

Dan glanced over at Sue. "How's the eye?"

"I'll survive."

"You have some explaining to do."

"I'm sorry. Let's just leave it at that."

"Impressive, by the way. I'm usually good at spotting liars. I'm beginning to think, however, that it may be a perishable skill."

"It wasn't an even playing field. You were in mourning."

"What is your real name?"

"My real name is Sue."

"Convenient."

"You have a plan to get us out of here?"

"Working on one."

"You want to share it with me?"

"Nope."

CHAPTER 38

—

Major picked a stun gun off the wood table and smiled at the arc of electricity as it jumped between the two conductors protruding from the top of the handheld device. He returned the stun gun to the table, smiled, and rubbed the knuckles on his hand, alternating between fists. Still grinning, he slowly walked over to his subjects, restrained in their respective chairs, and continued his deranged rendition of foreplay.

"Pathetic really," Major said. "I expected so much more from you, Dan."

"Sorry to disappoint. I didn't know there was a level of expectation."

Major stepped in front of Sue and slapped her across the face with an open palm, her neck snapping violently to the side.

"Any other smart comments, Dan?"

Dan looked at Sue as she straightened her head, a large red handprint on her cheek. "Keep your teeth together. You won't bite your tongue," Dan whispered.

Major looked down at Sue and smeared the blood that was on Sue's lip with his finger. Sue pulled her head away in disgust.

"You know, killing people is really overrated. The warm-up, the foreplay, that is where the joy is," Major said. "Men have been killing each other since the beginning of time. There is no creativity left to it."

"I agree. I am sure I speak for both of us when I say we can skip the killing part of the show," Dan replied.

Dan grunted as Major landed an elbow to the side of his head.

"I thought you were smarter than that," Major said.

"So did I," Dan mumbled.

"Here is how the next few minutes are going to play out. We are going to get to know each other a little better. Then, I am going to take that rope over there and hang Dan from one of these ceiling beams. We will all watch as he unceremoniously shits and pisses himself. Then he will die."

"Good thing these aren't my dress pants."

Major stepped in with his left hand and Dan gritted his teeth through the effects of a punch to face.

"Once you stop twitching, your face gruesomely contorted, frozen in the effort for another breath that will not come, I will put the semi-automatic .45 in your hand, aim it at the princess's head, and pull the trigger. That will provide good crime scene evidence. A nice little murder-suicide. Man takes girlfriend to his secret little abode. Man gets violent. Man shoots girlfriend. Man hangs himself."

"I already told you, technically it would be a murder-murder."

Major reached down and grabbed Dan's wrist. He slowly undid the rubber strap, pulled sharply upward, and removed Dan's new watch from his tied arm. He eyeballed his latest souvenir, flashing the timepiece for his limited audience.

"You won't need this. I have a nice spot for it on my mantle. Right next to a police detective's badge and a very cool alligator-skin wallet."

"It was Australian crocodile, asshole. And I am going to want that wallet back."

"You know, your nephew was also a little upset when I took the wallet. Now I understand why. A personal gift from Uncle Dan. I may have to put it in its own little showcase."

"Fuck you."

Major moved behind Sue and gently massaged both shoulders. Then he ran his hand up to her hairline and yanked on the gold chain around her neck, pulling off her necklace in one quick motion. He looked at the cross with the silver metal beams of sunlight streaking from the sides.

"You piece of shit," Sue said.

"I think she is going to want that back, too," Dan added.

Major dropped his latest acquisitions off at the old wooden table and then pulled a large knife from his pocket. He looked at his prized captives and smirked as he cut the packaging off the thick rope. He whispered something to Ridge and the large man's hands moved to the .45 semiautomatic on the table. Ebony removed the magazine, cleared the chamber, and then began a full weapons check and wipe down.

Major continued. "How much rope do you think we need here, Dan? We have low ceilings and you are probably six foot one or so. We may have to move to the other side of the main support column. I think the ceiling is a little higher on the other side of the room. Tough to hang someone with their feet hitting the floor."

"We could try," Dan replied.

"Oh, I am sure you would appreciate that."

Major used his arms to measure off a length of rope suitable to the task at hand and then stepped to the other side of the room, his eyes focused upward in search of an appropriate location to hang a noose. "I haven't lynched anyone in a while. Probably a couple of years. Ridge did your sister-in-law, but I was busy with your nephew at the time."

Major set the rope on the ground and jumped upward with extended hands. He hung momentarily from a large floor-support beam and then lowered himself back to the ground. "That one should work."

Major threw the rope over the top of the beam and pulled the noose downward. He admired his knot-tying skills and adjusted the opening on the noose. Looking through the circle shape at the end of the rope, Major smiled at Dan. "Think your head will fit?"

"Try it out."

"I think not," Major replied. "Ridge, could you prepare Dan for his demise?"

"Just a moment," Ridge replied wiping his fingerprints off the handgun on the table. He tossed a white towel to the side and swiped a loaded syringe off the table as he turned.

Dan's pulse increased as he alternated glances between death by hanging to the left, and mysterious drug injection on the right. On the other side of the room, Major began describing the sequence of the body's reaction to being hung as he searched for an appropriate location to affix the non-business end of the noose.

Ridge, syringe in hand, passed behind Dan first and then Sue. Major, relishing his expertise in incessant speech and the systematic shutdown of organs, didn't take his attention off the rope or his pontification until Ridge had sunk the syringe into his neck and depressed the plunger.

Dan glanced at Sue, who returned the look of surprise.

Ridge looked over at Dan and Sue as he dropped Major's body to the floor. "Orders," Ridge offered, taking the pulse of his partner. As Major's chest rose and fell in slowing increments, Ridge turned away from Dan and Sue. He grabbed the end of the rope and pulled it in the direction of the far wall.

CHAPTER 39

—

Dan glanced at Sue and nodded.

Ridge was twenty feet away, tying the support end of the rope to a vertically running cast-iron pipe. Major was on the floor, the syringe in his neck still slowly twitching.

Now or never. Dan took a deep breath and stood, his lower legs still attached to the chair, his wrists tied to each other behind his back. Before Ridge looked over, he threw himself forward, headfirst.

The somersault and resulting break-fall had the desired effect as the old chair Dan was sitting on splintered into pieces. Ridge turned, registered what he was seeing, and started to move as Dan struggled to get his hands over his feet and back in front of his body.

Using Dan's gravity experiment as an example, Sue leaned over in her chair, falling at Ridge as he passed, momentarily tripping the big man and providing enough time for Dan to get his hands in front of him.

Dan stood as Ridge regained his balance. Dan stepped back to gain distance and then turned away. He drove his zip-tied hands forward until his arms were straight in front of him. He reversed directions on his arm thrust and pulled his elbows back as far as they would go with adrenaline-pumping force. The law of physics did the rest as the zip ties on his wrist snapped at the point where they were joined.

Dan turned and Ridge's massive right hand contacted with his forehead, causing the gash on his eyebrow to re-open. The blood flowed more freely with the second injury to the same location and Dan strained to see through the crimson lens of his left eye.

The next moment Dan was in a bear hug, his breath evacuated, his ribs crushed. Through his impaired vision, Dan stared into the darkness of Ridge's black pupils.

Face-to-face, Ridge held Dan in his arms, his muscles straining, veins bulging on his neck. Holding Dan in a bear hug, Ridge walked steadily in the direction of the hanging noose. Dan unleashed a battery of assaults on Ridge's head. He used open palm slaps to burst the eardrums and thumb thrusts to the eyes. Ridge was unfazed. Dan tried to breathe as he looked over his shoulder at the fast-closing destination. Feet and arms flailing, Dan felt the edge of the noose slip over his head and onto his forehead.

Dan thrashed his neck violently and the noose fell off to the side. Dan jammed his fingers into the base of Ridge's throat and Dan heard a small groan. Again Dan smashed his open palms into the side of Ridge's ears. Ridge squeezed tighter and readjusted his aim on the noose. Every move of Dan's arms opened his torso to more assault. His diaphragm was compressed to its limit. The physical exertion combined with decreased lung capacity took its toll. Frantic, Dan saw stars. Somewhere in his oxygen-deprived brain a countdown began. *Eight seconds before unconsciousness,* he thought. *Eight seconds before the end. Eight seconds before Ridge here can do anything he wants to me.*

In one quick motion, Dan moved both his hands to Ridge's face and shoved his thumbs into opposite corners of the big man's mouth. Ridge's eyes bulged as Dan drove his thumbs into the crease between Ridge's molars and the inside of his cheeks. With three seconds before blackout, Dan released a primal yell and yanked his thumbs outwards and back towards Ridge's ears.

The flesh on Ebony's face ripped like blood-sewn fabric, his cheeks now open wounds, molars visible. Dan's feet hit the floor as Ridge reached for his own face. The guttural scream that exploded from Ridge sent the hair on Dan's neck up at attention as he gasped for air.

Ridge's eyes flashed open in horror at his blood-soaked hands. Dan raised his foot and stomped downward, meeting Ridge's shin and powering downward to crush the top bone of Ridge's foot. A second stomp to the end of Ridge's toes was next, followed by a kick to the groin and an outside knee to the side of the thigh.

Ridge regained his posture, face open, blood flowing. He reversed the assault, swinging wildly at his smaller opponent. Dan sidestepped the raging bull and then reached up for a support beam in the ceiling. Hanging by his arms he kicked both feet as Ridge turned. The soles of Dan's shoes met the middle of Ridge's face. The big man stumbled back and Dan charged forward, shoulder first. The impact drove Ridge backwards, leaving him teetering on the edge of the small, covered well. Dan moved in for the final assault and the deafening discharge from the .45 handgun silenced the room.

Dan slowly looked over his shoulder and found himself staring down the barrel of the .45. Sue's face was perfectly aligned down the center of the handgun on the other side of the sights.

CHAPTER 40

—

The sound of snapping wood planks ripped Dan's attention away from the business end of the handgun and back at Ridge, who was now grasping his chest. The inertia of the gunshot provided enough energy to tip the ex-marine over the lip of the old well. His backside hit first, momentarily resting on the wood planks as if the big man was choosing to sit down. Dan felt a moment of guilt as he took one final look at a life wasted. Then the wood-planked top of the well cracked and Ridge disappeared, his feet folding upward towards his bloody face as the darkness below welcomed him.

Dan stood and Sue's hands started to shake. He stepped off the firing line, raised his hand slowly, and repeated what he had been taught when confronted with an armed adversary. "Relax. I am un-armed. Lower the gun," he repeated soothingly.

Sue slowly dropped her hands before releasing her grip on the weapon. The gun thudded softly on the dirt cellar floor. Her hands were still bound together at the wrist with zip ties. Her unbuckled belt hung from the restraints between her still-bound hands, the black leather accessory dangling down to her knees.

"Nice escape."

"My hands were tied in front of me, looped around the belt. All I had to do was unbuckle it and pull. The gun was loaded on the table."

"And I kept him occupied for you. Are you OK?"

"I will be."

Dan retrieved the knife Major used to cut the rope for the noose. He sliced the remains of the zip ties off each wrist and then cut the final tie off his calf. Freed, he turned his attention towards Sue.

After several additional precision cuts with the knife, Sue joined Dan in emancipation. Hands still shaking, she rubbed her wrists. Dan crouched and approached Major's unmoving body. He checked for a pulse on Major's carotid. "He is still alive."

"What do we do?"

"Get the hell out of here."

Dan rifled through Major's pockets, tossing car keys, a wallet, and a cell phone into a pile next to the knife he had just used. He looked up momentarily at the noose dangling above and performed a sign of the cross, silently mumbling something to himself. He moved Major's belongings from the ground to the wood table as Sue carefully approached the top of the well. Not trusting her coordination with a body full of adrenaline, she lowered herself onto all fours and peered over the edge into the blackness. "How deep is it?"

"About thirty feet. You shot him center mass at pointblank range with a .45. He did not survive."

Sue's face turned pale with a mix of emotions. A combination of guilt, disgust, and admiration. "You tore his face open."

"He was trying to kill me. It was a move of last resort. I was told the technique was called 'the Joker.' The reason is obvious."

"Where did you learn that?"

"A special forces soldier. I was told it was most effective as an escape technique. Something to be used when you need to remove yourself from a situation with multiple assailants. To divert the attention of an angry mob, for example. I wasn't sure it would actually work."

"It was the most awful thing I've ever seen."

"Certainly in the top ten," Dan conceded, before starting to parse the inventory on the old wooden table. He reacquired his cell phone and turned the volume back up. He lovingly retightened the strap on his newly purchased watch. He picked up the vial of liquid that had been injected into Major and held the small glass bottle to the light.

"What do you think it is?"

"I don't know. But my guess is Major was never going to walk out of this basement. Ridge had a plan and Major didn't know about it. Reed Temple is cleaning up after himself. Paid Ridge to take care of Major. And you can bet there was a plan to end Ridge as well."

"I guess we did Temple a favor."

"You did him a favor. I merely injured him. You shot him."

Sue rolled her eyes and then grabbed her necklace, glanced at the broken clasp and carefully slid it into her pocket.

Dan grabbed a handful of zip ties and shoved them into the thigh pockets on his pants. He pocketed the knife Major had used to cut the rope and retrieved the gun from the floor, releasing the magazine into his hand and ejecting the round in the chamber. He grabbed Sue's cell phone off the table and held it up. "Is this yours?"

Sue reached for the phone and Dan retracted his arm. He deftly turned and tossed the phone into the well. A single clank reverberated from the open hole as the phone hit the stone wall on the way down.

"What the hell did you do that for?"

"Insurance. I don't want you to disappear again and claim you have no knowledge of what transpired here."

Dan pulled Major's driver's license from his wallet and held the ID up to eye level. "Says here Major's real name is Steve Jackson. Lives in the West End, near Georgetown. " Dan poked through the rest of the wallet and then slipped Major's driver's license into his pocket. He plucked a set of car keys off the far end of the table and held them up. "What car did you come in?"

"The burgundy four-door sedan," Sue replied, sulking. "The same one you took pictures of during the stakeout at the coffee shop."

"Were you blindfolded?"

"After they put me in the car, they bound me and blindfolded me."

"When you arrived, how long was the walk from the car to the house?"

"A few seconds."

"Good, then the car is in the driveway or on the street in front of the house. We need transportation."

"What happened to my car?" Sue asked.

"I traded up and Reed Temple took the new one." Dan gripped the keys in his fist and joined Sue in taking a panoramic glance around the basement.

"I don't think we are going to be able to clean this up," Sue said.

"Not you and I. Broken furniture. Blood. A body in the well. Another unconscious on the floor. Footprints . . . Forget it. Time to go."

"Where?"

"Outside. I need to make a couple of calls."

CHAPTER 41

—

Dan opened the passenger door and with a swoop of the hand, gestured for Sue to enter Ebony and Ivory's burgundy sedan. She grudgingly accepted the offer, still miffed over the demise of her phone and the possible implications of the dead man in the well with a gunshot wound in his chest.

As her derrière found the passenger seat, Dan grabbed her wrist with his vise-like grip. A second later her arm was strapped with a zip tie, attached to the handle above the passenger door frame. Her arm extended upward as if stuck in a perpetual pose of asking a question.

"What the . . . ?"

"Additional insurance."

"You still don't trust me?"

"Not yet."

Sue struggled with the tie-down, frantically pulling her arm as Dan walked to the front of the car, staring at her through the windshield. He stopped near the front left fender and started to dial.

—

The National Harbor's new casino drove the commoners back to their middle-class neighborhoods on the weekends with a fifty-dollar-per-hand minimum. The policy kept the welfare checks away from the chip-and-cash windows between Friday night and Sunday night when bigger fish were likely to swim by and test the waters of the new establishment.

Joseph Cellini exchanged five thousand dollars at the roulette table and the dealer slid five stacks of hundred-dollar chips in his direction using both hands. Cellini peeled a few chips off the top and placed them on red and even.

The neckless muscle he kept in tow was standing behind him, uncomfortable in his spruced-up, on-the-town attire. His slacks pulled at his thighs, his shirt stretched at the seams, his poorly knotted tie lashed around his massive neck.

The dealer set the roulette wheel in motion and with a flick of the fingers the white ball jetted around in the opposite direction. As the two opposing forces of the roulette wheel performed their dance, Joseph Cellini stood from his seat. He motioned for his neckless accomplice to take his place and surveyed his environment for a quiet corner. A dozen paces away, Joseph Cellini found a modicum of solitude near a group of senior citizens at the Pai Gow poker table.

Joseph Cellini flipped open his phone and simply said, "Speak."

"You know who this is?" Dan asked.

Joseph Cellini took a moment to process the voice and responded. "What do you think?"

"I'm going with yes."

A slot machine in the distance dispersed a ten-thousand-dollar jackpot, accompanied by flashing lights, buzzes, beeps, and the shriek of a lone victor celebrating with a standing pelvic thrust.

"You at the new casino?" Dan asked.

"I am," said Joseph Cellini.

"Well, if you are still interested in the guy responsible for injuring your daughter, the bomb maker himself is currently unconscious in the basement of a house in Old Town Alexandria named for a Civil War General. The front door is open."

"Will he be expecting me?"

"Depends on how long it takes you to get there."

"Something you did?"

"No."

"Do I need to provide maid service?"

"There won't be time. You can be at the house I described in less than fifteen minutes from your current location. If you are interested, you need to hurry. And if you can make it, ignore the problem with the water supply."

"I assume that is self-explanatory."

"Should be. I can delay calling the police but not all night. So if you are interested, get moving."

"What about a financial settlement to cover my art gallery losses?"

"As I said in the hospital, these guys were never going to negotiate a settlement."

Joseph Cellini breathed heavily into the phone.

Dan continued. "But in the spirit of good neighbor relations, I have a solution to your financial concerns that you will find amicable. I'm requesting a meeting. Good Time Charlie in Prince Georges County. Be there. Sunday. High noon."

"I'll be there."

—

Dan slid into the driver's seat and put the key into the ignition. "Secret phone call?"

"I don't think we should be talking about secrets."

Sue pulled at her wrist and scowled.

"Probably not going to break the zip ties with that angle," Dan said flatly. "Sit there while I make another call."

Sue scowled again and Dan dialed another number. Detective Wallace answered on the second ring and Dan recognized from the sound of the detective's voice that he was smoking a cigarette. Dan imagined the detective in his car, one hand on the wheel, one hand on the phone, a cloud of smoke, and a cancer stick hanging from his lips with an ash tail that was ready to drop. Dan pushed his own sudden desire for a smoke from his mind.

"I see you called," Dan said.

"I did."

"I was occupied. Did you find the gray BMW?"

"Are you aware that the gray BMW M5 is a particularly rare vehicle?"

"I heard that rumor. I didn't have time to check it out myself."

"Well, it was an important piece of information."

"Do you have an address?"

"I can do better than that."

"You have eyes on it?"

"Two cars ahead of me. We crossed the Key Bridge five minutes ago. Unfortunate for the driver. Now we are in my jurisdiction. My rules."

"I remember your rules. See if you can give them an hour in a cell at DC general."

"Still complaining about that?"

"Did you get an ID on who owns the car?"

"I called it in as soon as I picked up the tail and had the tags in sight. It is owned by Michael and Kate Smith. Leesburg, Virginia."

"There is no way those are real identities."

"I was thinking the same thing. The names seem a little too generic."

"How did you find the car?"

Detective Wallace took a long drag on his cigarette and exhaled slowly. Dan recognized the sound and buried a pang of envy.

"I followed the car from a gas station at Kirby Road and Route 123."

"You must have spoken with Alex the Russian."

Detective Wallace took another long drag. "Da."

"Very funny."

"I told you I was still on the case. Alex told me where I could likely spot the car and which direction it would be heading."

"Why would he tell you that?"

"Let's say I owe him one."

"I'm sure that is a story in itself. Where are you?"

"Wisconsin North. Turning onto Idaho."

"The next turn is going to be a right onto Porter."

"How could you know that?"

"They are heading back to the scene of the crime."

"Your sister-in-law's house?"

"On my way."

—

Dan turned the engine, checked the mirrors, and put the car in drive.

"What about the guys inside?" Sue asked.

"I don't think we have to worry about them. When they don't check in with Reed Temple, you can bet someone will show up to sterilize the location. They won't be there in an hour."

"You're probably right."

Dan checked his mirrors again and noted the empty street behind him. "Time to hear what you have to say. Who do you work for?"

"I am employed by the Central Intelligence Agency. I was assigned to follow you and to provide daily reports in order to ensure your safety."

"Reports to whom?"

"A superior. Someone I've never met. I was called into my director's office and ordered to an offsite location. I was given hard copy orders from an administrative assistant who provided a file for me to study. The file was about you. After I studied the file, I was briefed by someone behind a two-way mirror."

"What were your orders, exactly?"

"I was told that contact with you had already been established and I would be meeting you under the auspice of an internship. It was my understanding you had interns in the past."

"How did you know about past internships?"

"Standard operation. Your email account was compromised to identify access opportunities—a way to enter your life without raising undue suspicion. Your email history was dissected at the most granular level. We found references to past interns. We researched your friend, Professor Davis. The relationship between you and the professor was examined in detail. Once we felt comfortable about our chances, we created a student that fit our description. That student was me."

"My private emails are encrypted."

Sue cocked her head to the side. "Really?"

"What if I had called the professor?"

"Could have. But I think we've learned enough about phone manipulation to acknowledge there are ways to circumvent that possibility. If we didn't want you to reach the professor via phone, we could have made that happen. But all that aside, it was an acceptable risk. No cover assignment is perfect. No assignment is risk free. And if you did catch me in the lie, so what? We would have looked for another access point."

"What was in the file you were given at the time of your assignment?"

"Most of the things I learned about you I disclosed last week when I was trying to impress you with my research skills."

"I am no longer impressed. You had the CIA database at your disposal."

"Actually, a majority of the information I shared with you was supplied to me in hard copy. There is surprisingly little information available in the standard agency databases on you and your background. At least not at my level of security clearance."

"So you were reading from hard copies?"

"Yes."

"Which means someone was controlling all of the information you had. Everything you know about me could have been completely fictitious."

"It could have been, I guess. But it wasn't. I could tell by your reaction."

"But you didn't know that until after the fact."

"True. But I am not sure why it matters. All-in-all, nothing in the file given to me about your background would surprise you."

"The existence of the file surprises me. Why would I have one at all? The content is less intriguing."

"Never thought about it. I was just doing my job."

"Was there any information beyond what you have already told me?"

"Several additional items were discussed at the assignment briefing. A few other tidbits of a more subjective nature. Likes and dislikes. Sexual orientation. Alcohol and drug use tendencies. On

328 Favors and Lies

the whole, the file portrayed you as a bit of a loner. I am sure there is some additional information I do not have access to. Access at the Agency is limited by a variety of parameters. It is not unusual to have limited access or partial access."

"Hierarchical controls and compartmentalization."

"That's how it works."

"What about your knowledge of forensics and death? You were pretty convincing in your conversation with Tobias on the great killers and afflictions of humankind."

"I studied both subjects in real life. Well, uh, in college. Real college. The college I went to."

"I get it."

"I was told one of the reasons I was selected for the assignment was based on my educational background. But it had been a while since I graduated. I had to re-study. I downloaded all the syllabi from all the classes I would have been required to take if I were a student at Marymount. Crammed for eighteen hours a day. I was even assigned a tutor. Took a few exams."

"And the story about your parents passing away? The pimp with the whiskey bottle in the neck. I checked the legal records for you and the information was verified. There was also a brief mention of it in an old issue of the *Baltimore Sun*. Or was that information all planted?"

Sue looked Dan in the eyes. "Oh, that part was true."

"So your name is Sue Fine."

"I was told it was likely you would do a background check and that you had access to information normal people may not have. I also have a legal record, and was fingerprinted, so it was decided I would use my real name. It was more plausible to create a background for my real name, to augment what is already publicly available, than to create a fictitious person you would likely debunk. Of course, your background check would have no way of identifying me as a CIA employee."

Dan nodded as the car passed Reagan National. Minutes later, they approached the onramp to the Roosevelt Bridge, heading into the District.

"Do you know our man, Reed Temple . . . Clyde Parkson?"

"I don't."

"You are aware you both receive paychecks from the same employer."

"I was not given any information on him. After you took pictures of Ebony and Ivory at the coffee shop stakeout, I submitted the photos for analysis and identification. I never received a reply."

"Convenient."

"Yes."

"So your task was to follow me?"

"Yes. You can trust me."

"That is to be determined."

"If I wanted you dead, I would have put a bullet in you while you were in the cellar. I had a loaded handgun at your back. I could have easily shot both of you."

"Maybe you were aiming for me and you missed."

"From fifteen feet? I doubt it."

"Maybe you don't want me dead. Maybe you want me captured."

Sue had no rebuttal. Under the same circumstances she would be equally suspicious.

"What happened after you left the hospital? How were you acquired by our two dead guys?" Dan asked.

"I took a cab from the hospital. You had my car, mind you. I needed to check in with my superiors. I returned to my apartment and was acquired before I could get inside."

"So they followed both of us from the hospital," Dan said.

"It would seem so," Sue responded.

"I was checking for a tail."

"Not very well. Or maybe you were being tracked somehow. I had to travel by cab. There was very little I could do about surveillance."

"You could have driven the cab."

"I won't justify that with a response. Where are we going?"

"To my sister-in-law's house."

"Why?"

"Because that is the location of the car the Russian told me to follow."

"According to the DC police?"

"According to a DC detective."

"The same one who threw you in jail?"

"Great friendships start in unusual circumstances."

There was a long, uncomfortable moment of silence and Sue knew further elaboration was not in the cards.

"What's the story with your nephew?"

Dan grunted. "What intelligence did you have on him?"

"None. I only know what you have told me. And what I have pieced together. My orders were very specific. My primary objective was to provide intelligence on your movements in order to keep you safe."

"Sounds like a couple of agents received conflicting primary objectives from the Agency."

"Yes it does."

"And you didn't do a good job of keeping me safe."

"You are still alive. My objective has been met."

"How often did you check in with your superiors?"

"Daily. Usually a brief write-up sent via an encrypted email system. I also had voice-drop alternatives."

"Voicemail?"

"Essentially yes, but with a greater security element. Voice verification and some other security bells and whistles."

"Do you carry a weapon?"

"Not on this case, though I am fully trained. I have several thousand rounds through a variety of handguns and assault rifles. Keep in mind this is a domestic assignment. Highly unusual. Different rules."

"Rules for a game that shouldn't even be played. It is illegal for the CIA to operate clandestine programs domestically."

Sue paused for another moment. "I know you don't owe me anything. But it seems everyone involved with you is more informed than I am. Tell me about your nephew. Maybe I can help."

Dan stared straight ahead. The car was now heading north on Rock Creek Parkway. Lights from the back patios and decks of million-dollar properties on the cliffs overlooking the park flashed through the trees.

"My nephew had a rare disease called CIPA," Dan said, voice cracking almost imperceptibly.

"I've never heard of it."

"I'm not surprised. There have been fewer than two dozen cases reported worldwide since it was identified. Most patients don't survive to school age. Only a handful of cases have lived past the age of eighteen."

"What is it?"

"The official name is Congenital Insensitivity to Pain with Anhidrosis. The first part of the name is self-explanatory. Anhidrosis means the patient does not perspire."

"Insensitivity to pain and the inability to perspire?"

"That's right. My nephew could not feel pain in the conventional sense."

"Jesus. Sounds awful and great at the same time. At least you never had to worry about him getting hurt."

"On the contrary. We all had to worry about him being hurt and not knowing. When he was in elementary school he broke his wrist skateboarding. It wasn't until he dropped a couple of glasses in the kitchen days later that my brother realized he was injured."

"I can see why the life expectancy is so short."

"The body is a well-designed machine. Multiple systems exist to perpetuate the body's own survival. Think about it. Fevers are designed to kill off infection within the body. Sweat enables the body to cool down. Swelling helps to protect injuries. Eyes produce tears to keep them lubricated and protected. The list goes on and on. Pain is a major component of the body's self-protection system. Pain informs you something is wrong. Take away all of those warning systems and it's like driving a car with no dashboard. No check engine light. No gas level indicator. No door ajar warning. Like driving down the street with no seatbelt, the doors open, running on fumes with a malfunctioning engine, and being oblivious to the danger."

"When did they discover your nephew had the disease?"

"Shortly after he began to teethe. As an infant he cried for emotional reasons. When he wanted attention. Wanted to be picked

up. Those episodes of normal emotional display masked any serious physical ailments. I mean, the baby cried so the parents didn't
worry. What his parents didn't recognize was the baby never cried
because he had gas, or because he had a fever. Those instances were
masked by my nephew's unusual medical condition."

"So what changed when he had teeth?"

"My brother found him one day in his bed, face covered in
blood. As a toddler, he had chewed through his tongue, lips, and
nibbled on his fingers. He had no sensation of pain. Nothing to tell
him to stop. It scared the shit out of my brother. My sister-in-law
was beside herself."

"But your nephew survived."

"He had a diligent family. Checked his temperature twice a
day. Inspected his body constantly. Installed plastic windows in the
house. Taught him how his body should react to certain things, extreme temperatures. Explained and showed him that hot objects
would burn him. Showed him cold objects could also be dangerous.
He was well-versed in anatomy. Basically, they tried to give him the
tools to self-monitor."

"To give him his own dashboard."

"Exactly."

"Did he have injuries growing up?"

"Many."

"And . . ."

"They were managed. Treated normally. But what wasn't normal was the attention his condition attracted. A broken arm was
not a simple broken arm when the patient was one in a billion and
couldn't feel pain. There was a lot of medical interest."

"Must have been hard to grow up like that. To keep the implications of that in check."

"It was a mental challenge, to be sure. I taught him martial arts,
hoping more than anything that he would realize he didn't have
to fight. To teach him to take the high road. Boys are boys and I
wanted to remove the curiosity associated with any potential physical altercation. I hoped if he knew he could fight well, he wouldn't
be curious to show others he could fight well. I hoped to filter out
some of the natural adolescent bullshit."

"I can see where teaching him to fight would have some danger to it."

"For both of us. I learned it's not easy to fight someone with no pain reception. Pain submission holds were worthless. He wouldn't tap out. And he also knew I wouldn't hurt him. He used all of those to his advantage."

"He beat you."

Dan smiled. "On occasion."

"So what has Reed Temple been doing with him?"

"That is the million dollar question."

CHAPTER 42

—

Dan pulled the burgundy sedan to the curb behind Detective Wallace's unmarked police car. He walked around to the passenger side, opened the door, and cut the zip tie on Sue's wrist.

"Thanks. I think I've had enough restraints for the evening."

"That's what happens when you lie. No one trusts you. Out of the car."

Seconds later, Dan opened the passenger side of Detective Wallace's unmarked car and Sue sat down. Dan shut the door and Wallace rolled down the passenger window. The detective flicked on the interior light and surveyed Sue's face. The bruise and swelling had worsened. A broken blood vessel colored the corner of her eye a deep red. "Did he hit you?"

"No."

Dan squatted on the strip of grass between the sidewalk and the curb and rested his forearms on the frame of the passenger window.

"The guy responsible for the shiner on her face was involved in Detective Nguyen's death."

Wallace turned serious. "Enough games, Dan. I am going to need a name."

"I can do better than that." Dan reached into his pocket and pulled out Major's driver's license with his real name and address on it. He flipped the ID onto the detective's lap. "But there is still one loose end to snip. The man giving the orders to kill is still on the street."

"You're going to force me into behavior that could make me lose my job."

"No offense, but you have to be close to retirement age. Now, what do we have on the BMW?"

Wallace pointed in the direction of Dan's sister-in-law's house. "It pulled in the driveway ten minutes ago. I didn't want to blow my cover, so I watched from down the block and then moved to this spot. There are good lines of sight from here. The BMW is in full view. We can observe several lights on in the residence. We have a straight shot into half of the living room. You can almost read the books on the built-ins on the far wall."

"Did you see who exited the car?"

"Not really. I caught a glimpse of the door as it shut."

"Did you see anyone else?"

"No one arrived by car or entered through the front."

"That doesn't mean anything."

"What's your next move?"

"I am going inside."

"That's the plan?"

"I'm winging it."

"What should I do with the girl?"

"Keep an eye on her, but if she wants to leave, let her go. If she tries to come in the house, arrest her. She does not have permission to enter the residence and I am the executor of the estate."

Dan stood and then added, "Don't believe her innocence for a second. I may try to keep you from losing your job, but the people she works for won't."

"I'll keep that in mind."

"I also need you to call the Alexandria police. Tell them two individuals were held captive in the basement of the Stonewall Jackson House in Old Town and that lethal force was used in order to escape. Tell them the two victims are now with you."

CHAPTER 43

—

Dan walked up the driveway and stepped onto the front porch. He reached behind a decorative street-number sign on the wall next to the porch light and brandished a key used for emergencies. A moment later, he opened the front door and stepped through the foyer, gun drawn.

A standing pedestal light illuminated the corner of the living room near the window, on the far side of a wingback chair. Dan edged towards the living room, garnering a glimpse of a reflection of a person seated in the chair. The face was distorted by the window panes, the details concealed in the shadow cast by the edge of the chair. Dan registered a metal object to his right as he entered the room and his eyes momentarily averted from his target. A walking cane rested against the skirt of the person in the chair, a small leg brace wrapped around the ankle.

Dan stepped forward, gun at eye level, and pivoted towards his target. The person in the corner chair didn't flinch as Dan acquired a direct line of sight. He lowered his aim, the sights on his weapon falling to a point directly between the eyes of the woman who had brought him into the world.

"I had a feeling it was you."

Dan's mother—ten years deceased—tried to smile and failed. "I had a feeling you would have that feeling."

Dan shook his head, tears involuntarily forming in his eyes. His mother's hair was up, tied neatly behind her head. The salt-and-pepper color he remembered was now fully gray. Wrinkles rippled across her forehead and dripped from the corners of her eyes.

"Where is he?"

"Who?"

"Don't start. I'm in no fucking mood."

"I was hoping you hadn't lost your manners."

"I think we're a little beyond that, don't you. Planning to wash my mouth out with soap?"

Dan's mother eyed her son from his shoes to his head. "You are injured."

"Been better. Been worse. I want Reed Temple. Or at least that was his name earlier this evening when he was tying me up in a basement, ordering me to be killed."

"He is gone."

"Destination?"

"Somewhere you can't reach him. He was reassigned. New passport. New identity. New cell phone. Cash. He will be in the air in a couple of hours. By dawn he will be in another country. With a new life. More accurately, his old life back, reissued with a new identity."

"He killed Conner."

"It was an accidental death."

"He also tried to kill me."

"You survived."

"He is a murderer."

"He is a patriot."

Dan stepped back as if his thoughts of revulsion manifested into muscle movement. The gun was re-aimed, finger now on the trigger.

Dan's mother slowly raised and lowered her right hand, hushing her son as if trying to calm a dog. "Put the gun down. Have a seat. Let's talk."

"I'll stand." Dan moved his finger slowly to the side of the trigger guard but didn't loosen his grip. The veins in the back of his hand bulged.

"Your eyebrow is starting to drip," his mother said.

"And now the concerned mother routine?"

"Very well," his mother said. "We can discard the niceties. When did you know it was me?"

"I've known for a while. My first clue was the initial police report on Conner. According to a dead police detective, there was nothing in his medical records regarding CIPA. We both know how substantial his medical files were. Dozens of visits to multiple hospitals for myriad reasons. All of them included references to pain insensitivity and CIPA. But when the police obtained the medical records, only the injuries were included in the files. How could a very pertinent piece of his medical records disappear from multiple medical files? And why? From that, I knew his death was related to his condition and I needed to find someone who had the knowledge of the illness and the ability to have records erased. On top of that, there was the incident involving the disappearing phone call. No phone record of the call to my house Vicky made the night Conner died. Coincidences like that do not occur. It was obvious it was the work of an intelligence operation."

"You couldn't have suspected me at that point. As far as you knew, I was an English teacher and I was deceased."

"I suspected Dad. I had him pegged for it, really. It wasn't until I talked to a helpful gentleman from the Russian Embassy that I considered it was you. He mentioned how the Russians identify agents working under diplomatic cover at embassies overseas. It was something so simple perhaps I should have realized on my own. He said official cover operatives at foreign posts have to perform two jobs. One is a legitimate job, albeit a cover job, and the other is spycraft. This is common knowledge. What he said next was not. He said if you want to identify a foreign intelligence agent working under diplomatic cover, just keep track of the employees putting in the longest hours at the embassy. Dad never worked at the embassy. You did. And you always stayed up late. I didn't think much about it when I was growing up. I always thought we moved when Dad found a new job with better pay."

Dan's mother laughed a quiet cackle. "Oh, my dear Dan. I wasn't following your father around the globe. He was following me."

"So I have realized."

"Your father was a geologist. He was very good at what he did. He loved his job. And big companies with unlimited resources are scouring every corner of every country for oil and gas deposits. It was a perfect marriage. He could work anywhere. I could teach anywhere."

"Except you weren't teaching."

"I wasn't *only* teaching."

"How does the CIA capitalize on an English teacher?"

"My official cover was as a foreign service English language officer. We establish English programs in foreign countries to ultimately facilitate better relations with the US. We teach teachers how to teach more effectively and try to positively influence the lives of students through the expansion of English."

"I understand the diplomatic perspective. I am not sure I follow the intelligence side."

"Take a poor African country, for example. The establishment of English programs, as with most aid programs in Africa, is rife with corruption. The ruling party and those in power want their children to learn English. Rules will be bent, broken, and created to serve those in the inner power circle. After the program is filled with the children of the elite, there will be some elements of the general population who will be offered a place in some classrooms."

"Sounds like a wonderful program."

"It serves two purposes. One, it provides an opportunity to interact with the offspring of the power elite in a manner that cannot be accomplished through standard diplomatic channels. It helps mold these children to view the US and other English-speaking countries in a more favorable light. Two, when properly leveraged, one can get meaningful intelligence of the lives of those in the inner circle of power through their children . . . all under the auspice of learning English."

"Using children to spy."

"At no risk to the children."

"It is a little thing called 'principle.' Africa doesn't have the best track record regarding the treatment of their children. Chopping off arms, forced labor camps, using them as soldiers. And now you have the US, employing these children as spies."

"The world is not black and white. And the Belgians started the African custom of limb-chopping."

Dan changed the subject. "Tell me about the plane crash that killed you and Dad." Dan nodded towards his mother's injured leg. "And if you tell me my father is still alive, I will shoot you right here, right now, mother or not."

"No, son. He is dead. Your father and I were, in fact, in a plane crash. That is the truth."

"Don't call me 'son.' Again. Ever."

"I understand you are angry."

"You have no idea what anger is. I want the details of the crash."

"It was a small single-engine plane taking off from Johannesburg in heavy rain. It crashed less than a minute after takeoff. Your father and the pilot died on impact. There wasn't much left of the aircraft. The last thing I remember is looking over the wing as the plane banked left and the ground closed in at a great speed."

"And you survived. Conveniently."

"I was in a coma for two days. Another half a year in rehabilitation. Broken back, legs, pelvis. I have more metal below the waist than I do bone. Cold weather does me in. Hate winter."

"And you decided to leave me and my brother without parents? Clean it up with a closed casket funeral?"

"You were grown men. You had lives of your own. Lives you were free to live. Your father was dead. What you see in this chair is my life. My life to lead. The agency and its mission are in my blood."

"More than your own children, apparently. So who knew about your secret life as a spy? Did my brother know? Dad?"

"Your father knew. Your brother did not." His mother glanced out the front window. "I saw to it that you were taken care of."

"It isn't about the money."

"But it gave you the opportunity to do what you want with your life."

"Maybe I would have preferred the opportunity to have a life with you in it."

"I wasn't going to be around forever. My death was an inevitable eventuality, as it is for everyone. My departure from your life was only premature. The airplane crash reminded me that life can end at any moment."

"What about Connor, did he know you were alive?"

"He did not."

"What happened to him?"

"He died serving his country."

"Explain."

"He was recruited by the CIA under the premise of a medical study. Contacted regarding his medical condition and asked whether or not he would be interested in participating in a program to advance the interests of the United States."

"For money?"

"We appealed to his patriotic convictions. And he also got paid."

"You use the word 'patriotic' as if it is a get-out-of-jail-free card."

"Conner chose to help his country. The choice was his. We merely opened the door to him. He was eighteen at the time. He was able to make the decision for himself."

"You recruited your own flesh and blood and it killed him."

"He volunteered."

"He didn't know any better. He was a child. I see a recurring theme."

"Eighteen, Dan. If that is a child then we need to re-examine our definitions. The military is full of children. Wars are won with children. Tanks are driven and fighter jets are flown by children. Bombs are dropped by children. And the new drones, well, most of the really talented operators are not too much older than twenty. Who knew the video game generation would prove to be such an advantage?"

Dan shook his head, unable to believe what he was hearing.

His mother continued. "Connor understood that in all likelihood he would not survive long-term. He wanted to help."

"Help with what?"

"Do you remember 9/11?"

"Of course."

"How did you feel that morning?"

"Sick. Shocked. Sad. Disgusted. Angry."

"Angry. Every red-blooded American was angry. And if you would have asked any American on that fateful morning if we should use any method at our disposal to bring those responsible to justice, every American would have said yes. Yes to torture. Yes to drones. Yes to occupying foreign countries. Certainly yes to working with American volunteers in the name of creating super soldiers. Super spies."

"Do you know how mentally unstable you are?"

"I am not talking about science fiction, Dan. This is very real. We are close. We are very close to medical advances that will provide advantages to the way wars are fought, the way intelligence is gathered. And if we don't accomplish it first, the Russians or the Israelis will. Imagine a soldier who can feel no pain. Combine a soldier or a spy who can feel no pain with one who has a superior memory. A soldier or spy who is not slowed by the elements. These are no longer far-fetched. They are doable. We are not talking about superhuman, mutant capabilities. We are talking about replicating capabilities of a very select number of individuals with very special skills. Imagine adding soldier enhancements like an exoskeleton. Smart bullets. Now you are talking about humans who are no longer purely human. Humans who can serve as virtual robots—robots we can use without relinquishing security controls to the binary whims of computer systems, programmers, and hackers."

"So what happened with Conner?"

"He had a reaction to one of the experiments. An allergic reaction to pain-inducing medication. We were testing pain thresholds, using compounds that exponentially increase pain reaction in humans. Imagine an injection that could create a pain reaction so great that the pressure of a simple handshake could bring crippling agony."

"I can imagine the implications."

"Yes, you can. Torture. With a single injection, we could extract meaningful intelligence through extreme pain, without any physical implications. Grab an arm, squeeze, and get the answer to your interrogation question. Release the arm and there is no damage. No long-term effects."

"I'm sure it's great."

"We were testing this medication on Conner as an ancillary evaluation of his pain receptors. He showed no discomfort when injected with this compound. He had no pain reaction to the test compound, unlike the discomfort demonstrated by normal humans in the control subject groups. Unfortunately, the allergic reaction to the injected compound wasn't realized until it was too late. He didn't suffer."

"Of course he suffered. He suffered mentally. He suffered with fear. It may have not been painful, but he suffered. Don't confuse the two."

"It was an accident. You act like I didn't care. I had him under near-constant surveillance. He was being observed at school. Supervised by the Resident Assistant in his dorm. He was being watched here."

"This house?"

"It was under surveillance."

"What kind of surveillance?"

"Electronic. Human."

"Human who?"

"The elderly man next door. He is a retired colleague."

"What else did you have? Cameras? Video? Audio?"

"Yes."

"Then you have evidence and I want it."

"It has been destroyed, or will be shortly. The last bit of evidence left this house with Reed Temple minutes ago."

"Who is Reed Temple?"

"A talented agent with a distinguished career."

"What is his real name?"

"I cannot divulge that information."

"Does he know who you are?"

"No. I met him in person for the first time tonight. Of course, I refrained from divulging my true identity."

"You mean he doesn't know you are Connor's grandmother?"

"I told you we met for the first time this evening. We have spoken before, anonymously."

"Is Reed Temple a prodigy of yours?"

"Not my prodigy. Certainly my peer when it comes to being convincing. Believable. As you have witnessed."

"Why are you protecting him?"

"Because our country needs him. We need people like him. People who are willing to do what is asked, and sometimes willing to do what is not asked. This country is becoming a land of whiners, lawyers, and pussies. Excuse my language."

"I always knew I got my propensity for cursing from you."

Dan paced the living room, never taking his eyes off his mother. He glanced out the front window and could see Detective Wallace in his police car. Sue was still seated next to him.

"Who is Sue Fine?"

"An agent. We infiltrated your email and set up the internship. It wasn't difficult. It wasn't without risks, but it wasn't difficult. I sent her to protect you. To keep an eye on you."

"That is what she said."

"Is she still alive? She neglected to provide an update today."

"She is alive. Thanks to an old wooden chair and a bit of luck."

"For what it's worth, she reported that she was uncomfortable with this assignment after spending a few days with you. She inquired about reassignment."

"Maybe she should have been reassigned. She did a poor job of protecting me."

"It was not from lack of effort. You know, as hard as this may be to believe, I tried to keep you insulated. After Connor's death, I ordered the sterilization of most of your existence. Access to the majority of information about you now requires a top-level security clearance. Your medical history. Your employment records. Your tax records. Birth records. You were cleaned up, redacted, removed from various databases where normal people have their lives stored."

"I discovered the lack of medical records."

"Outside of the witness protection program, there are few people in the civilian population with less history than you. It was not a trivial undertaking. And it was done to protect you."

"And yet, why do I think this was done for you? I mean, if you wanted to protect me, you could have handled Reed Temple. I'm sure you were aware of the seriousness of the situation when you saw my face on the news after the bomb at my office. I don't think you were trying to protect me very hard, if at all. I think you assigned Sue to the case so she could keep an eye on me and inform you when I got too close to the truth."

Dan watched as his mother stared stoically ahead.

"In fact, you know what I think? I think Connor died and you hit the panic button. You didn't want anyone connecting the dots between your domestic pain study and the fact that experiments were being performed on your own flesh and blood, on US soil. I imagine, even in the CIA, people would protest the perversity of that dynamic. I also imagine, someone, somewhere in the food chain at Langley would be able to connect the dots between Connor and his not-so-dead grandmother. Birth records, the last name of Lord. Someone could have figured it out."

Dan's mother remained silent and he knew he'd hit the nail on the head. "I think when Connor died, you ordered a cleanup. But thanks to Reed Temple and his sidekicks, it got out of hand. Somewhere along the way your cleanup became a cover-up. And you decided to see it through to the end."

Dan's mother turned away and glanced out the window into darkness. "I'm not the only one covering their tracks. We all have secrets. Even you. For a period of five years, you do not exist. Not even a credit card or utility bill in your name. Nothing. Even a CIA agent struggles to imagine how you pulled that off."

"My life is my life."

"I am still curious about my son. It's a mother's job."

"As is deception, apparently, which you excelled at throughout your life."

"You were always perceptive as a child, Dan. You would have made a great operative. For years I was certain you would be the one to discover my real occupation. But you didn't. All that time you spent doing martial arts and hanging out with diplomatic security and marines at all those embassies kept you occupied. And the times you weren't in the dojo, you were out with your father on some expedition or you were studying."

"Your life was a lie."

"But my love was not."

"Your definition of love has no basis in reality."

"I am sorry you feel that way."

"And I'm sorry my mother is going to prison for the rest of her life."

"Good luck, my son. I don't exist. Shoot me now or chase a ghost forever."

"Ghosts are becoming my specialty."

Dan stared into his mother's eyes, wondering how the woman who raised him had lost her moral compass. Maybe she'd never had one.

"The only solution with a happy ending includes you telling me where Reed Temple is. I know he must be close," Dan said.

"Why do you say that?"

"It took me twenty-some minutes to get from Alexandria to this house on the night Vicky and Conner died. In that time, someone had to get here, remove Conner, and kill Vicky. In twenty-five minutes, tops. Someone had to be close."

His mother remained silent.

"Last chance for directions to my friend Reed Temple."

"I cannot help you."

Dan looked down at his watch and then out the front door at the gray BMW in the driveway. Then he smiled.

"Yes, you can," Dan replied. He reached into his pocket and removed a handful of zip ties. "And it won't require you to move."

CHAPTER 44

—

Dan removed the key ring to his nephew's Nissan hatchback from the *Welcome Home* plaque near the back door of his sister-in-law's house. He plotted out the plan in his head and checked the time on his watch.

He opened his cell phone and dialed.

"Sensei, it's Dan."

"How do you like the SUV?"

"Oh, it's great. Rides like a charm. Any chance you have LoJack?"

Gary Raven fell silent, but Dan could hear bodies falling on the mat in the background, dispersed intermittently with a combative yell.

"What happened?"

"Your SUV was borrowed. I need you to provide its current location. You claimed it had all the bells and whistles. I assume that includes LoJack, and whatever version of remote-access software you installed."

"Give me a second," Gary Raven replied. "I am on the mat. I have to boot up the computer."

Dan stood in the dark near the entrance to the back door of his sister-in-law's house and counted the seconds until he heard Gary Raven's voice. He eyed an old sweatshirt of his nephew's hanging on a hook near the back door and looked down at himself and his attire. Tattered, dirty, and bloodied. He removed the sweatshirt from the hook and pulled it over his head while he waited for Gary Raven to return to the phone.

"You there?" Gary asked.

"Yep. Tell me you got it."

"In the alley behind Twenty-Ninth Street, a block south of R Street, Northwest."

"Thanks," Dan answered. "Is your insurance on the vehicle current?"

"Yes. And I don't want to know why you are asking."

"If you don't hear back from me in the next forty-five minutes or so, report the car as stolen."

"Will do."

"Thanks, Sensei," Dan said. He hung up, placed his cell phone on the top of the refrigerator near the back door, and walked out the rear to his nephew's car.

—

Reed Temple pressed the lock release button on the key ring for the security-laden Mercedes SUV and threw his bag in the rear hatch of the vehicle. One bag was enough. Everything else he needed on his new assignment would be packed with white gloves and shipped to his final destination at taxpayers' expense. It was a perk of the job. Diplomatic personnel, official and unofficial, spent half their lives waiting for the arrival of their furniture. He whistled quietly as he closed the lid on the trunk. He patted the breast pocket on his suit jacket one more time, smiling broadly. A forty-minute ride to the airport, an overnight flight to Kuala Lumpur with a connection in Tokyo, and he would vanish into a new assignment in Southeast Asia. In forty-eight hours he would be sweating through his pressed linen shirt, sipping an umbrella drink on a sidewalk café somewhere between Jakarta and Bangkok.

He threw himself behind the wheel of the car, turned the ignition, and straightened his tie in the mirror. The car's engine went silent and he turned the ignition again. No clicks. No chugs.

Reed Temple's eyes danced across the displays on the dashboard looking for an indication to the car's mechanical hiccup. By the time he saw the thin wire drop from above his head and disappear beneath his chin, it was too late. Reed Temple clamored for his neck, his fingers insufficiently strong to pry the wire away from his crushing larynx and constricted jugular. Dan, behind the driver in the backseat of the SUV, pulled downward, his body weight sinking into the foot well. His forearms, beneath his nephew's old sweatshirt, were taut with strain.

Reed Temple's flailing arms scratched at the headrest. For a brief moment, Dan allowed himself to be seen in the rearview mirror. His eyes locked with Reed Temple and there was recognition that it was over. There would be no escape.

Reed Temple's flailing right hand found his coat pocket and managed to remove his semi-automatic government issue as blood filled his throat. His head arched back, beckoning for room that was not available. Grappling for life, Reed Temple raised the gun and fired backwards, aiming at Dan through the headrest, the only available angle on his assailant. The gunshot illuminated the car for a split-second and Dan's heart rate increased. Blood slowly began to drip from the back of Reed Temple's head, running down the back collar of his suit jacket.

Bulletproof headrests, indeed, Dan thought.

Dan held tightly until Reed Temple stopped twitching. Then he maintained pressure for another ten seconds. When he released his grip on the wire around Temple's neck, a sharp crease remained in the dead man's collar, neatly dissecting a spot just above the double Windsor.

Dan moved the wire, raising his hands back over Reed Temple's head. He retracted the garrote to the wristwatch and returned the bevel to the face of the timepiece.

He looked around once and exited the car, sweating, pulse elevated. He walked towards the dark end of the alley and turned right where it intersected with another alley running perpendicularly. He was back in his nephew's Nissan hatchback ten seconds later. Six minutes after that, he pulled into the rear parking spot behind his sister-in-law's house.

He entered the backdoor near the kitchen, took off his nephew's sweatshirt, and put it back on the hook. He reached up and removed his cell phone from the top of the refrigerator and checked the time. Twenty-seven minutes, round-trip.

CHAPTER 45

—

Dan walked back into the living room and found the wingback chair in the corner empty. The zip ties were cut and lying on the carpet. He reached down and picked up the evidence, stuffing them in the same pocket he had removed them from earlier. He noticed the plantation shutters had been closed, concealing the view to the outside. Dan pushed open the shutters and eyed the gray BMW still parked in the driveway. He glanced away from the window and noticed his mother's walking cane resting against the wall on the other side of the chair. *Everything is a lie . . .*

Dan exited the front door with no attempt to conceal his presence or intention. He beelined it across the manicured lawn and crossed the street to the police cruiser. Detective Wallace lowered the window and Dan motioned towards the back door. Sue was still in the passenger seat and turned towards the rear as Dan landed in the back of the car.

"Did you see anyone leave the house?" Dan asked.

Detective Wallace adjusted the rearview mirror until Dan's face was in view. "No one left the house once you went in. But then again, you should know that given you were in the residence."

Dan rubbed the lump on the back of his head. "I was momentarily incapacitated. Someone hit me from behind. When I regained my faculties, the house was empty."

"You were ambushed from behind in a living room with the lights on?" Detective Wallace asked sarcastically.

"Yes."

"Who else was in the room? I could see a partial silhouette in the chair. Until the blinds shut."

"The woman in the house was my mother."

"The driver of the gray BMW, which I followed from Langley, is your mother?"

"That is correct."

"I thought your mother was dead," Sue responded.

Detective Wallace turned at the waist from the driver's seat and stared at Dan. "You want to explain?"

"It caught me off guard as well."

"And?"

"And what? For ten years I thought my mother was deceased. She is not."

"And she works at Langley?"

"Let's not act completely surprised. It is one of the few employers where death doesn't mean the end of your employment."

"Does she have anything to do with Nguyen's death?"

"Not in any way that could be proven."

"She could be charged with illegal entry."

"She probably had a key and it was her daughter-in-law's house. But it doesn't matter. You have to find her to charge her, and she won't be found."

"What about the guy who ordered Nguyen's murder?"

"He was gone by the time I got inside. My mother implied that I missed him by a few minutes."

"Where did he go?"

"Don't know."

Dan felt the heat of the detective's stare and knew his lies were transparent. Dishonesty by those being questioned was a shared occupational hazard both men could smell in high wind.

"Take us to the nearest hospital, Detective. We need to be treated for shock. We have been through a lot this evening. We need medical treatment. I am starting to feel cold. Dizzy."

Dan looked at Sue and winked subtly.

Dan watched as Detective Wallace eyeballed Major's driver's license resting on the dash of the cruiser. Then his eyes again met Dan's in the rearview mirror. "Let me call it in."

Dan closed his eyes as the car moved down the street. At the stop sign at the end of the block, the radio in the detective's car chirped out a BOLO for a stolen black Mercedes Benz SUV.

CHAPTER 46

—

Dan relaxed in a chair at a round table in the back corner of the bar room. From his vantage point, he had a complete view of the room—every entrance, every exit, every table, every chair, every TV screen, every character.

Detective Wallace entered the room through the arched doorway and Good Time Charlie himself acted busy, shining glasses with a white towel at the bar. Wallace nodded at Ginger who was sitting on the same barstool where she had launched her sales pitch on their earlier encounter. Ginger winked and asked, "Did you change your mind, Detective?"

"Not yet," Wallace replied, looking around for Dan and spotting him as Dan raised his hand. Detective Wallace assessed the room and its patrons as he approached the table, belly arriving first.

"When I said I wanted to meet with you, I didn't expect to meet here," Wallace said, now surveying the football games on the TV screens.

"I wanted to catch the games. I had a couple of people to talk to. And a detective friend of mine wanted to meet. I thought I would handle it all at the same time."

"Are we friends now?"

"We did smoke a peace pipe, if I recall."

"We did."

"But I think we can do it for real this time," Dan said, smiling. He pulled two cigarettes from his pocket and pushed one across the table.

Detective Wallace looked down at the temptation and then up at Dan.

"I hear you quit," Dan replied.

"Every month."

"Three years for me. But I've been battling a strong craving for one lately. And I don't like smoking alone."

"It's against the law to smoke indoors in a public venue in the state of Maryland."

Dan glanced around at the necks of patrons cranked upward towards the TVs. "You are outside of your jurisdiction and I don't think the owner would mind if we smoked just one."

Wallace pulled a lighter from his pocket and leaned over to light Dan's cigarette. Dan inhaled slowly and blew the smoke upward. "Holy crap that is good."

"Don't blame me if you pick up the habit again."

"Just one. Just today."

"Celebrating?"

"Something like that."

Wallace leaned back in his chair and inhaled.

"So what's on your mind, Detective?"

"You can call me Earl."

"I could, but I like the sound of 'detective,' Detective."

"I had a few questions for you."

"Shoot."

"You want to tell me what *really* happened on Friday night?"

"You know I spent most of the afternoon yesterday with the Alexandria police and a roomful of suits who didn't identify themselves. I'll tell you the same thing I told them. I was drugged, kidnapped, and held hostage in the basement of a house that I own. My intern, who was really an employee of the CIA, was also held captive. We escaped. Fled for our lives. One of the kidnappers was shot. Another was incapacitated by his own man. A third kidnapper departed the scene. We thought there was a connection between the car you were following and the kidnapper who escaped, and we followed that assumption to my sister-in-law's house. There I met my deceased mother. You can imagine my surprise. I was obviously not in the right frame of mind. I was in shock. My behavior was clearly erratic. We were subsequently treated at Georgetown

University Hospital for shock and stress, as you are aware, being you provided transportation."

"Helps to have an intelligence agent corroborate your story."

"She corroborated a story that no one believes. The entire crime scene was sterilized. There is no report of any bodies being found at the Stonewall Jackson residence. There is no official police report at all."

"So you are just being labeled crazy."

"Crazy and alive. I can live with that."

"I have friends on the Alexandria police force who tell me there was only one body found in the house. Took three guys and a winch to get him out of an old well. All off the record, of course."

"I believe that."

"They said his face was torn open."

"It wasn't pretty."

"Things could have turned out worse for you. You got lucky. You could have easily been killed. Dumped under the Promenade. Who knows, your body could have been found in a stolen car with a gunshot wound to the head and a crushed larynx."

"That would be one way to go."

"There seems to be a lack of interest from the press on that story as well. Curious circumstances, really. A man in a stolen vehicle dies of a gunshot wound while on his way to death by strangulation. From what could be determined at the crime scene, the victim was being strangled from behind and attempted to shoot his assailant who was to his rear. The bullet ricocheted off the bulletproof plate in the headrest and entered the victim's skull."

"Incredible," Dan said, inhaling another drag and tipping the ash from the cigarette into an empty beer bottle on the table. "Sounds like a murder-suicide."

"I have been investigating death and dismemberment for a quarter of a century. Never seen anything like it. Have you?"

"No."

Detective Wallace leaned forward and stared at Dan through the smoke trailing off the cigarette in his mouth. "You sure you don't have any information on the subject?"

"You aren't implying I was involved, are you? I was inside a house you were observing."

"I am aware."

"And I was incapacitated. I had the injury on my head to prove it."

"Yes, you did. Of course, that injury could have existed already. A fresh injury."

"What about other evidence, Detective? Strangling a person from behind takes strength. It would also require some kind of weapon. A rope, perhaps. I mean, you could strangle someone from behind with a standard chokehold, but not if the headrest was in the way. Certainly not if the victim had a handgun at his disposal."

"No weapon. The ligature marks indicated something thin, but strong. Like a piano wire."

"I don't play the piano. Nor do I own one."

"Me neither."

"I guess that is two suspects down. You know, DC is a dangerous city. Another reason I live in Virginia. One bridge crossing away, but another world entirely."

"Hmmm," Detective Wallace replied, exhaling.

Dan put a finger in the air, pointed at the beer bottle on the table, and then changed his finger configuration to order two more drinks. The two men smoked in silence until drinks arrived. As the waitress walked away, Dan reached into his pocket and removed a thumb drive.

"You might find this interesting."

"What's on it?"

"Voice recordings. Everything you need for everyone involved. I have the person responsible for Nguyen's death admitting that he has the detective's badge sitting on his mantle at home."

Detective Wallace's eyes watered. "I already got his badge back. And his detective's notebook."

"You would have needed a search warrant for that."

"I only needed an address and you gave me his driver's license."

"Skirting the law?"

"No more than you."

Dan nodded and then took his hand off the thumb drive. "I assume you can get that to the right people. I understand you aren't very popular with the federal agencies already. Maybe you know someone at the *Washington Post* who would be willing to write up a story and run it for you."

"Who made the recordings?"

"I did. Virginia and DC are single-participant jurisdictions, meaning that only one party to a conversation needs to give permission for that conversation to be recorded. Being that I made these recordings, the legal authority has been satisfied."

"You were wearing a wire?"

"I owned a fancy watch that could record up to twenty-four hours of voice. I downloaded the audio files to a computer via a simple USB connection."

"And where is this watch now?"

"I lost it."

Detective Wallace picked up his beer and took a long slug. Then he casually slid the thumb drive off the table and slipped it into his breast pocket next to his detective's notebook. "Have you been doing a background check on me? Or is it just coincidence that I have a nephew-in-law who writes for the Metro section of the *Post*?"

"The world is full of coincidences."

"And what if I choose not to do anything with the recordings?"

"Doesn't matter to me. My interest has been satisfied."

"Has justice been served?"

"Justice is decided at the individual level."

"There is a system for justice. Most rational people would say justice can only be satisfied through the judicial system. Faith in the legal system is what keeps this country from ripping apart."

"It is a nice idea, but it's not reality. Do you know who has the most power in the legal system?"

"I imagine you are going to tell me."

"Judges and the guy at the police station handling evidence. Either one can win or lose a case single-handedly. Either one can determine the course of a life. The rest of the judicial system can be banished to irrelevancy pretty quickly if either of those two people have been compromised, fall asleep at their post, succumb to emotions."

Wallace took another long draw of his beer and then extinguished his cigarette in the remaining liquid in the bottom of the bottle, swirling the container briefly. "Another way to sabotage justice is to have no fingerprints."

Dan smiled. "That would be a neat trick."

"A nice trick, indeed. I followed evidence regulations with regard to the fingerprints taken when you were admitted into the DC jail. According to the letter of the law, I accessed the fingerprint system and deleted the prints we acquired when you were processed on entry."

"Thank you for following the law."

"But there is a discrepancy. The prints initially entered into the system were not the same as the prints that were deleted."

"I'm not sure I understand, Detective."

"When I processed you into the system, your fingerprints were taken electronically. I requested and received hard copies of those fingerprints, printed at the time of your incarceration. I wanted to compare those prints to other evidence."

"To see if I killed Nguyen?"

"Yes. But here is the interesting part. When I went back to the system to delete the records, in accordance with the law, I asked for another hard copy of the prints. This copy of your prints was different. The fingerprints entered into the system are not the same ones that I deleted."

Detective Wallace looked around the room cautiously and removed two folded pieces of paper from his pocket. He slid them across the table in the direction of Dan. "Seems like something is wrong with the computer system when it comes to your prints. Input does not equal output."

"That is a curious error. You should have the IT department look into that. A computer issue like that could wreak havoc on the wheels of justice."

"Yes, it could." Detective Wallace stood and extended his hand. "It's been a pleasure and an adventure."

"Likewise, Detective. Keep my number. If you need anything on the other side of the river, let me know."

"I just might do that."

Detective Wallace waved to Ginger on his way out. As he disappeared through the arched doorway, Ginger slipped from her stool and headed towards Dan. A large red leather purse hung from her shoulder. She reached the table, and Dan stood to pull out her chair.

"Well, what do you know, gentlemen still exist," she said.

"Only on Sundays."

"Everything OK with you and your detective friend?"

"I understand you two have met. Haley told me he was in here asking questions last week."

"He was. I kind of like him. For a cop."

"Thanks for keeping an eye out for me."

"You were good to Haley. You were always good to me. Nice to me. Normal to me."

"People are people."

"In my profession, people have a tendency to look down at you. Look at you like an object. Guess some of that is a hazard of the profession."

"It seems like the least of your occupational concerns."

Ginger looked at the butterfly bandages on Dan's eyebrow. "Looks like you have some occupational hazards yourself."

Dan nodded. "You said you have something for me?" he asked.

"I'm glad you could make it. I didn't want to carry this around anymore. Didn't feel safe with it. Was too nervous to keep it at home and too nervous to keep it in my car."

"What is it?"

Ginger glanced around nervously as a group of men in the corner screamed in celebration to a touchdown being scored on one of the games. Dan noted the sudden outburst made her even more jittery. As the celebration subsided, she reached into her purse and pulled out a black leather-bound book. A large strap held the cover closed.

"This was Haley's. One of her girls got it from her apartment after she, uh . . ."

Dan removed the strap and cracked the cover of the leath-er-bound book. His eyes opened wide as he read through pages of entries, names, services, preferences. "Holy shit."

"That is exactly what I said. And then it got worse. By the time I made it through the first dozen pages, I started to get nauseous. Needed a little weed and a little wine to calm my nerves."

Dan flipped through the pages, recognizing names from the news, people of prominence, lawmakers, and judicial guardians. He counted the lines per page and then estimated the thickness of the book at 150 pages. "There are thousands of entries. Thirty-four lines per page, 150 pages, front and back."

"I figured you would be the best person to have that."

"Why me?"

"Because you will do the right thing with it."

"I don't always do the right thing."

"More than most."

"You could sell this for a lot of money," Dan said.

"As soon as I mentioned that book to anyone, I would be dead."

"It might have the same effect on me."

"Then burn it."

"Not a bad idea."

"It's yours now. If anyone ever asks me about it, I will deny I ever saw it. Don't know anything about it."

"Thanks, I think."

"Do whatever you want with it. I am sure Haley would smile knowing you had it." Ginger checked her watch and pushed her chair away from the table. "I gotta run. Somewhere to be."

"You know how to reach me."

—

At halftime, Dan left the comfort of his corner table in the bar area and crossed the restaurant to the private dining room on the opposite side of the establishment. He pulled the burgundy drapes to the left and slipped into the room through the arched doorway. Tobias and Joseph Cellini looked up, the top of their round dining table covered in papers. Two laptops were opened and plugged into the outlets at the base of the wall. Thick notebooks full of data sat in stacks near the front table leg. Cellini's neckless accomplice was staring up at the television on the wall, cursing at the results of the games as they flashed across the screen.

Dan approached the table and Joseph Cellini and Tobias both smiled. "Look at the happy couple. Does that mean the two of you were able to work something out?"

"I think we have a mutually acceptable agreement," Cellini responded.

"And you, Tobias? Are you happy with the arrangement?"

"Not the billion dollars I was looking for, but retirement is in my immediate future."

"So we are even? Clean slate?"

"Your debt is cleared. We are good."

"Glad to hear everyone could walk away happy."

"And Mr. Cellini, are things between us on the up and up?"

"You keep an eye out for my daughter and you won't have any problems with me."

"Good."

Dan looked over at Mr. Neckless, who raised his wrist to show off his new gift. He pulled on the face of the watch and smiled at the wire as it unfurled. "Thanks for the watch, Danno."

"Don't mention it. Well, if we are all satisfied, I have a date with a doctor tonight. Take out in the hospital's doctor's lounge."

Joseph Cellini spoke. "Danno, we are planning to do a little fishing later this afternoon, if you are interested. Head out on the Chesapeake Bay for a couple of hours. I hear the rockfish put up quite a fight. You are welcome to come with us."

Dan stared into Cellini's eyes and he could see the flicker of the devil dancing. "Fishing?"

"Yep. We've got our tackle in the car."

"Deep-water tackle?"

"Something like that."

"I'll pass. I've been known to have motion sickness."

Dan shook hands with the three men and nodded at various

staff members on his way to the front door. A minute later he strolled to his car in the parking lot and started the ignition. He drove around the restaurant and eyed the large black sedan with New York plates parked in the corner of the lot, not far from the Dumpsters. A large, well-dressed man with dark sunglasses stood at attention next to the rear of the car, smoking a cigarette, scanning the environment. As Dan drove by, the man stepped forward away from the car. For an instant Dan was certain he saw the rear of the vehicle bounce, the rear shocks under the trunk rocking slightly.

CHAPTER 47

—

Dan wiped the new front glass window of the art gallery as Lucia sat behind her massive stone desk giving him directions to the last streaks. Dan allowed the nit-picking, the fiberglass cast on Lucia's arm a reminder of what he owed her.

"Anything else?" Dan asked.

"Nope. That wraps it up. This place looks as good as new."

"New was a hundred and sixty years ago. It looks better than new."

"Have you started painting again?" Dan asked.

"I have been dabbling. Business has picked up. The little explosion we had in here has put this place on the map. People are curious. The newspaper did an article on the gallery. I've sold most of the art that was hanging on the wall when the explosion occurred."

"Who knew that shrapnel was the key to a good promotional campaign?"

"I am thinking about adding it to my art repertoire."

"I will leave the art decisions to you," Dan said, followed by a long moment of silence. "I am sorry for everything that happened. For the explosion. Your arm. Levi."

Lucia nodded. "And I am sorry I lied about my father. About who I was. I know he can be a problem. Difficult."

Dan thought about his mother. "Let's agree not to talk about our parents."

"Done."

Lucia turned her head as the front door to the art gallery opened. Sue Fine, dressed in professional attire, approached the desk, managing to flash a meek smile. Lucia returned the smile and then looked over at Dan who was staring stoically ahead.

"I'll leave you two alone," Lucia said, excusing herself to the rear of the gallery.

"I quit," Sue blurted before Dan could say anything. "Retired. Officially. The paperwork has been processed."

"Why did you quit?"

"The job wasn't what I expected it to be, after all. I didn't want to look back in twenty years and be proud that my greatest asset was my ability to lie."

"I think it's OK as long as you cloak it as patriotism."

"OK for some. Not for me."

"You were good at it."

"Thanks."

The front door to the art gallery opened again. A man hidden under a scarf and a hat, walking arm-in-arm with a woman in a fur hat, entered the room and began to move around the perimeter wall, admiring the artwork on display. Dan glanced at the backside of the patrons, poked his head into the rear of the gallery, and let Lucia know she had customers. A moment later she engaged the couple in the far corner of the gallery as they discussed a large piece of shrapnel art hidden in a painting of a girl riding an old-fashioned tire swing.

Dan turned back to Sue. "So what's next?"

"I'm not sure. I am still weighing my options. I was thinking about getting a private detective's license."

"Unsavory characters. Unusual hours. Low pay. Not sure that would be my first choice."

"It's the only experience I have, other than being a spy."

"That is a short resume. You have any references?"

"Not really."

"Maybe I can offer you an internship. Unpaid."

"For how long?"

"Until I trust you. Come back in a couple of weeks and we will see if you're still serious."

—

Dan watched Sue through the front window as she disappeared into the sidewalk crowd. He sighed deeply and a voice boomed behind him, shaking him from his focus. "Can you trust her?"

Dan turned and smiled. "Alex Stoyovich."

"As far as you know."

"What are you doing here?"

"I wanted to check on you. See how you were doing. I also wanted to bring you a gift." Alex opened his long overcoat and pulled out a bottle of vodka plastered with Russian letters. "You can't get this outside of Russia. It is made in a small town three hours from Moscow. Made with the best water in the world."

Dan took the bottle. "I'm not sure why you're giving me a gift. I should be giving you one."

"I am giving you a gift for being the impetus to my retirement. My wife has been patient for forty-two years."

"You said your wife died. That you only had a cover wife. You couldn't have been married for forty-two years."

"And you believed me? If you did, then I failed as a teacher."

"Or I failed as a student."

"You were an exceptional student."

"I still have one remaining question."

"I hope it is a question about art or vodka. Those are my new passions. Well, one is an old passion. One is new."

"I would believe these are your new interests, if not for the fact you just reminded me not to trust you."

"What is your question? I will try not to lie."

"As you probably know, one of the people involved in my nephew's death escaped. I would like to locate her."

"The woman."

"Yes. I believe she was the big fish you referred to when you mentioned the gray BMW."

"Da. What do you want with this woman?"

"You don't know?"

"Don't know what?"

"Who she is?"

"I know who she claims to be. I know what name she traveled under on her trip to Russia. I can assure you it is not her real name."

"She is my mother."

Alex began to laugh, big choking bellows heavy enough to get the attention of his wife and Lucia still in the far corner of the gallery. "Oh, dear. That I did not see. I am sorry for laughing. The greatest thing about this profession is the surprises."

"I have reached my quota on surprises."

"When you get older you will once again look forward to them. When the days begin to blur into one another."

"Can you find her? Tell me where she is?"

"I am sorry. I cannot. What I can tell you is what the Americans are likely to do under the circumstances. This woman, your mother, will be offered reassignment or early retirement. If she receives a reassignment, she will be transferred overseas to a small diplomatic post for a couple of years. Nothing too extreme, just a nice cushy assignment in a small embassy or consulate for a couple of years to let her career wind down. If and when retirement comes, she will be permitted to select a suitable location, provided that location is outside of the DC area. I doubt seriously the Agency would allow her to choose Washington. Not in her case. Not for her sins. Think medium-sized town in the Midwest somewhere. That is far more likely."

Dan absorbed every word of the advice. "So she is gone?"

"She can be found. But it will take time and money. And luck."

"What would you do if you were me?"

"Let it go. Move on. Sometimes a victory doesn't have to be a total victory. You proved your nephew wasn't on drugs and that your sister-in-law didn't commit suicide. That is what you set out to do. You had an article in the *Post* that exposed an illegal domestic intelligence operation conducted on American soil. You pulled back the curtain of the puppet show. You have nothing left to prove."

"Thank you," Dan replied. "For your help and for the vodka."

"You are welcome." Alex looked over at his wife who had moved on to the next picture on the wall and was receiving personal input from the artist. "So . . . Where are you going to start?"

"Start what?"

"Start looking for her?"

Dan smiled. "I was thinking about taking a trip to Namibia. She always liked Namibia."

ABOUT THE AUTHOR

Mark Gilleo holds a graduate degree in international business from the University of South Carolina and an undergraduate degree in business from George Mason University. He enjoys traveling, hiking and biking. He speaks Japanese. A fourth-generation Washingtonian, he currently resides in the D.C. area. His first two novels, *Love thy Neighbor* and the national bestseller *Sweat* were recognized as finalist and semifinalist, respectively, in the William Faulkner-Wisdom creative writing competition.